Highlander Unchained

by

Donna Fletcher

This is a work of fiction. Names, characters, places, and incidents are either the product of the author's imagination or are used fictitiously, and any resemblance to actual persons, living or dead, business establishments, events or locales is entirely coincidental.

Highlander Unchained
All rights reserved.
Copyright September 2012 by Donna Fletcher
Published by Donna Fletcher, 2012

Cover art
Marc Fletcher

Visit Donna's Web site
www.donnafletcher.com
http://www.facebook.com/donna.fletcher.author

Table of Contents

[Chapter 1](#)
[Chapter 2](#)
[Chapter 3](#)
[Chapter 4](#)
[Chapter 5](#)
[Chapter 6](#)
[Chapter 7](#)
[Chapter 8](#)
[Chapter 9](#)
[Chapter 10](#)
[Chapter 11](#)
[Chapter 12](#)
[Chapter 13](#)
[Chapter 14](#)
[Chapter 15](#)
[Chapter 16](#)
[Chapter 17](#)
[Chapter 18](#)
[Chapter 19](#)
[Chapter 20](#)
[Chapter 21](#)
[Chapter 22](#)
[Chapter 23](#)
[Chapter 24](#)
[Chapter 25](#)
[Chapter 26](#)
[Chapter 27](#)
[Chapter 28](#)
[Chapter 29](#)
[Chapter 30](#)
[Chapter 31](#)
[Chapter 32](#)

Chapter 33
Chapter 34
Chapter 35
Chapter 36
Titles by Donna Fletcher
About the Author

Chapter One

Scotland... the Highlands 1200c

Dawn was carried along with the throng of excited villagers, pushing at those around her so as not to get crushed. News had spread fast about the capture and soon now the warriors would return with the prisoner in tow and she, like others, was eager to have a look.

The village folk continued to compete for positions along the route into the Village Dowell, elbowing and shoving, each wanting a good view until a woman yelled out, "I see them."

The scrambling stopped and all heads turned.

Dawn stretched her neck to see past the swarm in front of her. Luckily, she was taller than many of the women and even some of the men, so it took only a bit of a stretch and a turn, and she had a clear view of the road.

The troop had crested and was descending the last of the rolling hills that lead to the village. The warriors wore smiles; their chests puffed with pride. Several hands shot high waving weapons and victorious shouts filled the air. This was a joyous day for the village and for Colum in particular. He was liegeman for the feudal lord, Roland Gerwan, Earl of Carrick who no doubt would be pleased with the capture of the infamous warrior Cree.

His name ran shivers through Dawn as it did to

anyone who heard it. Cree was feared like no other warrior and woe to those who believed otherwise. Where he tread, rivers of blood flowed, those he touched suffered greatly, and those who survived his attacks prayed not for mercy, but for death.

Dawn crossed her arms over her chest and rubbed, a chill prickling her flesh, though the early autumn air was warm. She cast a quick glance to the sky and saw that a dark cloud had blotted out the sun and more clouds rushed threateningly to blight the sky.

A boney grip on her arm startled her, and she shot a quick glance down to see Old Mary beside her. She had been old as long as Dawn could remember. A good, caring soul Mary was, though many thought her a bit touched in the head and avoided her.

"A bad portent, bad indeed." Mary frowned and released Dawn's arm, then shuffled her stooped body through the crowd and disappeared.

Her ominous prediction only served to chill Dawn more and once again she rubbed at her arms, the flesh beneath her gray linen shift cold with fear. She could not say why she did not take to heart Old Mary's warning and leave as the old woman had done. Perhaps it was curiosity that kept hold, since Dawn wondered if it was the devil the warriors had captured and with him locked away peace could possibly prevail.

The shouts grew louder, the crowd cheering, and applauding their victory. Dawn smiled along with the others proud of the warriors as they marched by with stains of battle—dirt, sweat, and blood—heavy upon them.

Moments later, dead silence struck the crowd. Not a gasp or startled cry, not even a breath was heard, though many were held.

And Dawn? She stood unable to move, as if a winter wind had swept down and frozen her solid. Never had she seen a man the size of Cree. She stared unable to take her eyes off him. He walked behind Colum's horse. His wrists were bound and tethered by shackle and chains, though he looked fit enough to break free from his solid constraints. He was massive in size, both height and width and his bare chest was a mass of thick muscles and spotted with dried blood. More muscles bunched along his arms and dark leather leggings could not hide more of the same. Dark boots were the only other thing he wore.

Dawn hesitated to glance at his face fearful of what she would see. Curiosity; however, had her turning and taking a peek.

Her heart slammed in her chest, and then lurched in her throat. He was so handsome that she could not take her eyes off him. Even grime and blood could not hide his fine features. God had surely favored him for the more her eyes drank in, the more beauty she saw and only God could have made someone so splendid. His long brown hair was not only threaded with strands the color of gold, but also mixed with the bright white yellow color of the sun.

Her eyes caught his then, and her breath left her in a heavy whoosh. They were dark like the blackest night. She wanted to look away but she couldn't. There was something about his eyes that completely absorbed her, held her, and bound her to him like the chain that tethered him. Then like a startling slap in the face, she realized he was staring back at her.

His eyes had caught hers and held them captive even as he continued walking. She wondered then if it had been the devil, rather than God, who had given him his handsome features. She tried to tear her glance away, but it was impossible. Something kept her mesmerized. Where before she felt chilled, now a heat began to take hold and spread quickly through her body. Where it had begun she could not say, perhaps her toes or her breasts, her nipples having turning hard. It spread rapidly, and it was not long before it entirely consumed her.

The sensation was warm and soothing, not at all distasteful. Yet she sensed it was wrong. She should not feel this sense of pleasure from this mongrel who butchered like a savage dog.

Whatever strangeness tethered them was broken by the crowd that pushed forward, sweeping her along as they kept pace with the warriors who moved further into the village. Once the warriors stopped the crowd circled them. Dawn warned herself to take her leave and yet once again she paid no heed. She remained enthralled like the others, while wondering if the devil had already doomed them all.

Cree. She shut her eyes for a moment. His name echoed through her, not like a tolling bell, but a whisper that tingled along her flesh, and she feared that the mere thought of his name might hold the power to conquer. She could not imagine what the power of speaking it would do.

Dawn opened her eyes and her glance fell on him. He stood proud and tall, looking not at all fearful or concerned by his capture, though the warriors around him did. They kept their distance, some even inching further away.

Colum dismounted his mare and kept a firm grasp on the chain that restrained the prisoner. His short height and barrel-shape did not threaten, but his stinging voice and quick hand to those who displeased him left no doubt to his indisputable authority. Besides, he had his troop of near fifty warriors to protect him.

Upon his arrival, he had made it clear to all in the village that he was to be obeyed, and the land worked hard for the feudal lord. He had demonstrated on a hapless farmer what would happen to anyone who proved unruly. He had beaten the man so badly that it had taken him weeks to heal.

All had worried that they would suffer greatly under his command and though he demanded long hours of toil and strict obedience, he did not starve them. Life was not easy under his rule, but at least no one went hungry.

"You see my strength now," Colum shouted, "I captured the mighty Cree and I shall make a gift of him to the liege lord. We will wait on the Earl of Carrick's word to see what is to be done with him."

"He stays here among us?" Timmins, the smithy, asked with concern.

Dawn saw Timmins cringe, realizing his mistake too late, and those around him quickly moved away.

Colum stomped over to him and spittle sprayed from his mouth as he shouted, "Do you doubt my ability to protect you?"

"Nay. Nay, my lord," Timmins said his head bent in supplication. "I question my own ability to forge more sufficient chain to hold him."

Dawn was not surprised by Timmins's apologetic response. He had a wife and two young *bairns* to worry about. He would not be so foolish as to insult Colum.

"This chain will do," Colum boasted. "I have kept him secured with it thus far, and I will continue to do so. He will give us no trouble. His warring days are done. Now go. All of you get back to work."

She turned to take her leave, though she found herself unable to stop from taking one last peek at the prisoner.

His dark eyes latched onto hers as bold as could be and a jolt of heat hit her and rushed through her with such fury that her cheeks felt on fire and no doubt flamed red. She startled and nearly stumbled when she turned and as soon as she secured firm footing, she made haste.

She hurried to see to her duties, while trying to shake Cree free from her thoughts. He lingered there like a bad dream she had trouble escaping.

Familiar high-pitched shouts managed to penetrate her foggy mind and had her running. Dawn was one of many helpers to the cook Flanna who ran her kitchen with a strict hand. She was probably annoyed that everyone had deserted their duties so they could not only greet the returning warriors, but have a look at the notorious Cree for themselves.

Cree again? Dawn could not seem to keep her thoughts off him. It was as if one look had branded him to her every thought and that disturbed her. Slaves were branded, and she had no desire to be a slave to anyone. Though she was far from free, at least she wore no one's mark.

Another sharp shout hurried her steps and when she rounded the back of the keep Flanna was berating two workers who paled as she shook a large wooden spoon dangerously close to their faces. They scurried off without a word to do her bidding. She then turned and had at Dawn.

"You will be working extra hours along with the

others for deserting your duties," she shouted and threatened Dawn with the same wooden spoon. "Lord Colum will no doubt want a fine celebration feast this night, and I cannot prepare a pleasing one with just two hands. Now get busy. See that we have enough dried dandelion root for drinks and make certain there is enough thyme, and then see to cleaning the root plants for the stew."

Thyme. Brewed, it chased away nightmares. Could it rid her of thoughts of Cree?

"What are you standing there for?" Flanna shouted.

Dawn got busy in the kitchen, though not out of fear of Flanna. She was quick to punish many of the workers with a whack of her spoon across a hand or back of a head when angered by their laziness or lack of sense, but never once had she ever raised it against Dawn. She had threatened with a shake of the spoon in Dawn's face, but had gone no further.

Dawn wondered if it was her height that put Flanna off, since her head barely reached Dawn's chest. Then she thought that perhaps Flanna empathized with her. While not alike in height and weight, she short and skinny and Dawn tall and while certainly not thick in weight, not slim either, alike they were. They both possessed plain features, not faces that turned men's heads, indeed not memorable. Their hair was even similar in color, dark red like that of dried blood and straight without a wave or curl, though gray strands ran through Flanna's, since she was nearer to thirty years, while Dawn had barely turned ten and nine.

And worse, there was not a man ready to love them. Lay with either of them for sure, but love them, make a home with them, have babes with them? None wanted the two women for that. Dawn believed Flanna had accepted her lot and lay with men of her choosing, but Dawn could not do the same. She had been lucky that no man had ever forced himself on her, though some of the young women, who lay freely with men, laughed when they didn't think she heard. Dawn knew they believed her commonly features were not the only thing that stopped a man from taking her and spilling his seed.

After all, who wanted a woman who had no voice?

Chapter Two

"Dawn! You may not be able to speak, but I know you are not deaf," Flanna shouted.

Then why did she yell? Dawn turned to face her. Most believed her deaf. After all, she was struck dumb, so it would only follow that she could not hear as well, but she heard fine, better than most.

"The wild onions need replenishing. Go collect more and be quick about it."

Dawn grabbed a basket from the many piled by the door and hurried out past the cook's garden and to the field beyond. She didn't waste a moment. She yanked out bunches, and the pungent scent rushed up to sting her nostrils.

She could smell well enough, see even better, but she had been born without a voice. Her mother had told her that she made no sound when entering the world. She had wondered over why it was so. Why had she been born with no voice? She could not make a sound at all. No grunt, no moan, nothing.

She could not cry out for help. No sobs were heard when she shed tears. Her laughter was forever silent, and she could not cry out in the throes of pleasure, which was the reason the other young women so often laughed at her.

"What man wants to rut with a silent woman?" She had heard Dorrie, certainly no friend, remark and those with her had laughed as well. Of course Dorrie had continued, encouraged by the agreeable responses of her cohorts.

Dawn could have turned away and heard no more of her hurtful remarks, but she had been curious. Dorrie had spoken with such confidence that it had been obvious she had experience coupling. While Dawn was not ignorant of the act itself, she had no firsthand knowledge of it and wanted to know more.

"Men want women who moan, cry out, and pant with pleasure, for it gives them just as much pleasure. A silent woman cannot even grow a man hard. A needy man would never force himself on such a woman. There is no excitement in it, for she cannot even scream when she explodes with pleasure."

Dawn's heart had hurt then, for she had wondered the same herself. Hearing it only confirmed what she had suspected... no man would ever want her.

A smile tempted her lips. She recalled how Lila, her closest friend since her arrival at the village ten years ago, had put a quick end to the insults. She had rounded the cottage unexpectedly and assaulted Dorrie with a stream of verbal arrows that hit well their mark. Dorrie had run off in tears, no one following her.

Lila had told Dawn not to worry that someday a man would love her, for he would see how very special she was. Dawn wanted to believe her, though recently turning ten and nine years without a single man having ever shown any interest in her, had her believing that her life was destined to be a solitary one. Fate had declared it so.

Lila was two years younger than her, ten and seven years and already round with child. Paul, Lila's husband, two years older than her, had loved Lila as long as Dawn could remember. Paul, Lila, and she had fast become friends upon her arrival. They had liked the pictures she would draw in the dirt or on the sand along the shoreline. And it hadn't taken Lila long to understand her hand gestures.

When Dawn's mother died two years ago Paul made it known that he would look after her and that she would be no burden to the village. She had worried when Colum and his men had arrived a year later. She had thought for sure that the warriors would have their way with her. But as soon as Colum had discovered that she could not speak, he kept his men clear of her, declaring that none of his warriors would seed idiots.

Dawn did not understand why people thought her ignorant simply because she could not speak. She heard and learned so much by listening, and those who chose to converse with her found a way to do so.

She laughed silently thinking how perfectly matched Lila and she were, Lila an endless chatterer, and she unable to say a word. Paul often reminded her how blessed he was to have her in their lives, for Lila had someone who would never interrupt her never-ending tongue.

Dawn stretched the ache out in her back and a drop of rain splat on her cheek. Rain or not, she did not want to return to the kitchen knowing that a long night lay ahead, only to fall exhausted on her pallet afterwards, wake, and begin again tomorrow.

It would be such a pleasure to have a day to simply do whatever she wished, but that was a dream that surely would never see fruition.

"Dawn! Dawn!"

Flanna's screech prickled her skin sending gooseflesh running over it. Dawn shuddered, grabbed the basket full of wild onions and before she could turn Flanna gave another shout.

"Hurry your steps. Lord Colum demands your presence."

Dawn almost tripped over her feet and her stomach roiled. Why would he want to see her? It never bode well when Lord Colum demanded to see a villager. She struggled to recall if she had done anything to offend him.

Nothing came to mind, and when she was a few feet from Flanna it suddenly struck her. Had Lord Colum or one of his warriors seen the way she had stared at the prisoner? How the heat had risen to blotch her cheeks? How their eyes had remained connected far too long?

Fear sent her hands trembling, and Flanna saw it when she reached to take the basket from her.

"What have you gone and done?" she asked in a low voice so heavy with concern that it sounded foreign, and Dawn stared at her wondering if someone else had spoken.

Flanna grabbed Dawn's arm and walked her far enough away from the kitchen door so no one would hear. Her voice remained low when she said, "Tell me you have done nothing foolish." She shocked Dawn even more when she grabbed her hands, shook them, and demanded, "Tell me."

Dawn could not believe that Flanna wanted her to respond with hand gestures. She had never thought that Flanna had paid heed to them. Dawn tapped her chest and shrugged.

"You do not know," Flanna said understanding.

She nodded to confirm, though wondered if her own folly was the cause.

Flanna genuinely looked worried for her and that

worried Dawn all the more. She would have never expected Flanna to care and yet she did. The revelation startled her.

"Go wash your hands in the rain barrel, and then crumple some heather in them. Lord Colum will not like it if you present yourself with the stench of onions upon you."

Her sharp tone had returned, though the worry remained.

Dawn nodded and went to walk around her to do as she had ordered when Flanna grabbed her arm once more.

"You come back here when Lord Colum is finished with you, and let me know what he wanted of you."

Showing her appreciation the only way she could, Dawn nodded and smiled.

"Hurry, he does not like to be kept waiting," Flanna ordered, and Dawn thought she caught a tear glisten in one eye. After giving Dawn a shove to send her on her way, Flanna hurried off herself.

Dawn worked fast. All too aware of the suffering Colum could inflict if his summons was not answered quickly enough. She did not want to think of the punishment he could order if she had somehow offended him. It was best she hurry and be done with the ordeal as quickly as possible.

When she finished removing the odor of onions from her hands she entered the kitchen. Silence struck and all stared wide-eyed at her until Flanna ordered the workers to tend to their chores. Dawn continued to pass through, it being the only assigned entry way for the servants to the Great Hall.

She tucked her long, dark hair behind her ears and silently recited a prayer of mercy as she walked through the narrow stone passageway until she finally came to the wooden arch. Once she stepped past, she would be in the Great Hall.

Dawn prayed for courage, but fear remained her companion as she forced herself to step forward. It was not a large room. The keep had been built small, since the feudal lord had not been in residence here since long before she had arrived. It had sat in disrepair until Colum had appeared. He had the hall repaired first and a small dais erected the large chair in the middle more representative of a throne.

"Dawn!"

The shout startled her, so loud was it that it echoed off the stone walls. She realized Colum—like others—assumed that along with being dumb she was also deaf. She hurried over and bobbed her head respectfully and kept it lowered.

"Look at me," Colum said, though it sounded like a shout.

She raised her head cautiously. Her heart beat ever so wildly that she thought it would burst. This was the closest she had ever been to Colum. She was surprised to note that his pudgy face wore a pinched expression, and there were many more lines and wrinkles than could be seen from a distance. His lips were so narrow that it appeared as if he had none at all. And his shoulder length brown hair was sparse on top and sprinkled with gray.

"You listen well, woman," he ordered with a stinging tongue, "and you find a way to let me know that you understand what I say."

She nodded and swallowed her fear, though it stuck in a lump in her throat.

"You were present at our victorious return with

the prisoner Cree."

She nodded again and dread swelled like a rising ball of fire ready to scorch her. Had Colum seen the exchange between Cree and her? Was she to be punished for gazing upon him too long?

"Cree is to be held prisoner until I receive word from Lord Gerwan as to his fate. I have no doubt that Lord Gerwan will order his execution and will want to journey here to be in attendance for it."

Her stomach tightened thinking of the horrible suffering Cree would endure before he died. Torture always preceded executions and in no time he would scream for mercy. It would not be given; it never was. And then there were those who would cheer at his pain. A shiver ran through her, and she wondered why she should care. He certainly had not cared when he himself had slaughtered so many innocent people.

"Cree's wounds need tending. I will not allow him to die before Lord Gerwan arrives and condemns him to death. But Cree is a wise warrior, and I have no doubt he already makes plans to escape."

Why was he telling her this? This was not something for a servant to know. What did he expect of her?

"He will try to retrieve information from whoever I send to tend him, for he knows all too well that I will see no harm come to him just yet."

A dreadful thought hit her. Could Colum be thinking of appointing her Cree's caretaker? Her worst fear was confirmed when next he spoke.

"He can get no such information from you." Colum sneered. "For once your evil affliction will serve a purpose."

Evil? He believed evil had something to do with her inability to speak? The thought disturbed and worried her.

"Your duties are now that of caretaker to the prisoner Cree. You will see that he is kept well fed. I want him to believe himself safe, and a full stomach will make him feel such."

Suddenly, Dawn understood his reasoning, for he had used the same logic on the villagers. Keeping everyone well fed gave them a sense of security when truly there was none. It made her realize just how powerless she and the villagers were.

"Do you understand," he shouted.

Dawn nodded rapidly while trying to comprehend what he expected of her. She simply could not foresee herself tending Cree. Those dark eyes of his had seemed to consume her from a distance. How would his intense glare affect her in close proximity?

Already the heat started rising in her body and prickled her skin. She grew anxious that it would rush to stain her cheeks and embarrass her. This was not good, and yet how could she escape it?

"You will report everything he says to me." Colum's hands flew around him in a poor imitation of her precise gestures. "Those signals of yours, someone must understands them —" He pondered a moment, and then it struck him. "The woman Lila; she will interpret."

A sickening sensation settled in the pit of her stomach. She did not want Lila part of this. There was no telling what she would suffer being involved. And Paul? He would be insane with worry for his wife. She would do her best to make Colum understand her, so there would be no need to rely on Lila.

"You will gather food and whatever is necessary to tend his wounds, and you will spend as much time with him as possible. With you unable to speak, he will do most of the talking and you will report what he says. Do you understand all I've said?"

Dawn bobbed her head.

"One more thing." His sneer grew wide and made his narrow lips grow narrower until it looked like he had no lips at all. "You will keep the prisoner satisfied in whatever way is necessary."

Dawn stared at him not certain she understood.

Colum shook his head annoyed and leaned closer to shout in her face. "You will rut with him if he wants. You do know how to rut do you not?"

The few warriors that were present laughed.

One shouted, "I can show her."

Colum glared at him. "What did I tell you about spilling your side in a dumb one? I will have no warrior of mine seeding an imbecile." He grinned. "Cree on the other hand can leave his seed in her belly before he dies knowing he leaves an idiot in his memory." The warriors laughed again and Colum shouted at her. "Now be gone and do my bidding or suffer my wrath."

She fled his presence. Fear now a shadow that clung heavily to her. He was sending her to willingly submit to be ravished by Cree and even hoped he would get her with child. Feed and satisfy his lust and the prisoner would what? Trust her? How did Colum think that such a savage would trust anyone?

She stood in the kitchen not even realizing she had entered it.

Flanna snagged a basket from the floor, shoved it at her, and pushed her out the door shouting, "You forgot the thyme."

Once outside Dawn stood bewildered as a light rain fell on her. She was unable to comprehend what had just passed with Colum. Flanna joined her only a moment later and hurried her away from the door.

"You are deathly pale. What is wrong?" Flanna asked anxiously.

Dawn shook her head not believing what she had just been told.

Flanna grabbed her hands. "Tell me."

Dawn raised her hands and started to explain. She outlined someone large, and then locked her wrists together. Flanna understood instantly.

"The prisoner Cree."

Dawn nodded and went on to tap her chest and gestured tending his wounds and feeding him, and then she suddenly stopped and stared wide-eyed at Flanna. Reluctantly, and with heat rushing her cheeks red, she bent her fingers just enough for the tips to touch her palm and with one finger from the other hand shoved it repeatedly in and out of the hole.

Flanna gasped. "Good lord, no. He cannot expect you to rut with the savage."

Suddenly, there was a shout from the open door and they both turned to see Goddard, Colum's most trusted warrior. He was broad and tall, though nowhere near the prisoner's size. His face and arms were scarred no doubt from endless battles, though the women seemed to favor him. Dawn had seen him talking with many of the village women, though mostly with Dorrie.

"Here! Now!" he shouted, and they both hurried to enter the kitchen after him.

Flanna went to speak, but Goddard raised his hand and silenced her.

"The dumb one will be seeing to the care of the prisoner. She is to take what food or items she wants and answers to no one but Lord Colum. Is that understood?"

Flanna gave a quick nod.

Goddard turned to Dawn. "Be quick and see to your new duties." He snickered and raised his voice. "Understand?"

Dawn bobbed her head knowing that he reminded what was expected of her.

Goddard left the room and there was silence. No one moved. No one spoke. They stood and stared at her.

"To work," Flanna ordered the others and turned to Dawn. "Take all that you need." More quietly she whispered, "May God help you."

Chapter Three

Dawn approached the hut with reluctant steps. It was a confined shed used to house those Colum felt needed punishing. A slit no more than three fingers wide had been placed near the top of the door. It allowed the only light to enter and the guard to have a look.

Usually only one warrior stood watch. Two now stood outside in front and two others stepped from around back, snickered when they spotted her, and returned to their posts.

She gripped the one basket and the bucket of water she carried and stopped a couple of feet from the warriors.

One stepped forward, equal in height to her though heavy in weight, and if she recalled correctly his name was John and the other warrior, who had not moved, she believed was Angus. Spending all her time in the kitchen and not permitted to serve in the Great Hall, she had little contact with the warriors and was not familiar with them all. And she preferred it that way.

John gave a quick look in the basket, nodded, and stepped back to open the door.

It was Angus, pale of skin and bright red hair, who snorted and said, "We were told you were to take your time. So you will be leaving none too soon."

With that, John gave her a shove and as she

stumbled through the open door, fighting to remain standing, she heard the wooden latch lowered firmly in place.

Trapped with a savage.

Her heart beat madly in her chest and her breathing turned labored. If she could speak, she knew she would scream with fear. With the hut so small, she had hit the far wall only a few steps from the door leaving her to assume that the prisoner was on the other side and barely a few feet from her.

The gray skies and light rain allowed for little light to enter through the slot, so the confined space was mostly dark with a sprinkle of shadows. A slight stench stung the nose and she knew it would grow worse, for the hut was only cleaned out after someone served their time.

She heard the rustle then and moved along the wall to the door, hoping what little light was available would reach into the shadows if she looked from a different angle. There was another movement, another rustle, and fear prickled her skin.

It took a moment to make sense of what she saw and when she finally did, she shivered. To her left in the corner a huge shadow loomed. It moved slightly, and she pressed herself back in the corner by the door. Her only means of escape yet by no means accessible.

"I can smell your fear."

His voice was deep and tinged with menace, and her legs went limp. She struggled to keep from collapsing and tried to calm her trembling hands. But he was right, for her fear was potent, her courage slim.

Cree stepped out of the shadows and her breath stalled. He was so very large, more so at this short distance than seeing him from afar—and so sinfully handsome—even in dismal light one would never think him a savage. But evil was a cohort of deception, and she would do well to remember that.

"Colum sends me a plain one."

For once Dawn was relieved to be thought plain, perhaps then he would not find her to his liking. At least she prayed he would not.

"Come over here."

Though his voice low, it was no less a command. One that Dawn had no choice but to obey. It was seeing that his wrists were no longer bound that caused her to hesitate.

"I give an order only once."

The threat in his tone left no doubt that she should pay quick heed to his warning. With limbs that refused to stop trembling, she stepped forward. Three small steps and she stood in front of him, her head lowered, daring not to glance in his eyes.

"Look at me," he snapped so sharply that her head shot up.

If she could have gasped she would have, though in a sense her eyes did for they spread wide. His dark eyes intoxicated and as before she felt a tingling warmth take hold of her flesh.

"You will tend me."

Not a question, but another command. She nodded and placed the burden of the basket and bucket on the ground. Reaching in the basket, she snatched a hunk of cheese to hand him.

He took it and as he broke off pieces to eat he walked slowly around her, at times so close that his bare arms brushed against her. Even through her linen shift she felt his rock-hard muscles and knew his strength must be unfathomable.

He stopped in front of her. "You will need to stop trembling to see to my wounds."

That he saw she quivered and smelled her fear, left her feeling exposed and vulnerable. She often felt that way without a voice to defend herself. But what good would a voice do her now. Even if she screamed the guards would not come to her aid.

He grabbed her chin roughly and his dark eyes bore into hers. "Do you understand what I say?"

Dawn nodded as best she could, his grip strong, and he quickly released her. She tore off a chunk of bread from the loaf to give him and hoped it would keep him from talking while she saw to his wounds.

He took it and remained standing where he was, a wise choice, since it was the only spot that had a modicum of light. She got busy and prayed that once she finished tending him the guards would let her leave.

Dawn scooped up a full dipper of water and held it out to him. He drank it and handed it back to her. She then poured water over a clean cloth she retrieved from the basket and proceeded to gently clean his chest of the dried blood. She continued to wet the cloth from the dipper and wring it out on the ground, so that the water in the bucket would remain clean to drink and use for cleansing.

With each swipe of the cloth, she saw that his wounds were nothing more than scratches. While it was unlikely that his chest could deflect arrows, axes or swords, the taut, hard muscles certainly felt to have the strength of an impenetrable shield.

She moved around to his back and was met with more muscles. What truly amazed her was that his body bore no scars. There were few, if any, warriors who did not bear a battle scar and many thought the more scars the more courageous the warrior. But was the true mark of courage for a warrior to walk away from battle without blight on him?

After wiping his chest and back with the wet cloth one last time, Dawn took a fresh cloth and rubbed him dry. Her bare hand followed the cloth making certain she had cleaned away all dried blood.

"You have a gentle touch."

Dawn yanked her hand away and froze.

Cree spun around and grabbed hold of her hand. "Swallow that foolish fear of yours or you will suffer for it."

Dawn could do nothing but stare into his eyes and their darkness only served to frighten her more. How could she be brave against a man of his size? Even now his hand could easily crush hers. She would be a fool not to fear him.

"You forgot one wound," he said and took her hand and shoved it down into the top of his leggings.

Shocked by his actions, she fought to control her panic. She pressed her fingers along his flat, hard flesh just below his waist, but found no wound. She glanced back up at him.

"Lower."

She looked again, but even the dim light she saw nothing and reluctantly loosened the ties so that she could ease his garment down lower on his hips.

"Keep going," he said.

She gently worked the leather down, her fingers brushing along more muscled flesh. She soon noticed the large bulge between his legs and though she near froze again, she fought against it. Was there truly a wound or was this a ploy to have her touch him intimately?

"Go on," he urged.

His flesh was not only hard but warm, and there was a scent about him that she favored, though she could not say what it was, and it was unseemly for her to even think such a wicked thing.

Please. Please let me find a wound.

Just as her fingertips grazed the hair that nestled his shaft, she saw it. Low on his right side, a bruise much too dark that she feared it could prove a problem. Without thinking, she dropped to her knees to take a closer look. She had seen some wounds like this, cut and forced to bleed, but the person always died.

Her fingers probed it gently, and he did not flinch, though it had to have pained him. There was nothing she could do except apply salve as she would to his scratches. She reached for the small crock in the basket just behind him and lost her balance. She tried to right herself fearful that her face would land against his groin.

His hands were quick, yanking her up clear off the floor. "When I am ready to have you between my legs I will let you know. Now tend my wounds."

He dropped her to her feet and this time she made certain to keep her balance. He had actually thought she intended to—her stomach rolled over not only at his wrong assumption, but the vision it evoked. Could he possibly expect such wickedness from her?

Not wanting to give it another thought, she hastily applied the salve, giving the bruise a quick dab, and not daring to linger. With deft hands, she tended his minor scratches.

His words persisted in disturbing, running wildly in her head. His intentions were all too clear. He would have her *when he was ready.* If not today or tomorrow, one day he would have his way with her. And there was naught she could do about it. She was as trapped as he was.

"What other food have you?"

He walked to the door and sat, bracing his back against it. He rested his head back and took a deep breath, as if his ordeal had suddenly tired him and he needed to reclaim his strength.

When he lifted his head and saw her staring, he went rigid and snapped, "Be quick about it."

Dawn scrambled to gather the food items. For a moment, a sheer moment, she thought she caught sight of the fatigue that had surely claimed him and yet it took a mere instant for him to regain his strength.

She had brought plenty of food recalling how Colum had told her to keep the prisoner well fed, much like an animal fattened before slaughter. She intended to leave all she had brought setting it on a cloth beside him along with a flask of ale.

She turned, intending to sit by her basket, and once again prayed she could soon take her leave.

"Eat with me," he said.

She looked at him oddly. No women dared eat until the warriors finished their food. And besides, she had no stomach to partake of any sustenance.

He shoved a piece of bread at her and, fearing the consequences should she not obey, she took it. She did, however, pretend to nibble at it. If she even dared take a bite, she would surely choke, for her mouth had gone dry.

Silence followed and she wondered if he waited for a response from her. She dreaded the moment he found out she had no voice. How would he feel that Colum had chosen a *dumb one* to tend him? Would he be angry and lash out at her? She was surprised that it had gone this long without him questioning her lack of response, though she supposed he believed fear held her tongue.

"Colum sends me a quiet one. One who listens rather than speaks."

She made no move to explain. Better he thinks what he wishes to think and save her from explaining.

"No doubt there is a reason he chose you in particular to tend me."

On that point, he was surely right.

"Shy, quiet, not one to gossip, but one who allows others to speak while she listens."

True she was shy, not able to gossip, though she doubted she would if she could, having seen the hurt and damage it could cause. Naturally, she had no choice but to listen.

"When one truly listens, one truly hears."

That he understood that surprised her. Being immersed in silence had forced her to listen, truly listen as he had said. And she heard, heard far more than others were aware of, but no one with a voice would understand that. Yet this savage did.

"Your name."

Dread descended over her. The moment she feared was upon her.

"Stop being cowardly and tell me your name."

A name was so easy for a person to recite, to make an introduction. She had never had that opportunity and with the discovery of her affliction people shied away or were rude.

"Have you no tongue," Cree snapped.

Thankfully, she did have that, and she stuck out

the tip to prove it.

"So you do have some courage."

His grinning laugh surprised her and made him appear all the more handsome, but at the moment that did not matter to her. What did matter was that he had found her response amusing, and it would be wise to take advantage of his levity and make him aware of the truth.

Dawn pressed her fingers to her throat and shook her head.

"You cannot speak?"

She nodded and waited apprehensively for his response.

"How long before you can?"

He did not understand. He assumed her ill.

Trepidation mounted as she shook her head.

He looked with puzzling eyes on her and leaned forward away from the door and closer to her. His face was so close to hers that his warm breath brushed her cheek. "Are you telling me that you cannot speak at all?"

She answered with one quick bob of her head.

"Not a grunt or groan?"

She shook her head and waited.

"How long have you suffered this," —he shook his head— "I am asking you questions you cannot answer."

She was about to gesture that she could speak with him in her own way, but recalled Colum telling her that she was to report everything Cree said to her. If he knew that she could communicate, then he might be averse to saying anything to her. Colum would certainly punish her if she had no information to give him, so she chose not to let Cree know.

"Colum was wise for sending me a dumb one."

Dawn was aware that anyone without a voice was referred to as dumb, but along with it came the assumption that the person was also ignorant. Her mother had made certain she was anything but that. Though she could not speak, she could understand French, Latin, and various Gaelics. Her mother had taught her and had encouraged her drawing. She had insisted that Dawn had been given such a generous talent as a distinct way of communicating.

"He believes he has bested me."

Did he suddenly think her deaf too? Would he chatter away and give her news to take to Colum?

"You do have a name, do you not?" Cree asked.

She nodded.

"Is there some way you can express it to me?"

She didn't see any harm in letting him know her name. She turned her gaze on the ground beside her and cleared the dirt of the few leaves and stones, grabbing one as she finished. She drew a horizontal line and above it a half circle. She finished it with lines bursting from the top of it.

Cree studied it a moment, and then glanced up at her. "Dawn. Your name is Dawn."

Pleased that he understood so quickly, she smiled and nodded.

"Dawn," he said curtly.

Her name was so abrupt on his lips that she thought him angry. However, she did not shiver, though she remained still.

"It is time for you to take your leave."

He stood then and returned to the shadowy corner.

She did not hesitate to stand and hurry to the door. She wanted out of the small prison and away from Cree.

"Dawn."

Not a shout, and yet the potency of it had her cringing and reluctantly turning around. She could not see him. The shadows had swallowed him whole. She waited hoping he had not changed his mind.

"When you return with my evening meal bring a blanket."

Relief trickled all the way down to her toes, and she nodded.

"Make it a large one. You will be sleeping with me tonight."

Chapter Four

Night fell and pitched Cree into total darkness. A chill came with it, but he did not shiver or bemoan his circumstances. He remained strong and focused on what must be done next. He needed to learn as much as he could.

He had had no doubt that the stout leader Colum would send him a woman or ply him with food in hopes of retrieving information from him before he had him tortured mercilessly, and then finally executed him. It appeared his fate was inevitable, or at least his enemies believed so.

He had counted on their ignorance, and they hadn't failed him. Though he had been surprised to see that Colum had sent him a woman who could not speak assuming he could learn nothing from her. However, Dawn was not as dumb as probably many assumed. In the short time he had spent with her, he had learned that she was capable of communicating, and he doubted that Column was aware of the extent of her soundless speech.

She would serve him well, and he would see that she did, though he couldn't allow lust to interfere with his plans. He had grown hard when her face accidentally met his groin. He had not bed a woman in a while. His mission had kept him busy, so it had only been natural that Dawn's mishap had grown him hard.

While he could easily abate his need between her

legs, he had no intention of bedding her. He favored women who could moan, groan, and scream quite loudly with pleasure from his mighty thrusts.

He would make Colum think Dawn was serving his purpose, while using her to his advantage. Then when the time was right...

Night shadows scurried away from him when he grinned, the dark even fearing him.

He had fought many battles in his bid to get here and now that he was here he would let nothing stand in his way—especially not a plain woman without a voice.

Why his thoughts lingered on her he could not say, perhaps it was the fact that though the smell of fear had weighed heavily on her, she had not let it consume her. She had remained stoic, shedding not a single tear nor begging on bended knee. She had done what was expected of her in spite of it all.

Still, he had no intentions of involving himself with a voiceless woman. His lust would have to wait, and then he'd find himself a woman that he'd make scream with pleasure. He'd need one. He'd always had a woman after battle, a willing one. He could not abide, nor would he condone his men forcing any woman. If they could not find a willing one, then they could assuage their own lust.

He shook his thoughts away. He had no time to waste on such trivial musings. His mission came first and foremost and that was what he needed to concentrate on. His time was limited, and he needed to be prepared. He could tell upon entering the village that his scouts' information had proven accurate. They had mapped the area well, designating buildings, estimating the populace, and detailing the workings of the village. He was familiar with it all, and so when he had arrived at the Village Dowell it was as if he was returning to a place he knew well.

Dawn had caught his eye not soon after entering the village. How could she not? She stood out in the crowd being taller than most men. He couldn't say what made him focus on her. Her features certainly didn't captivate, though neither did they repel. Her body was pleasing enough, a narrow waist and full hips just as he liked them, though her breasts didn't even look to be a handful. Her hair hung long and the color wasn't particularly appealing—dark red—and without a curl or wave to it, though it shined. And the scent had been quite pleasing. It reminded him of the heather covered hills on a fine autumn day.

He forced the smile from his face as soon as he realized it had surfaced. He didn't need to be thinking about Dawn. But there had been something about her when their eyes had met that had stirred him unexpectedly. He had nearly gotten hard and that was unusual for him. He controlled his lust never letting it rule him. That a woman, plain and voiceless, could tempt him so easily disturbed him.

The latch creaked and Cree jumped to his feet annoyed that he had been so engrossed in his thoughts that he hadn't heard anyone approach. He silently berated himself for not paying heed and losing himself in foolish musings.

The door sprung open and Dawn stumbled in, the guard's laughter trailing in after her as he forced it shut. Cree clenched his fist, angry with the man for shoving her and promising himself that the idiot would suffer for it.

Cree walked over to her stopping so close that their bodies almost touched. "Are you all right?"

She nodded.

He stared at her lips wondering what it must be like to never be able to speak a word, never make yourself known, never to cry out in pleasure. He turned hastily away from her.

"I'm hungry."

With her hands trembling and her thoughts in turmoil, she hurriedly set to work. She knew lust when she saw it. She would see it in Paul's eyes for his wife and in other men when they sniffed after women.

Even though the hut was dark, they had stood close enough for her to see the lust in Cree's eyes. And while she feared what she saw, it also troubled her that she felt a quickening in her stomach. Was it because she had never lain with a man that her body had responded? Was it nothing more than her body's need that she felt? Had it been unnatural for her to go so long without mating?

She didn't like these thoughts that buzzed like a swarm of bees in her head, and she tried to keep focused on her task at hand.

Cree watched her work. Her hands trembled, though she kept good control not allowing it to interfere with her chore. She fumbled with the pouch that hung from the belt at her waist, but got it open quickly enough. He was surprised when the scent of heather filled the confined space. She sprinkled handfuls of the scented sprigs around, and he was grateful. It helped mask the lingering pungent odor.

She spread a blanket on the hard earth and placed two folded ones on it. She then emptied the basket of food setting generous amounts in the middle of the blanket.

He almost grinned. Colum planned on keeping him well feed and his lust appeased in hopes Cree would speak freely to Dawn. Cree had other plans. He would be the one to learn from Dawn. Though mute, she had obviously found a way to communicate with those who bothered to pay attention, and he would pay her attention.

She waved her hand over the blanket inviting him to partake.

Cree walked around to where she stood on the opposite side of the blanket. He sensed her apprehension as he approached and admired her fortitude to keep a stoic stand, though she obviously wished to run. Where would she run? There was no place for her to go.

He held his hand out to her. "Allow me to help you sit."

Her eyes turned wide and if she hadn't been mute, he had no doubt that his unexpected mannerly action would have turned her speechless.

Hesitantly, her hand stretched out to him.

He didn't wait; he snatched hold of it. Her chilled hand soon turned warm in his heated one, and he was surprised that her skin felt soft. He had thought with all her chores that calluses would mar her hands, but not so.

With his grip strong, he assisted her to the ground. He then returned to the other side and sat down.

"Did you cook any of this?" he asked.

She shook her head.

"You don't work in the kitchen?"

She nodded.

"What do you do there?"

Dawn stared at him a moment surprised that he attempted to converse with her and surprised that she favored the idea.

She pointed to the thyme in the bread and the onions in the stew and with her hands demonstrated picking and chopping them.

"You gather and help prepare."

She nodded.

"Many work in the kitchen?"

She held up her two hands and then closed one.

"Fifteen," he said and she confirmed with a nod.

He was impressed that she could count and did so without hesitation. She obviously was familiar with numbers or she would have hesitated.

"Column must love to eat."

Her hand moved back and forth to her mouth as if shoveling in food, and it caused Cree to laugh and Dawn to smile.

Even with the bare amount of light they had he could see that her smile had turned her otherwise plain face quiet lovely. She would never be a beauty, but he found something about her attractive that was just too damn hard to ignore, and so did his groin. It stirred much too much to his liking.

"Does Column feed his people as well as he feeds himself?"

Her smile faded, though she nodded.

"He feeds his people, but does not treat them well."

She shrugged and Cree understood that she would dare not betray the man who could cause her great harm.

"Have you lived in Dowell since your birth?" he asked deciding to take a different tactic. He'd learn more about her, thus learning more about the workings of the village and in essence Column.

She shook her head and held up both hands spreading her fingers.

"Ten years you're here?"

She nodded and smiled.

He noticed that her dark eyes lit along with her smile. "You came here with your mum and da?"

Dawn held up one finger.

"You came with only one—your mum?"

She nodded and again her smile faded as she shook her head.

"Your mum died?"

She nodded surprised he understood. She hadn't been trying to tell him of her mum's passing. She always saddened at the memory of losing her mum. She loved her dearly and mi—

"You miss her."

Again he caught her by surprise understanding her thoughts, as if he could read them. She gave a quick nod.

"You are alone now?"

She shook her head and smiled.

"Column sends me a wedded woman?" he snarled.

Dawn drew back fearful. He sounded like a snarling dog ready to bite, and she hastily shook her head.

"Explain," he snapped.

Her skin turned hot and her stomach churned as panic began to rise inside her. How could she explain to him? Would he understand her gestures or would he grow angry with her?

She quickly held up two fingers.

"You have two friends?"

With a nod, she continued. She pointed a finger at him, and then turned it on her.

"A man and a woman?"

She gave another nodded as she linked two fingers together.

"They're wed."

She grinned, joined her hands together and extended them passed her stomach.

"The woman is with child."

She nodded.

"Are they you're only friends?"

Dawn thought a moment. While there were many villagers who were pleasant to her, she couldn't call them friends, and then there were a few who made fun of her and far too many who simply ignored her.

She nodded and patted her chest.

"They are the only ones who you care for and who care for you."

Her smile grew, and she was disturbed to see him grow angry. His eyes narrowed, his jaw tightened, and his nostrils even flared.

"No men force themselves on you do they?"

She gave a fast shake of her head.

"Have you taken any man willingly between your legs?"

Her body flushed with heat, and she was glad for the darkness that she hoped concealed her red-stained cheeks.

"And don't lie to me," he snapped, "for I will learn the truth myself."

Her stomach churned at his words. He intended to have his way with her, and there was nothing she could do to prevent it.

"Answer me," he snapped again.

She patted her chest and shook her head.

"You've never given yourself to a man?"

She continued shaking her head.

"You're a virgin?"

She nodded slowly, as if perhaps she shouldn't admit the truth to him.

"How have you managed," —he laughed and shook his head— "Column has ordered his men to stay away from you. He'll have none of his men sire a du —"

He bit his tongue as soon as he saw the hurt surface on her face, though she turned away from him quickly enough.

"You will not turn away from me," he ordered and she had no choice but to obey.

Her chin went up just a bit, but enough to be noticeable. And though the hurt remained in her eyes, her face and the pale column of her neck had grown taut with courage.

"No one will lie between your legs, but me."

Her mind went silent and for a moment she knew what was meant by someone turning speechless. His edict had so shocked her that no thought came to her head.

"You belong to me now."

It took her a moment to form a clear thought and when she did his words struck her hard.

Belong to me.

She was nothing but chattel to him, to be owned and worked like the burdensome beasts who toiled for their masters. She would be expected to spread her legs for him whenever he ordered, and she would not be able to object. Had she expected any different? Had she foolishly thought, if only for a few moments, that because he had attempted to converse with her that he would be kind and treat her as kindly as her friends?

A spark of anger misplaced her fear and suddenly she wanted to lash out at him and tell him she was not a woman to be used at his whim. But even if she had a voice, she would not be able to speak her mind or she would face Colum's wrath. And a beating from him was something she might not survive. So she would deal with the lesser of two evils... and spread her legs for the infamous Cree.

Chapter Five

Cree watched Dawn as she gathered what was left of their meal and placed the remnants in the basket. He could tell by her fumbling movements that she was nervous, and it was his fault.

His body certainly made no attempt to conceal his desire for her. He had grown hard telling her that it would be him who would lie between her legs. He found her features plain, though her creamy skin looked soft to the touch, and while her breasts were small they were pert enough to garner attention.

Damn if he wasn't hurting with how hard he was swelling.

He had to stop this. He had no intention of coupling with a mute. He'd not spill his seed and worry that it would take root in her. He had worked too hard to throw away his dream for one night of lust.

Still, he could not take his eyes off her. The sway of her generous hips, the slimness of her waist, and the gentleness of her movements proved too much to ignore. Try as he might, he could not help but wonder how she would respond to him if he coupled with her.

He shook the tormenting thought from his mind so hard that he stumbled.

He felt her hand on his arm and when their eyes met he saw concern in hers. She didn't have to speak for him to know that she worried over him, and his desire for her grew. Never had he seen a spark of concern for him in any woman's eyes, and it startled him to the point that he pulled away from her, as if her touch had burnt him.

Her head went down and she turned away.

He grabbed her arm, and she swung her head around.

"I will warn you one more time only—never—turn away from me."

She bobbed her head, kept her eyes on his, and shrugged as she pointed at him.

He easily understood that she was asking how he was. "Tired," he said.

She slowly eased her arm from his grasp and set about arranging a sleeping pallet. He saw that she had saved some sprigs of heather and after bunching some of the rushes together, she added the heather to them, and then laid a clean wool blanket on top. She spread another blanket on top of that one and folded the top back.

"Well done," he said with a nod to her.

She bobbed her head, and he was sorry to see that she did not smile. He liked when she smiled. It made him smile.

What was the matter with him thinking of smiles? He had no time for such nonsense. He had a mission to accomplish and foolish musings would not help him. He had to use her for what she was worth, and then be done with it and yet...

The thought did not set right with him. What little he could surmise, she was a good woman and did not deserve to be treated badly and yet...

Whatever was the matter with him? He had done far worse than using a lone woman to achieve victory. He could not allow himself to feel for this woman, mute or not. She was but a pawn in a high stakes battle and he would do what was necessary to be the victor just as always.

Cree motioned for her to lie down on the blanket.

She hesitated and he caught the fear in her eyes, dark as it was, he could still see it stirring there. Then with reluctance that was all too obvious, she surrendered to what she believed was her fate and slowly lay down on the blanket.

He was quick to join her and wanting done with this, he settled himself around her and drew her back against him. She fit nicely in the crook of his curves, though she bristled when his enlarged member rubbed against her. She didn't help matters any when she attempted to avoid contact with it. Her actions only grew him larger.

He finally tightened his arm around her waist, yanked her harder against him, and whispered harshly in her ear, "Stay still or I'll bury myself deep inside you."

She froze stiff against him, and he warned himself to ignore the sweet scent of her soft hair that tickled at his nose, the warmth of her body that seemed to feed his heat, and the feel of her rounded backside that made him swell to an aching hardness.

He forced his thoughts elsewhere. He refused to succumb to lust when so much depended on his success here.

"While a nod or shake of your head answers simple questions, there may be times when your response is best left between us," he said, "in which case you will find a way to touch me once for yes and twice for no. Do you understand?"

He was pleased when she pressed her finger once against his arm.

"Good, now go to sleep." He yanked her harder against him to let her know that she was to stay where she was, closed his eyes, and in no time drifted off into a much needed slumber.

Dawn listened to his steady breathing. His cheek was pressed against the side of her head, his arm tight around her, and his leg clamped over her two. She couldn't move, but then where would she go. The guards had no intention of letting her out until morning.

She wished sleep would have claimed her as quickly as it had claimed Cree, but the worries that continued to mount kept sleep at bay. She certainly was relieved that he hadn't force himself on her, though she had no doubt that he had considered it. His lust weighed heavily in his eyes as did the way his glance drifted far too intimately over her more than once. Then, of course, there was the bulging size of him that was finally abating. It had dug into her when he had heaved her against him. She had thought he would take her there and then and was surprised when he hadn't.

This was one time she was glad to be mute. He probably wanted nothing to do with a voiceless woman and that was fine with her, though she didn't know how it would fair with Colum once he found out, but who would tell him?

Would Cree request another woman to tend him? Had the guards watched through the narrow slit in the door? She sighed inwardly wondering what to do, and then realized there was nothing she could do. She hated being helpless. It left her feeling vulnerable, and she felt that way much too often.

It had troubled her when he had spoken of a time

when he may wish to communicate with her without others noticing. She had no idea when such a time could possibly come, or why their communication should be private. But she let him have his way and did what he had asked.

What troubled her even more was that she had not a bit of news to take back to Colum, and if she didn't find something out soon he would surely punish her for disobeying him.

She closed her eyes and wished this was all a nightmare and that she would find herself waking in her cottage. Though small, it was a fine home to her with a soft sleeping pallet and single table and chair and that was where she wanted to be right now... home.

A tear quickened in her eye and she forced it away. Tears would do her no good and besides crying seemed a waste, since it only brought more suffering to her silence. No one could hear her cry, and so her cries seemed louder inside her head.

Sleep began to intrude on her endless musings, and she could no longer keep her eyes open. She fell asleep, though woke periodically throughout the night finding herself in the same position, Cree not having moved a muscle.

She startled once in her sleep, and Cree was quick to tighten his hold on her.

"Do you try to flee?" he whispered.

She tapped his arm twice.

"Then settle yourself. You have woken me too often this night."

She tensed fearful of disturbing him.

A moment later he asked, "Did a nightmare frighten you?"

She tapped him once.

"Was I in it?"

She again tapped his arm once, though he truly wasn't in her nightmare... he *was* her nightmare.

1.   ~~~

Sunrise found Cree still asleep and Dawn awake and ready to take her leave. She was relieved when she woke to find that he had released his hold on her and had turned on his side away from her. She had gotten quickly, though quietly, to her feet, grabbed the food basket, and knocked on the door to draw the guard's attention.

He opened the door and with a grin ordered, "You're to go directly to liege lord Colum. Don't stop anywhere."

Panic rose to tighten Dawn's throat, and she nodded and hurried off. Colum looked for news already and she had none to give him. Whatever was she to do?

Dawn hurried around to the back of the keep to the kitchen, since it was the only way she was allowed to enter the Great Hall. Colum would fly into a rage if she dared enter the hall through the front of the keep.

Flanna caught her eye as she entered and shifted her eyes to the left, as if directing Dawn's glance behind her toward the archway that lead to the narrow hall connecting to the Great Hall.

Dawn followed her glance, and there stood Goddard. He grinned when their eyes met, and he motioned her to him.

"Colum waits to speak to you," he said.

She dropped her basket and followed him through the narrow passageway and into the Great Hall.

Colum sat in the chair at the dais with his grin growing as she approached.

"The scent of him best be on her," Colum said as she got close.

Goddard gave a hard sniff and snorted. "His stench is heavy on her."

Colum waved her closer and Dawn took cautious steps forward, while Goddard walked around her and took a seat at the dais.

"What have you learned?" Colum demanded.

Dawn clenched her hands to keep them from trembling and tried desperately to think of something, anything, that might appease him.

It came in a flash to her. She made an angry face, tapped her chest, and pressed a finger to her lips.

Colum stared at her a minute and then grinned. "Cree was angry because you cannot speak."

She nodded as relief ran through her.

"Good. This is good," Colum said rubbing his hands together, and then stopped and shoved a shaking finger at her. "Now get me information."

Dawn wasn't sure what information he wanted, and her expression showed her confusion.

"Not only mute, but an idiot," Colum grumbled and then shouted at her. "Find out why he was in the area where we captured him and if his men are nearby. I want to know his plans. His kind always has plans. Now go and get me answers."

Dawn bobbed her head, turned, and hurried out of the hall.

Flanna was quick to jump at her when she entered the kitchen. "You're a sight and need cleaning you do." With that, she took firm hold of Dawn's arm and rushed her out, though not before shouting a warning to her staff that they better keep working in her absence, or they'd be hell to pay for their laziness.

Dawn felt as gray and dreary as the overcast sky. She didn't object as Flanna hurried her along a footpath that led to her cottage a few feet away. Flanna gave her a shove inside. While this was her first time ever in Flanna's home, she didn't care to take note of anything. She was too tired and distraught.

"Are you all right?" Flanna asked.

Dawn was still stunned by the woman's sudden concern, though perhaps it was as she had thought. They were two kindred spirits that no men wanted.

Dawn pretended to yawn.

"You're tired. Didn't the devil let you sleep at all?"

The idea that the villagers would now believe Cree had ravished her upset her, and she was about to confide the truth to Flanna when she thought better of it. It was necessary that everyone assume what Colum already believed. She could not take the chance of anyone discovering the truth.

Dawn shook her head, for the devil hadn't let her sleep, though not for the reason Flanna thought.

"You need to get yourself washed and some good food into you. I have fresh warm bread that just finished baking, bramble jelly, and oatmeal porridge. I'll arrange a tub of hot water for you right here in front of the fire, and then you can eat."

Dawn touched the woman's arm and Flanna stilled. She rubbed a hand over her face and chest to demonstrate washing and nodded, and then she motioned shoveling food into her mouth and shook her head.

"You can wash here, but you must eat with the

devil," Flanna said understanding.

Dawn nodded and yawned.

"Fine," she snapped. "Have a wash and then a nap, since I was wrong about that bread. It won't be done for a while."

How she wished she could crawl in Flanna's bed, not a pallet but a bed with a good-stuffed mattress and sleep for a few hours, but it was not meant to be.

Dawn shook her head. She rubbed, as if washing herself and then pointed at the door.

"You must return to him after you're done washing."

Dawn nodded. She didn't want to hurry back to him, but she had to see what she could discover or Colum would do her harm.

Flanna seemed to understand and sorrow filled her eyes as well as her words. "You have two devils you must answer to." She shook her head. "I'll have a tub filled for you. At least you can get his scent off—for a time."

Dawn sniffed at her garments and noticed that she did carry a scent on her, and she buried her nose in her sleeve for a minute. It was a woodsy scent mixed with Cree's body scent. Some men's scents were hard on the senses causing the nose to wrinkle in distaste, not so Cree. His scent actually appealed to Dawn. She couldn't define what she favored about it. She only knew she liked it.

The realization startled her, and she stopped sniffing her sleeve just in time, since the door swung open. Flanna marched in with servants who carried a round wooden tub. Others followed carrying buckets of steaming water.

Dawn was grateful for Flanna's fussing and more so for the tub of steaming water. After they all left, she disrobed and climbed over the rim into the tub and sunk into the blessed hot water. Being tall didn't help, and so her knees almost touched her chin, but she didn't care. The hot water was most welcoming. The heat soaked into her every limb and began to ease the stiffness away.

She had slept so rigid last night and rushed so this morning that it wasn't until she had watched the tub being filled that she had realized how her body ached. She wished she could sit and soak until the water turned cold, but there wasn't time.

Cree would be waiting for his morning meal. He had questioned her during last night's meal, so perhaps this morning she could pose her own questions to him. She scrubbed herself with the soap that Flanna had left for her including her hair.

She smiled favoring the scent of lavender that covered her. That was until she reached for her clothes. They smelled of Cree and the strong, not unpleasant, scent sent a quiver through her body.

The door swung open and Dawn was quick to wrap the towel around her. She smiled wide when she saw that it was Lila, her best friend.

Lila was everything Dawn wasn't. She was beautiful with soft red hair that curled gloriously down her back, lovely green eyes, cream-colored skin, petite and slim, and a lovely voice that could chatter on forever.

"I was stunned when Flanna showed up at my doorstep and expressed concern about you needing fresh garments. She struck me speechless she did, being kind and thoughtful to your—" She stopped and hurried to give Dawn a quick hug. "When Paul heard what Colum had ordered you to do, he wanted to go to him in your defense."

Dawn shook her head and waved her hand.

"I know," Lila said grabbing tight hold of Dawn's hand. "I told him you would not want him to do something so foolish."

Dawn nodded and tapped Lila's rounded stomach, and then slipped her hand out of hers and backed away.

Lila got teary-eyed. "I know you tell me that Paul must worry only about the babe and me and not to worry about you, but Dawn..." A tear slipped down her cheek. "Are you all right? Did that monster hurt you?"

It would have been easy to turn to Lila and wrap herself around her knowing she would hug her in return just as they had done when they were young and something had troubled either one of them. They had always sought solace from each other, and it had been no difference as they had gotten older. They had always been there for each other.

This time however was different. This time if she shared the truth with Lila it could prove dangerous for her and Paul. Dawn refused to take that chance, so she did something she had never done... she lied to Lila.

She tapped her chest and smiled.

"You tell me you're fine, but I don't know if I believe that."

Dawn hurried into a brown, worn wool skirt and slipped a faded green linen blouse over her head.

"You won't look at me, which means that there is something you're not telling me."

Dawn turned, walked over to her, pressed a finger to her mouth, and shook her head. Her eyes pleaded for understanding.

"I know what you're doing," Lila accused another tear slipping down her cheek. "You're trying to keep Paul and me safe."

Dawn joined her hands, as if in prayer and placed them to her lips. Lila knew the sign all too well. It meant please no more and please trust that I know what I do.

"I don't like it, but—" Lila shook her head. "I know there is nothing that Paul or I could do without suffering for it, and it pains me not to be able to help my friend who is more sister to me and who I love dearly."

They hugged then. Dawn close to tears herself, but refusing to surrender to them. She stepped away, crossed her arms over her chest, patted her hand to her heart, and pointed to Lila.

"You express your love so beautifully."

Dawn smiled. Lila always made her feel as if she could speak, and she didn't know what she would do without her. That was why she wouldn't take a chance of getting her friend involved with the situation.

She kept her smile, tapped her chest, and gave one good nod.

"I know you feel you can handle this, but," — another tear slipped down Lila's cheek— "Cree is a monster and how can you fight a monster all by yourself?"

Chapter Six

Cree paced the confined cell impatient for Dawn's return. She could not speak, yet he felt as if she had spoken to him. Her hand gestures and facial expressions spoke more plainly than words and more honestly than people with voices. He had been surprised as to how comfortable he had slept wrapped around her last night. He rarely slept without waking several times, but not so last night. He had slept soundly. He could blame it on the long walk tethered to Colum's horse, but that would be nonsense.

He stopped and stretched to ease the taut muscles in his back. His stamina was beyond the ordinary; he had made sure of it. He pushed himself beyond the limits of endurance with the intention of being prepared to survive anything; the harshest of battles, unpredictable elements, and intolerable pain. Many believed him oblivious to pain, though the truth of it was that many believed he lacked a soul. That he had long ago bartered the devil for it, or as some had whispered... he was the devil's own.

He welcomed the rumors. He wanted people to fear him. Fear prevented people from taking action, which allowed him to win many a battle that could have otherwise been lost. Of course, being feared by so many left you with little or no friends. And women? No decent woman would give herself to him and even the indecent ones hesitated. After all, anyone who lay with the devil's progeny would surely bear his mark. Those who chose to lay with him could not resist but to return for more. The devil's son skilled in the ways of the flesh and once tasted—was impossible to resist.

That mattered little to him now. His plans were what mattered most. They had been laid and set in motion. He would have what he wanted and that included a noble woman as his wife. He may not have been born of nobility, but it could be bought for a price, and he had done just that... bought it.

He stretched again twisting at his waist to limber his muscles. It would do him no good to simply sit. He would keep himself well limbered.

His thoughts drifted to Dawn and a low growl rumbled deep in his chest. It was a habit of his when he grew annoyed, and annoyed he was, for he grew hard with the thought of her. He could certainly keep himself limber coupling with her. Not that he had any intentions of doing so. He had told her that he'd be the one to lie between her legs merely to frighten her. He couldn't imagine bedding a woman who could not utter a sound. What pleasure would there be in that? He enjoyed the moans and groans of a woman in the throes of passion. He grew harder thinking of the groaning screams of a woman in climax. He could not fathom finding any pleasure in silence.

And yet...

Dawn was excellent with gestures. Her hands spoke what her voice couldn't. Would her hands speak as loudly when making love? Would her touch say what she couldn't?

He stilled. His growl grew deeper as the thought of her touch turned him rock-hard. If he did not rid himself of this torment, he feared what he might do and no doubt what Colum expected... rut with the mute and take the chance of leaving his seed to grow in her.

He was angry with Colum for using an innocent young woman who could not voice her fear or objection, and he was even angrier with himself for thinking of bedding her. She needed protection from the likes of Colum and even from the likes of him.

He had told her that she belonged to him, and what belonged to him he protected... he would protect Dawn even from himself.

Voices drifted in from outside, and he went to the door and stood a few feet in front of it. His feet braced firm and ready.

The door swung open and with a laugh the guard shoved Dawn in only this time Cree was there to catch her. His arm swiftly wrapped around her waist, and he drew her firmly to his side in a display of not only protection, but possession.

"Shove her again and I will kill you." A primitive snarl followed Cree's warning, and the sunlight falling in from the open door glistened off every taut muscle in his toned body.

The guard's eyes rounded like full moons, and he turned deathly pale before quickly shoving the door closed and slamming the latch.

Dawn trembled in his arms, and he turned to face her. His lips were so close that they grazed her cheek, and then her lips and she shuddered.

"I will not hurt you," he whispered her tremble sending a shiver to his loins.

He wisely, though reluctantly, stepped away from her.

She did the same hurrying to the blanket to spread the food she had brought in her basket. He could see that her hands trembled as she worked, and she did not turn to look at him. Perhaps she thought if she avoided his eyes that he would ignore her, as no doubt many did.

But he was not like others, and so he approached her.

Dawn heard him move, and she was not at all comfortable being on her hands and knees with him behind her. She quickly set to finishing her task.

She wished her hands didn't quiver so, but she couldn't stop them. Being in his arms, pressed against him, his muscles tight and hard, and feeling the animal snarl rumble through his chest put the fear of the devil into her and into the guard as well. She had almost half expected Cree to turn into a fierce animal, but then wasn't he already one?

He attacked and devoured everything in his path and she suddenly wondered how Colum ever could have captured such a cunning and fearless animal. The strange thought got her speculating, and she turned to him not realizing how much her eyes questioned.

Cree joined her on the blanket and reached out to take hold of her chin. "I see a question in your eyes."

She almost startled, but quickly contained her surprise and pointed to the food.

Cree nodded. "I am hungry, but why do I sense that wasn't the question so prominent in your eyes?"

Lila and her husband Paul, to some extent, were the only ones good at reading the look in her eyes. But then few bothered to meet her eyes directly. It was as if they feared by doing so that somehow, they too, would be cursed and lose their voice.

He caused her to jump when he demanded, "Tell

me."

Dawn thought quickly and realized this would be the perfect time to try to learn something that she could possibly give to Colum. She eased his fingers off her chin and slowly reached out to give his thick arms a squeeze, then pointed around the shack and shrugged.

Cree stared at her a moment amazed that he could so easily understand her. "You wonder how someone like me, so big and strong, could be captured."

She nodded, pleased that he had no trouble interpreting what she expressed.

"An error in judgment," he said.

She frowned and shook her head before realizing that she was telling him that she didn't believe him.

He reached for a hunk of bread. "You think I lie?"

She was about to shake her head, but instead nodded. She needed something to give Colum, or she would suffer the consequences of her failure to gather information for him.

"Why?"

He sounded as if he issued her a challenge that she would much rather not accept it, but she was left little choice.

She looked to her left, and then to her right, and then she placed one finger to her lips.

"You believe I harbor a secret."

The more she thought about it the more it made sense. Cree was an infamous warrior. Unbeatable. Soulless. The devil's own. How was it that a man like Colum could capture him?

Only if he wanted to be captured.

The thought startled her, but she sensed it to be true and if it was... what did it mean?

She nodded and reached for a chunk of bread,

then broke several pieces off leaving one large one. She placed the smaller pieces in rows with the large one in the lead. She pointed to it and then to Cree, then shrugged.

Her astuteness amazed Cree. She might not be able to speak, but she was far from dumb. But then either was he. He knew that she was searching for information to bring to Colum.

He decided to answer her without truly answering her. "My men are where they should be."

Dawn wondered if *he* was where he should be as well. Could his capture have actually been planned? But why would he want to be captured by Colum? If he wished to attack the village, he could have easily done so. It made no sense. She needed to learn more, but she didn't want him to grow suspicious of her. She didn't know who she feared more Cree or Colum. Either one could hurt her, but hadn't Cree told her that he would never hurt her?

Why didn't she believe him?

"You express yourself more clearly than I would have thought for one without a voice," he said turning the conversation away from him to her. It was his turn to learn some things. "How long have you had no voice?"

She cradled her arms and made a rocking motion.
Cree frowned. "From when you were born?"
Dawn nodded.
"You have never uttered a single sound?"
She shook her head.
"Yet you understand so much."

Dawn turned and reached a few inches beyond the blanket to brush the dirt clear and began to use her finger as an artist would a brush.

Cree watched amazed once again. She drew a picture of a woman, so lovely that it brought a smile to his face. "Your mum."

Dawn beamed. Her face lighted with joy as she pointed at the woman and then at herself.

"Your mum taught you."

She continued smiling and threw her hands up stretching them out in a circle.

"Your mum taught you a lot."

Dawn nodded as sadness washed over her face, while she brushed the portrait of her mum away and dusted her hands together to rid herself of the dirt before pointing to him.

She asked about his mum and he laughed. It sounded foreign to him. How long had it been since he last laughed? He couldn't recall.

He leaned close to her and whispered, "It's rumored that the devil hatched me."

Dawn didn't know what made her do it. Perhaps it was pure instinct, or the need to protect not only herself, but him from such an evil thought. He had to have had a mother and she had to have loved him. Someone somewhere had to have loved him. How horrible to think otherwise.

She placed her hand to his cheek, and shook her head to let him know that she didn't believe that.

How foreign, and yet how comforting her cool, gentle touch felt. He had forgotten how a gentle and caring hand felt, or to be comforted for the simple sake of it. Dawn expected nothing. She gave generously of herself and all to let him know that she didn't believe such nonsense.

Her fingers grazed slowly along his cheek as she removed her hand. Cree felt the loss of her caring touch down to the pit of his stomach. It was almost as if she had branded him, and now he belonged to her.

He belonged to no woman and never would.

Irritated that she had affected him so foolishly, he struck at her with words, "I am not a pet you can comfort with a tender touch." Her response surprised him and quickly had him regretting his words.

She placed her hand to her face, pointed to him, and then waved her hand back and forth while shaking her head. She was telling him that she would not do it again and regret washed over him.

And so did anger.

He stood and yanked her up by the arm and propelled her to the door. He pounded on it and when it opened he shoved her out. "Do not return until this evening." He closed the door with such force that a board cracked.

His hand fisted so tightly that his knuckles turned pure white, and he restrained himself from punching the door. He turned and went over to the blanket, but didn't sit. He opened his fisted hand and placed it to the cheek she had touched, and his hand tingled.

What had it been about her simple touch that affected him so? Never had he felt anything like it before, but then it had been far too long since he had felt such tenderness. And he regretted even more his response, for she would never touch him again. That meant he would never again feel such pure loving tenderness.

He sat and was about to push the food away, his hunger gone, when he changed his mind and grabbed a piece of bread. Food kept one strong and he had to stay strong. What nonsense for him to waste time on a mute. The only purpose Dawn served for him was to learn what he could from her. And seeing that she was more astute meant that there was much she knew about the village and Colum.

Tonight they would talk and only talk. There would be no touching, and tonight he would send her home to sleep. Regret once again pinched at his gut, and he shook his head. He would not have her sleep with him, not now, not ever. The thought grew him much too hard, and the consequences were much too unacceptable.

Chapter Seven

Fear prickled every inch of Dawn's skin. She knew the moment that Cree threw her out that she was in trouble... serious trouble. John, the guard, grabbed her arm and squeezed it so tightly that her breath caught in her throat.

"You're in trouble now."

Her breath returned with a soundless gasp as he dragged her off after issuing orders for Angus to stay alert, while he took her to Colum.

The villagers stared at her, their mouths agape, as John forcibly dragged her through the village yanking her up whenever she stumbled, but not before rocks skinned her leg and brought a silent grimace to her face.

That was when Lila caught sight of her. Dawn quickly shook her head in warning, for she knew her friend would rush to her aid and suffer for it. Paul realized the same and hastily hurried to his wife's side to quickly wrap his arm around her and hold her tight.

The fearful expression on Lila's face and tears pooling in her eyes sent a chill through Dawn. As she was dragged and pulled up the steps to the keep, she knew her situation was direr than she had imagined, for John was taking her through the front doors of the keep.

The Great Hall turned silent as soon as John

tossed her at Colum's feet. Dawn didn't get up or raise her head. She kept it down fearful of what she would see in Colum's eyes.

"He threw her out he did," John said, "and ordered her not to return until tonight."

"Get up," Colum screamed.

Dawn scrambled to her feet, and the fury she saw in his eyes ran her blood cold. Goddard stood beside Colum in front of the dais grinning. All were aware that the man enjoyed inflicting pain, and he was anticipating what Colum would do to her or, if she was lucky, what he would order Goddard to do to her.

Colum continued screaming. "What did you do?"

"Perhaps it's what she didn't do," Goddard suggested.

Colum's face contorted in rage, and his hand came down hard across Dawn's cheek. She stumbled, and Goddard grabbed her before she could fall. His hand closed like a band of steel around her arm that already ached from John's abuse. She fought against the pain that radiated through her arm and feared it was only the beginning of her suffering.

Spittle flew everywhere as Colum continued his tirade. "You were given specific orders. You were to give him whatever he wanted. Are you too stupid to understand that? Did you refuse to rut with him?"

"Maybe she doesn't know how?" Goddard said.

"Is that it?" Colum yelled in her face spittle hitting her cheeks and eye. "Do I need to have someone teach you?"

"I can do it right now, right here," Goddard said with a smile that disgusted Dawn.

She had to think fast. She could not let Goddard take her like an animal in front of everyone. She could not bear the thought of such humiliation or the consequences. Would other warriors feel that she was now free territory for them to enjoy and toss aside?

The thought turned her stomach, and she shook her head and tapped her chest to get Colum's attention.

"You better tell me something good, lass, or I'll let Goddard take you until you beg him to stop." Colum leaned in close to her. "He likes to play rough with his women."

"It's the only way," Goddard said proudly. "You give a woman a good rough tumble that she never forgets, and she obeys you quick enough the next time. I'll have the dumb one obeying Cree's every touch in no time."

Instinct had Dawn wanting to cringe, but instead she bravely stood her ground. Though with her legs trembling so badly, she had no idea how she remained standing.

She didn't know where the thought came from, but she thanked the heavens for it. She eased her arm free and frantically patted her chest, and then quickly demonstrated shoveling food into her mouth. Then she stopped and shook her head making a sour expression and threw her hands up in the air repeatedly.

Colum scratched his head. "What are you trying to say?"

Dawn tried again. She held her wrists together trying to show that she spoke of Cree and went through the process again.

"I don't understand the idiot," Cree yelled. "Go get her friend so that she can explain her senseless ranting."

Dawn panicked. She didn't want Lila involved at

all. Before John could do as Colum bid, she ran to the table grabbed a piece of meat and pretended to chew, and then spit it out and made a face that showed disgust.

"Cree didn't like the food," John said.

"Is that it?" Colum asked without yelling. "He didn't like the food so he tossed you out?"

She nodded vigorously, and her stomach turned in relief. That was until Colum spoke.

"Who prepared the food for him?" Colum asked with anger.

Dawn couldn't let Flanna take the blame for this so she was quick to tap her chest. She wasn't prepared for the slap Colum delivered to the same cheek as before, and she stumbled to her knees.

He grabbed her by the hair and yanked her up. "You will spend the afternoon preparing Cree a decent meal and tonight you will rut with him and tomorrow... you better have information for me or I'll hand you over to Goddard to enjoy."

She could have sworn that Goddard licked his lips.

Colum gave her a hard shove. "Go and prepare."

She stumbled though remained on her feet and hurried to the archway leading to the kitchen. She almost reached it when Colum stopped her yelling out her name. She turned fearful she would not escape further wrath.

"You'll take candles with you tonight," he ordered. "The devil's son will enjoy the flames." Laughter erupted in the hall, though stopped abruptly when Colum raised his hand. "And least you think to lie to me then think again, for it's the smell of rutting I will be looking for on you tomorrow."

Laughter burst loud again and followed her out of

the hall and down the narrow passageway. She stopped a moment to lean against the stone wall and take a breath. How she wished she could scream and cry, but with no voice that wasn't possible and silent tears would not help her. She had a choice to make, though it really was no choice, for either way she would lay with a devil. It only mattered which devil she could tolerate, and she already knew the answer to that.

Tonight she would give herself to the devil's son, and she prayed that God would help see her through it.

2. ~~~

Flanna hadn't been in the kitchen when Dawn had entered, and so she got busy preparing a good stew for Cree's supper. No one stopped her or offered help, especially when they caught sight of her bruised cheek. It was swollen and growing ever darker and hurt when she chewed. But there was no time to tend to it now or to her leg that continued to sting. She had to get the stew cooking and make fresh bread, and then she would clean herself up and tend to her wounds.

She had just gotten the stew cooking when Flanna entered the kitchen. As soon as she caught sight of Dawn, she issued orders for her staff to finish what Dawn had started, and then she ushered Dawn outside.

"Did Cree do this to you?" Flanna demanded once away from the eyes and ears in the kitchen and pointed to her cheek.

Dawn sighed, though it was soundless as if forever stuck inside her, and she could never release it. That was how she felt—stuck—captured like her sigh. Dawn shook her head.

"Colum did it."

Dawn nodded.

"Why?"

It took some doing, but Dawn was finally able to explain in gestures what had happened.

Tears sprang to Flanna's tired eyes. "You lied to protect me."

How did she explain to Flanna that she had lied to protect herself and in so doing had placed Flanna in danger, which in turn had her lying again? In the end her lies were meant to protect, and so she simply nodded.

"You know you have no choice," Flanna said sadly. "You must couple with the monster."

Dawn was pleased that at least Flanna had been kind enough not to tell her that she had to rut with Cree. It sounded more like what animals did rather than humans. She was certain that Lila and Paul didn't rut and, while they coupled, it was more like they made love. Dawn never expected to find a man she would make love with, perhaps couple, but she doubted that she would ever find love. No one would ever want to make love with her let alone want her.

Dawn nodded reluctantly.

Flanna leaned in close to whisper, "Lie there and let him have his way and be done with it. It will hurt less, and he will want you less if you don't respond. Play dead beneath him and he will leave you be, and you will have the scent of sex upon you to satisfy Colum.

The scent of sex was unknown to her, and she wondered if she had ever smelled it on others and had not known what it was. Tonight she would find out, for she had to or she would suffer for it.

Flanna placed her hand on Dawn's arm and her face winced in response. Flanna was quick to push up Dawn's sleeve to reveal a dark purple bruise going around her arm just above her elbow.

"Where else do you hurt?" Flanna asked with concern.

Dawn raised her skirt, and they both winced, though only Flanna's was heard. Her left leg was scraped from knee to ankle with a purple bruise slightly below her knee.

"Go to your cottage and clean up and then rest," Flanna ordered like a concerned mother. "I will let you know when the food is ready." She almost turned to leave, but stopped and looked to Dawn. "I have heard tell that once a woman tastes the devil's son there's no satisfying her. She returns to him again and again. Do not taste of the devil. Do not touch him. Do not become a slave to his evil passion."

Dawn made her way to her cottage with her thoughts in turmoil. She had spent little time with Cree, though more than anyone else here. She certainly couldn't say that she didn't fear him. He was a man to be feared by the sheer size of him alone, not to mention his strength, which was something she sensed whenever she entered the small shack where he was imprisoned. She wondered how the weak structure could hold him.

Most of all she wondered what she had done that had upset him so much that he had thrown her out. She worried that it was because she had touched him. She had meant no harm by it. She couldn't explain why she had done it. She only knew that she could not stop herself. It was as if he needed her comforting touch.

She entered her cottage to find a crying Lila and Paul there.

"Are you all right?" Paul asked.

Dawn nodded. She could tell that he was upset and knew why. He had felt helpless to help her and had to restrain his wife from helping her for her own good, and it had not sat well with him.

"I'll leave you two to talk," he said and stopped next to her to give her shoulder a squeeze. Then he whispered, "Thank you, Dawn. You are a true friend."

She understood that he thanked her for shaking her head at Lila, warning her not to interfere, and her eyes grew misty. As soon as the door closed behind him Lila flew at her, and they hugged tightly.

"I feared greatly for you and for me, for I do not know what I would do without you," Lila cried.

Dawn kept hold of her. She needed Lila's comfort as much as Lila's needed hers. Lila often spoke for Dawn especially when she had been taunted by others. Lila was always there to verbally defend her with remarks that struck as sharply as an arrow's point. Dawn on the other hand had been there for Lila if anyone should attempt to physically taunt her. Being taller than most women had helped intimidate, which usually resolved the issue. But there had been times when they were young that they both got into scuffles, neither ever leaving the other to fend for herself.

That was why this was so hard for Lila now. There was nothing she could do to help Dawn and that was precisely what Dawn explained to her in gestures that Lila easily understood, but objected to.

Dawn in return patted Lila's protruding stomach.

Lila sighed. "I know, Paul reminds me of the same, the babe comes first."

Dawn nodded vigorously.

"At least let me tend your wounds," Lila said.

Dawn nodded and smiled. It would do them good to share this. It would make Lila feel that at least she had done something to help Dawn. And Dawn needed this calming and caring time with Lila before she faced Cree once again.

Unfortunately, Flanna burst through the door out of breath. Lila and Dawn helped her to a chair, and she struggled between breaths to deliver her message.

It turned Dawn pale when Lila said, "Cree wants her now?"

Flanna quickly explained that Colum searched for her, and that he was pleased that the prisoner Cree had requested her return. He had ordered a basket of food to be prepared quickly and that candles were to be added to it. He had then sent Goddard to the kitchen to collect Dawn. When he didn't find her there, someone in the kitchen suggested that she was probably at Flanna's cottage. As soon as Flanna had returned to the kitchen and heard, she had rushed to Dawn.

Dawn wanted no contact with Goddard, so she and Flanna immediately left Dawn's cottage and hurried to the kitchen. She snatched up the waiting basket and was on the way to Cree when she met up with Goddard.

He sneered at her and leaned close to whisper, "The scent of him better be strong on you along with some information, or you'll soon find my scent heavy on you."

She didn't acknowledge his remark with a nod or

a gesture. She simply continued walking, though her legs trembled terribly.

John, the guard, said nothing to her when she stopped in front of him. He opened the door and kept his distance from her letting her enter of her own accord, and then closed and latched it behind her.

Dawn heard Cree stir in the corner where he usually sat. The food she had placed on the blanket was still there, though barely touched. He didn't acknowledge her presence, so she moved to the blanket and began gathering the food to place in the basket she had left there. Keeping her hands busy also kept her mind occupied, since she would rather not think of what was to come.

Rain clouds had fast moved in obliterating the sun and promising rain possibly for the remainder of the day. That meant the hut would lack light and though she had the candles she didn't know if she should use them. She feared that the more clearly she could see Cree the more frightening he would appear.

The decision was made for her when she removed the candles from the basket to get at the meat pie beneath. Once Cree saw them he grabbed them.

"Finally light," he grumbled and quickly set to lighting them.

He took a hunk of bread and scooped out the middle and inserted a candle creating a holder for it. He lit three more and did the same placing them around the blanket. He then turned his dark eyes on Dawn.

His murderous glare sent a chill racing through her clear down to her bones. He appeared ready to kill, and she had no doubt that his look alone could send a man to his knees and have him begging for mercy.

"Who did this to you?" he demanded.

It was a harsh whisper that warned of retribution if not answered and Dawn reacted instinctively. She scrambled to her feet and backed away from him hoping the shadows would swallow her and protect her.

He was on his feet before the first shadow wrapped around her.

Chapter Eight

Cree grabbed her arm and her face pinched in pain. He cursed, releasing her, and scooped her up to carry her back to the blanket. He sat her close to the candles and gently pushed up the sleeve of her blouse.

His temper soared once again upon seeing the handprint that had left a large purple bruise, bound to grow worse by morning, around her upper arm. On closer examination, he thought he saw two different prints, and it fired his temper even more that two men had laid hands on her.

He then wondered if she had been hurt elsewhere or worse... "Has someone forced himself on you?"

She shook her head.

"Where else have you been hurt, and don't bother to lie to me or I'll strip you bare and see for myself."

She had no doubt that he would, so she lifted her skirt to show him her right leg.

He winced at the skin that had been rubbed raw from her knee down along her shin with a substantial bruise forming just beneath her knee. He didn't hesitate. He reached for the bucket of water and placed it beside him. He then took the cloth that had covered one of the baskets, soaked and rinsed it in the bucket, and began to clean her leg.

Her leg jumped from the pain.

"It needs cleaning, and I do not have a light touch," he said unapologetically and continued cleaning it. "This wound appears as if you were dragged. Who did this?"

It was not a request. And while she did not wish to answer him, she knew she had little choice. She also knew this was only the start of his questions. But why should he care what happened to her? Then she recalled him telling her that he protected what belonged to him. And for some unfathomable reason, he believed that she belonged to him.

She did what she had to do; she answered him. She pointed to the door.

"The one called John?" Cree asked.

She nodded.

"It looks as if two men left their prints on your arm. Who?"

She pointed again to the door.

"John and who else?"

She held her left hand up to a short height and placed her right hand next to it at a higher height.

Again he easily understood her. "Colum's right hand man Goddard?"

She was not surprised that he understood her gesture, but she was surprised that he knew the man's name, though he probably had learned about Goddard when he had been captured.

She confirmed with another nod.

Cree looked up at her now and again as he worked on her leg to see if he was causing her too much pain. But she appeared to bear his brute tending with patient courage. Her shin looked much better once he cleaned it, though the bruise had darkened and would no doubt pain her until healed as would her arm.

Once he deposited the cloth in the bucket, he rested a gentle finger to her bruised cheek. "Did Colum do this?"

She nodded.

"How many times did he hit you?"

She held up two fingers.

"Why did he hit you?" He saw the hesitation in her eyes. "You'll not keep it from me. I'll have my answer."

Somehow she thought that he always got his answer and with whatever means possible, though she had never expected that he would tend her. And she never expected that he would care that she'd been hurt... though as he had told her... she belonged to him.

She answered, pointing to him and then to herself, then she held up her hands and gave a shove in the air.

Cree had already surmised that he had been the cause, but to hear it? He almost laughed at the absurdity of hearing a mute, and yet he had heard her as clearly as if she had spoken aloud. He did not like the idea that she had suffered because of his own foolishness.

"I sent you away so Colum punished you," he said to confirm what he had suspected.

She nodded, though much too slowly for Cree.

There was more than she was telling him. "Why else did he punish you?"

Dawn felt trapped more than she ever had in her life. And having no voice to speak her mind, cry out her sorrow or pain, or even laugh made her feel trapped beyond measure. But now stuck between Colum and Cree she wasn't sure who to fear most. Lying to either one of them could bring her suffering, but what was she to do?

Cree gently caught her chin with his fingers. "You will tell me and I will protect you."

But who will protect me from you?

Dawn didn't know what to do and thankfully Cree saved her from having to make a choice.

"Colum expects you to get information from me, doesn't he?"

She nodded with relief. She hadn't told him. He had realized it himself, so she did not feel guilty of divulging the truth. But what happened now that he knew? Surely he would not share information with her.

He released her chin, though his fingers drifted to her bruised cheek and faintly traced the purple area. "I will not see you suffer for me."

Dawn didn't know what he could do to stop Colum. He was locked away, a prisoner, while Colum was free to do as he pleased. And he was one man against many, though if his reputation proved true that would matter little. It was said that he alone could kill dozens of men, and yet he touched her now with tenderness that surprised her. She had not thought him capable of compassion, but his gentle caress told her differently.

"You will obey me and I will see that you are kept safe."

Obey. It seemed as if she forever had to obey someone, but then it was necessary to survival, and she would do what she must to survive. Her mum had taught her that and so much more. She had taught her that to survive she had to have patience, listen, hear, and learn.

Was she not hearing something he was trying to tell her?

She took his hand that rested on her cheek, and she thought she felt him startle, though it was such a brief reaction that she couldn't be certain. She squeezed it, and then pointed around the confined space and at the locked door.

He leaned close, his hand resting in hers, and his warm breath fanning her face. "You wonder how I can protect you while locked away in here."

His lips were only inches from hers, and his eyes were fired with a heat that set her own temperature rising and her heart beating madly against her chest. She had never laid eyes on a man as sinfully handsome as Cree. His looks alone could turn a woman's thoughts wicked, not to mention the size and strength of him.

"Worry not," he said his breath whispering across her lips. "Trust me and I will always protect you."

Dawn shivered, for she feared that if she trusted him that it would be like surrendering her soul to the devil.

She released his hand and shrugged.

"You still wonder how I could protect you, since I'm locked away."

She nodded.

Cree returned to tending her leg as he spoke. "I will give you information to give to Colum."

Her brow rose with suspicion.

"You may not be able to talk, but your expressions speak clearly."

The thought that he could read her so easily disturbed her. It had taken Lila years to be able to read her expressions. How had he been able to do it so fast when he barely knew her?

"It is information that will satisfy him."

But be no threat to Cree. That would appease Colum, but how long before he found out the truth? What would happen to her then?

"That is all you presently need to concern yourself with," he ordered. "Take what information I give you to Colum, and you will suffer no more."

Doubt surfaced on her face.

"Do not question your good luck," Cree snapped and tossed the cloth into the bucket. Then he provided her with a tad of information, which she assumed was a lie, but would probably appease Colum.

"Now rest. You have suffered enough this day," he said.

Dawn wasn't sure what to do. Never had she rested during the day. There were always chores to be done, whether in the kitchen for Flanna or in her own small cottage. Not that she would mind having a rest. She had barely slept last night, and she was beginning to feel the pain of her wounds.

"Have you yet to learn that I don't give orders twice?"

She yawned, though no sound came with it, and he stared at her oddly. Most people did when they realized that she never issued a single sound.

"Your body agrees with me," he snapped annoyed and blew out the candles moving them aside. "Now lie down and rest."

What else could she do? She stretched out on the blanket on her side and in no time was sound asleep.

Cree braced himself against the wall and stared at her. Little light was available, since the skies outside had darkened and rain had begun to beat against the hut. He bent his knee resting his arm on it and continued to stare at her.

The more he stared the angrier he grew, and he fought to contain it. It didn't help that his eyes remained focused on her bruised cheek. His hand fisted when he thought of the pain she had endured when Colum had hit her not once but twice. He wished the man was standing in front of him right now, for he would squeeze the life out of him.

He dropped his head back against the wall and shut his eyes for a moment. It would do him no good to lose his temper now. He'd make Colum pay for what he did to Dawn, just not yet. But when the time came, he would enjoy making the man suffer.

It did him no good to worry over Dawn or to place more importance on her than was necessary. She was a pawn like so many others and was to be used accordingly and yet...

He shook his head letting his glance linger on her once again. He couldn't help but feel protective of her. When she had yawned and not a sound came from her mouth he realized, though could not comprehend, the prison that she lived in. He felt trapped in the confines of this shack, but to be trapped in the confines of your own mind was incomprehensible. Perhaps that was why he felt the need to protect her. Though if he was honest with himself he would admit that for some unexplainable reason he was attracted to her. Even in his anger at her injures, he had found himself admiring her slender leg. She had height to her for a woman, though he still stood a head over her. And she was more shapely than thin, and he liked that in a woman.

He grew hard with the thought of her, and he cursed beneath his breath. He needed a woman that was the problem, or so he tried to convince himself. He shook his head. He had more important matters to dwell on. He would see that she spent most of her time with him, and then shook his head.

That might not be a good idea. Having her in such

close proximity and having an aching need for a woman could prove a problem. He wasn't interested in coupling with her, whether she had a body that enticed or not.

He let his eyes wander over the swell of her hip as she lay on her side, and the way it curved to a slender waist and...

With a bolt he got to his feet and turned his back on Dawn. He shook his head and forced his thoughts elsewhere, anywhere but here. He heard her stir behind him, and he turned to see that she had sat up.

Sleep lingered in her drowsy eyes, then she pointed to him and her eyes turned wide. He knew that she asked if he was all right, and he wanted to warn her not to do that, not to worry over how he felt, but he kept silent and let her concern stir his desire for her.

She waited patiently for an answer even though her eyes were still heavy with fatigue. He growled and snarled that she should be more concerned about him than the much needed sleep she obviously required.

He told himself to keep his distance, order her to return to sleep, and most of all turn away and not linger on her eyes that looked more languid with passion than with sleep. It was wishful thinking. She would not want him to touch her. She would startle and scream if she could. Or would she do what Colum expected of her and rut with the prisoner?

He was tempted to find out, though he warned himself against it.

Keep your distance. Keep your distance. The words echoed in his head, but did he pay heed?

Not for long. He stomped over to her in two easy

strides, dropped to his knees in front of her, and brought his mouth down on hers. She did what he expected and leaned back away from him. He followed her down until she lay flat on her back, then he braced his hands on either side of her head. And then he kissed her.

Chapter Nine

Dawn had feared this moment, the anticipation of it causing her endless worry and yet it was necessary to her survival. If she didn't couple with him and have his scent upon her, then Colum would make her suffer.

Cree's powerful strides had startled her as he had advanced and dropped down beside her. His intentions were obvious; he would have his way with her and be done with it. Instead he kissed her and the unexpected happened. It sent a pleasant shiver rippling through her.

His hand took hold at the back of her neck and his lips pressed against hers with a strength that turned her shiver to a tingle. She startled again when his tongue invaded her mouth, and she braced her hands on either side of her to steady herself. Surprisingly, the more her tongue sparred with his the more she enjoyed the kiss. It hadn't been intentional. She had meant to avoid his brash invasion, but instead she seemed to have fueled something inside herself.

His other hand slipped around her waist and eased her back on the sleeping pallet following down on top of her, the kiss uninterrupted. The heat from his hard body drifted into her and strangely enough comforted her. Fear tingled at the recesses of her mind, but his kiss held it at bay.

When he drew his mouth away she felt a moment

of loss, but then he brushed his lips over hers as if teasing her.

"My kiss is the first you have ever tasted?" he asked in a whisper that sent tingles rippling across her passion-plumped lips.

She nodded realizing a heathen had been the first to kiss her and, oddly enough, she wished he would kiss her again and as if hearing... he did.

She couldn't lie still a minute longer. It was as if something inside her nudged her and without thinking her arms wrapped slowly around him. She had never felt such strength before, his thick muscles as hard as stone and yet his flesh smooth to the touch. She didn't think. She wanted only to explore, so her hand slipped up beneath his long hair and along his neck where her fingers began to roam ever so gently.

Cree was off her in an instant, his bare chest heaving as if he was breathless. She couldn't be sure if it was anger or passion she saw in his eyes. And she quickly scurried to sit up suddenly feeling defenseless lying prone while he stood so close towering over her.

She waited and as she did fear began to crawl over her turning her skin damp and causing her heart to pound. What had she done wrong? He had kissed her, but when she had touched him... the thought struck her like a slap in the face.

He doesn't want me to touch him. Most everyone avoided being touched by her, as if she would inflict them with her horror. And yet he had wrapped himself around her to sleep or had it been because he didn't trust her and so kept watch over her that way?

Whatever it was she had been a fool to respond to his kiss. He was a heathen; he cared for no one. He would have his way with her simply because there was no other woman but her to assuage his need. And there had been need, for she had felt it swell against her as they kissed. Why hadn't she kept her hands to herself? He would have taken her and it would have been done with or would it? Could she truly admit to herself that she had enjoyed his kiss and had been sorry to have it end? Then she recalled Flanna's warning not to touch the devil or she'd become a slave to his passion.

She quickly recited a prayer for her sinful action and turned her head away from him. Lord forgive her, she wished Colum had never caught Cree, for then life would have gone on as always. And she could have continued to pray and dream that somewhere there was a man brave of heart and soul who would love her.

Not knowing what to do and not wanting to see anger or disgust in his eyes, she stretched out on her side, her back to him, and shut her eyes. There was nothing she could do. She was trapped here with him just as her voice was trapped somewhere never to be set free.

Cree stared at her back fighting to control the urge to rush over to her and... damn but he had had his way with more woman than he could remember, so why not have her and be done with it. He made a fist and pressed it to his gut. He had felt as if he had been punched quick and hard when he had kissed her, for the kiss had stolen his breath.

She tasted sweet and so delicious that he could have drunk of their kiss forever. He had known in an instant how innocent she was, her kiss unsure, her tongue darting in fright and uncertainty. He had felt the wild thumping of her heart against his chest, felt when her body grew languid with passion, and knew that she would surrender to his touch, but then... she had touched him and everything had changed.

Never, not since the first woman whose legs he had laid between had he gotten so quickly and so thoroughly aroused. He had grown so hard, so fast that he was still fighting the urge to join her on the pallet and make love to her.

He turned away in disgust. What was the matter with him? He made love to no woman. He'd give a good poke and be done with it. Not that he rushed, which was why he always sought a woman with stamina and one that would make no demands on him.

He had plans for his future and it didn't include a peasant woman who couldn't speak.

Innocent.

The thought had him growing even harder if that was possible. Never had he taken a woman's innocence. Just the thought that he had been the first to kiss her and taste her sweetness made him feel all the more protective of her. It was as if with that kiss he had laid claim to her and she now belonged to him and no other... ever.

He heard her stir and he turned. She lay so that the sparse light barely caught her face, and he shook his head. She was plain of features. No one would look twice at her, though no one would turn away. One thing he did notice about her was that she kept herself cleaner than most other woman he had known. There was a fresh scent about her and her hair was soft and shiny and her skin was soft to the touch.

Damn, if he didn't excite himself again with thoughts of her. This had to stop. He could not let his need for a woman interfere with his plans. It had taken many years of sacrifice and endless bloody battles to finally get here and he would not throw it all away on a voiceless, peasant woman.

If need be he would take her innocence, but make certain his seed took no root, and then see that she was protected. He would never let anyone hurt her; she would be safe under his rule.

He sat a safe distance from her and forced his thoughts to focus on his plans. His arousal faded, while his mind swelled with battle scenarios. He searched and found a twig and began drawing in the dirt. Not satisfied, he would erase some and start again.

He was so engrossed with maneuvering his troops that he didn't hear Dawn stir awake. She lay quiet watching him. His brow was knit tightly in concentration, his eyes intent on the ground, and his hand busy drawing.

Drawings she understood; drawings gave her a voice.

She got to her feet and his head shot up. She remained where she was, tapped her chest, and pointed to his dirt drawing requesting permission to take a look.

He waved her over and she went to him. He held his hand out and for a moment she hesitated, but only a moment, and then she slipped her hand in his. He assisted her as she lowered herself to sit crossed-legged, as he did, beside him. Her eyes went to the drawings. They were a bit crude, but she was able to make out the mountains, valleys, trees and the squares that she understood represented cottages while the Xs were warriors. And there were many warriors.

She squinted, tilted her head, and realized that she was looking at a battle plan. She glanced at him, held up fisted hands and knocked them together.

He nodded. "Aye, battle plans forever fill my thoughts."

She leaned her elbow on her folded knee, rested her chin on her hand, and considered the drawing once again. She reached out and wiped away a couple of troops of warriors relocating them in different spots. She then pointed to the advantages of the moves.

Cree studied the changes she made and was surprised that the slight shift in location did actually give his troops a better advantage, an element of surprise that could mean an easier victory. He was impressed by her quick mind. She had sized up the plan and immediately spotted a flaw... and corrected it.

She pointed to the mountains and raised her hand.

"You're asking if the mountains are high."

She nodded and pointed to the valley, then held her hands out at different levels moving them up and down.

"The height of the mountains and depth of the valley can make a difference." Again he was surprised at her perception, though suddenly realized that it could present a problem if he allowed her to continue to study the drawing.

He ran the stick through the drawing several times and Dawn turned questioning eyes on him.

"I'm hungry," he said and stood, then reached down and grabbed her at the waist and hoisted her up. She winced and his nostrils flared. He had forgotten about her wounds.

She didn't seem to let it bother her. She slipped away from him and lit the candles she had brought with her and then got busy arranging food on the sleeping pallet.

He watched her amazed by her graceful movements and the way she took pains to arrange the food for him. But then she was a servant and it was her duty to please him.

The thought struck him hard. Had she responded to his kiss out of duty? And if so, why did it disturb him? She had been given orders and she had suffered the consequences of those orders when she had no information to give Colum. So had she been doing her best to please the man who could cause her great pain and not him?

Anger boiled up inside him, though it made no sense. Why should it matter to him one way or the other? She meant nothing to him, though... he felt a tug in his gut. She was a pawn in a dangerous game, being played by everyone around her, and she was doing her best to survive. How could he fault her for that? Actually he had to admire her. She did what she had to do and spoke not a complaint.

She couldn't speak.

It still astonished him that she could not make a sound, not even a grunt. He had seen others who could not speak, but they at least were able to grunt or make some type of noise. He had never known anyone who had lost their voice entirely. And to think she had this since birth. He wondered if any children she birthed would be afflicted with the same horror.

It also surprised him how she had adapted so well to her affliction, though some would think it more a curse. She appeared to communicate with anyone who paid heed to her, though he doubted many did. They more than likely assumed her ignorant and cast foul words upon her rather than a pleasant word.

She smiled at him and pointed at the blanket where an array of food spread out invitingly upon it.

He joined her sitting opposite from her eager to partake in the meal and perhaps conversation. Strange that he actually thought of speaking with her when she could not say a word, and yet it seemed that he had discussed things more with her than any other woman he had known.

She handed him a piece of meat and bread.

"Eat," he said, though it sounded like an order to his ears.

She reached out and tore a small piece of bread off the loaf and nibbled on it.

He was about to tell her to eat more when he decided against it. With the day she had been having he wouldn't be surprised if she had no appetite at all, and he would not force her to eat.

He reached for more bread and she quickly moved to help him, ripping several pieces off the loaf and placing them in front of him. Her duty was to serve him and she was seeing her duty done. The thought gave him pause and he wondered what else Colum expected of her this day.

"Is there anything else that Colum wants from you?"

She didn't need to speak, for the way her body turned rigid spoke louder than words.

"Tell me," he said.

Dawn stared at him. How did she tell him that Colum expected the scent of coupling to rest heavy upon her? That she would be handed to another man if he did not mate with her this night. The thought of Goddard having his way with her caused her stomach to roil, and she let the piece of bread fall from her hand before she pressed it hard against her stomach.

Cree didn't care for the way Dawn paled or how her hand clenched at her stomach. Whatever Colum had threatened her with had sickened her to think about and that angered him.

"You will tell me," he ordered firmly.

If she had to choose who she wanted to take from her that which should only be given to her husband, the man she would love with all her heart, then it would be Cree she would choose. She could not bear the thought of Goddard taking her like an animal in front of others.

"Now!"

Dawn jumped at his stern command. What choice did she have? Reluctantly, she pointed to Cree and then to her.

He saved her from going any further. "Colum expects us to mate."

She nodded, though she knew she needed to make him aware of what would happen if they didn't.

He seemed to understand the situation and asked, "And the consequence if that doesn't happen?"

Dawn raised her arm high and hoped he would recall the last time she had referred to Goddard that way, and then she pointed to herself and then to her raised arm.

He didn't respond immediately and she feared he did not understand her. But then she watched as that murderous look rose in his eyes and turned her cold once again.

"Are you telling me that if *we* do not couple that Colum will give you to Goddard?"

Her shoulders slumped with relief that he understood and she nodded.

"How would he know if —"

His sudden silence frightened her all the more.

"He wants my scent upon you."

It sounded to Dawn as if he growled beneath his breath like an angry beast.

"The bastard will pay for treating me like a dog and for using you without care or thought."

It dawned on her then that Cree had no intentions of dying that somehow he would escape and make Colum pay. What then would happen to her village? Would he and his warriors pillage it and the people? This was news she could take to Colum, but with no proof, what good would it do?

What made her anxious was that he turned completely silent. He finished eating and then quickly retired to the corner of the hut where the shadows devoured him. Dawn didn't know what to do, so she cleared away the food and sat on the edge of the blanket, found a stick, and began to draw.

She loved to draw and had since she was little. Her drawings said what she couldn't, and they spoke of beauty and joy. She wished she had had a permanent way of recording her drawing, but paper was costly as was paints and materials. So she made do and would draw in the sand only to brush her creations away or have the wind take them.

She drew a familiar scene. A place she often went to when she had a rare moment to herself. It was a glen not far from the village. She, Lila, and Paul shared grand adventures there when they were children. It was a safe place to her. A stream ran through the glen, hills rose on either side and trees dotted the landscape. She loved the soothing sound of the trickling stream. The water was in no hurry, making its way slowly along its path. She would sit for hours there if she could, but her work in the kitchen gave her little time to spare. Drawing the familiar scene at least let her visit it.

Two candles flickered out and when she looked up to see that the candles had burned completely down, she realized that she had spent several hours drawing in the dirt. She had a couple of more candles in the basket, though she didn't want to waste their precious light on her drawings. Reluctantly, she swept her hand across her creations, and they were gone.

The hut's door swung open causing her to jump and for Cree to quickly emerge from the shadows and stand protectively in front of her.

"She's to come fetch supper," John said standing outside the door and, dare not, letting his foot pass over the threshold.

"I have other plans for her," Cree said never taking his eyes off the guard. "Have someone else fetch it."

John couldn't seem to find the right words. He fumbled around, his tongue unable to work properly, until he finally gave up and shut the door.

Dawn slumped with relief. When the door had opened she feared she would be forced to leave and forced to endure Goddard. She gladly remained behind with Cree and was more than happy that he refused to allow her to leave. It bought her time. How much she didn't know, but for now she was pleased with this short reprieve.

Cree turned as soon as the door closed. "Take your garments off."

Chapter Ten

Dawn stood frozen to the spot. Her eyes rested on him as he slipped out of his leather leggings and removed his boots. In a matter of seconds, he stood before her naked and her breath caught. He was more than a fine specimen of a man; he was magnificent.

Toned and hard, not a thickening spot on him, and devoid of scars, a rarity for a warrior or perhaps a badge of honor. She was eager to see all of him and so her eyes roamed. He was solid, large, and hard all over. His precise lines and angles had her hand aching not to touch him, but to draw him. He would make a beautiful subject to draw.

He stretched his arms out to his sides. "Do I please you?"

She dropped down to the ground without thinking and grabbed the stick she had been drawing with. Her hand began moving and her eyes darted back and forth between him and the ground.

Cree shook his head. The woman confused him. He had expected her to tremble in fear at his command, perhaps hesitate to obey then eventually acquiesce. But what does she do? She drops to the ground and starts drawing.

He gave her a few minutes and then hunched down beside her. He was stunned at what she had so quickly drawn. It was him... from the chest up. He stared shocked at her skillful hand.

"You are talented."

She smiled at him and it struck him that she may be plain, but there was a loveliness to her that he doubted many were aware of.

He reached out and took the stick from her hand. "You must remove your garments now."

There was no point in protesting, weeping, or fighting. She had made her choice; this had to be done. She would submit willingly to Cree to save herself from being taken by Goddard.

Cree stood and offered his hand to her. She took it and got to her feet, then stepped away. With shaking hands, she fumbled her way through removing her clothes. She kept her back to him fearing that he would turn away in disgust at her naked body. Some of the women had made fun of her and let her know that her voice was not the only thing she lacked... her body left a lot to be desired. Lila had told her to ignore their remarks that they were jealous, but Lila was her friend and always defended her.

Why it mattered what he thought of her body she didn't know, and she shouldn't let it bother her, but it did, and it kept her from turning around when she finally stood completely naked.

Cree had watched how her hands trembled as she attempted to remove her garments. He had grown annoyed at first, wanting her to hurry, but as he watched her remove one garment at a time, revealing creamy skin and luscious curves, he changed his mind and continued watching her disrobe.

Her body was lovely, perfect curves, slender limbs, and a taut backside his hands itched to touch. He wanted to see more of her and when she didn't turn around he said, "Turn."

She gathered all the courage that she could and

with a sturdy lift of her chin, she turned around.

His loins tightened at the sight of her. Her breasts were but a handful, her waist slim, her hips curved and her legs long. Damn what was wrong with him? He favored thicker and well-endowed women. Why did this woman affect him so? He had grown hard watching her disrobe and he grew harder when she had turned around. Now he was annoyed with himself. He controlled his passion, his passion didn't control him. It was a rule he had lived by.

He had seen too many men lose all they had fought hard for because they had allowed their desire to override common sense. He had no intention of letting that happen to him. He had worked hard and sacrificed much to get where he had gotten, and he would not lose it all over a woman and a voiceless one at that.

He almost cringed at his words. It wasn't Dawn's fault that she had no voice. She had bravely faced life with the infirmity and had thrived in spite of it. In a way she was a conquering warrior herself.

Cree stretched his hand out. "Come here."

Dawn wanted this done, so she didn't hesitate, she went to him. It did help that he hadn't turned his eyes away from her, but kept them steady upon her. And being as hard as he was he obviously desired her. At least she told herself that to make it easier for her to join with him.

As soon as her hand touched his, he yanked her against him and she felt a jolt through her body that caught her breath. His body was hard and warm and the strength of him overpowered.

He lowered them to the blanket and covered her with his body. He stared at her and she thought he would say something but he didn't, he just stared.

Then he began to move against her and she felt his shaft hard between her legs. He continued to stare at her as he did.

She realized than that he had no intentions of kissing her. He would take her and be done with it. She would lay there and do what she must... suffer the lesser of two evils.

A tingle started between her legs and flourished and grew stronger as his movements grew stronger. And still he kept his eyes on her. She tried to remain still, but it was difficult. She could not stop herself from moving against him and the more the tingle grew pleasurable the more rapid her movements.

Dawn shut her eyes against the building passion and grabbed hold of his arms.

"Open your eyes," he ordered, his breath rapid.

She did as her own breathing grew heavier. She waited for him to enter her, to be done with it, to have his way and stop the unbearable ache that would not stop building inside her. When suddenly, she felt herself explode with extraordinary pleasure.

She gripped his arms tight and wished at that moment that she had a voice, for if she did she would scream with the sheer pleasure that consumed her.

Cree let out a groan as he rode against her hard, and then finally collapsed on top of her.

She didn't quite understand what had happened. Cree had never entered her and when in the throes of it all—God help her—she had actually wanted him to. Hadn't he truly wanted her?

Voices outside the door had Dawn pushing at Cree's chest.

"Stay as you are," he said.

Dawn's eyes turned wide. She didn't want anyone

to see them like this, see her naked, though Cree's body covered hers as well as a blanket would, though not him. His backside lay bare for anyone who entered to see.

The door sprung open and Flanna walked in with a basket in each hand. John stopped at the threshold as usual, though both of them froze when they caught sight of the naked couple on the ground.

"Blasted, woman, put the baskets down and get out," Cree screamed at her.

Flanna fumbled, dropping the baskets to the ground and cast a glance of pity at Dawn before turning and hurrying past the guard.

John laughed and nodded and as the door closed he could be heard saying, "Colum is going to want to hear about this.

Realization struck Dawn... Cree had done this to protect her. The guard would tell Colum that the prisoner had rutted with the dumb one, and Flanna would spread the news as well. And she would have his scent upon her.

Tears threatened her eyes, but she forced them away. He had saved her from suffering at Colum's hand and saved her from Goddard and, while the villagers would certainly gossip about it, she at least would be safe. She knew she should be grateful, but she could not help wonder why he had not actually coupled with her.

Cree got off her. "Get dressed."

It was a curt command and she hurried into her clothes.

He slipped his things on and sat on the blanket, not glancing her way.

A crack of thunder had her jumping, though had not disturbed Cree in the least.

"Food," he said.

She went to the baskets Flanna had brought and as she rifled through them she recalled the look of pity in Flanna's eyes. Would she see that in others' eyes? Would the villagers pity her and avoid her more now for having copulated with evil?

Pity is for fools, her mum used to say. *Do what you must and be done with it. Get on with life for it will not wait for you.*

She had to remember that and do what she must. She smiled seeing all the food Flanna had brought. If anything good came of this misfortune it was that she was eating better than she ever had and for that she should be grateful.

She picked up the baskets and walked over to the blanket where she began spreading out the food. She didn't look once at Cree, and she wondered if he bothered to look at her.

Cree watched her closely. He liked watching her movements and he had liked feeling her move against him. The thought annoyed him, though what had annoyed him even more was his climax. Never had he experienced such an intense one and he hadn't even been inside Dawn. He wondered if it would be more intense if he had been and, if so, would the climax be unimaginable and more satisfying than anything he had ever known?

She may not have been able to scream out when she came, but he had felt her release. Her body had grown taut like a string on a fine bow when stretched to release an arrow, and her hands had squeezed his arms growing ever tighter until she had finally burst with pleasure. It had caused him to burst with satisfaction as well. He had nearly entered her several times. It had taken much control on his part not to, but he wondered how long that would last, for he was already thinking of coupling with her again.

This would not do at all. He needed his wits about him and he needed to concentrate on the plan. Dawn had supplied him with relevant information without realizing it. The fool Colum was doing exactly what he had expected... prancing with pride. He gave no thought to the consequences of capturing Cree. He assumed that he had the evil-doer in his hands and he had no more to worry about. That was obvious by this small hovel Colum considered an adequate prison to hold the mighty Cree.

He had had enough of this forced confinement, not that he could not bear more if it were necessary. He had trained himself to endure most anything and had many times. However, this short time spent with Dawn had tested his will, and he did not care for the fact that he was having difficulty maintaining control. It was time to implement his plan.

That night as he lay wrapped around Dawn, her body relaxed in his arms, he had the sudden realization that he would miss sleeping with her. She was not a fitful sleeper, pushing away from him during the night, or jabbing him with flailing limbs. She remained tucked against him as if she was content being in his arms. And he had slept more peaceably than he ever had.

He tucked Dawn closer to him, resting his leg over hers, and she didn't protest. She snuggled contentedly against him.

He had to be done with this. There was too much at stake. This was the last time Dawn would ever lay in his arms. He would make sure of it.

Chapter Eleven

Dawn left Cree the next morning not sure what to think. All he had said was go, nothing more. It had sounded so final, as if he never wanted to lay eyes on her again. She didn't have long to waste her thoughts on the matter, since the guard John poked her in the back with a long stick urging her to the keep.

The sneer he wore told her all she needed to know and the stares, snickers, and whispers from the villagers who watched confirmed that news had spread that Cree had had his way with her.

Colum was waiting for her in the Great Hall. Goddard sat to his right, and those warriors he trusted the most occupied the other chairs on the dais.

"She stinks of rutting," John announced proudly, as if it had been his doing.

Colum and his men laughed.

"Finally, you do something right," Colum chortled. "Let us hope he left his seed in you and you bear him a voiceless son. It would be a fitting legacy for him to leave behind."

Her legs went weak at his remark. Had that been why Cree had not entered her? He didn't dare take the chance of leaving her with child? She admonished herself for letting the thought upset her. She should be glad such a monster did not leave his seed in her.

He was no monster.

Did she truly believe that? If he was a monster he

would not have made certain she carried his scent. If he was a monster he would not have covered her naked body with his to keep from prying eyes. If he was a monster he would have taken her with no thought or care and he hadn't. Cree was no monster. He couldn't be... he cared.

"Now tell me you have learned something and you will have served me well," Colum said.

Dawn was not foolish enough to believe that the information Cree had given her was accurate, and she did not care. Colum wanted something and she would give it to him. She quickly pointed to the bread on the table.

Colum shook his head.

She pointed to herself and back at the bread.

"You've hungry?"

She shook her head.

"Make yourself understood," Colum shouted.

She pointed to the bread again and motioned as if she were tearing it apart.

Colum waved his hand at her. "Show me."

Dawn quickly approached the table and just as quickly tore several pieces off the bread. She lined them up, pointed to them, and then pointed at all the warriors in the room.

"Warriors," Goddard said understanding. "The pieces represent warriors. Cree's warriors?"

Dawn nodded and then moved half of the pieces away crumpling them in her hand.

"He has fewer warriors than we think," Colum said with a broad grin.

"Why would Cree tell her such a thing?" Goddard asked suspiciously and Dawn's heart nearly stopped from fear.

"Why else?" Colum laughed. "He thinks her

dumb like most and incapable of communicating."

Goddard nodded, agreeing.

"You've done well," Colum said. "Now go get more food and get back to him and find out more."

Dawn didn't hesitate. She hurried out of the room to the kitchen. All movement and sound stopped as soon as she entered.

"Get back to your chores or I'll see the lazy lot of you punished," Flanna threatened and everyone did as she said. She then walked with Dawn outside.

There was a nip in the air. Soon the last of the harvest would be picked and the ground turned for winter, which would be upon them soon enough. Why Dawn should be thinking on mundane things she did not know. Life was no longer mundane. Life was vastly different, and she doubted it would ever be the same.

"Are you all right?" Flanna asked.

Dawn nodded and her hands moved letting Flanna know that she needed more food. She also wanted to let Flanna know that she wanted to wash up, but thankfully the woman was perceptive.

"You'll want to wash up before returning to him."

Dawn smiled and tapped her chest. Those familiar with her gestures knew it meant she was grateful.

Flanna grabbed her hand. "Are you sure you're all right? I saw—" Her eyes filled with tears, though she didn't let one fall. "He's powerfully built. Are you sure he didn't hurt you?"

She could tell Flanna the truth but, odd as it seemed, it would be better to let things remain as they were. Otherwise gossiping tongues would be wagging about how the mighty warrior Cree wouldn't waste his seed on her. She would be ridiculed even more.

She cupped both hands and, with palms down, ran one over the other.

Flanna confirmed she understood with a nod. "It's over."

Dawn smiled.

Flanna shook her head sadly. "It's only just begun."

Dawn walked to her small cottage keeping her head down and avoiding glancing at anyone. She heard the whispers, the chortling, though she was surprised when Old Mary grabbed her arm and stopped her.

"They should all be grateful to you. You saved them from his wrath."

Dawn watched Old Mary hobble away and wasn't sure if it was Colum or Cree's wrath she meant.

She continued to her cottage and wasn't surprised to see Lila waiting in her doorway. As soon as Drawn was a few feet from her, Lila spread her arms wide and Dawn hurried into them. Lila ushered Dawn inside and the two cried together.

When their tears were spent, Lila sat dawn down at the table and fixed a hot brew for them both and they talked.

"Did he hurt you?" Lila asked as if she would kill Cree if he had.

Dawn shook her head and motioned that she was fine.

"I wished your first time could have been different and with someone you loved."

How did she make Lila understand that that was never meant to be? No matter how much she wished for it or her friend wished for it, it was not something she would ever have. And it was best she accepted it and continued to survive. And that meant not lingering on something that could not be changed.

Dawn motioned that she desperately needed to wash and Lila hurried to set a pot of water to heat. Within the hour, she was freshly washed and wished she had a change of clothes, since the scent of Cree was strong on her garments.

Lila had talked the whole time, though Dawn had expressed a gestured or two regarding the babe Lila carried. It wouldn't be long now, and she wanted to make certain her friend was feeling well. She, herself, may never have children, but Lila's children would be like having her own and that pleased her.

Dawn walked Lila to her cottage two doors down. Lila was a spinner and a fine one at that. She worked daily on her spindle and distaff in her cottage producing the fine yarn that Colum traded with the aristocracy, while leaving the villagers to wear threadbare garments. Lila had made sure to keep the scraps and from them had made several garments for her unborn babe.

They were just a couple of feet from Lila's cottage when the village alarm bell tolled sending fear through the villagers. Men, women, and children began rushing about, while the dire warning continued to clang ominously.

Lila shouted, "Look."

Everyone followed her pointing finger to see smoke rising in the cloudy sky, and they all ran toward it.

The prison hut was on fire and the flames growing out of control.

Dawn stared in shock and disbelief. What had happened? Was Cree inside?

Lila huddled beside her and they watched as John,

the guard, shouted at the men who had formed a bucket brigade, Paul among them.

"Faster," John screamed.

The men did their best to rush the pails down the line more rapidly, but it didn't matter. Flames engulfed the small hut and in minutes it collapsed sending tendrils of fire and sparks spiraling into the air.

John ordered the women to join the men and Dawn pushed Lila away when she went to follow her. She pointed to a spot by one of the cottages where Lila could watch but not be seen and shoved her toward it. Lila didn't argue; she went.

They couldn't let the fire spread. They had to extinguish ever last ember or chance losing other buildings. The whole village could go up in flames if they didn't stomp out what remained of the fire. It took hours of hard work, but every last spark was finally snuffed out. Men and women let their buckets drop from blistered hands and aching limbs. Husbands and wives hugged each other in relief and children clung to their parents' legs as they all headed to their individual cottages.

"Stay where you are," John shouted.

Everyone froze and Dawn saw that Paul sent a warning look to Lila to stay put and not show herself.

"The prisoner has escaped. Your liege lord and his warriors have gone after him and will return victorious. Now get to your duties."

Exhausted from their ordeal, their bodies too tired to move, they inched along to their perspective chores knowing that John would report those who refused to obey. And Colum would show no mercy upon his return, especially if Cree could not be found.

Paul took Dawn by the arm and ushered her over

to Lila, then hurried both women away and didn't stop until they reached the relative safety of his and Lila's cottage.

He turned to Dawn. "I will walk you to the kitchen, and then later I will come and walk you home. Don't go anywhere alone."

Dawn knew why Paul warned her not to venture anywhere by herself. He worried that some would blame her for Cree's escape and see that she suffer for it. Though he probably worried more, just as she did, that Colum would blame her and punish her, and his punishment would be far worse.

Flanna was waiting outside the kitchen door for her, and Paul stopped a distance away and waited until she reached Flanna, then he turned and ran off to hurry to the fields.

"In the kitchen and stay there," Flanna ordered obviously thinking the same as Paul.

Dawn didn't argue. She'd keep to herself and tend to her duties. She preferred it that way. She didn't know whether to be relieved or worried over Cree's escape. Would Colum somehow blame her? Would he punish her? And what of Cree? If escape was so easy for him why had he waited? Why hadn't he escaped his first day here?

Something nagged at her, but she couldn't quite catch hold of it. She lost herself in her work not wanting to think of what might happen. All the while that nagging bit of something jabbed at her.

Night came but Colum and his warriors had not returned. Paul came for her as he said he would and he tried to convince her to spend the night with him and Lila. But Dawn wanted time alone and insisted she would be fine, he was not to worry.

She made herself a hot brew, slipped out of her clothes and into her night dress, and dropped down on her sleeping pallet. She was exhausted and though she fought to remain awake and see if she could discover what it was that nagged in the recesses of her mind, she couldn't. She fell asleep as soon as her head rested on the pillow.

The next morning she popped up in bed and realized what had plagued her. It was the drawing Cree had made in the dirt. She recognized the area, and she realized that the drawing had been a plan of attack and she, not realizing it, had helped him strengthen his forces' positions to attack the Village Dowel.

She jumped out of bed and dressed quickly. She wasn't sure what to do. Would anyone believe her? They would want to know why she hadn't said something sooner. She wanted to protect her village, but she feared no one would pay heed to her warning. And yet if she didn't, what would be the consequences?

Would there be anything left once Cree got finished with the village? What of Lila, Paul, and their unborn baby? She had to at least warn them. She opened the cottage door and stood staring. Villagers rushed past with worried expressions.

Was Colum returning? Had he recaptured Cree? Were her worries over or were they just beginning?

She followed along with the crowd. Lila and Paul joined her when she reached their cottage. The villagers lined the entrance waiting to greet their liege lord, but this time he was not returning the victorious hero. Colum and his warriors looked worn and defeated.

Silence followed the troop, not a word was

whispered, not a sound heard. Dawn feared that Colum would lay blame on someone and that someone could well be her.

Colum halted and glared at the sea of faces, many turning away in fear. "You're a worthless lot. Get to your chores now."

Everyone scurried off keeping their distance from Colum as he and his men traveled on to the keep. They all knew someone would suffer for this and many an eye turned on Dawn and whispers followed her as she walked along with Paul and Lila.

Paul could not walk with her to the kitchen. He had to leave with the other men who worked in the field. But he urged her to be careful and warned his wife that she had their unborn babe to worry about, so fearful was he that she would do something foolish in defending her friend.

Dawn was nearly to the kitchen when she heard the first scream. She turned and her blood ran cold. Charging down the hill was a troop of warriors their faces streaked red and as they reached the bottom they were joined by two other troops charging in from the right and left.

And in the lead rode Cree.

Chapter Twelve

Dawn's first thought was of Lila. The workers in the field would have been the first to spot the approaching warriors. Paul could have had time to get to his wife. She prayed that he did as she ran to find her friends.

She made her way through the madness, ducking, bobbing, and jumping to stay out of the way of the battling warriors. Even in her haste, it was easy to see that Colum's men were no match for Cree's warriors. It would not be long before Cree claimed victory and with it lives.

Children cried, women screamed, knowing what was waiting for them. Once Colum's men were conquered, the true horror would begin for the villagers. She wanted to tell them to run and hide in the woods, but would it do any good? Would Cree send his men to search for them? And where would they go from there?

Dawn finally spotted Lila on the side of a cottage. She was kneeling on the ground crouched over something, and Dawn sped to her side. She dropped down beside her friend, her heart pounding when she saw that it was Paul on the ground and he was wounded.

"He's hurt badly," Lila cried.

"Forget me, help Lila, the babe is coming," Paul said with such fear that it sent a shiver through Dawn.

She looked to her friend.

"I will not leave my husband," she insisted, and then doubled over in pain.

Dawn took stock of the situation. Paul had suffered a leg wound that was still bleeding. She tore a piece off the hem of her skirt and wrapped his leg. It wasn't enough to stop the bleeding, so she ripped off another piece of her skirt and one of her sleeves and wrapped both around the wound. Blood seeped through, but not as fast as before.

Lila went to do the same, but Dawn stopped her and patted her stomach, letting her know she would need it for the babe.

"Get her out of here," Paul insisted.

"No, I won't leave you," Lila cried.

The chaos in the village grew worse, the clang of swords, the moans of the injured, the screams of the dying shivered Dawn down to the bone. Paul was right... this was no place for Lila to be with the babe coming.

Dawn took charge. She motioned to Lila that she would get her to the safety of the woods, and then return for Paul. Lila wanted Paul to go with them, but Dawn argued with exaggerated motions that it could prove fatal to them all. Then she held up three spread fingers and snapped them close together, reminding Lila of something the three had long ago agreed to.

Lila shed more tears. "We made a pact when we were young to always help each other no matter what."

Dawn crossed her chest with her finger.

Lila nodded. "You promise to help Paul and you have never broken a promise to me."

It was Dawn's turn to nod, and she helped Lila to stand. Dawn then bent down and shifted her shoulder beneath Paul's and, with a strength born of determination, dragged him closer to the side of the cottage where he'd be less noticed. She then motioned to Paul that she'd be back for him soon, and the three would then hide in the woods and help Lila with the birthing.

Paul tried to argue but Dawn dismissed him with a wave of her hand, then pressed a finger to Lila's mouth, warning her to remain silent and took off with her, Dawn's arm around her waist to help move her along.

Once Dawn found a spot in the woods, Lila grabbed her arm and with labored breathing said, "Please, Dawn, bring him safely to me."

Dawn squeezed her friend's shoulder and nodded.

She took off again, not wanting to leave Lila alone too long and needing to get to Paul before it was too late. She didn't know where she found the courage to keep going in spite of her fear, though fear had become a constant companion of hers lately. She had come to know it well. It had clung tightly to her from the first moment she had laid eyes on Cree. He was not a man to trust or to care for. Why then was she relieved that he had not died?

The battle had worsened. More of Colum's men lay wounded, dead or dying. The stench of blood and death hung heavily in the air, and she knew the end was near. Cree would claim victory over the Village Dowell this day.

She hurried to where she had left Paul, weaving, bobbing, and jumping to avoid the battling warriors. She finally reached Paul and with a bit of a struggle she got him up. He leaned heavily on her, his wound painful and making it difficult for him to walk.

They shuffled along and several oaths ran through

Dawn's head. She was unable to take the easy path to the woods that she had with Lila. The battling warriors had blocked it and so she had to make her way around it.

Paul grew heavier with each step they took, but she managed to keep firm hold of him. When there was finally a break in the fighting, she hurried him, as best as she could, across the center of the village, giving her a direct path between the safety of two buildings and to the woods beyond.

Unfortunately, the pain had worn Paul out, and he staggered, weighing down more heavily upon her. She stumbled and fought to regain her balance and for a moment she feared he would propel them both to the ground, landing on top of her.

Just as she got him steady, she spotted a lone rider baring down on them... it was Cree and fury blazed in his eyes.

Dawn did not think twice, she dropped Paul to the ground and threw her body over him.

Seconds later, she was yanked off him with such force that it made her head spin, and then she heard Paul cry out, "Please no, Dawn is helping me."

The point of Cree's sword stopped within inches of Paul's chest and Cree looked to Dawn to confirm Paul's plea, and she nodded. He then pointed to her ripped sleeve and tunic. "Who did this to you?"

She tapped her chest and looked to Paul who hurried to explain that she had used the torn pieces to wrap his wounded leg. He then continued detailing what had happened and the whole time that he did, Cree never let go of her. And while Cree listened to Paul's plea for mercy and help for his wife who was about to give birth, several of Cree's warriors formed a protective circle around them.

Cree finally ordered Paul to be silent. He then turned to one of his men. "Take this man to the keep for the healer to look after." He looked to three other warriors and ordered, "Take this woman and let her lead you to her friend in the woods and bring them both to the keep as well."

When he released Dawn, he said to the three warriors, "This one hears clearly enough, but she has no voice to protect herself, let no harm come to her. And make sure she is returned directly to me."

The three nodded, and then formed a protective wall around Dawn, and she found herself running to keep pace with them as she pointed the way.

Cree mounted his horse and glanced around. The battle was near over, his warriors tending to the last of Colum's men who were quickly laying down their swords. As usual Cree was victorious. It had been an easy battle as he had thought it would be, Colum's men no match for his skilled warriors. They had fought brave and hard as always, though the stakes were much higher this time... for them all.

He watched as some women huddled in fear over their injured men while others ran wildly with babes in their arms. Where he did not know, for there was nowhere for them to go. He could understand their fear. It had gripped him when he had seen what he thought was a warrior attacking Dawn.

He had known it could not be one of his. Death waited for any who dared to disobey his orders and rape was something he would not tolerate. Rage like none he had ever known before had rushed through him when he had spotted Dawn's ripped garments, and he had been ready to kill the man who had attacked her with one swift blow.

Pride quickly replaced anger when Paul explained what had happened. That Dawn would put herself in danger to help her friends spoke generously of her nature. She was a good person, and he was pleased to see that she was safe, and he intended to see she remained so.

A wave from his most trusted warrior Sloan caught his attention, and he rode to where he stood on the keep steps to join him. As soon as Cree dismounted his stallion one of his warrior's was there to tend the animal.

Annoyance plagued Sloan's usual pleasant countenance, and Cree suspected he was not going to be pleased with the news.

"We cannot find Colum or Goddard."

Cree was not happy. He had lain awake last night thinking of how he was going to make both men pay for what they had done to Dawn. He thirsted for revenge, and he would not be satisfied until that thirst was quenched.

"Send a group of men to scour the surrounding woods. If they have not found them by nightfall, have them return. He is probably on his way to Gerwan, his feudal lord, to deliver the news and gather troops.

Sloan grinned. "Will the news have reached Gerwan by then?"

"It will have, and Colum will no longer be of use to him."

"Colum will seek revenge against you."

"I am counting on it," Cree said. "Now see to the injured and before nightfall I want the villagers gathered here in front of the keep."

"Has Turbett arrived yet?"

Sloan laughed. "The men argued over who would

go fetch him."

"I expected no less from them. It is another victorious battle, and Turbett will prepare a scrumptious feast for all to celebrate."

Sloan nodded slowly. "That he will, though it will not be just another victorious battle we celebrate. It will finally be having a permanent home that we celebrate."

A shout to Sloan had him running and left Cree standing on the steps of the keep alone. This was his now, hard won and a longtime coming. But he and his men had earned it and they would protect their new home with their lives. No one would take it away from them; no one could. The King had decreed it.

He cast an anxious glance over the village to see if his men had returned with Dawn yet. She was nowhere in sight, and so he turned and entered the keep, wondering how he would stop himself from taking the silent one to his bed tonight.

3. ~~~

Lila would not stop asking about Paul as the warrior carried her out of the woods. Dawn reassured her over and over that he was fine and being tended to by Cree's healer. And still she questioned until a pain gripped her and she cried out.

Dawn pointed toward Lila's cottage as they neared it.

The large man shook his head. "Cree ordered her to be brought to the keep and you to be brought directly to him."

"Paul is at the keep. I want to—" Lila screamed and the warrior carrying her stumbled, but never let go of her. "The baby," she cried out her hands going to her rounded stomach.

Dawn rushed to Lila's cottage and the warriors did as she had hoped, they followed after her. She was ever so grateful that the cottage suffered no damage during the battle. She hurried inside and yanked the blanket down to the bottom of the bed and gestured for the warrior to place her there.

"We must go to the keep," he insisted and turned assuming Dawn would follow.

Lila cried out again. "The baby is coming."

The warrior hurried to the bed, placed Lila on it, and rushed over to the two other warriors who had entered. They whispered amongst themselves.

"Please bring my husband to me," Lila called out to them.

Dawn walked over to them and shooed them toward the door.

The large one protested. "We are to remain with you until we can get you to the keep."

Dawn shook her head and shooed them again, forcing two out. The big one wouldn't budge until Lila let out another earth-shattering scream.

"I will be right outside," he said and hurried out, closing the door behind him.

Dawn rolled up her one sleeve and returned to Lila's side ready to help her friend.

4. ~~~

Paul entered the cottage a short time later supported by two warriors. Dawn was quick to move a chair by the bed so that Paul would be close by his wife, and the warriors eased him down on it.

The large warrior had followed them in and motioned to Dawn. "You are to come with me now.

The healer will be here shortly to help birth the babe."

Dawn shook her head, her hands motioning and the warrior scratched his head.

"Dawn says she is staying here and helping her friend," Paul said.

"Cree has ordered her return to the keep," the large man explained.

Dawn shook her head and waved her hands, signifying that she was not going anywhere.

The large warrior shook his head and scratched his graying beard. "You have no choice, lassie." And he stepped toward her.

Dawn grabbed the broom, resting against the fireplace, and swung it at the guard.

"She's warning you to stay away from her," Paul said. "Can you let her stay until the babe is born, and then she will go with you?"

Dawn nodded vigorously.

"It is not my choice."

The healer entered the cottage the same time that Lila let out another blood-curdling scream, and Dawn foolishly let down her guard. The large warrior lunged, grabbing the broom and tossing it aside as his other hand grabbed for her. With a tight grip on her arm, he dragged her to the door.

Lila screamed at him to let her go that she needed her there with her. The healer, an older woman as round as she was short, attempted to assure Lila that she would help her and all would be well. Lila would hear none of it; she continued to cry out to Dawn.

Paul pleaded with the warrior to let Dawn stay but he paid no heed to the pleas. He dragged Dawn out of the cottage. She fought him every step of the way, but try as she might his grip was too strong for her to break.

Once he got her into the Great Hall, Cree's voice rang out, quivering the rafters. "Dawn, cease your struggles."

She stilled and turned to face him, and her heart hammered in her chest. He was more imposing and more handsome in full light, and it sent her knees trembling. Whatever did he want with her? And did she truly want to find out?

She wanted to run but where? As much as she wanted to return to Lila, she dare not for fear that her friends would suffer for her disobedience. She was trapped, always trapped, and she could do nothing but face her fate.

"Come here," Cree ordered.

She walked over to him and as much as she wished to walk with her chin high, she kept her head bowed in respect and out of fear of punishment.

"Look at me," he snapped.

She raised her head.

"You are safe now. You have nothing to fear."

Did she believe him? Did he truly mean her no harm?

"I gave you my word, and I will keep it. I will let no harm come to you."

She nodded and placed her hand to her chest in a show of appreciation. She then anxiously pointed toward the door, and then herself, and back to the door again.

"You want permission to leave."

She nodded vigorously and rocked her folded arms as if she held a babe."

"I forgot. You're friend has birthed the babe?"

Dawn shook her head.

"You want to be there when she does."

Another vigorous nod.

"Go, but return later. I wish to speak with you."

She nodded apprehensively, bowed her head, then turned and hurried out of the keep."

Sloan walked over to Cree. "Do you truly wish to speak with her or ease the ache of lust?"

"Watch your tongue, Sloan, or I'll cut it from your mouth."

"I think not. You have never punished anyone for speaking the truth."

Sloan walked off to tend to his duties, and Cree silently cursed him.

Chapter Thirteen

Dawn smiled at her friends and their newborn son. Lila had delivered Thomas not long after she had returned to the cottage. Elsa, the healer, had done a fine job of calming Lila and delivering the babe with more ease than Dawn had thought possible.

The babe was swaddled in a soft wool blanket his mum had made and slept contentedly in her arms. He had full cheeks and a few sprouts of red hair on the top of his head. He was the most beautiful babe that Dawn had ever seen.

"Elsa tells us that Cree will treat the villagers well and that we will not be sorry that he is our new lord," Lila said with a smile.

"It is true," Elsa said. "He is the new lord of this land and he will do right by the people. Speak truthfully to him and do your fair share, and you will have a good life under his leadership."

"He will explain to all at the gathering in front of the keep not long from now," Paul said. "Lila will be excused from attending since she just gave birth, but I must attend."

Dawn didn't wait for him to ask, she motioned that they would go together.

Paul gave an appreciative nod and turned his attention on the babe who was yawning.

"Let us talk. I am curious about your loss of voice," Elsa said slipping her arm around Dawn's and moving her along, right out the door.

Dawn shivered when Elsa closed the door. She understood that this time was for Paul and Lila and their newborn, so why did she suddenly feel left out?

"There's a good place," Elsa said pointing to a bench on the far side of Lila's garden.

Dawn followed along, recalling how she and Lila had often worked in the garden together. And how Paul had built the bench from a fallen tree branch he had found in the woods. It was sturdy enough, though he would have been sturdier if Paul had been permitted to cut down a tree instead of picking from the decaying ones on the ground. But the villagers were not allowed to cut the trees or hunt the animals. The woods, and all in it, belonged to their feudal lord Roland Gerwan, the Earl of Carrick.

Elsa sat, the bench creaking under her ample weight. "So you have been without a voice since you were born?"

Dawn nodded.

"You made not a sound when you were born? Not a cry, grunt, or groan?"

Dawn shook her head. Elsa looked perplexed as most people did.

"Usually, at least in my experience, a voiceless person can still manage a grunt or a groan. Never have I known someone to be completely voiceless. It is quite odd. How do you manage to speak with others?"

Dawn held up her hands, and then snatched up a stick off the ground and did a quick drawing of the cottage.

Elsa smiled, her full cheeks plumping. "Amazing. Your drawing helps you to communicate. You are talented."

Dawn gave a nod of thanks.

"I wish there was something I could do to help you. But I fear that since you were born voiceless, there is nothing that can be done. It was simply meant to be."

Dawn had never thought, hoped, or prayed that one day she would suddenly start speaking. She had accepted her lot a long time ago. This was who she was, a voiceless person, not that she could not make herself heard, though she had learned that silence had its own rewards.

"I look forward to getting to know you, and I would be pleased to have you visit my cottage as soon as I am settled in," Elsa said.

Dawn pointed to the cottage and back at Elsa, and then shrugged.

Elsa smiled again, though Dawn realized it was simply an extension of the warm smile that she seemed to constantly wear.

"I understand you perfectly," Elsa said with joy. "You want to know where my cottage will be."

Dawn nodded, fearful that perhaps someone would be forced to give their home to Elsa.

"Cree will find a suitable and an unoccupied one for me and make repairs if necessary. He will want me to make a place available to all who require healing."

Dawn tapped her chest, pointed at the cottage, and then all around.

"You do make it easy to understand you. Yes, available to everyone, villagers and warriors alike. I am here to serve the ill and needy."

Dawn wondered if her words would prove true. Colum had his healer serve him and his warriors. No villager had dared approach the healer for help. They relied on the older women in the village who had some knowledge of healing.

"I would love to sit and talk with you more, but a brief reprise is all I can spare. I must go and see how the wounded do and if anyone else needs me." Elsa stood. "And I'm sure your friends are wondering where you are. Lila would not stop worrying about you. She was frantic for your safety. It was only when I reassured her that Cree protected the weak and afflicted that she finally calmed. We will talk soon, Dawn." And with that she walked off at a brisk pace.

Dawn remained on the bench. She had thought Cree an unfeeling soul, and yet he had not been cruel to her. He had not caused her harm. Were the tales about him just that... tales? He certainly had to have done something to have people fear him so badly or where would the rumors have come from?

She was curious to hear what Cree would have to say to the villagers. She did not have long to wait since Cree's warriors were walking through the village, herding the people toward the keep. A warrior waved her toward him, and she stood and hurried to the cottage door and gave a knock.

Paul opened the door, his finger pressed to his lips. Then in a whisper said, "Mum and babe just fell asleep though—"

Dawn tugged on his arm, and Paul hurried the door closed behind him after catching sight of the warrior making his way toward them. Dawn slipped her arm around his shoulder to lend him support. He was pale and obviously in pain and no doubt had not wanted to leave his wife and newborn son, but he, like her, knew they had no choice.

The warrior halted his approach when he saw that

Dawn helped Paul and returned to herding the crowd that was growing larger as more and more villagers joined the others in walking to the keep. Everyone searched the crowd for family and friends to see who had survived. Some husbands just now were reuniting with their wives and crying children found their tearful parents.

Dawn looked about for Old Mary, not many bothered with her and Dawn feared she may not have survived. She did spot Flanna, though did not catch her eye. She appeared dazed and unsure as did many in the crowd.

A poke to her arm had her turning quickly, and she smiled down at Old Mary smiling back up at her.

The old woman poked her again. "Changes come; good changes."

With that she made her way through the crowd toward the front, her steps sprier than Dawn had ever seen. She was pleased that the old woman was hopeful, but she was more pragmatic. What would happen when their feudal lord, Roland Gerwan was told of the attack? Would he send his warriors to retake the keep and reclaim his land? Were more battles on the horizon? Would there be more suffering?

"I hope Elsa is right and our lot will improve with Cree as our leader," Paul said.

Dawn heard doubt creep into his words and understood. The liegeman that had overseen the village before Colum arrived had been old and had not driven the people hard. Life had been fairly good. Everyone in the village had seen to doing their share and had shared when necessary. Upon that liegeman's death the Earl of Carrick had sent Colum to oversee his land and life had changed and not for the better. Now it would change again, but *how* was the question on everyone's minds.

"Elsa is such a generous woman. She's returning to the cottage later to check on Lila and the babe, and she says that she will bring food for us."

Dawn felt a catch in her stomach. She had planned on preparing a meal tonight for her friends and having some time with them. She was aching to hold the newborn and get a chance to talk with Lila.

"Silence!" the rough shout stilled everyone instantly, and the tall man with the golden hair whose voice had echoed over the crowd stepped back behind Cree.

Her stomach didn't have a chance to settle seeing Cree standing on the top step of the keep. He was a sight to behold; broad and tall and as handsome as he was imposing. His dark eyes roamed the crowd slowly as if committing every face to memory. Some shivered while others looked away, and mothers shoved their children behind them fearful that the devil himself was marking each and every one of them.

"Listen well for I will not repeat myself," Cree said his voice strong and echoing out across the crowd. "This land now belongs to me. I am your new feudal lord and the title Earl of Carrick will soon be mine as decreed by the King."

Grasps and whispers circled the crowd.

"Silence!" Cree yelled. "Work and keep a truthful tongue to me, and I will see that you have a good life with food aplenty. You will be able to hunt the forest for food not only for me, but for yourselves as well. You will bring your complaints to me, and I will deal with them fairly. But my word is law, and I will have no one protest it. I will see not only this land prosper, but the people as well. Pledge your fealty to me, and I will see you kept safe. If not... gather your things and leave now. You are free to go."

The villagers mumbled among themselves, many wondering if they could trust a man they thought evil.

"For those who stay," Cree called out, "we celebrate. There will be food, drink, and merry making, for tomorrow we forge a new life together."

Several villagers cheered, which led to more cheers until it seemed as if everyone cheered... even Paul joined in. Dawn, of course, could not, but if she could, she did not know if she would. Cree was a puzzle to her. He had not raided the village leaving destruction in his path as the tales claim he always did. Women had not been brutalized and children had not been harmed. It seemed that it had been Colum's warriors who had suffered the most. But then Cree claimed this land as his, and he would not want to destroy it or the people that would tend it for him. And why would the King decree this land as belonging to Cree?

As the crowd began to disperse smiles replaced frowns and laughter could be heard. Cree had dispelled their fears and worries and even invited them to celebrate in the new life he offered. Why wouldn't they accept his terms? What would they have if they packed their meager belongings and left?

Dawn once again assisted Paul as they returned to his cottage.

"Don't expect he'll want the likes of you now that he has a choice of who will warm his bed."

Dawn didn't need to turn and look behind her to know who made the comment. Dorrie's voice was distinct and always resonated with self-importance.

"He will want someone who will excite him with squeals of delight and pleasure."

"Enough, Dorrie," Paul said.

"I agree," Dorrie laughed. "Cree has had enough of the dumb one and will look for a good woman to please him."

"Then that leaves you out," Paul chuckled, "since everyone knows that you're not good."

Dawn grinned and silent laughter rippled through her.

Dorrie rushed past them in a snit purposely bumping against Paul and causing him to stumble. Dawn held tight to him to keep him from falling, he weighing heavily upon her. Suddenly he was lifted off her. A warrior, big and broad had taken hold of Paul.

"I'm to help him; Cree's orders," the warrior said.

Dawn followed along as the warrior easily helped Paul to the cottage. At the door the warrior turned to Dawn. "Cree will see you at the celebration." With that he turned and left.

Paul stared at Dawn. "It sounds as if you are not to miss the merrymaking."

What Paul truly meant, and he well knew it, was that Cree had commanded her presence there. She had no thought—or want—to go and participate in any form of merriment. She didn't understand how anyone would want to. The village had been attacked, people had been harmed, and this called for a celebration?

"Cree is providing a celebration tonight, which means there will be food and drink aplenty. He has seen the injured tended to, and he has freed anyone who wishes to leave. That is far better than what

Colum did when he had first arrived here."

Was Paul trying to convince her that Cree was a good man and she should not worry or was he trying to convince himself that she would be safe with Cree?

They entered the cottage to find Lila up and about, though moving slowly. Her cheeks glowed rosy red, her blue eyes sparkled with joy, and her favorite green wool shawl was wrapped snug around her shoulders covering her warm wool night dress. The babe lay sleeping in the cradle that Paul had fashioned for him.

Paul went straight to her. "You should be abed resting."

"I feel well enough, and I cannot abide to lay abed too long. Besides, it is time you rested. Your leg must be paining you something awful." She hustled him over to the bed. "There is time for you to rest until supper."

Paul grinned, sat on the bed, and took his wife's hand. "You want to talk with Dawn."

Lila nodded and leaned down to give him a quick kiss. After which he stretched out on the bed and closed his eyes. It wasn't long before he was snoring lightly.

Lila went to Dawn and threw her arms around her and with tears in her eyes said, "I owe you our lives. If it hadn't been for your courage Paul would not have survived and either would I or the babe. You are a true friend, and I am grateful to have you in our lives."

Tears tickled down Dawn's cheeks and any previous worry that she was being shut out of her friends lives faded. They sat at the table and Lila went to fix them a brew, but Dawn stopped her and pointed to the chair for her to sit.

Dawn shook her head. When Lila went to argue, she pointed sternly to the chair.

Lila laughed softly. "Since you put it that way." She sat and sighed gratefully.

Dawn appreciated the way she and Lila conversed so easily, and no different from anyone else. They began talking about the babe, Lila's delivery, and how grateful she was that Elsa had been there. Dawn had agreed. The woman truly was a gifted healer, and her friend had been lucky to have her birth Thomas.

When they were on their second brew Lila asked, "Tell me what Cree wanted with you."

Dawn had not intended to speak about Cree even though she wished to share some of her apprehension with her friend. It was better left for another day.

"Do not think to keep it from me," Lila warned in a whisper. "I know it concerns you; I see it on your face."

Dawn playfully ran her hand over her face.

"You cannot rub it away that easily."

No, that she could not, and Lila would not let her. Dawn sighed, though no sound was heard, and Lila reached out and took her hand.

"What does Cree want from you?"

Dawn gestured as if she held up a shield in front of her and a sword in her other hand.

"He wants nothing from you, but he offers you protection?"

Dawn nodded slowly.

"You have your doubts though, don't you?"

Dawn nodded again and shrugged.

"But you don't know why."

Another nod from Dawn turned Lila as silent as Dawn for a few minutes.

"There are women in the village who I am sure will keep Cree entertained, Dorrie being one of them."

Dawn smiled and nodded vigorously.

"Ah, Dorrie has already made her intentions known. That is good, let her have the beast, she no doubt will service him well."

Dawn barely nodded, a vision of Cree rising naked over Dorrie invading her thoughts and unsettling her stomach.

Lila grabbed her hand, chasing the disturbing vision away. "Do not think on what happened between you and Cree. It is a new start for all of us. Perhaps there will be a warrior among Cree's men who will fancy you, and you will have a chance to love."

Dawn forced a smile and was glad the babe started fussing, ending—before it could start—a discussion of how Lila just knew Dawn would find love one day. She was also glad that Lila asked her to fetch the babe for her. He calmed as soon as Dawn scooped him up and held him close. Once his eyes stayed open, he would not take them off Dawn. He seemed pleased and content there in her arms, and so she continued to stand in front of the hearth holding him.

A knock sounded at the door a few minutes later, and Elsa entered with a large basket and a smile.

Happily holding Thomas, Dawn listened as the two women talked. The delicious scents of the generous amount of food Elsa had spread on the table woke Paul.

His eyes turning wide, he stretched himself out of bed and hobbled over to the table. "This is all for us?"

"Of course, you both need to regain your strength," Elsa said.

"You will join us," Lila said to Elsa.

"Thank you, but Dawn and I will be attending the celebration at the keep, and we should be getting ready for it." Elsa walked over to Dawn and slipped Thomas out of her arms and into Lila's arms.

Lila looked with worried eyes to her friend as she took her son.

Dawn did not want her friend to worry over her, so she smiled and gestured how excited she was to attend the celebration. Lila appeared relieved. With a hug and a kiss to Lila and a nod to Paul, Dawn followed Elsa out the door.

"I will see you at the celebration," Elsa said and hurried off.

Dawn could not help but think that she was being reminded that her presence was not a request. She was expected to attend, though an order had never been directly issued. It had certainly been implied. She entered her cottage only a short distance from Lila's and immediately stoked the fire that had burned down to almost nothing but embers.

Her cottage had gotten a chill to it with the fire dying down, and she rubbed her arms. She realized then how she must look. Her one sleeve was completely gone and smudges of dirt marred her naked arm. Her skirt was ripped, and she realized that she did not have another one to replace it. The one other blouse she had was worn beyond repair. And her gray shift wasn't much better.

How could she go to the celebration tonight when she had nothing proper to wear? Besides who would bother with her? She would stand alone and be ignored as usual. There would be no joy in it for her.

Dawn decided there and then not to attend. She reasoned that although it seemed she had been instructed to attend, no one had explicitly ordered her to do so. With her decision came a sense of relief. She would set something to cook, wash up, change into her night dress—a garment well past its prime—and spend the evening repairing her clothes as best she could.

She chopped what kale and wild onion she had left, added water, and set it to stew in a crock. Then she filled a bucket with water from the rain barrel outside her door and bathed herself with the chilled water. With a silent sigh, she slipped into her worn nightdress, plaited her long brown hair, and gathered her sewing basket. She moved the lone chair closer to the hearth and set to work on repairing her skirt.

It wasn't long before her eyes grew weary. She sought her pallet, thinking a brief nap would be good before supper, and surrendered to sleep.

She did not know how long she had been sleeping when a loud sound startled her out of her peaceful slumber. She jumped up off her pallet, her eyes quickly turning wide when she saw Cree standing in the open doorway.

Chapter Fourteen

Cree didn't know if he wanted to strangle her or hug her so relieved was he that Dawn was safe in her cottage. With the villagers pouring in and out of the Great Hall and his warriors remaining on guard for any disturbances, it had taken time to search though the many faces to find her. When he had finally concluded that she was not present, dread rose in him.

Had something happened to her? Had she been harmed? She would not be able to scream out for help and the thought had fired his blood. He would kill anyone who raised a hand against her.

It had been Sloan who had suggested that perhaps the woman he searched for had decided not to attend the festivities.

Cree had not even given that thought, and the idea fueled his anger even more. He had ordered Sloan to find out where her cottage was located and then had taken off to find out if Sloan had been right.

His anger had mounted with each step he had taken, so that by the time he reached her door he hadn't bothered to knock. He gave it a shove, sending it swinging open.

His heaving chest slowed as his anger dissipated, and he shut the door behind him, wanting no one to disturb them. Not that anyone would. They feared him too much to offer the silent one protection, and they were wise in doing so.

She stood next to her sleeping pallet, which

annoyed him even more to think that she had no decent bed to sleep on. Her eyes were wide and her body tense. She obviously was frightened and she need not be, though giving it second thought... perhaps she should be.

He took only two steps and stopped, casting a glance around the small room. It was neat and orderly, though threadbare. Her table size could serve only one and one chair sat near the hearth. A lone crock sat in the hearth and no doubt was the reason for the pleasant scent. A worn wool cloak hung on a peg near the door and the only other garments he spied were the bundle on the chair. Her pallet barely held room for her, and her wool blanket had been patched in more places than he thought possible.

He approached her with quick, purposeful strides and she hastily hurried to stand behind the chair near the hearth. He almost laughed at her maneuver to shield herself. Did she truly think a pitiful chair would stop him?

"You were to attend the celebration," he said stopping only a few inches away from her and seeing that the fire's light silhouetted her naked body beneath her nightdress. He hardened so fast that he silently cursed himself.

Dawn caught the spark of lust in his eyes and to her surprise and fear her body responded with a tingle between her legs. She warned herself that no good would come of mating with the devil, and yet the tingle grew stronger.

"You disobeyed me," he said, taking a step closer.

Dawn clung to the chair, though she knew it was a useless shield against him. But at least it separated them and once she let go, and she would need to let go to be able to communicate with him, that separation would be gone.

She should have attended the celebration and been done with it. At least at the keep she would have been surrounded by people, unlike now with him standing here in her cottage and she in her nightdress. But then she had never expected him to come after her. Why would he? She was of no importance to him?

"I do not take disobedience lightly."

She bowed her head and placed her hand on her chest over her heart.

"You are wise to apologize, but tell me why you disobeyed."

What explanation could she offer him that he would deem acceptable? He would dismiss her claim that she did not feel her presence at the keep had been mandatory. He obviously felt he had made himself clear. And he truly had. She had simply not wanted to partake in the festivities, though if she was being completely honest, she had stayed away because she thought it best to keep her distance from him. So how did she explain her actions?

Cree waited, wondering what excuse she would offer and the longer she remained silent the more he assumed she was attempting to think of one. He took note of what now appeared obvious. She stood in her nightdress and had been in bed when he had entered. Her garments lay on the chair, a small sewing basket on top. And a bucket of water and wet cloth sat not far from the hearth. It became clearer to him. She had washed up, slipped into her nightdress while she repaired her torn garments, and she had grown sleepy. And rightfully so after the day she had and thought to nap before attending the celebration. But the day had taken its toll and she slumbered longer than she had planned.

A reasonable explanation, but if he had learned one thing about Dawn in the brief time they had been forced together it was that she delayed responding if she believed her answer would annoy him. Since she had yet to answer him, he viewed the scene differently.

"You had no intentions of returning to the keep even though I ordered you to do so, did you?"

Lying would get her nowhere, and so she shook her head.

"Why?" he asked, taking another step closer.

Rather than an answer, she asked her own question. She pointed to him, then to herself and shrugged as she tossed her hands up.

"You wonder what I want from you."

She nodded and once again grasped hold of the chair.

He had asked himself that very question repeatedly since his escape. His plans had changed because of her. He had moved up the attack on the village fearful that Colum would blame her for his escape, torture, and then kill her. Now that she was safe, there was nothing for him to worry about... nothing except the ache in his loins that surfaced fast and furiously whenever she was in his presence. And why could he not banish her from his thoughts? She lurked there haunting him, never leaving him alone.

And what was it that he would think on over and over again? Her naked beneath him, her hands touching him, and her body speaking to him as she wrapped her long legs around him and took him deeper and deeper inside her, squeezing him tighter and tighter—

He shook his head and stared at her and had to restrain himself from reaching out, scooping her up, and taking her to bed where he would—

Cree backed away, turned, and went to the door. "Work like everyone else and keep a truthful ton—" He swung the door open and without glancing at her said, "I will only warn you once; never dare question me again."

He stormed through the village, people scurrying out of his way. He kept his footfalls firm and straight and refused to turn and look back. He knew if he did all would be lost. One glance back and he would return and not only appease his lust, but hers as well.

He could not tell her to keep a truthful tongue, for if he did she would then be obliged to tell him that she lusted for him as much as he did for her. He had seen the innocent passion in her dark eyes, and he had known that if he didn't get out right there and then, he'd be buried deep inside her in no time.

And then what?

He shook his head. He had plans, and Dawn was not part of those plans. She was an innocent, and he would not use her for his pleasure, and then discard her even if he saw passion in her eyes. It would not be right; she suffered enough having no voice.

He stomped to the keep determined to push the voiceless woman from his thoughts.

Sloan took one look at him and shook his head. Everyone cleared a path to let him through, his scowl was so frightening. Sloan continued shaking his head, grabbed hold of the young blond lass, Dorrie, who had asked repeatedly about Cree, and walked her over to his solemn leader.

"I have a gift for you," Sloan said and was about

to shove Dorrie at him when she stepped forward of her own accord and without an ounce of fear.

"I know how to please a man," she said, throwing her shoulders back so that her large bosoms rested near his face.

Cree stared at her chest and thought about burying himself in her and easing his ache.

She stepped closer, her thin fingers reaching out to him. "And I will scream out with pleasure unlike the dumb one who makes not a sound."

Cree snatched her wrist in his hand before she could touch him and she cried out. "Speak ill of Dawn and you will suffer for it." He shoved her away from him, and she stumbled and attempted an apology.

Sloan signaled one of the warriors and Dorrie was quickly carted away.

Sloan turned to Cree.

"Keep your warnings; I have no need of them," Cree said and walked out of the Great Hall.

Chapter Fifteen

The next morning the villagers were roused early from their beds and told to report to their daily duties. Dawn was surprised to see repairs already being made to the buildings and cottages that had suffered damage during the battle. She had hoped she would have time to stop at Lila's and see how everyone was doing, but she didn't want to chance being late.

She hurried along with everyone else to their perspective chores, only to find that Flanna was no longer in charge of the kitchen. A large, burly, bald man was lining everyone up as they arrived, including Flanna who quickly reached out to Dawn and yanked her to stand next to her.

When everyone was accounted for the man addressed them. "I am Turbett, and I am now the cook in charge. I will assess and decide if the present kitchen staff will continue in their chores or be assigned duties elsewhere."

Dawn listened more closely than others and while he appeared pleasant enough, his round, chubby face wearing a continuous smile, she could detect that he was a man who would expect much from his staff. He was probably not much different than Flanna, and she lashed out with a wooden spoon when displeased with her workers. Dawn hoped that Turbett did not do the same.

"You will each tell me what your assigned kitchen chores are," Turbett said.

Flanna spoke up. "I was the cook here and I have a good staff. I am sure they will serve you well."

Turbett smiled as he said, "We will see about that. Go cook me a meat pie... without any help from your staff."

Flanna gave a nod and turned to Dawn beside her. "This is Dawn—"

"Let her speak for herself," Turbett said.

"She cannot; she has no voice. I will speak for her."

"Do not bother," Turbett said with a dismissive wave of his hand. "She is no use to me without a voice. She will be given work elsewhere."

Flanna stepped forward. "The kitchen is all she knows, and she takes orders well and is quick in accomplishing her tasks. She is an asset not a hindrance."

"To you perhaps, but not to me, she will be assigned work elsewhere."

"Where?" Flanna demanded.

"That is no concern of yours."

"It most certainly is."

Dawn watched as the two went back and forth at each other, her stomach tightening. Flanna was right. She knew only kitchen work, no other. If he did not allow her to remain there and work she did not know what she would do. Flanna had been accepting of her, but few others would be.

"My word is final," Turbett yelled, his smile gone. "And if you don't watch that sharp tongue of yours, you'll be gone along with her."

Dawn would not see Flanna lose her work. She stepped forward and tapped her on the arm.

The woman turned.

Dawn patted her chest, smiled, and pointed to the open door.

"What will you do?" Flanna asked with concern.

"Something will be found for her," Turbett answered and turned to Dawn and raised his voice. "Go outside to the front of the keep. There is probably a line already there of people who are waiting to be reassigned chores."

"She has no voice; she's not deaf," Flanna snapped.

Dawn hastily slipped out the door, leaving Flanna and Turbett arguing. She walked to the front of the keep and Turbett was right. There was a line of villagers waiting to enter the keep and a longer line then she had expected. She wondered if Cree would be assigning chores. If so, she had no desire to see him, especially after last night.

She had berated herself most of the night for having made such a foolish decision in not attending the festivities as Cree had ordered. She had never expected Cree to come to her cottage, and she had not at all expected to find herself aroused by his presence and the lust she had seen in his eyes. She had to keep her distance from him or else she might do something she would regret. Silent laughter shook her chest. What difference did it make if they coupled? Everyone had assumed that they had already done so. And when she stood on line with the others they would all assume that the mighty Cree had found her lacking and now paid her no mind. She would suffer their wagging tongues whether she had coupled with him or not.

But not just yet, she decided to make a quick visit to Lila and see how they all were doing. Then she would return and stand on line with the others.

She jumped when she was poked in the back and quickly turned around.

"Have you been assigned a chore?" a large warrior with a ragged scar running across his cheek asked.

She shook her head.

"On line with you then," he ordered and gave her a shove. "There will be no idle hands in Cree's village."

Dawn reluctantly joined the others waiting on line and was surprised to see Old Mary a few people ahead of her. She wondered what possible chore the old woman could be given, her hands too gnarled to be of any use.

The line moved slowly and Dawn was grateful that she had worn her wool cloak, a late autumn chill stinging the air. She glanced around the village and noticed several hunters returning with fresh kills while villagers eyed the meat with hungry eyes. They had existed mostly on porridge, kale, and berries. Meat had been for Colum and his men alone.

She also spotted Elsa with two women from the village who appeared pleased to be following her. Dawn wondered if they had been assigned to the healer. It got her wondering where she would be placed, and how she would be treated in her new position.

Finally, she entered the keep and was relieved when she saw that it was the tall, blond man who she noticed had been by Cree's side more than any other warrior. She heard someone call him Sloan and assumed that he was Cree's right-hand man.

She listened as chores were assigned particularly when Old Mary stepped forward.

"And what do you do, Old Woman?" Sloan asked.

"I listen, I hear, and I know things," Mary said her head nodding in cadence with her words. "No one pays an old woman mind." She laughed.

Dawn would have laughed along with her if she could. Old Mary was right. No one paid her mind, just like no one paid attention to a woman without a voice. She and Old Mary had always been invisible to most.

She expected Sloan to dismiss her and so she was surprised when he inquired.

"What do you know?"

"I know where Colum keeps a locked chest and I know how he escaped."

Sloan summoned a nearby warrior with a flick of his finger and whispered something to him that had him making a swift exit. He then directed Old Mary to take a seat by the hearth and told her to enjoy the hot cider. The woman turned a toothless grin on him and shuffled over to the table.

The next few people that followed took longer, Sloan thorough in his assessment of where to place each one. Dawn grew nervous as her turn neared. Sloan asked many questions, and she wondered if he would understand her gestures or grow impatient with her.

She was one person away from it being her turn, and she prayed that it would go well for her when suddenly Cree walked up to Sloan, his back to Dawn. After a few whispered words, Sloan nodded toward Old Mary, and Cree turned and was about to approach the woman when he spotted Dawn.

His eyes met hers and he stared unblinking. No one made a sound or moved.

Finally, he summoned her with a crook of his

finger, and she obediently approached him.

"Why are you not in the kitchen attending to your chores?"

She pointed to her mouth and shook her head.

"Turbett doesn't want you because you have no voice?"

Dawn nodded.

Cree scowled and nodded at a table two away from where Old Mary sat. "Go sit and wait for me."

Dawn did as he directed, though she heard Sloan whisper, "Do not force her on Turbett or our meals will suffer for it."

She was not surprised at Cree's response.

"He obeys or he will find himself as voiceless as Dawn."

Sloan quickly returned to his own chore and summoned the next villager in line.

Cree joined the old woman. "Tell me what you know."

"In the solar there are loose stones in the upper right corner of the fireplace where Colum kept a small chest. What is in it I do not know and only Colum and Goddard knew of the secret hiding spot. There is also a secret passageway leading from his bedchamber to the back of the keep. That is how he escaped. I saw him sneak out with Goddard close behind while his warriors continued to fight and die, the cowards."

"How did you come by this information?" Cree asked.

Colum dismissed me as old, feeble, and deaf since I never answered him when he spoke to me. He was right about one thing... I am old. As for the other two?" She shrugged. "People see what they want to see. " She gave a nod to Dawn. "Many villagers keep their distance from her. They don't see her true beauty, her true worth. Dawn is a rare woman and it will take a rare man to love her, but once he does; he will know true happiness."

The thought of another man coupling with Dawn angered him, and he snapped at the old woman. "I want no predictions from you just the truth or you will suffer the consequences."

Old Mary shrugged again. "What can you do to me? I have known love and sorrow, pain and suffering, laughter and happiness. I have lived long, sometimes I think too long. If I die tomorrow; I die in peace and I will meet my maker with no regrets. Can you say the same?"

Cree had thought about that with each battle he had entered. He knew it would be the fires of hell that would greet him if he did not live to see another day, and he would die without truly having lived for he had known more sorrow than love.

He glanced over at Dawn, her threadbare cloak closed tightly around her, her head held high and her eyes curious as she watched Sloan assign chores. He noticed she shivered, and he wondered if she was worried about her fate. Then he realized that she was chilled, and he cursed her silent suffering.

He summoned a servant to him and ordered food and another pitcher of hot cider to be brought to the table. The servant nodded and hurried off.

"I have decided on your chore, Old Woman," he said. "You will be my eyes and ears, and you will tell me all you see and hear and... you will keep a watch over Dawn and let me know if anyone mistreats her."

"I will gladly serve you, my lord. And gladly keep watch over my friend."

The food arrived and Old Mary eyed it with appreciation.

"Enjoy and you will take your meals at the keep from now on," Cree ordered and snatched two tankards off the table, along with the extra pitcher of hot cider, as he stood.

"Thank you," Old Mary said with a grin and a nod, "now Dawn will have more food for herself."

"What do you mean?"

She held up her gnarled hands. "I can no longer keep my own garden or cook my meals. Dawn saw that I did not starve. She shared from her garden and cooked for me. She has a generous heart."

"Eat," he ordered gently and with tankards and pitcher in hand, he walked over and joined Dawn.

Dawn wrapped her chilled hands around the tankard he handed her after he filled it. She was grateful for the heat that seeped into her hands, though nervous that he had sat and joined her. His brow was knitted, and she wished she could reach across the table and rub the tight, deep lines away.

Something had happened to her being locked away with him for that short time, though she could not make sense of it. She assumed it had only been lust she had been introduced to, but why then did she want to reach out and comfort him? And if it was just lust why did he care what chore she was assigned? Why had he not left her to stand on line and let Sloan decide her fate?

Her questions disturbed her, for they suggested something she was not prepared to face. She could not be, dare not be, falling in love with the devil.

"Do you wish to remain working in the kitchen?"

Was he actually giving her a choice when others

had none? And how would Turbett react to her being forced on him? But if she did not work in the kitchen, where would she work?

"You're not sure are you?"

She shook her head.

"Cree," Sloan called to him and Cree turned.

A short, slim man with graying hair stood beside Sloan, a rolled parchment tucked beneath his arm. Cree signaled him over to the table.

"Show me," Cree ordered and the man spread out the parchment with trembling hands.

Dawn's eyes turned wide and she smiled.

"This is a rough facsimile of how you wished your castle to be designed. There is more work to be done on it," the man explained.

Cree studied it, his chest swelling with pride. It had taken many years and the lives of many good warriors to reach this point, and he intended for this stronghold to be a monument to all who had sacrificed with him and a home for those who had survived. And he would rule over it all.

"I am pleased with this, William," Cree said.

William smiled with relief. "You have chosen a perfect spot for the castle. It sits high on the bluff overlooking the Kyle of Tongue. The Kyle will make it easier for the needed material to be transported here, and the various craftsmen that will also be required."

Dawn listened to the conversation, but was far more fascinated by the drawing. She itched to make some changes, but it was not her place to do so.

Cree saw the way Dawn studied the drawing and how her hands gripped her tankard. She appeared anxious to reach out and add her touch, and he wondered what that might be.

"Do you have a piece of charcoal, William," Cree asked.

The man shook his head.

Dawn did not hesitate, she scurried off the bench and snatched up a piece of kindling from the basket near the hearth. She used it to poke a piece of wood that had burned, as much as it was going to, out of the fire. She tested it with her finger and scooped it up after determining it was not hot. Once back at the table, she held it out to Cree.

So that was what she used to draw with, he thought and shook his head. "It is not for me or William. It is for you to show me what changes you would make."

She could not hide her joy, and William could not hide his annoyance, though when she began to carefully adjust his drawing William soon sat on the bench beside her amazed.

"You are very talented," William said with a pleasant smile.

Dawn nodded and returned his smile.

"Dawn cannot speak," Cree said abruptly.

"Oh, I am so sorry," William said, "but you speak through your drawings, do you not?"

A slight blush rose to stain her cheeks, pleased that he recognized that.

"Enough," Cree said annoyed, "William has work to do and so do you, Dawn."

William hurried to roll up the parchment. "I will work on the changes." And off he went.

Dawn wondered over Cree's dark scowl. He had encouraged her to make changes to the drawing. Why now was he annoyed?

"You will return to your cottage and wait until I

decide what your daily chore will be."

She contained her surprise and before he could change his mind, she bowed her head and hurried out of the keep.

Sloan walked over to the table and handed a tankard of ale to Cree and took a generous swag from the tankard in his other hand. "You best settle this with her and be done with it."

"This does not concern you."

"Aye, it does," Sloan said, "and I will tell you why. I have never seen you look at a woman the way you look at the silent one. If you are not careful you will lose everything that you have worked so hard to achieve. And since when do you not rut with a willing woman after battle? Go take her and ease your loins that must be as hard as rocks."

"Much harder," Cree mumbled and Sloan laughed, stood, and returned to his chore.

Cree remained where he was, finished his tankard of ale and poured another. Sloan had been right. He had always bedded a willing woman after battle and usually all night long, so great his lust. But not so last night even though one had offered herself to him.

What was wrong with him? There were plenty of women who would rut with him and come back for more. He had never lacked for a woman, and yet he had turned one away.

There was a simple solution to his problem. He would bed a woman, satisfy his lust, and be done with it.

Chapter Sixteen

Dawn did not know what to do with herself. It had been three days since Cree had sent her from the keep, and he had yet to assign her a chore. She spent some time with Lila, Paul, and the babe, but she had not wanted to intrude on this rare time that they had to spend with each other.

Paul had been told that he was not to return to the fields until his leg had healed and that it was up to Elsa to decide when that would be. Lila had been up and about the day after giving birth. She was now busy fussing over both Paul and the babe and working her magic with the wool on her spindle and distaff.

They were happier than Dawn had ever seen them, and she was happy for them, though she did miss spending time alone with Lila. That was why she was so very glad to hear the knock at her door the same time it swung open.

Dawn watched as Lila carried a chair into the cottage, and then shut the door.

"A gift," she said and placed the chair at the table opposite of where Dawn sat. She slipped her cloak off and draped it over the chair and then sat. "Time to share one of your tasty brews and time for us to talk and as for the chair," —she grinned broadly— "Paul is making us a sturdier set from the wood that has been left for the villagers to use. Taggart, the miller, stopped to tell Paul about the wood, knowing what a skilled hand he has in building things. Taggart saw to having his son cart some pieces to Paul. I tell you, Dawn, it has been but a few days since the attack, and the village is already prospering."

Dawn listened as she prepared a hot brew for them both.

"It is remarkable that few villagers were seriously hurt in the attack. It was Colum's men who suffered the most, many losing their lives or sustaining serious wounds that no doubt will take their lives. Those left behind have willingly pledged their fealty to Cree and now work alongside his warriors and seem happier for it."

Lila voiced what Dawn was thinking.

"Cree is far different than the tales told about him, though wagging tongues insist that Dowell has been spared Cree's usual rampage because the land is now his. And most are pleased that Dowell now has a fierce leader to protect them, though he is still feared."

Dawn caught the way Lila shivered as she handed the tankard to her.

"He walks the village with a scowl and none approach him, and if he should approach any—" Lila shook her head— "they tremble with fear."

Dawn made a punching motion that Lila quickly understood.

"No, Cree has not hurt anyone, though," —she grinned— "I hear that Dorrie offered herself to Cree and he turned her down."

The thought of Cree coupling with Dorrie upset her, though she did not let it show. She tugged at her ear. It was her way of asking how Lila had heard this.

"Several villagers had not only seen it, but heard the exchange. Gossip was quick to spread after that.

Some are saying—" Lila stopped talking and her smile faded. "We need to talk."

Dawn nodded. Lately, the villagers had been avoiding her more than usual, and she noticed how they would turn away and whisper when they saw her. She had wondered what they were saying about her.

"Dorrie could not let anyone believe that Cree did not find her desirable, and so she has been telling everyone that he has taken you as his mistress since you cannot speak, therefore you cannot reveal any of his plans or secrets." Lila reached over and laid a gentle hand on her arm.

Dawn shook her head before Lila could ask her if it was true, though Lila did not smile at the news.

"You have not been assigned a chore like everyone else?"

Dawn shook her head, concern knotting her stomach.

Lila squeezed her hand. "I fear he intends to lay claim to you, to make you his mistress, for you to serve only him."

Dawn pulled her hand away and shook her head while patting her chest, letting Lila know that Cree did not want her.

"Then why has he not assigned you a chore? Everyone in the village has been assigned a chore, even Old Mary. You are the only one who has no chore. Haven't you asked yourself why?"

Dawn raised her chin, shook her head, and tapped her chest with both hands.

Tears came to Lila's eyes. "It is not true that no one wants you."

Dawn nodded vigorously. It was true and Lila

knew it. There were those who acknowledged her with a nod, but no one ever attempted to talk with her, and mothers mostly kept their children away from her out of ignorance more than fear. And then there were those like Dorrie who belittled her every chance she got.

Dawn had enough talk of gossip particularly about her, and so she smiled and rocked her arms as if holding a babe, wanting to hear about baby Thomas.

Lila's face burst with a bright smile and for the next hour that was all they talked about. Lila left in a hurry, realizing that feeding time was near and insisting that Dawn come by and spend more time with Thomas. She had nodded in agreement and looked forward to it, though having held the babe and felt him cuddle close to her with such contentment had had her wishing that someday she would have children of her own. The one fear that she had, though had never expressed, was that her child would be born voiceless like her. And that she would never inflict upon anyone.

She grabbed her cloak from the peg and decided a walk in the woods would serve her twofold. It would clear her thoughts while she foraged for wild onions to add to the soup she planned to make herself tonight.

After grabbing her basket, she headed out the door going around back to enter the woods behind her cottage. She stopped to restack two logs that had slipped off her wood pile and realized that it would need replenishing soon. Paul had always seen to it for her. She then gave a satisfied nod at her garden as she passed it, pleased with the work she had done there. It was in good shape thanks to the last couple of days with nothing to do, though she had been anything but idle.

She had harvested the last of the vegetables and herbs and had set them to dry, and then she had turned the soil so it would be ready for winter rest. Her hands held proof of her strenuous labor, blisters just beginning to heal.

Pleased that she had accomplished the chores she had set for herself, she hurried off eager to complete a new task and making certain to keep to herself, the reason she approached the woods from behind her cottage.

She had no want to be avoided or to hear whispers that were not truly whispers since most thought her deaf as well as dumb. She would go and enjoy her foraging and even thought to find the right twigs to begin fashioning a winter wreath for the door.

With a light heart and a determined step, she entered the woods.

5. ~~~

Cree watched her every move from where he stood with Sloan on the small hilltop. The spot gave him a vast view of the fields and a good view of the village. Sloan and he had been discussing the expansion of the planting fields. He had wasted no time in seeing to improvements and expansions for the immediate future. There was much more to come, but first he had to tend to present needs and that meant more food for his people.

Dawn had distracted him, her patchwork cloak catching his eye. It was threadbare and would do her no good this winter. And her wood stack was low, though her garden was well tended and prepared for winter.

"Have you assigned her a chore yet?" Sloan asked with a laughing grin.

"You know damn well I haven't."

"And why not?"

"Wipe that grin off your face or I'll wipe it off for you," Cree cautioned.

"A fight will not satisfy that burning need in you," Sloan said completely ignoring the warning. "What you need is to sink yourself deep into a woman and not just once... and it appears not just any woman."

"What do you mean?" Cree snapped.

"That was a buxom lass last night who served your meal and made it clear that she would be willing to serve you another way. Yet, you ignored her even when she made certain to brush your face with her breast."

"Enough," Cree warned through gritted teeth.

"Enough is right," Sloan said. "Go after her, sink yourself in her and if she pleases you make her your mistress until you tire of her. But do something before she robs you of your sanity."

Sloan walked away as if Cree would pay heed to his words, but he stood there watching Dawn disappear into the woods. He had been busy these last few days, too busy to give Dawn a thought, though that was a lie. She had invaded his mind and his senses day and night. There was not a time he had not thought about her.

At first he told himself it was because she needed to be assigned a chore like everyone else, but the chore he had in mind only served to make his task more difficult. No matter how hard he tried, he could not stop images of her naked beneath him from assaulting him. He could almost feel the way she would squeeze his arms, tighter and tighter, her body bucking against him as he drove into her and he exploding in a blinding climax just as he had that time in the shed... only this time he would be deep inside her.

The groan started deep in his chest and would have developed into a deeper roar if he hadn't curtailed it. He stood a minute more, and then, with powerful strides, he walked down the hill and into the woods.

6.

Dawn felt more content than she had in days perhaps weeks even though the sky was overcast it did not dampen her spirit. Rarely, did she have a chance to explore the woods at leisure. There was always work to be done. Today was hers to enjoy, for she did not know what tomorrow would bring.

She had come upon an area where there were several small broken branches and twigs and pine cones that would make a splendid winter wreath. She began to fill the basket, wishing she had had the sense to bring two; one for the twigs and one for the wild onions. She did not want the scent of onions greeting her every time she entered her cottage.

She paused at her task to listen. Something had changed in the woods. It had turned silent. She stood straight and that was when she saw him, tall and unmoving, staring at her. The animals had scurried away sensing a predator had entered their home, but he was not there for them... he was there for her.

He kept his eyes riveted on her and even at this distance she could see that they steamed with lust. She did not know what to do. Running would do her little good and even if she could scream, it would not matter. No one would come to her aid. He was the lord of this land and no one would question his actions.

What choice did she have but to wait and let him come to her and take her, or did she offer herself to him and fully taste what he had only given her a sample of?

Her answer came easily. She smiled, raised her arm, and held her hand out to him.

Chapter Seventeen

Cree stared for a moment, wondering if she knew what she offered him or had she offered it feeling she had no other choice that it was inevitable, and she could do nothing but accept it.

What did it matter? It only mattered that he would finally ease the unrelenting ache that tore at him. He walked over to her, his powerful and determined strides growing more eager with each step he took.

She stood her ground, though her legs trembled, her stomach grew anxious. and she wondered if she had made the right choice. But she had made a choice and that was what was important. It had been her decision; she had made it for herself.

He reached out, his hand going around the back of her neck, his arm slipping around her waist, and his lips descending on hers. It was not a gentle kiss; it was a hungry one. It did little to appease his appetite. It only made him hunger for more.

The power of his kiss overwhelmed Dawn. He feed on her with an urgency that intoxicated her senses. His lips pressed to hers in a way that demanded and provoked her to join him. And when his tongue surged into her mouth, her body bucked, and he yanked her hard against him.

Her arms wrapped around him of their own accord, as if that was where they belonged. As soon as she did, his one arm grew taut around her waist and with one swift lift, her feet were off the ground. With his kiss growing ever stronger, he walked them to a large oak tree. Her feet crunched on a bed of leaves as he lowered her down and pinned her back against the tree with his body.

He was hard and warm and smelled of fresh earth and pine, and she drank in his scent, thirsty for it.

He ended the kiss abruptly and rested his brow to hers. "Bloody hell, what is it about you?"

His lips went to the crook of her neck. He kissed and nipped along it as his hand reached up and pushed the neckline of her blouse down to scoop up one breast and free it. His mouth went straight for her nipple, his tongue teasing the already tight bud until it was rock hard, and then he took it in his mouth and suckled.

Dawn gripped his arms, squeezing tight as a rash of tingles rushed through her to settle with a throb between her legs. He leaned his hips into her, his arousal settling hard against her, and she felt herself grow wet.

His hand slipped down and hoisted up her skirt and stopped suddenly when he realized she wore...

"No stockings."

His growl reminded her of a primal beast, and she startled when his fingers slipped between her legs."

"Damn, you're wet and ready for me."

Ready for him? That surprised her. She would have never thought she would want to couple with the infamous Cree, but at the moment she wanted it badly.

She dug her fingers into his arm when she felt him slip two fingers inside her, and when his thumb began to rub her soft nub, she pulsated with pleasure. Her hips began to move against the rhythm he set, urging her to respond, to enjoy.

He ground his mouth against hers, demanding a kiss. She gave it to him, her hunger as ravenous as his. She thought she would die when his fingers slipped out of her, but then she felt his thick, hard shaft rub against her. And she never wanted anything more than at this moment to have him buried deep inside her.

He rubbed harder against her, his rhythm increasing, and she squirmed trying to get him to enter her and end her torment. His hands quickly went to her backside and took firm hold. He plastered her against him, increasing his rhythm and forcing her to join him.

He growled low in his chest, though she heard it clearly enough, and she knew then that he had no intentions of coupling with her. He did not want to spill his seed in her and risk it taking root. Her pleasure faded quickly and was completely gone by the time she felt him burst against her.

Her hands slipped off his arms to rest at her sides, and she turned her head away not wanting to look at him, just wanting him done and gone and to leave her in peace, though she wondered if she would ever know peace with him as feudal lord.

He grabbed her chin, forcing her to look at him. "Why? Why did you stop yourself from coming?"

Her eyes turned wide, wondering how he could possibly know that she had not climaxed.

He scowled. "I can feel your passion for me. It burns hot inside you. I can feel when it cools and fades but... I do not know why it cooled and faded. Tell me."

Dawn shook her head. She would not, could not,

tell him how she felt.

Anger rose in his dark eyes. "You will tell me."

"Cree!"

Dawn was relieved to hear Sloan shout out for him, though he did not release her right away.

"You will answer me; I will see that you do." He released her then, and she watched him walk away to join Sloan who waited a distance away.

When they were both out of sight, she let herself crumple to the ground. Tears gathered in her eyes, but she refused to let them fall. It would do her no good to feel sorry for herself. And why should she be upset that he hadn't coupled with her? She still had that part of herself to give to someone, if by some chance, someday, someone fell in love with her.

Her mother had told her once that the heavens had made her special and that someday, someone special would come along and he would love all that was special about her. She had believed her mum when she was young, but as she grew older she realized that her mum had told her that to help ease the pain of being voiceless and unwanted.

At the moment, she wanted desperately to be that young lass who believed every word her mum had told her. *Someone special was waiting for her and someday someone would love her.*

Dawn wiped the tears from her face and gathered her basket. She would return to her cottage and keep herself busy. Idle time did little good for anyone. She plucked a few wild onions on her way home and as she rounded her cottage, she stopped surprised by the flurry of activity around the keep.

A troop of Cree's warriors were gathered in front of the keep, some of their horses prancing eager to make haste. Cree stepped out of the keep and Dawn felt her stomach quicken. Villagers stopped in their tracks to stare and gasps could be heard along with whispered mumblings. He was a sight to behold dressed all in black, his leather tunic studded with metal along the shoulder seams. Black leather cuffs were held in place at his wrists by crisscrossed leather strips. And his sword was sheathed at his back.

He looked ready for battle and, without thought, Dawn recited a silent prayer for his safety. He spoke for a moment to Sloan who nodded, and then he mounted his horse and led his men out of the village, though...

Dawn could not believe that he stopped at her cottage, and she clutched her basket tightly worried what he might say.

"Do not go into the woods until I return and give you permission."

Dawn nodded and he rode off.

She did not have to look around to know that people were staring at her, and so she hurried into her cottage away from curious eyes and gossiping tongues.

It was only a few minutes before the door opened and Lila hurried in.

"What is this I hear?" Lila asked.

Dawn smiled and reached out for Thomas who went contentedly into her arms. She looked from the babe to Lila and back again.

"Do not think to distract me by asking about Thomas." She beamed proudly. "He is doing wonderful, and he barely fusses. He is such a good baby. And Paul has returned to the fields, though he tells me that he has been giving the task of helping to plan next year's crop, and he says it will be much larger with the fields being expanded."

Dawn smiled seeing her friend happy and hearing the hope in her voice. Thomas gurgled at her, and she caressed his soft cheek. His eyes lighted and he smiled. Her heart soared, and she wished— oh how she wished—she would one day have children of her own. She feared though that her affliction would pass to one if not all her children and that would break her heart. She would not want one of her children to suffer as she had.

"Now back to my original question," Lila said and Dawn knew she would not be able to avoid answering it this time. "Did Cree actually stop and order you not to go into the woods until he returns?"

Dawn nodded.

"He worries over you."

Dawn frowned and shook her head.

"Yes, he does," Lila argued. "Some of Colum's men have been spotted a distance from here, and there is talk that Colum may be among them. That is where Cree goes now to find them. And he has not ordered anyone to stay out of the woods except you. As I said he worries for your safety."

Dawn did not bother to shake her head again. Lila would continue to argue the point while she was trying to comprehend it.

"The women gossip," Lila said and paused.

Dawn waited, knowing that any time Lila hesitated to speak that she was about to deliver troubling news.

"They say that you are the devil's mistress and that is why you do not have to toil as others do. Your chore is to please the devil, and he wants nothing interfering with his pleasure." Lila paused once again before asking, "Has he had his way with you again?"

What did she say to her friend? Did she let her go on thinking that Cree had taken her virginity or did she confide how their new feudal lord will not spill his seed inside her? The answer came easily. She was too embarrassed to let anyone know the truth... even her dearest friend.

Dawn nodded, for what did it matter? People would believe what they wanted to. The truth would be hers and hers alone.

Lila spoke low when she said, "You do realize that you could be with child already?"

Dawn glanced down at Thomas sleeping contentedly in her arms, and her heart ached to know the pleasure of cradling her own child in her arms.

"You are like the sister I never had," Lila said. "I am here for you no matter what happens."

Dawn smiled and pressed a hand firmly to her chest.

Lila got teary-eyed. "I love you too."

The subject was changed then, nothing more needing to be said, both women understanding the depths of their friendship. Lila moved from subject to subject, being her talkative self. Dawn would interject with hand motions now and again or to answer a question.

Lila left a couple of hours later and Dawn got busy soaking the branches she had gathered in water so that they would soften enough to bend and fashion into a wreath. She refused to allow her thoughts to linger on Cree, though she did give thought to going to the keep tomorrow and seeing if she could be assigned a chore. Perhaps if she had a chore like everyone else people would cease to gossip about her.

Day gave way to night and Dawn soon found

herself seeking the solace of her bed. She was about to slip into her only nightdress when a knock sounded at her door. She was hesitant about answering it with the lateness of the hour. If it was Lila, she would have simply entered by now or Paul would have called out to her. So who was it at her door?

She cautiously opened the door, though just a crack and was surprised to see Dorrie standing there.

"Old Mary has need of you," Dorrie said annoyed.

Dawn nodded and when she opened the door and stepped out Dorrie was gone. It was just as well, she had no desire to have Dorrie accompany her to Old Mary's place. She hurried along, the village quiet this time of night and the air chilled. Autumn would soon be gone and winter upon them. She wrapped her threadbare cloak more tightly around her and hurried along worried over Old Mary. She lived removed from the village, her cottage set back in the woods.

As she trekked through the woods, she recalled Cree's warning; *do not go into the woods until I return and give you permission.* She was disobeying him, though how would he know?

Dawn stopped abruptly, thinking she had heard footfalls behind her. The thought suddenly hit her; what if this was a ruse? What if there was nothing wrong with Old Mary?

Fear prickled her flesh, and her first thought was to run for home, but she thought of Old Mary. What if the old woman was ill and needed her help? She had no choice but to proceed to her cottage and see for herself.

The attack came so fast that Dawn had no time to react. One minute she was standing and the next she was on the ground. Her heart pumped violently in her chest as she tried to hurry to her feet, but he was on her before she could even try.

Fear would tie you in knots if you let it, her mum would always say. Action, Dawn, action, her mum would remind. And so Dawn listened to her mum.

She swung hard, catching her attacker in the face. He grunted and fell off her, and she scurried to her feet. She didn't get far, his hand grabbing her hair, knotting it in his fingers and yanking her back. She stumbled, though made sure to remain on her feet. She turned around, swinging and caught him in the side of his head. He swore and swung, catching her in the jaw and sent her stumbling. If she could scream, she would have, not from the punch, but from the way it felt, as if her hair was being ripped from her head as he stopped her from falling with a yank of her hair.

He swung again, only this time she was quick to react, and he caught the corner of her eye, though not as hard if she hadn't moved. They scuffled and she went down, he on top of her and when he fumbled with her skirt, pulling it up, her fear escalated.

She had to stop him, too much had been taken from her, and she would not surrender a single thing more. She clawed at his face, and he slapped her hard, stunning her. Frantically, her hands searched along the ground for anything to use as a weapon, and she blessed the heavens when her hand connected with a large stone. She didn't hesitate. She wrapped her hand tightly around it and brought it up against the side of his head with as much force as she could muster.

He tumbled off her, and she hurried to her feet, throwing the rock at his face before she took off. She didn't stop. She flew like the wind until she reached her cottage and once inside she latched the door and collapsed against it.

She didn't cry, though her body trembled, and she comforted herself with a tight hug. With the darkness of the woods and being busy fighting her attacker off, she had had little time to see his identity. But for one brief moment when a cloud had drifted off the partial moon, she had caught sight of him.

Only now did she have time to digest what she had seen. It had been Goddard, and she shivered at the thought. And worse Dorrie had helped him. But why? Why would Goddard attack her and why would Dorrie help him do such a thing or did she know his plans? And who would she tell of the attack? Who would care?

Cree.

She closed her eyes and rested her head back against the door. His name had sprung instantly to mind. What did that tell her? Did she believe he would truly care or did she hope he would?

An hour later after debating the issue, she picked herself up off the floor and took herself to bed wondering if she should even bother to tell Cree of the incident. Would it make a difference?

She slept fitfully that night and woke shortly after dawn. She winced when she yawned herself awake and her hand quickly went to her jaw. She could feel the swelling and she had no doubt that it was bruised, though how badly she couldn't say. The corner of her eye also pained her and she wondered if that was bruised as well.

Dawn debated about paying a quick visit to Lila. She would be able to determine the extent of her injures. She dressed quickly and threw her cloak on, pulling the hood up. No soon as she stepped out of the cottage then she saw that Cree and his men were returning. They were not far off, a few more feet and they would be upon her, and she did not want Cree to see her before she knew how bad her wounds appeared.

She hurried around to the back of her cottage waiting for the noise of the galloping horses to pass by. She waited a few more minutes to be certain, and then she crept around to the front of the cottage ready to take off for Lila's place.

A hand reached out and grabbed her arm and with the memories of last night fresh in her mind, she fisted her hand ready to protect herself.

Her fist was swallowed in Cree's strong hand, and he laughed until her hood fell back and he saw her face.

Chapter Eighteen

"What happened? Who did this to you?" Cree demanded not letting go of her arm and glaring at the two bruises on her face. Someone had struck her hard, and he was going to make him pay.

Dawn tried to free her arm and when Cree realized that he was preventing her from communicating with him, he released her. "Tell me," he demanded once more.

He caught the way her glances darted past him, and he turned to see several villagers staring at them and whispering. He took her arm once more and directed her to his horse. He grabbed her around the waist and hoisted her up on it. Then he mounted behind her, his one arm firm around her waist, and his other hand taking the reins, and they rode to the keep with many eyes following them.

Dawn had pulled up her hood so that no one could see her wounds, but Cree had seen them all too clearly, and he was burning with such a raging anger that he was ready to kill. Who had dared to touch her? And how far had he gone? He wanted answers and he wanted them now.

He dismounted as soon as he brought his horse to halt in front of the keep. Then he reached up and with his hands around her waist pulled her gently off the horse. One of his warriors took the reins and led the horse away as they climbed the steps.

Once inside Cree entered the Great Hall and when

he caught sight of Sloan, he gave him a nod, and the man followed beside him once Cree reached his side. Not a word was uttered until they were in the solar and the door closed.

Cree reached for Dawn's hood and shoved it off her head. "I thought I ordered you to keep an eye on her."

Sloan stood speechless for a moment, then he shook his head. "I had a warrior watching her cottage until late, and he returned this morning."

Cree felt Dawn trembling beside him, and he silently cursed himself. He released her arm, slipped her worn cloak off her, cursing silently again that she had no decent cloak to keep her warm, and with a gentle hand to her back guided her to a chair by the fire.

Sloan went to the door, opened it, and shouted, "Hot cider now."

A pitcher and tankards were delivered in seconds, and Sloan filled one tankard and handed it to Cree.

He took it and said so only Sloan could hear, "Go get the healer, but do not hurry."

Sloan nodded, knowing that Cree wanted time to talk with the lass. He left, closing the door behind him.

Cree went to Dawn and handed her the tankard. Her hands trembled as she took it from him, and he silently cursed again. What had she been through and would she be truthful about what happened to her?

He scooped up a small bench near the fire and placed it in front of her and sat. His anger mounted when he once again laid eyes on the two bruises. The one at the corner of her right eye wasn't too bad and from the look of it he assumed that she hadn't taken the full blunt of the punch. Her right jawline, however, was a different matter. It was dark purple and swollen. The blow had to have knocked her down and possibly out.

His hand suddenly stilled. He had not realized that his fingers had explored her face along with his eyes. He did not recall raising his hand or touching her face, but there he was, his fingers gently exploring her wounds.

Her skin was so soft, a pleasure to touch, and he quickly dropped his hand away. He needed answers and he needed them now. "Tell me what happened. Tell me everything," he said sternly and took the tankard from her hand so that she would be free to communicate with him and placed it by the hearth to keep it warm.

The warmth of the cider and the fire had eased her trembling, though not her trepidation. She was familiar with his anger from her time spent with him in the hut, though the anger she saw burning in his eyes now surpassed anything she had seen then. And his harsh tone made her worry that some of his anger was directed at her.

"I am not a patient man."

Dawn nodded and began. She patted her chest and then pressed her hands together as if in prayer, tilted her head, and rested her hands to her cheek, then made a gestured as if she knocked on a door.

"Someone knocked on your door late when you were asleep?"

She made the same sleeping gesture, but shook her head.

"You were getting ready to go to sleep?"

She nodded.

"You were still in your clothes?"

She nodded again.

"Who was at the door?"

Dawn hesitated, fearful for Dorrie, but then Dorrie had not cared what happened to her.

"Was it a man?"

Dawn shook her head.

"A woman, though certainly no friend."

Dawn nodded her head slowly.

"You will point her out to me. Continue."

Dawn moved forward in the chair and gestured with a raised hand that she wanted to stand. Cree stood, moving the small bench out of her way and stepped aside. Dawn hunched over and pretended to walk slow, curling her fingers as if gnarled and old.

"Old Mary?"

Dawn put a hand to her stomach and frowned.

"Of course," he said understanding. "This woman told you that Old Mary was ill and asked for you. She knew you would not hesitate to go help her. But did you not think for once it might be a ruse?"

She nodded and walked her fingers along in the air.

Cree nodded as well. "That's right, Old Mary leaves a bit further in the woods. You realized after a while that it could be a trap," —he scowled— "but you could not be sure and worried for Old Mary so you continued on."

She nodded, and then shivered.

"Someone jumped out of the woods and attacked you."

She gestured how she fought the attacker and how he hit her and how she fell, and she brought her hand down on top of her other hand to show how he had landed on her, and she could not stop herself from shuddering.

Cree was at her side in an instant, his arm coiling possessively around her waist. "Did he—"

She shook her head knowing what he would ask and not wanting to hear it, not wanting to recall just how close she had come to having Goddard have his way with her. She hadn't realized that she had rested her head to Cree's chest and when she did, she lifted it quickly to stare into his heated eyes.

"You are telling me the truth, Dawn?"

She nodded.

"How did you get away from him?"

She slipped out of his arms and went to the fireplace and patted one of the stones and fisted her hand as if she held one, then swung it at her head. She then pumped her arms.

"You knocked him out with a stone and took off running."

She nodded and did something she questioned afterwards. She returned to his side, his arms going around her once again.

"Confirm for me again that he did not take your virginity."

Dawn shook her finger from side to side in front of him, tapped his chest, and then tapped her own.

"I'm the only one who has ever touched you."

She nodded, and she thought for a brief moment that he smiled and for some reason it warmed her heart.

There was a knock at the door and Cree walked Dawn over to the chair and had her sit and before he bid the person to enter, he leaned down and placed a gentle kiss on her lips. And it soothed her more than she ever thought possible.

Sloan entered first and stepped aside for Elsa to

precede him and behind her came Lila who flew past them both and headed straight for Dawn.

"Good lord, what happened?" Lila asked bending down in front of Dawn and reaching out to hug her. "Elsa was at the cottage checking on Thomas when a warrior came for her with news that you were injured. I left Thomas with one of Elsa's helpers and came with her. Why didn't you come to me for help?"

"Silence!"

Lila realized her mistake and immediately sought to rectify it. She stood and turned to Cree, her head bowed. "Please, my lord, forgive my disrespect for not acknowledging your presence and asking permission to speak with my friend. I was so worried about her that I foolishly gave thought to nothing else."

Fearing Cree would punish Lila, Dawn stood at her friend's side and began gesturing fast.

"Dawn says that I speak much too often when I shouldn't, but that I am her dearest friend and she would appreciate it if you would forgive my bad manners. And that since I am here you should take advantage of the fact that I can understand her better than anyone."

Dawn was not happy to see Cree's scowl deepen.

"Since you understand her so well, Lila, ask her if she knows her attacker and who the woman was who came to her door last night and told her that Old Mary was not well and had asked for her," Cree said annoyance edging his voice.

Dawn made two gestures and Lila said, "Goddard and Dorrie, my lord."

Cree turned to Sloan and without a word exchanged between them, Sloan nodded and left the room.

"The healer will examine your bruises now, Dawn," Cree said then turned to Lila. "You are no longer needed. You will leave."

Lila bowed and turned to leave, but Dawn stopped her, gave her a hug, and gestured something to her. Lila smiled and hurried out of the room.

Elsa spent a few minutes looking Dawn over and told Cree that it appeared Dawn was well and that the bruises would heal with time. She then left, quietly closing the door behind her.

"Rest," he said to Dawn and handed her the tankard of cider kept warm by the fire. "And do not leave this room until I give you permission."

She nodded and he walked out of the room in no rush and yet Dawn thought she sensed his need to hurry off.

Dawn sat staring at the fire, her thoughts on Cree. How could he be angry and demanding and yet at the same time have a tender touch? At least that was how his arm had felt around her waist tender and— possessive. But then she was his property, and he had warned her that he protected what belonged to him.

She sighed, though it could not be heard, only felt deep down inside her. She took a drink of cider, rested the tankard on the small bench, and let herself relax in the chair. The quiet and warmth lolled her as did the sense of safety and, having had a troubled sleep last night, her body surrendered to the peaceful quiet, and she drifted off into a contented slumber.

7. ~~~

Cree glared at the shivering woman, though did not feel an ounce of sorrow for her.

"Please, my lord, I beg you, I did nothing wrong. I only took a message to the dumb one's cottage," Dorrie pleaded.

Cree pushed away from the dais he leaned against and approached her. "Dawn. Her name is Dawn."

"I meant Dawn no harm, I but delivered the message," she said her eyes downcast.

"Who gave you the message?" he asked stopping only inches away from her.

"One of Colum's warriors who pledged allegiance to you after the attack, my lord."

"You know his name?"

She shook her head. "No, my lord."

"That's odd, I hear you know all of Colum's warriors."

Dorrie's cheeks flamed red.

"I don't give second chances, Dorrie," he warned.

"I believe it was Seth, my lord," she said quickly.

"It is good that you recalled his name," he said, though he had already known it. Sloan had taken stock of all Colum's warriors who had remained after the attack, and there was one missing—Seth. He had his men searching for him now.

"I am sorry, my lord," Dorrie apologized again. "I truly meant no harm."

Cree doubted that very much. "Whether you meant it or not, you were the cause of one of your own being harmed and that cannot go unpunished."

Dorrie fell to her knees in front of him, her head bowed, tears streaming down her cheeks. "Please, please, my lord, I am sorry, so very sorry," she pleaded through sobs.

"I'm sure you are and will be even more so when you are made to suffer for your misdeed."

Dorrie's sobs stopped, and she raised a stark white face to him.

Cree turned to Sloan. "Put her in the stocks until I say otherwise."

"No, no please, my lord, I meant no harm," Dorrie begged and continued to do so as two warriors dragged her away.

Sloan poured them each a tankard of ale and handed one to Cree as he rounded the dais and sat.

"You know what you need to do if you want the silent one protected," Sloan said.

"Dawn," Cree snapped. "Her name is Dawn."

"You must make *Dawn* your mistress, then no one will dare do her harm."

"Mistresses can be a troubling lot," Cree said after a swallow of ale.

Sloan raised his tankard. "They can also prove beneficial. But we're not talking about whether she would truly be your mistress or not. As long as others believe that she is, then it is enough to keep her safe."

"So I give her the title without the benefits?"

"Are there benefits in bedding a woman without a voice?"

"Watch what you say about her. She did right by me while I was held prisoner here."

Sloan nodded. "True enough, and I must admit that I respect and admire her."

Cree quirked a brow.

"She has strength and courage for one who cannot speak up for herself, though from the way her friend understood her I'd say she communicates more clearly than some who have voices. She also protected herself admirably against her attacker and did not even seek help from anyone after the deed was done. "

"I doubt many would have helped her, the fools that they are."

"The fools belong to you now and are yours to protect," Sloan reminded. "And there is one more thing you must consider, though it has probably already crossed your mind."

Cree nodded. "Why did Goddard return to attack a voiceless woman?"

8.

Silence greeted Cree when he returned to the solar, though what did he expect, for Dawn to have suddenly found a voice. He approached the chair where she sat quietly and, sensing no movement, he realized that she had probably fallen asleep.

He stared down at her. Her head lolled to the side, and her arms were wrapped tightly around her middle as if shielding herself, though from who... him?

She was wise to fear him, most, if not all, did. He had let nothing stand in the way of his mission, making a home for him and his men and their families. And most of all gaining respect of those that had used him to further their ends. He would hold a title now and have a proper wife who would bring with her a worthy lineage.

He had refused to allow himself to care for any woman, not wanting one to get in the way and ruin his plans. He had seen too many powerful men fail for want of a woman, and he had no intentions of having that happen to him. A woman was a means to an end to him. There were those women who satisfied his lusty needs, and he wanted no more from them, and then there was the one who he would make his wife and who would bear his heirs. He would treat her with the respect she deserved, but he had given no thought to loving the woman he would wed.

And this woman? His eyes had remained on Dawn. She was no beauty, though there was something about her that caught his eye and would not let go. Every time he looked upon her, his breath would catch and he'd find himself getting aroused. No woman had ever affected him that way, and he wondered why this one did.

His anger spewed through him like raging fire at the thought that another man had dared to touch her, dared to take her innocence, dared to rob him of what was his. She was his property, she belonged to him, and her innocence was his and his alone to take, if he so chose to take it.

The thought of making her his fired his loins and the consequences of such action did little to cool him.

He shook his head. Never had he debated a matter with himself. He always knew what had to be done, what must be done, whether difficult or not, and he would see that it was done. And he knew what must be done if she was to be protected.

He leaned down and gently scooped her up in his arms. She stirred and opened her eyes.

"Sleep," he ordered sternly and she obeyed resting her head on his shoulder as he carried her out of the room.

Chapter Nineteen

Dawn woke with a start, blinking her eyes rapidly to bring herself fully awake, for surely she was dreaming. The scent was strong in her nostrils; earth, pine and something else she could not quite grasp. She breathed deeply of the familiar scent trying to recognize it, but for some reason it eluded her. She inhaled as if she could not get enough of it, as if it soothed her, and she wanted to linger in its comfort.

Cree.

The scent was all Cree, but how could that be?

Her eyes spread wide, and she realized that it was no dream and that she was in a rather large room in a bed that could easily sleep three people. She hastened out of it relieved to see that she was fully clothed, though her boots had been removed.

She spun around growing dizzy at the size of the room. It was larger than her cottage. A fire burned brightly in the stone fireplace. A narrow table sat against one wall and on top sat a small chest, rolled parchments and several candles, though none were lit. Larger chests sat about the room as did two chairs and two tables, the smaller one tucked close to the side of the bed, unlit candles on top as well.

It did not take Dawn long to realize that she was in Cree's bed chamber, and she hurried to put her boots on, grab her cloak draped over the one chair, and head for the door slipping quietly out of the room after peering out in the narrow passageway to see that no one was about.

She pulled her cloak up over her head and carefully made her way down the stone stairs, listening to make certain no one was headed her way. When she reached the Great Hall, she was relieved to see that only a couple of servants lingered about, and so she hurried through and once outside she released the breath she hadn't realized she had been holding. She also noticed from the activity in the village that it was late afternoon, close to dusk. She had slept much longer than she had thought, though her nap had given her strength, and so she ran to her cottage seeking its solitude and its safety, or was there any place that would be safe for her now?

She stopped abruptly when she saw Dorrie locked in the stock, her eyes swollen and red from crying, and her garments and hair already filthy from villagers throwing whatever was handy at her, mostly mud & dirt.

"I'm sorry, Dawn," she cried out. "Please, please, I beg you to speak on my behalf and ask Cree to free me. Please, please, oh God, I will never treat you badly again. Please, please."

Dawn stared bewildered while villagers took a wide berth around her as if they too feared they would suffer Dorrie's fate if they should speak wrongly to her.

Dawn hurried along, keeping her face concealed and ignoring the whispers that surrounded her, so many whispers. Tongues were wagging and Dawn could only imagine what they were saying.

At the moment she didn't care. Dawn wanted nothing more than to get home and lock herself away from everyone. But most of all she wanted to wake from this never-ending nightmare.

She halted in her tracks when she saw the warriors tossing things out of her cottage. The little she had was being set to flame. She ran, praying they had not found the wrapped cloth that contained the only thing her mum had passed on to her.

She flew past the men before they could stop her, and her heart slammed into her chest when she saw that not a stitch of furniture was left in the cottage. She ran to the hearth now cold from the water that had been doused on it. She shifted the one stone in the fireplace until it came free and reached in to rescue the cloth she had hidden there.

"You're to come with us, Dawn."

She turned to see Sloan standing in the doorway. Fear rippled through her entire body. What would they do with her? Was she to be punished like Dorrie or would her punishment be worse for not obeying Cree and going into the woods when he had ordered her not to?

She hugged the pouch to her chest and shivered.

"There is nothing to fear," Sloan said. "You have been given a different cottage."

His comment caught her unaware, and she instinctively shrugged.

"I understand that gesture," Sloan grinned. "You're asking why."

Dawn nodded, her fear receding, though just a bit.

"Cree's decision," he said and stepping to the side he swept his hand at the door. "After you."

Dawn felt a tightening in her chest. This was her home. The one she and her mum had shared. She did not want to be moved to another cottage. She wanted to stay here where she was familiar with the drafty spots and the way the door rattled when the wind caught it. And from here she could take a few steps and be at Lila's cottage. No she did not want to leave her home.

And so she stood firm clutching the cloth and shaking her head.

Sloan took a step toward her and she took a step back. He stopped and smiled. "It is a nice cottage that has been made ready for you."

Dawn shook her head and pointed to the ground, and then to her.

"I understand that gesture too," Sloan said surprised. "This is your home and you do not want to leave it."

She nodded.

Sloan winced. "Unfortunately, it is not truly your home or your decision. Everything in the village belongs to Cree, and he decides where each person will reside. You have no choice but to reside where he commands."

He was right. There was nothing she could do but obey. She cast one last sorrowful look around the small room, her home since she and her mum had arrived here and breathed a silent farewell. Fearing it was not only her cottage that she was bidding farewell to.

Dawn stopped just outside the door. Several women were gathered in a huddle a short distance away. They were whispering and pointing in her direction.

Sloan stepped past her and shouted, "You have chores to attend to, be gone."

They scurried away, whispers trailing behind them.

Dawn followed Sloan, though gave one last

glance behind her and was sorry she did. She watched as her only garments were thrown on the fire. Her stomach knotted and her hands began to tremble. She turned around not wanting to think of what all this meant, though she was no fool. Cree was making it clear to all that Dawn was his.

What she could not understand was why? Why did he want a woman who he refused to couple with? She was more confused than ever.

A strong wind blew sending the shivers through her meager cloak and gray clouds raced overhead. She shivered again. A storm brewed and she did not care for storms. They frightened her, though she could not say why.

Dawn halted when Sloan did and cast a wary eye at the cottage in front of her. This certainly could not be where he meant her to live. It was much too large for just her and was meant for one in service to the keep, which was why it sat close to the keep and tucked back a bit in the woods. This way the person would have easy access to the servants' entrances in the back.

It struck her then what her living here would mean. It would say to all that she was in service to the lord of the keep.

"This is your home now," Sloan said and waved her forward.

Her legs trembled so badly that she didn't think she could move. All she could do was stare at the cottage and all it represented. How in such a short time could she have gone from being ignored by most and unwanted by a man to being the main fodder of gossip and being a kept woman?

"Are you all right, Dawn? You have gone pale,"

Sloan said.

She took a breath, and she could see the pity in Sloan's eyes when there was no sound to be heard. She hated when anyone pitied her. Her mum had taught her that pity never did anyone any good.

Deal with your lot with strength and courage and you will know no pity. Her mum's words rang clear in her head and gave her the courage to toss her head up and march forward.

Sloan followed, though stopped just before they reached the door. "Cree will be here to see you shortly."

Dawn turned to him and nodded. Then she smiled and bowed her head in thanks. There was no point in being rude to him. He followed Cree's orders as did all.

Sloan returned her smile and looked about to say something, then stopped, nodded, turned, and walked away.

Dawn lifted the latch on the cottage door and walked in. It wasn't until a good wind wiped past her stirring the fire in the hearth that she hurried to close the door behind her. She stood eyes wide and mouth agape. The room was twice the size of her cottage with a table and four chairs in front of the hearth. A narrow table sat against one wall and on it sat wooden bowls and crocks while beneath sat stacked baskets. A long bench sat to another side with pegs above it along the wall. Two cloaks hung from the pegs, both wool, one dark green, the other dark blue and lined with fur. Before she did anything she hid the pouch with her cherished possession behind the baskets until she could find a better place for it.

She was surprised to see another doorway, though no door blocked its entrance. She wandered over and entered, coming to a stop just inside the room. It was a fairly good-sized room with a bed that could hold two people and a flat-topped chest at the foot. The lit hearth kept the room more than comfortably warm and the wooden shutters on the lone window were closed, the latch firmly in place.

The fire's light flickered across the bed, and Dawn stared at the fresh bedding and the lovely wool blankets not to mention the two overly stuffed pillows. It was much too elegant for her and much too large.

The thought startled her. Of course the bed was too large, it was not meant for her to sleep in alone. Actually, it wasn't meant for sleep.

She took a quick step back and bumped into something solid. She turned even more quickly and scurried back away from Cree, the size of him filling the doorway.

He glared at her for a moment, then walked straight for her. He still wore all black and his size so over powered that he appeared the devil himself rushing at her. When he reached her, he simply grabbed her cloak and pulled it off her shoulders.

"You'll not wear rags anymore." He rolled it up and tossed it into the fire. It caught and burnt quickly.

She inched her way toward the door, not feeling comfortable with him in such an intimate setting.

He scowled when he turned and saw what she was doing. He walked over to her, took hold of her arm and shoved her in front of him and through the doorway. He let her go once in the other room.

"You will live here now." He stared at her, a spark of passion glinting in his eyes.

She gave a nod, not knowing what else to do. It

was a command, after all, and she had to obey. Her life was not her own. It belonged to him and as Sloan reminded, all in the village belonged to him.

He did not like the frightened look in her eyes. He had seen it there too often, though he had to admit it was tinged with courage. Even though she feared, she fought it and bravely battled through whatever ordeal she faced.

She had done that in the hut, and what disturbed him was that there were times he wished he was back there with her, just the two of them. When he had stepped into the other room it had given him that sense of confinement with her, and he had found himself growing aroused at the thought. Could he have that here with her, the feeling of being locked away from everything, only having each other? He had found certain contentment with her, though he did not understand it and did not want to try. He did however wish to experience it again and that was why while she slept he had issued orders to have her moved to this place, though Sloan believed it was because he had no choice but to make Dawn his mistress.

It had been some time since Cree had done anything because he'd been forced to. His reputation alone was enough to make people fear and obey him and fear him they should, for he had no qualms about making those who disobeyed him suffer. As Dorrie was finding out now, sitting in the stocks where she would remain for at least a week. Others would learn from her misfortune... learn not to mistreat Dawn.

"You may take whatever food you wish from the kitchen or have meals brought here to you. I have already spoken with Turbett and he awaits your visits."

Her eyes turned wide and she went to gesture, but he held up his hand.

"I will brook no argument. You will do as I say."

This would not bode well for her with the villagers, receiving special treatment, especially when it came to food.

"I'm waiting for a response."

Again her eyes widened for no one except Lila or Paul ever expected her to respond. She nodded, though she wished she could have protested. She would have much preferred to prepare her own meals.

"There are garments in the chest in the other room. Make use of them and make sure to get rid of the ones you wear now. They are nothing but rags, and I will not see you in them again."

He would expect a response, and so she gave him a nod. What else was she to do? And that was a question that had haunted her. What was she to do with herself? Everyone had chores and she wished to be as productive as the others.

She tapped her chest and shrugged.

Cree looked puzzled at first, and then he asked, "You have a question?"

She nodded.

"Ask me?"

She gestured slowly, hoping he would understand her. She made a half circle and turned her palms upward.

"The rising sun," he said pleased with himself.

She nodded, and then took a step to the side and turned her hands over and brought them down.

"The sun sets," he said.

She nodded and pointed back and forth between her hands, then at herself and shrugged.

"You wonder what you are to do throughout the day."

She nodded.

"That is an easy question to answer, Dawn." He stepped toward her, reaching out to slip his hand around her neck and ease her mouth to his and, just before his lips claimed hers, he said, "You will be available to me whenever I want you."

Chapter Twenty

How could she be upset and yet find his kiss so enjoyable? She was angry with herself and angry with him and yet his kiss had her melting against him as his arm coiled around her waist and he yanked her hard against him.

She had never been kissed by anyone but him and she doubted that any kiss could prove as wonderful as his kisses. He kissed with brutal yet tender possessiveness setting her heart to pounding, her stomach fluttering and between her legs tingling. And worse, the more he kissed her the more she wanted him to.

His tongue did not shock her when it surged into her mouth this time, though she was surprised when her own played wickedly with his. And his groan let her know that he was enjoying their kiss as much as she was.

As their kiss turned urgent, insatiable, he grew hard against her and she grew wet.

He ripped his mouth off hers and took several steps away from her and paced shaking his head.

She suddenly felt vulnerable just as she had when they had been in the hut. He could have done whatever he wanted to her there, no one would have stopped him and no one would stop him now. She was more a prisoner than he had ever been and she would never know freedom.

He walked over to her and grabbed the back of her neck, his grip firm. "I know not what you do to me but know this... you are mine until I say otherwise."

With that he stormed out the door.

Dawn felt her legs go weak and she wisely got herself to a chair to sit. How could she find such comfort and yearning in the arms of a man who with one command could decree her fate?

She glanced around the cottage. There was so much room for one person and the furnishings in good shape. It was truly a lovely place. And she need not worry about food; she would have as much as she wanted and then there were her new garments.

She got up and hurried into the other room lifting the lid to the chest at the foot of the bed. She could not believe her eyes. There were soft wool dresses and plush velvet ones that were not fit for the likes of her. She was relieved when at the bottom she found wool skirts and linen blouses and a pale blue shawl so tightly weaved that she could not resist wrapping it around her shoulders. She brushed her cheek against it, the wool so soft that it tingled her skin.

Dawn closed the chest and sat on it, tugging the shawl more tightly around her, needing its warmth.

Tingles.

All Cree had to do was look at her and her flesh would tingle. Most would say that the devil was introducing her to sins of the flesh and if she was not careful she would lose her soul to him. The thought sent the shivers racing through her and she stood ready to return to the other room and fix herself a hot brew.

She stopped and glanced down at the chest of clothes. Where had he gotten them from? Who had they belonged to and who were they intended for?

She didn't want to think of the possibilities; she wanted to run as far as she could and not look back. But there was no place for her to go. The village Dowell was and always would be her home.

Her stomach gurgled and she realized that she had not eaten all day. She could go to the kitchen and get food as Cree had instructed. But it did not seem right for her to simply enter the kitchen and take what food she wanted.

She could however see if she could get Flanna's attention and request a few items so that she could cook her own meal. Her stomach gurgled again and she smiled. She had no voice but her stomach certainly did and was protesting loudly its hunger.

With a quick deposit of her shawl to the chair and grabbing the wool cloak off the peg, she hurried out the door. She sniffed the air as she hurried to the kitchen... rain... you could smell its crisp scent and it was not far off.

Dawn smiled seeing Flanna outside the cookhouse and hurried over to her.

"Good lord, are you all right?" Flanna asked cringing at the sight of Dawn's bruises.

A nod and a smile assured Flanna that she was fine.

"Stop your gossiping and hurry with those onions, woman," came a rough shout from inside the kitchen.

Flanna shook her head and grabbed a basket from the stack outside the kitchen door. "Come with me so that we can talk."

Dawn frowned and pointed to the basket as they walked to the wild onion patch in a field beyond the kitchen.

Flanna shook her head. "I am nothing more than a helper now and Turbett is not an easy task master. He works everyone until bone-tired, though I must admit that his food is quite tasty. And he is generous in feeding his helpers. But what of you?" she asked reaching out to take hold of Dawn's hand. "Tongues are wagging about your attack and how Cree has punished Dorrie and how now you serve the—" Flanna bit her tongue.

Dawn slipped her arm free and brought her hands to her head and stuck two fingers up on either side.

Flanna nodded. "The devil." And then whispered. "Do you serve the devil?"

Did she serve the devil? She wasn't sure and so she shrugged and taking Flanna's basket from her, plopped down in the field to gather wild onions, wishing to talk of anything other than Cree right now.

Flanna joined her and wisely spoke no more of Cree, but rather of Turbett and his dictatorial ways, which had Dawn smiling since he sounded not much different than Flanna when she had been in charge of the kitchen. And though her stomach continued to gurgle with hunger, she didn't want this time with Flanna to end too soon. It reminded her of life before Cree had descended on the village and changed everything.

So she sat continuing to pick onions and smiling.

9.

"It is done and yet you continue to fret and scowl," Sloan said, pouring him and Cree more ale as they relaxed at the dais. "Dawn is now well protected. The villagers think that her chore is to service you."

"A *chore* you say?"

Sloan laughed. "*Fear* is a better choice since that scowl would send any woman running in fright."

"It didn't send Dawn running; she bravely stood her ground fearful or not," Cree informed him adamantly sounding as if he defended her. Not realizing it, though Sloan did.

"So then she is your woman now?"

"Yes," Cree snapped.

Sloan leaned closer so that the nearby servants would not hear and said, "You're a bloody liar."

Cree's dark eyes narrowed, his scowl vanished replaced by an ominous expression that had Sloan offering an apology of sorts.

"My tongue runs before I think."

Cree simply nodded, more annoyed that Sloan had seen through to the truth, but he would not admit that he had yet to actually couple with Dawn, not even to Sloan. And he and Sloan had certainly shared many tales about the women they have bedded.

Dawn, however, was different and he would not discuss the intimacies of what he shared with her and sully her character any more than it was already being tarnished.

Has there been any news on the search for Seth or Goddard?" Cree asked letting Sloan know that they would talk no more of Dawn.

"Not yet, though I cannot understand why Goddard would take the chance of returning to simply attack Dawn."

"He didn't," Cree said and Sloan stared at him waiting for an explanation. "Goddard and Colum are not men who would waste time on Dawn unless she had something they wanted.

Sloan nodded. "Information."

"No doubt they thought she knew more than she had told them when I was held captive, a ruse that worked well for us, and Colum would not want to return to the Earl of Carrick without a stitch of useful information that would help the earl to regain his land."

Sloan grinned and raised his tankard. "And little does Colum know that there is a new Earl of Carrick."

Cree raised his tankard as well. "To us all, living and dead who helped to achieve land of our own where we will now know some peace."

They drank and then Sloan asked, "What do you think Roland Gerwan, former Earl of Carrick will say when he learns that he is to give you his daughter to wed?"

"Gerwan is not a foolish man. He knows if he does not comply that the King will simply claim the rest of his land whereas his land, in a sense, remains with future heirs and he gains the extra advantage of having the infamous Cree as a son-in-law."

"And guarantee his safety and that of his holdings."

Cree raised his tankard. "And gain the King my presence in this area and firm obedience from the ruling lords."

"Do you think someone will try again to take Dawn?"

His eyes narrowed again, the crease between them deepening. "Colum is no fool, though he is desperate and desperate men can do foolish things. The fatal mistake he made was harming someone who belongs to me. Now," —he shrugged— "he will pay for it."

"You don't intend to stop hunting for him," Sloan confirmed.

"His time is limited. I will find him and..."

Cree did not need to detail what would be done to the man. Sloan knew all too well what happened to men who brought harm to anyone under Cree's protection.

"Have all the villagers been assigned chores?" Cree asked.

"You assigned the very last one yourself," Sloan smirked.

Cree glared at him, though issued no threats. Sloan had a quick wit and would not disrespect him, though he would be honest with him and Cree counted on his honesty.

"See how each fair at their chores and if any have any particular skills we can use. Have you taken Turbett to the miller yet?"

"Turbett's damn annoying to work with," Sloan complained. "If he wasn't such a great cook—lord his bread is delicious—I would run a sword through him."

"His bread is tasty because he works with the miller to produce a good ground grain. And see that the miller knows he is to follow Turbett's instructions without question."

"You put this on me so you do not have to deal with the insufferable man."

Cree quirked a brow. "I put this on you, for if I handle it Turbett will end up dead and we will end up with tasteless food."

"I will see that it is done," Sloan said without hesitation.

"I thought you might." Cree stood after downing the last of the ale in his tankard.

"You will stay with her tonight?"

"Since when do I have to keep you abreast of my actions?"

"Since I have never seen a woman who ties you in knots as this one has."

Cree sat again. "You evidently have something to say concerning Dawn so say it and be done."

Sloan leaned closer so they could not be heard, more servants having entered the Great Hall in preparation of the evening meal. "We have each had our fill of women, not growing attached to any particular one knowing what we had to do. You still have to finish what we've started. You must wed a woman for what she can bring to the marriage; more land and more power. And she in turn will produce heirs to guarantee the future of your name and holdings and those to come after us."

"I know all this; I don't need reminding."

"I think you do when I see the way you look at the silent one. You have not fully satisfied your lust for her. Be done with it, have your fill, enjoy and let her go. And be careful not to leave her with child and run the risk of having a son who cannot speak, for your enemies would take full advantage of it. Keep your heart as silent as it's ever been or risk losing everything you have fought and sacrificed for."

Cree stood and without saying a word left the Great Hall. He made his way to the front of the keep and stood on the steps surveying the village and the land beyond that now was his. Sloan had been right, they had fought endless battles, lost many good men and made many sacrifices to have a home and Sloan had assumed that he had turned his heart silent in order to reach his goal.

It had taken more than silencing his heart to become the infamous warrior Cree who killed, tortured, and conquered in the name of the King. His heart hadn't turned silent, it had turned cold and had remained that way much too long now and he doubted he could ever care, ever love. And he believed it was for the best.

Anger had been his steady companion along with frustration and annoyance and lust which he easily satisfied with a willing woman.

Lately though he'd been finding himself wanting only one woman... Dawn. The thought of her stirred him and he grew aroused and disturbed. Thoughts of rutting always aroused him, but lately all he had to do was hear Dawn's name and he would grow hard.

Perhaps Sloan was right. Perhaps if he took her and satisfied his cravings, enjoyed her for a while, it would be done and he would think of her no more. No doubt he would grow bored with her particularly since she could not speak, could not scream out in the throes of pleasure or release.

He stiffened recalling the way her fingers had dug into his arms as her passion grew and how she bowed against him eager for more. And he could not help but wonder how she would respond if he buried himself deep inside her.

Damn, if he didn't swell more.

He stormed down the steps as thunder rolled in the distance and went around to the side of the keep and stopped to stare at Dawn's cottage. It nestled against the woods giving the place a modicum of privacy and that was why he had chosen it for Dawn or had it been for him?

He shook his head and approached the cottage, entering without a knock or a shout to let her know he was there. He was surprised to find the room empty and he went to the small bed chamber and was annoyed finding that empty as well.

Where was she? He thought she'd be resting.

And that you could join her.

Then he recalled telling her to make use of the kitchen. He turned and left the cottage. He must have been scowling since everyone he passed hurried out of his way. It was good they feared him; they would then obey him without question or suffer the consequences as Dorrie now did.

It didn't take him long to reach the kitchen and when he entered all movement ceased.

"Is there something I can get you, my lord?" Turbett asked with a respectful bobbed of his head.

Cree glanced around the room overcrowded with helpers and not seeing Dawn asked, "Has Dawn been here?"

"I have not seen her but..." Turbett turned to his helpers. "Have any of you seen Dawn?"

A young woman spoke up. "I saw her a short time ago."

"Where?" Cree demanded.

The woman's voice quivered as she answered, "With Flanna in the field beyond the kitchen picking wild onions."

Cree's anger flared in his eyes and all saw it.

"I appointed her no chore, my lord," Turbett was quick to say. "And I will see Flanna punished for this."

"See that supper is prepared for two and sent to Dawn's cottage," Cree ordered. "And make certain that Dawn is greeted with no chore when she comes here looking for a meal."

Turbett bowed his head. "I will make certain that Dawn is kept well fed, my lord."

Cree left the kitchen his annoyance growing. He had not instructed her to return to her old chore, so why had she?

He stopped at the end of the cookhouse catching sight of her in the field with Flanna and filling an already overflowing basket with more onions. She was smiling and again he grew annoyed. He could never make her smile like that or could he?

He stood and watched her and let her have her fun.

Cree caught the quick movement at the edge of the woods at the far end of the field. He remained as he was appearing as if his attention was focused on Dawn. But it wasn't, his eyes were fixed on the spot where he saw the flash of movement and he strained to see more clearly.

He caught movement again and this time there was no mistaken what he saw... a bow being drawn... the arrow aimed at Dawn.

Chapter Twenty-one

Dawn turned at the shout of her name. The next thing she knew she was on the ground flat on her back with Cree on top of her, his body covering every inch of hers. She heard him yell at Flanna to get down and stay down. And then he let out such a terrifying roar that Dawn was certain it would cause the devil himself to shiver.

In no time they were surrounded by Cree's warriors, Sloan the only one being permitted past the human barricade.

"A skilled archer in the woods, find him." Cree's angry demand warned that he would brook no failure. As soon as Sloan took his leave Cree summoned one of his warriors and ordered him to escort Flanna to the kitchen.

Only then did Cree lift off her and not entirely so. He shifted his weight and lay partially draped over her, his hand remaining firm at her waist.

Worry, anger, and was that a touch of lust she saw in his dark eyes? He lay there staring at her and it did not take long for him to grimace in disgust. She was aware she looked a fright with her tattered garments and bruised face. Not to mention the quiver that refused to stop running through her body.

"Are you all right?"

She was a bit startled by how concerned he sounded... almost as if he truly cared about her. She nodded and patted her chest to let him know that she was fine, though her confirmation did not ease the deep crease between his eyes.

She furrowed her brow and shrugged.

Cree was amazed by how her gestures appeared much like a voice. A shrug and a wrinkle of her brow was basically a question and it was easy to understand in this situation what she was asking. She wanted to know what had happened.

"Someone took aim at you with an arrow."

Her eyes widened, she shook her head, and shrugged again.

"You wonder why, as do I."

She gestured as if drawing back an arrow in a bow and shrugged.

"A good question. Who would want to harm you?"

She stared at him. Most of the villagers simply ignored her. Some would acknowledge her with a nod. Then there were those who would amuse themselves by making fun of her like Dorrie. But serious harm? What reason would anyone have to harm her?

She shook her head letting him know that she had no answer.

His eyes roamed over her with annoyance, though lust still lingering in them.

He fingered her worn garments. "Don't let me see you in these rags again."

With that he stood, held his hand out to her and when she took it, he slowly eased her to her feet.

She swayed a moment, still a bit disoriented from him tackling her to the ground or had it been the way he had protected her with his body, keeping every inch of her covered with no concern for his own safety. The thought still startled her. No one had ever protected her so gallantly. And gallant was not a word anyone would use to describe the infamous Cree.

His hands went instantly to her waist. "Take a moment and regain your strength."

She nodded, attempting to gather and make sense of her confused thoughts and the best place to do that was alone in her cottage. Her cottage? How she wished she could go home to her small cottage. She had found comfort there. More so when her mum had been alive but even now it had been as if her spirit lingered there watching over Dawn and it made her feel safe.

"Are you all right, Dawn?" he asked lifting her chin with one finger.

She had not realized that she had lowered her head, but then it had been weighted with too many thoughts and no doubt had sunk on its own. Though she was not sure how she felt, she nodded.

"I want the truth. Not what you think I want to hear," he chided.

So he wanted the truth? She threw her hands up in frustration. Was that a smile? It had been brief, but she thought she caught a smile tempt the corners of his mouth.

"You need a washing, clean garments, food, and rest."

And time to herself, she added silently.

Cree was suddenly issuing orders and some of the warriors that circled them formed a line on either side of them. Another order had the circle parting and forming a line facing the woods while Cree and her kept pace with the warriors shielding them.

It wasn't lost to Dawn that Cree kept her tucked close against him with his arm around her waist. He held her with the ease of familiarity. And why? Simple. They had become more than familiar with each other while in that hut, and it hadn't stopped.

Dawn was never so relieved to walk into her new home, though she stopped abruptly once inside the door. The table was laden with food and her stomach gurgled with joy. Then she saw that the table was arranged for two people and her heart sank. She had hoped to be alone, have a chance to think, to make a modicum of sense of all that had happened to her in such a short time.

Cree gently nudged her forward so that he could shut the door. He slipped off her cloak and went and hung it on the peg. He then eased her down in one of the chairs at the table.

"I was going to join you, but first I must see to this incident."

How could she feel relieved and disappointed at the same time? She wanted time alone and here she was sorry that he was leaving.

"I will return later."

A tingle of anticipation settled between her legs, and she scolded herself for her body's wicked reaction.

Cree stopped beside her at the table and leaned over her. He raised his hand, though stopped in mid-air, as if he questioned his actions, and then as if resigned to the inevitable he stroked her bruised jaw with the back of his fingers.

"I will find who did this to you and I will see him punished."

The resolve in his voice sent a small tremor through her, but it was his kiss that made her shiver and tingle. It was so unexpected and so very tender that it made her feel cherished like never before.

"Until later," he whispered and brushed his lips lightly across hers, then walked out the door.

Dawn gasped, though no sound was heard, when she realized that she had been holding her breath.

Later.

He would return and what then would he expect of her? Her thoughts were quickly diverted when she eyed the meat on a platter. She stared in awe at it. She could not recall the last time she ate meat, though she did recall the delicious taste of it.

She stared a few minutes more, not believing that she could actually reach out and take a piece and not just one but many. She smiled and snatched a slice. It was more delicious than she remembered. She grew bolder and tasted from the other platters and bowls amazed at the tastiness of the food. Though she hated to admit it, Turbett was a far better cook than Flanna.

A crack of thunder caused her to jump and soon after that the rain started growing heavier by the minute. Dawn sighed inwardly feeling lucky that she was in a warm place with plenty of food.

She sprung up in her chair, struck by an unexpected thought. *Dorrie.* Good lord, she could not be left out in this rain all night. She would catch her death, and Dawn could never live with that. Dorrie might not be a friend to her, but illness and death was too much of a punishment to suffer for her foolishness. She hurried to the door not bothering to collect her cloak. The rain would soak it quickly enough, and then it would prove more hindrance than help.

As soon as she opened the door one of Cree's warriors blocked her from leaving.

"You are to stay here," he said. "Cree's orders."

She shut the door and stood in thought. Then she remembered the window and hurried into the other room. She pushed the flat-top trunk beneath the window, yanked open the heavy shutters and hoisted herself up and partially out the window. Once her waist cleared it, her weight took her down the rest of the way. The mud eased her fall, though didn't help with her appearance.

It didn't matter though, her priority was Dorrie. The woman may have treated her badly at times, but leaving her locked in stocks in a rainstorm was beyond horrific. It was inhuman.

She crept along the edge of the woods, steeling herself against the fright that ran through her when it stormed. When she was far enough away so that the warrior standing guard could not see her, she ran. The heavy rain had turned the ground quickly to mud and with dusk giving way to night and clouds covering what little moonlight there was, and it raining buckets, it would soon be difficult to see where one was going.

Dawn hurried through the empty village, everyone having retreated to their homes. She stopped briefly when she spied Dorrie. Her head hung down as if there was no life left in her and Dawn rushed to her side.

When she laid her hand on Dorrie's shoulder, the woman barely raised her head, though she did managed to say, "I'm sorry."

Dawn didn't wait. She grabbed hold of the metal spike that locked the stock and pulled. It was wet and difficult to keep hold of and it took much effort to pry it out. Her arms ached from the task and once done with the one, she worked on the other. The top part of the stock was heavy and she feared for a moment that she would not be able to lift it without hurting. Dorrie but after a struggle she got it off without harm to the woman.

Dorrie had trouble raising her neck and lifting her wrists, so Dawn helped her and once free of the stock, she collapsed against Dawn.

"Bless you, bless you," Dorrie said over and over.

Dawn nodded and slipped Dorrie's arm over her shoulder and forced her to walk along with her. The rain was so bad Dawn could barely see in front of her and supporting Dorrie's weight didn't help the situation. But Dawn did not give up. She had to get Dorrie to the cottage and get a hot brew into her and some food and get her into dry garments.

Dorrie was near to collapsing when they reached the cottage. Dawn didn't even think of returning through the window. She marched Dorrie right to the front door.

The warrior rushed to her, his mouth dropped open in shock that she was standing there and was not in the cottage. And when he caught sight of Dorrie...

"She belongs in the stock until Cree orders otherwise." He reached out to grab Dorrie from her.

Dawn swerved to avoid him while her other hand shot out and gave him a shove he hadn't expected. He went down hard, giving her enough time to get Dorrie inside the cottage and latch the door.

"He will punish you for helping me." Dorrie barely got the words out she was so weak.

Dawn didn't bother to respond. She would face that problem when the time came. Now she needed to help Dorrie. She set the pitcher of cider near the hearth to heat while she hurried to the other room and snatched a fine wool skirt, wool stockings and linen blouse from the trunk.

"So much food," Dorrie said. "Surely I am dreaming or," —tears ran down her eyes— "I have died and gone to heaven."

Dawn took a piece of meat and handed it to Dorrie.

Dorrie looked skeptical and glanced around, as if expecting someone to appear and punish her for even thinking of taking the meat.

Dawn shoved the meat into her hand and retrieved the pitcher of cider from the hearth and filled a tankard.

Once Dorrie took a bite of the delicious meat she couldn't stop. She reached for more and she followed it with several gulps of cider. Her shivers grew worse as she continued to eat. Dawn hurried to collect the rain water and set it to heat by the hearth. The she prodded Dorrie and yanked at her wet garments. When she finally got Dorrie's full attention, she held up the dry clothes and pointed to her wet ones.

"For me?" Dorrie asked incredulously.

Dawn nodded.

Tears rimmed Dorrie's eyes. "Why? I have treated you so badly, and yet you help me."

Dawn patted her chest, shook her head, and pointed at her.

Dorrie scrunched her brow and then as if understanding dawned on her, she said, "It doesn't matter what I've done," —tears trickled down her cheeks— "you cannot see me suffer."

Dawn nodded.

"I'm sorry, so very sorry," Dorrie cried, her body shivering.

Dawn shook her head and urged her to drink more cider. Then she brought the bucket of heated rain water to rest beside Dorrie's chair and once she put the tankard down, Dawn tugged at her blouse.

"I am soaked to the bone," Dorrie said hurrying to strip off her clothes.

Dawn and Dorrie worked together washing the mud off Dorrie while the woman cried. Dawn wasn't sure what to do. So when they finally finished and Dorrie was dressed in clean garments, Dawn ran and got a blanket from the bed and wrapped it around Dorrie hugging her, hoping to stop her shivers.

Dawn was shocked when Dorrie slipped her arms out of the blanket and hugged her tightly.

"I will not forget what you have done for me."

Dawn smiled and handed her another piece of meat. Dorrie took it, smiled, and reached for a piece of meat handing it to Dawn.

10. ~~~

Cree was ready to kill someone. "How did the culprit manage to elude my best tracker and warriors?"

Sloan rubbed his chin. "I don't know."

Cree glared at him. "Not an acceptable answer."

"I agree, but it is the only answer that I presently have for you, my lord. The rainstorm has hampered attempts to continue tracking. We will try again in the morning whether it continues to rain or not. But I do not hold any hope."

"You feel he has gotten away?"

Sloan nodded. "I do, though I wonder if he waits for another chance to get Dawn, not wanting to return to Colum having failed his mission."

"Dawn will have a guard with her at all times. She is to go nowhere without one." Cree poured himself another tankard of ale. "And make certain that the men are aware that she cannot scream out to them for help. They must keep an eye on her at all times."

"I cannot imagine the terror she must have felt when she was attacked and could not scream out for help."

Cree gripped his tankard so hard that his knuckles turned white and his expression murderous. That very thought had haunted him from when he had first laid eyes on Dawn's bruises. She could not scream out in rage or fear, though no doubt she had wanted to. Her voice was forever trapped inside her, leaving her much too vulnerable.

He did not like the thought of her being vulnerable to anyone but him. Perhaps a few lessons in how to defend herself would prove helpful.

"I must say I admire her bravery. She did not surrender or give into the thug. She fought, even though he pummeled her face. And what amazes me even more is that she sought no help afterwards. She saw to her own wounds." Sloan shook his head, as if he didn't believe it.

Cree slammed his fist on the table causing Sloan to jump. "She did not seek help because she assumed no one would care what had happened to her. This land and these people belong to me, and I want them all, every one of them, to know that they are now under my protection and that I will let no harm come to them. Dawn has been harmed and I want them to see with their own eyes what I do to those who attempt to harm what is mine."

"I believe that you have made yourself clear by

putting Dorrie in the stocks. Tongues have been wagging incessantly about it, though no one has dared speak against it."

"They will learn to follow my decrees or suffer the consequences. Speak with Dorrie tomorrow and see what she can tell you about this Seth that she claims is the one who delivered Old Mary's message. And have you spoken to Old Mary?"

"I have, and she was quite upset that someone had used her to hurt Dawn."

"Move Old Mary to Dawn's cottage," Cree ordered. "She is too old to be living removed from the village, besides her eyes and ears will better serve me here."

"She is old and set in her ways, she may protest—"

"Did I say it was a request? And are you implying that the old woman intimidates you?"

Sloan leaned closer and lowered his voice. "The men believe that she is a witch, sometimes knowing things before they happen."

"She is an old woman, no doubt wise for her years, and she watches and listens. That is how she is able to predict what will happen. And she is friend to Dawn unlike the villagers who ignore her. Dawn treats her well and sees that she has food when no one else cares."

"How is Dawn?" Sloan asked.

"You care?" Cree asked with a quirk of his brow.

"She intrigues me for one who has no voice."

"Do not let her intrigue you too much," Cree warned.

"Jealous?" Sloan grinned.

"I keep warning you about your tongue."

"And yet it is still whole in my mouth."

A commotion at the entrance to the Great Hall kept Cree from responding and when both men saw who had entered they jumped out of their seats.

"Elwin, are you not supposed to be guarding Dawn?" Sloan demanded hurrying around the table to stand in front of the warrior who stood dripping rainwater on the wood floor.

"Tannin is standing guard—"

"What has happened?" Cree snapped with anger.

Elwin took a step back and bowed his head. "The silent one got out of the cottage and went and freed Dorrie, then brought her back to the cottage. They are both there now."

Cree looked ready to choke the man. "How does a woman escape a man of your size and girth, and why didn't you return Dorrie to the stocks?"

"I stopped her when she opened the door. I told her that she could not leave—your orders." He hesitated reluctant to continue, though knew he had no choice. "I can only assume that she got out through the window in the other room. And as for Dorrie," —he took a breath— "I tried but the silent one tricked me and got into the cottage and latched the door before I could stop her."

"I'm admiring this woman more and more," Sloan said, though refrained from grinning.

Cree turned on him and Sloan was quick to raise his hands. "You must admit that it takes mettle and a generous heart to help someone who has wronged you."

"Or foolishness," Cree said, "of which I intend to put an end to. Sloan, go get Lila I have no doubt I'll have need of her. Elwin, you follow me. Dorrie will be returned to the stocks and Dawn...shall learn the consequences of disobeying me."

Chapter Twenty-two

Dorrie sat, in fresh garments, at the table with her hands wrapped around a tankard of hot cider while Dawn hung the wet towels by the fire to dry. Dorrie's garments were another matter. They would need washing, so Dawn placed them in basket for her to take home.

"I should be doing that," Dorrie said. "You have done more than enough for me already. And I cannot thank you enough."

Dawn shook her head and pointed to Dorrie's tankard, then her mouth, and then she smiled and rubbed her stomach and hugged herself.

Dorrie nodded and Dawn was glad to see her smile. "The cider does warm me, though I thought nothing would take the dreaded chill from my bones. It is amazing how when I watch you speak with your hands that I can truly understand what you're saying."

Dawn rolled her finger over and over in front of her mouth.

Dorrie giggled. "You talk a lot. That's funny."

Dawn lifted the bucket of water now dark from the mud she had washed off Dorrie and went to the door to empty it.

"Let me do that," Dorrie said but Dawn shook her head before the woman could move.

Dawn tugged at her wet garments.

"Oh, I suppose you're right. You're still wet while

I'm finally dry and warm. You must fill the bucket again so that I can help you wash up and slip into dry, warm garments."

Dawn nodded, unlatched the door and lightning struck just as she swung it open. It pierced the distant ground and electrified the sky outlining the dark figure bearing down on her cottage while another figure followed behind him.

She dropped the bucket outside and hurried back into the cottage, leaving the door open. Not doubting in the least that if she didn't, Cree would break it down. She rushed Dorrie out of the chair and brazenly took a protective stance in front of her.

"Oh my God, he's here isn't he?" Dorrie said her voice trembling. And she reached out and grasped Dawn's hand tightly, as if by holding onto her, she could save her from Cree's wrath.

Dawn kept her eyes on the open door. She did not rescue Dorrie only to see her returned to the stocks. How she would prevent it, she did not know. She only knew that she would stand her ground against Cree, for she did not believe Cree would do her harm.

Dawn heard Dorrie gasp behind her when Cree bowed his head to enter the cottage, the door not tall enough to accommodate his height and his shoulders so wide that they scraped the door frame. His leather tunic dripped rainwater as did his wet hair that appeared as black-as-night and his face wore such a threatening scowl that it had Dorrie inching closer to Dawn.

Dawn raised her chin determined to see Dorrie kept safe and then Elwin entered the cottage and Dawn's resolve suffered a blow. He was here to take Dorrie to the stocks and how could she, one voiceless woman, stop the large warrior from doing so?

"I do not know what you think you are doing," Cree said in a tone so cold that a chill circled the room. "But she,"— he pointed to Dorrie— "goes back to the stocks now. And you will answer to me for your insolence."

Dawn did not know what made her do it, perhaps it was all she had suffered through lately, or perhaps she was simply tired of constant threats and no longer cared what happened to her. Whatever the reason it didn't matter, her hands were moving before she could stop them.

She turned slightly, pointed at Dorrie, then to the door, and then she tapped her chest hard and pointed to the door.

Cree's eyes narrowed. "Are you telling me that if Dorrie goes to the stocks so do you?"

Dawn gave a hard nod.

Cree walked over to her, and Dawn moved quickly to shield Dorrie completely.

"You dare give me an ultimatum?"

Dawn nodded again and her hands started moving fast... too fast.

"Damn," Cree said annoyed and grabbed her wrists. "Slow down, I cannot understand you."

"Dawn, are you all right?"

She peered past Cree's wide shoulders and was stunned, though relieved, to see Lila.

Cree released her wrists and turned. "Tell me what she says."

Lila bowed her head and approached as Dawn sent her a nod to let her know that she was fine. Lila stopped beside Dawn, her eyes turning wide at the sight of Dorrie standing behind her friend.

Dawn didn't wait, her hands started moving and

Lila started interpreting. "Dorrie has been punished enough—"

"One day in the stocks is not punishment enough." Cree's brisk interruption had Lila inching a bit further away from him.

Dawn slapped her chest and began gesturing, and Lila hesitantly interpreted. "Let me finish."

Cree looked ready to strangle her, and this time Dorrie and Lila both inched further away from Cree and Dawn.

"What is she saying?" Cree asked, Dawn's gestures appearing as if she was chastising him.

Lila was quick to talk. "She says that Dorrie cannot be left out in a thunderstorm. She will get sick and die."

That brought tears to Dorrie's eyes.

"She says that Dorrie did not harm her that badly that she deserves to die and she, Dawn, could not live with knowing that she had been the cause of her death."

"I am sorry, so sorry," Dorrie said. "I truly did not know anyone would harm Dawn. I did not know the warrior who approached me, though he made it seem like I did. He told me his name and still I didn't remember him. He was insistent that I give Dawn the message, and he promised me,"— she hesitated a moment— "a night of fun if I did."

Dawn gestured again and Lila spoke. "It is not her fault. You cannot punish her for this."

Cree took a step closer to Dawn and brought his face to within an inch of hers. "I can punish her for no reason at all if I so choose."

Dorrie started crying.

Dawn poked him in the chest, and then made a gesture.

Lila remained silent and Cree did not take his eyes off Dawn when he threatened more than ordered, "Tell me what she said."

Lila did as she was told, though her voice trembled as she said, "She wants to know if you have a heart."

His dark eyes turned so cold and empty that Dawn grew frightened and took a step back. She didn't get far. His hand snapped out and grabbed hold of her wrist.

Cree didn't take his eyes off Dawn as he spoke. "Sloan, take Lila home and Elwin take Dorrie to her cottage, and she is not to leave it until I say otherwise."

"I won't, my lord, I won't," Dorrie said her head bowed as she slipped past Cree.

Lila hesitated, fear for her friend's fate evident in her wide eyes. Sloan stepped forward and tugged at her arm for her to follow. She reluctantly went with him, though her eyes never left Dawn until Sloan shut the door behind them.

Cree yanked Dawn closer, planting her hand hard against his chest. "You want to know if I have a heart—I don't. There is nothing there. It is empty. I feel nothing and care for no one. And it would be wise for you to remember who you deal with... a *heartless* warrior."

Dawn could not believe that Cree had no heart, perhaps a silent one, one that never had the chance to be heard... voiceless like her. But her hand felt no thump, no beat, no life, and she shivered.

"Damn it," Cree growled angry that she had paid his words no heed and angry that she was chilled. "Didn't I tell you to get rid of these rags?" He grabbed her blouse and ripped it down the middle. He did the same to her worn skirt, and then ripped the torn garments off her body, leaving her to stand naked, except for her boots, in front of him.

Dawn was too shocked to move, though not too shocked for her body to quiver and it wasn't from feeling chilled.

Cree stepped closer, his leather tunic brushing the tips of her nipples and hardening them in an instant while gooseflesh prickled her bare skin.

"My word is law, and you will obey it."

There was nothing left for her to do but nod.

"Stay as you are," he ordered and turned and went to the door.

She wondered what he was doing when he opened it and stepped outside. She found out soon enough when he returned with a bucket of rainwater.

He placed it on the table. "Clean yourself."

Surely, he did not intend for her to wash in front of him, but she learned quickly enough that he had no intentions of going anywhere when he removed his leather tunic and slipped off his black shirt beneath.

"What do you wait for? *Wash*," he ordered.

She could not stop her hands from shaking as she reached for the cloth that she had hung to dry by the fire. She told herself to be brave that he had seen her naked when they were in the hut together. But this was different, she argued with herself. The hut was dark with barely enough light for them to see each other. Here the room was aglow with the hearth's light, and her naked body was clearly visible to him.

And worse... he didn't take his eyes off her. They roamed over every inch of her as if he was inspecting her and determining her worth.

Hurry and be done with it, she admonished

herself. Her hands continued to shake as she dipped the cloth in the rainwater and began to scrub her body. The rainwater was cold and she could not stop from shivering as she scrubbed the dirt off her body. She worked fast not only wanting to be done so that she could don her garments, but to warm herself against the chill that felt as if it was seeping into her bones.

She undid the ties and slipped off her boots before bending over to wash her legs. She made sure to turn so that her back was to the hearth. Her breasts hung exposed, but it was better than having her bare backside facing him.

The more he watched her the more it unnerved her. But then she supposed this was her punishment for freeing Dorrie, too humiliate her by making her tend herself while he watched.

She shivered again and turned to face the hearth needing the fire's warmth.

She felt his presence behind her before his hand settled on her shoulder.

"Your back needs washing."

He could not mean to wash her back. But when she tried to turn, he squeezed her shoulder to still her.

"Stay as you are."

His stern command froze her, and she stiffened when she felt him rub the cloth over her back. When he dipped the cloth lower, running it over her backside much slower than was necessary, her body betrayed her, sending a fit of tingles rushing between her legs.

Oh lord, she was sinful for responding to his touch. Whatever was the matter with her? He had told her he had no heart. He did not feel or care. He did not care now. He was punishing her and in more ways than one. She had never tasted passion until he had touched her, and now she found that she wanted to taste more... but at what price?

She stiffened again when he ran the cloth down her legs, though gratefully he did not linger on them. A sigh rose in her chest, though remained locked there when she heard the cloth splash in the bucket. He was done.

Her relief was short-lived when he began to towel her back dry. And her tingles grew in leaps and bounds as he lingered on her backside.

By the time he finished, she was throbbing between her legs, and she was relieved when he handed her the towel and said, "Finish."

She quickly ran the towel across her chest, though his stern command froze her hand.

"Turn around."

Dawn did as ordered and turned to face him to finish drying herself. This time she could not avoid his eyes. It was impossible to, they gleamed with passion. And the sizeable swell beneath his leggings only served to confirm his craving.

That he would have her this night was obvious, but would it be as before? Would he spill his seed outside her, fearful of getting her with child? Would it always be that way when he took her? Would she never know the feel of him buried inside her?

"Your need is as great as mine," he said and her cheeks flushed red knowing passion gleamed as brightly in her eyes as it did in his.

She reached for the blanket draped over the chair at the table, suddenly feeling much too vulnerable standing naked in front of him.

"Don't," he ordered sternly. "I want you naked."

She shivered and felt herself grow wet. How could she want this man, who claimed not to care, so badly? He would take her and satisfy his need and that was all, but then wasn't her need being satisfied as well? And what did she expect from a mighty warrior like Cree anyway?

Love.

The thought startled her. Without a heart how could he love anyone, though if his heart was merely silent was there hope? She learned how to speak without a voice. Could Cree's heart learn to be heard? Or was she being foolish? After all how did one teach the devil to love?

Chapter Twenty-three

Cree walked over to Dawn, stopping barely an inch away from her. He ran his thumb over her lips as if readying them for his kiss. But he didn't kiss her. His hand drifted down to her neck and squeezed it gently before drifting to her shoulder and kneading it with strong fingers.

He did not understand his unrelenting need for this woman. He had never wanted a woman as much as he wanted Dawn. It was like a gnawing hunger in his soul that he feared would never be appeased.

All he wanted was to take her and bury himself deep inside her until he was lost in exquisite pleasure. Even then though, he worried that it might not be enough. He feared he would want her again and again. He felt completely out of control when it came to her and that did not sit well with him.

"You belong to me," he whispered.

She stared at him for a fraction of a moment before nodding, amazed by the thought that sprung to mind.

And you belong to me.

Without a doubt she belonged to him, everyone and thing in Dowell belonged to him. But that she should think that he belonged to her was utter madness. And yet the thought nagged at her that Cree belonged to her and no amount of reasoning seemed to matter. It was a thought strongly rooted in her and, try as she might, she could not uproot it. It had dug deep and would not let go.

"You know I will have you this night."

She laid her hand on his arm and pressed one finger against his hard muscles.

"You remember," he murmured. "This is good. One for yes and two for no." He took hold of her chin. "Tell me. I want you to gesture it. Do you want me?"

She thought he held his breath waiting for her answer and for the first time in many years she wished she had a voice. He wanted to hear her say it of her own accord, and she answered him. She pressed a finger against the hard muscle in his forearm.

His chest expanded with a breath and in the next second he lifted her up into his arms, and he carried her into the other room. He yanked the wool blankets back before placing her down on the bed, and then he quickly slipped off his boots and yanked off his leggings, tossing them carelessly to the floor.

He was a sight to behold. Hard muscle everywhere even between his legs. And she shivered wondering over the wisdom of her actions.

He stopped, his one knee resting on the bed. "Do you fear me, Dawn?"

At one time she feared him beyond reason, but now? She reached for his hand and turned it over pressing one finger against his palm, waited, and then pressed twice against his palm.

"Yes and no?" he asked perplexed.

This time she nodded.

He lowered himself down alongside her, their bodies touching, but he did not touch her. "You should fear me in some things, but I never want you to fear me when we are intimate."

His hand came up then to gently touch the bruise on her face. "Does this hurt?"

She turned her hand from side to side.

"Sometimes?"

She nodded.

He leaned down and kissed the corner of her mouth near the bruised area. "Does that hurt?"

She shook her head.

He brushed his lips across her mouth. "And that?"

She shook her head again, aching for more, so much more from him.

He took hold of her chin then and his lips took hers with such fervor that she thought for a moment she would climax, but he stopped abruptly.

"And that?" he whispered against her mouth. "Does that hurt you?"

She pressed her finger against his arm twice, and then twice more, and then twice more.

He laughed. She had never heard him laugh and it made her smile.

"Then you want more?"

She pressed her finger to his arm at least seven times and he laughed again, and she liked the sound of it.

He kissed her again feverishly, and she responded just as zealously. His hand roamed down to her breast while their tongues sparred like warriors hungry for victory. He cupped one and ran his thumb across her nipple, teasing it until it was rock hard. Then he tore his mouth away from hers to settle it over her hard nipple and tease it unmercifully with his tongue.

She gripped his one wrist and squeezed hard hoping it would translate into the moan that was trapped inside her that she so badly wanted to release.

He went to work on her other breast while his hand made a slow descent down her body as if making certain to touch every inch of her, claim every inch of her, mark every inch of her, and he did just that.

She was wanton and wicked for loving what he was doing to her, for what he was making her feel, for the pleasure he was giving her. But then the devil knew the sins of the flesh, and she was succumbing to each and every one of them.

When his hand moved to cup between her legs, she bucked against him. His mouth quickly descended on hers again and as his tongue charged into her mouth, his finger hastily slipped between her legs and right inside her.

She gasped, though it could not be heard, and he pressed his mouth more firmly against hers while his tongue took command. He inserted another finger inside her while his thumb settled over her sensitive nub and began to stroke it.

He set a rhythm then that had her moving with him and it wasn't long before she was ready to explode in a blinding climax. She gripped his wrist harder, tugging at it as she did.

He drew a breath when his lips left hers, then rested his brow to hers. "You're so wet and tight. I cannot wait to lose myself in you."

His words fueled her own passion, and her hand moved to grip his upper arm. The muscles were rigid, and she held onto them for dear life as he moved over her. His fingers slipped out of her and while disappointed, she was more eager for him to slip inside her. She had never felt so alive. It was as if she pulsed with a life she never knew existed. And she was greedy for more.

He rose over her, his hands on either side of her head. "Keep your hand on my arm. I like the way you squeeze it hard. " He spread her legs with his knee. "You will let me know if I hurt you."

It was an order, not a request, and Dawn nodded.

"You are so beautiful," he whispered.

Only her mother had ever told her that she was beautiful. She was so startled by his words that her mouth dropped open and as it did he slipped inside her, just a nudge at first, and then he pushed hard into her. She gasped deep in her chest and her hand squeezed his arm so hard she thought she would break it.

"Are you all right?" he demanded not moving.

Surprisingly, she felt wonderful and smiled.

He smiled back at her and kissed her quickly. "You're going to feel a whole lot better soon." And he began to move, pulling out, driving in, and Dawn matched his tempo wanting him deeper and deeper inside her.

"Damn," he mumbled throwing his head back as he drove in and out of her.

She didn't realize it, but her one finger kept tapping his arm over and over and over as if she was screaming yes, yes, yes, at him.

It was the most glorious feeling she had ever experienced and though sinful as it was, she hoped to feel it again and again with Cree... only with Cree.

Soon all thoughts vanished and all she could feel was the immense pleasure building and building until she was on the edge of exploding and seeing Cree's face contorted in pleasurable pain, she knew he felt the same.

Soon, very soon she would burst in fiery climax,

and he would do the same. She would finally feel him spill into her and that would truly join them as one. She felt it. She was coming. Oh lord was she coming. She squeezed his arm tighter and tighter and tighter.

Cree pulled out of her just as she was about to explode, and she deflated in an instant.

He collapsed on top of her, his arms going around her waist and holding her tight as his body shuddered in release.

Dawn wanted to scream, she wanted to cry, and she wanted to beat her fisted hands hard on his back. Why? Why did he do that to her? But she knew the answer. He did not want to take the chance of his seed taking root for fear he would have a child without a voice... like her.

She felt numb, empty, and she moved her hands off him not wanting to touch him, not wanting him to touch her, and not wanting him near her. Not when she was hurting like this.

He placed kisses on her stomach, light delicate ones, before raising his head to look at her. "Are you all right?"

She nodded.

He moved up alongside her and took her in his arms, tucking her against him. He was silent as she lay still in his embrace. She wished that he would go and leave her alone in her misery. To know that he would lie with her, have his way with her, and yet never come inside her tore at her heart. She was there for his enjoyment whenever he wished. She meant nothing more to him than a place to dip his wick—she laughed inwardly. He might dip it, but he had no intentions of extinguishing it inside her. That would be left for the woman he would wed.

"I must go," he said and nuzzled kisses at her neck. "Sleep and I will see you on the morrow.

She nodded and gave his hand a slight squeeze, not wanting him to suspect that she was glad to see him go.

He dressed quickly and, with one last quick kiss, he left the room. She fought back the tears that threatened to overflow. He still had to get his shirt and tunic on, and she did not want him to return and find her in tears. Once she heard the door close, she hopped out of bed, grabbed the soft blue shawl, and wrapped it around her.

She could not bring herself to return to bed, so she sat in front of the hearth, her knees tucked up under her chin and let her tears fall. She was being punished, punished for letting the devil have his way with her and enjoying it, and for thinking that somehow she could get his heart to be silent no more.

11. ~~~

Cree sat alone at a table in front of the hearth in the Great Hall his legs stretched out in front of him staring at the flames. He was only slightly wet, the rain having turned light. It was late and everyone was tucked in bed, if not asleep. He was sure that Sloan had found some willing woman, he always did.

He had thought of spending the night with Dawn. He had actually wanted to, but it would not have been a wise thing to do. He would have made love to her again and probably again before sunrise, he had enjoyed her that much. He had come so hard that he swore it had shivered him down to his soul. And still he had thought about taking her again. He had silently cursed himself for pulling out of her as he came, but what choice did he have. He could not risk her carrying his child. His bride would arrive soon and, hopefully, soon after the wedding she would be with child, and he would have a legitimate heir.

He wondered if he would enjoy his wife in bed as much as he enjoyed Dawn. It didn't matter though. He would have no love for his wife. She would be there to serve a purpose, as Dawn served a purpose.

Then why did he want nothing more than to return to Dawn, make love to her again, and afterwards curl around her and sleep beside her until morning?

Damn. Damn. Damn.

He stood and warned himself to go to his bedchamber and go to sleep. He did not need to complicate the situation any further. It would do no good. His thoughts of her had already aroused him, and he knew he wanted her at least one more time tonight or maybe two more times. With thoughts of different ways he could have Dawn, he left the Great Hall and headed for her cottage.

He opened the door as quietly as possible not wanting to wake her if she should be asleep, though he intended to do just that. He grinned at the thought of raining kisses all over her lovely naked body. He disposed of his clothes before entering the bedchamber and stopped abruptly when he saw her sitting in front of the fire. The way her shoulders shook he knew that she was crying.

Seeing her sitting alone crying silent tears tore at his heart so badly that he wanted to pummel someone with his fists, but then it would be him who deserved the beating for no doubt he was the cause of her tears. He was at a loss at what to do. He rarely dealt with crying women. They were usually pleasurably satiated when he left them, but then he had never taken a woman's virginity.

Was she upset that she had lost it to him? But she had given it willingly. What then could have brought on her tears? The sudden thought was like a punch to his gut. Could he not have pleased her? Had he left her wanting? He had to know.

He called out her name, and she turned wide, shocked, and wet eyes on him.

He immediately went to her, scooped her up in his arms, and carried her to the bed. He sat keeping her on his lap, his arms firmly around her. And damn if he didn't like the way her bottom nestled so perfectly against the hard length of him, growing him even harder.

"What's wrong?" he asked and kissed her gently.

She shook her head.

"That will not do," he said wiping away her tears. "You must tell me."

She swallowed hard and again shook her head.

He burrowed his nose in her hair. "Have I told you how I love the scent of you?"

Love. He loved the scent of her. Was his heart attempting to speak to her?

"I enjoyed making love to you," he whispered and nibbled along her ear. "Did you enjoy it?"

Making love. Was his heart opening? Trying to be heard? She did not need to think on his question, and so she nodded, for she truly had enjoyed *making love* with him that was until...

"I came hard, harder than I ever have. And you?" he gently kissed her bruised eye.

She nodded slowly.

He stared at her and his eyes narrowed. "You nod and yet your finger taps my arm twice."

She turned rigid in his arms. Had she done that? She hadn't realized she did, and she lowered her chin not wanting to look at him, not wanting him to see the truth.

He lifted her chin gently. "You didn't come did you?"

There was no point in lying to him, though she had no intentions of explaining why she hadn't come. She simply shook her head.

"I pulled out of you before you could come, didn't I?"

Her cheeks flushed red and she wanted to fade away. He shouldn't be talking to her this way. They were not husband and wife. And did husbands and wives even dare speak so intimately?

"Listen to me, Dawn," he ordered firmly. "Your pleasure is my pleasure and I will not have you robbing either one of us of it. We must establish a signal that lets me know when you are coming. I had thought by how hard you squeezed my arm that you were in the throes of coming."

He wanted a signal so that he would have time to make sure she climaxed before he pulled out of her. She couldn't help but wonder how it would feel for them to climax together.

Wicked.

She certainly had become wicked, but then the devil had led her astray, and there was no turning back now. She was doomed and no one could save her. She reached up and tugged at his ear.

"That could work," he said and smiled. "Shall we try it?"

He didn't give her a chance to agree. He stood, smiled, dropped her on the bed, and spread her legs.

Oh how she loved his smile, though rare it was, and how happy she was to see him hard and ready. Though he had been that way when he had planted her on his lap and knowing that he wanted her again had sparked her own passion.

He positioned himself between her legs, and then slowly lowered himself over her as he inched his way inside her. "Damn, but you fit as if you were made for me and me alone."

Her heart leaped for joy, not to mention how wet she grew, and her arms wrapped around him, hugging him to her. He moved his mouth over hers for a kiss, and she took hold of it hungry for the taste of him.

He drove into her over and over, though he stopped once to ask her if she was all right, and she smiled and nodded, which had him grinning.

Lord help her, she wanted him as deep inside her as she could get him and instinctively she wrapped her legs around his back and sure enough he sank deeper into her.

Their passion grew, their rhythm turning fast and furious.

Her climax was building even more powerful than before and she could tell that his was as well. And the thought hit her...what if she waited... waited until...

She tightened her legs around him and gripped his arms tightly.

He looked at her and breathlessly asked, "Soon?"

She nodded and tightened her legs around him even more and he moaned driving into her.

She was on the edge again, ready to come, ready to step off and plummet in pleasure. She saw the same in his eyes, felt it in his frantic rhythm, and she bucked hard against him driving him into her hard. And only then did she tug at his ear.

He cried out her name and at that precise moment she knew he was coming, and she stepped off the edge with him.

Chapter Twenty-four

Cree left Dawn just after sunrise. It was rare that he was not out of bed before daylight rose over the land, but today he had a reason to dally, and he had dallied. He had woken wrapped around Dawn. She had been so warm, her skin so soft, and her scent strong with last night's endless lovemaking. He hadn't been able to keep his hands off her and when he touched her she had been so very responsive that he had not wanted to hurry, and he hadn't. And damn if he hadn't found himself exploding with a never-ending pleasure deep inside her.

He wasn't sure how many times they had coupled, though it seemed that each time he woke throughout the night and found himself cocooned around her, he'd grown hard, and then his hands would begin to touch her and all was lost. Whether it was a quick joining or a lingering one, he had burst in a blinding climax.

He smiled, though it fast turned into a scowl, thinking what little control he had over himself when it came to Dawn. He had cursed himself, after he finally had gotten a breath, for coming inside her and had cautioned himself not to do it again. But he had paid no heed or perhaps it was that once inside her, he was lost... lost in pure pleasure. His scowl deepened as he entered the keep and made his way to the Great Hall where Sloan was talking with a group of warriors.

"Out for an early morning walk?" Sloan asked his grin much too wide to Cree's liking.

"Looking to see why you have yet to dispatch the men to find the culprit you failed to find yesterday," Cree said as he approached the group.

The warriors bowed their head and stepped aside, clearing a path for Cree to Sloan who had not stopped grinning.

"I've given final instructions to the men," Sloan said. "They were just about to take their leave."

Cree looked to each one of them. "I expect results. This is your home now, and I intend to see it kept safe for everyone."

The men nodded vigorously.

"Go and find who threatens our home," Cree ordered and the men took off.

Sloan shook his head. "They would follow you to hell."

"They already have."

"Drink and food for, my lord," Sloan called out to one of servant lassies who smiled sweetly at him, bobbed her head, and hurried off.

Cree went to the table by the hearth to sit and stretch his legs out, recalling a similar scene last night and the decision he had made. Though control for his never-ending desire for Dawn remained a concern, he could not say that he had regretted returning to her.

Sloan joined him, stopping to cast an inquisitive glance over Cree before claiming a seat opposite him at the table. "You had a good night."

Cree didn't turn around to face him. "Good enough." He would not discuss what had transpired between Dawn and him with Sloan. It was private, meant for Dawn and him alone and the thought surprised him. Sloan and he had shared numerous tales of women, but he had no want to share Dawn with him. Dawn was his and only his.

"Dawn's friend Lila talks nonstop. She spoke much about Dawn while I saw her home."

That had Cree turning and swinging his long legs over the bench to face Sloan. "Tell me."

Sloan waited until the two servants placed pitchers of hot cider, ale, and platters heaped with food on the table, only then did he answer Cree.

"She told me that Dawn is the bravest woman she knows. That she never let her affliction get in her way and that she has endured many taunts and endless ignorance with resolve and strength. Lila says that Dawn speaks better with her hands than most people do with their voices. That she is a loyal friend and has a caring heart and hadn't that been proven with Dawn freeing Dorrie, a woman who has taunted Dawn endlessly. It is obvious that she is worried about her friend."

"Dawn is far safer now under my protection than she has ever been," Cree said as if he waited for Sloan to challenge otherwise.

Sloan looked ready to take the challenge, though seemed to think better of it. "Dawn is a unique woman."

"You're right about that," Cree agreed and appeared to relax, reaching for a piece of bread. "She is unlike any woman I have ever met."

"And we've met many along the way," Sloan said, grinning and raising his tankard.

Cree joined him in the toast to their past conquests and realized he was toasting, with no regret, the end of them. He wanted only Dawn, no other. The surprising thought did not disturb him. It actually gave him a sense of indescribable pleasure.

"What are your plans for Dorrie? Back in the stocks?"

"Ask it the way you truly want to ask it," Cree demanded with a glint of anger in his dark eyes.

"Not how I want to, but how others will perceive it if you do not return Dorrie to the stocks."

"And it should matter to me what others think? Has it ever mattered before?"

Sloan seemed to give it thought, and then shrugged. "You're right. It never did matter to you. But it is different now. You now hold a title; you are the Earl of Carrick."

"Not officially. Not until I wed Gerwan's daughter."

"All the more reason to act like—"

"The men I despise?" Cree spat. "The men I pillaged and murdered for? I earned this land unlike them, but I will not treat my people with such careless disregard as they do."

"You will allow Dawn's blatant disregard for your orders to go unpunished?"

Remembering her silent tears had Cree saying, "She's been punished enough."

Sloan looked ready to argue, but Cree's dark scowl quickly stopped any retort that was on his tongue. "As you wish," he said respectfully. "Dorrie is to be allowed out of her cottage?"

Cree nodded. "See that she goes back to doing her share, and then some, for at least a week, though she is to be confined to her cottage, after her chores are done. Turbett can always use extra help. Send her there. Let her see what Dawn had to contend with."

Sloan nodded. "When do you wish to hear

grievances and permissions?"

"Not for a couple of weeks. Let the villagers have time to see the way things will go and learn that they can speak if something seems unfair or troubling without threat of harm."

The two men spent the next hour discussing what issues needed to be addressed over the next few days.

When they finished Cree asked, "Is Elsa set in her cottage?"

"She is and has two village women eager to help and learn from her. I'm still searching for someone to oversee the keep servants. Someone who eventually will report to your wife since the running of the keep will be her domain."

Cree stood. "I'm sure you'll find someone. I'll be going with William to the site where the new castle will be built. See that six warriors are made ready to accompany me in an hour's time."

"They'll be waiting," Sloan said. "What of Dawn? Is she still to have a guard on her at all times? Is she restricted as to where she may go?"

"Keep Elwin on Dorrie and shift the men around to watch over Dawn. And find the damn culprit who shot that arrow so we can lay this matter to rest."

Cree left Sloan to see to the day's matters. He hurried to his bed chamber pleased to see that a fresh bucket of water waited for him. He stripped off his leather tunic and black shirt and proceeded to wash himself. He could not abide being dirty. He had spent his younger years in such squalor and hunger that he swore he would do anything never to live that way again, and he had. He only wished his mother had survived long enough to benefit from his wealth and power. She had literally worked herself to death in order to see that he and his sister survived, she being their only support, his da having died from a fall when Cree was barely three years.

He had been relieved that at least on his mum's deathbed he could promise her that he would keep his sister Wintra safe. She was only nine years when their mum died ten years ago. She had never told him who Wintra's father was, but she didn't have to. He remembered all too well the day she had come in from the fields bruised and battered. He had been ready to kill the man who had harmed her, but his mum had insisted she had taken a fall and that she would be fine. She had protected him that day with her lies, but he had never forgotten. And when she began to grow with child, his suspicions had been confirmed.

He had never told Wintra. As far as she knew they shared the same da. It had been an unspoken agreement between he and his mum, and Cree never intended to break it. He had placed Wintra in an abbey following their mum's death and paid the Abbess a goodly stipend to see to her care and teach her what she needed to know to wed well. When all was settled with his title, he would take his sister out of the abbey and bring her to live with him. Then he would arrange a good marriage for her with a good man.

When he was finally dressed in clean garments, dark brown leggings and shirt with a chestnut brown leather tunic and his boots wrapped securely with leather ties, he made his way to Elsa's cottage. He did glance to see that a guard had been posted at Dawn's cottage, though he hadn't doubted there would be. Sloan never failed to carry out his orders, whether he agreed with him or not.

The sun shined brightly and there was less of a chill in the autumn air, though that wouldn't last. Winter would be upon them soon enough, and he wanted the people and land prepared. Sloan would see to it. He was good at seeing that things got done with little to no problems. And if a problem arose, then Cree would step in and settle it. Sloan and he had fast become friends after Cree had saved his life. He had come upon Cree trying to defend himself against a band of motley thieves. And though he had been doing an excellent job at keeping them at bay, there was just too many of them, and he would have eventually been defeated. Sloan had joined his crew that day and had been an asset ever since.

Cree came upon Elsa's cottage not far from the keep. He had had the men repair and add onto an existing cottage that had long been neglected. The men continued to work on it, most having volunteered for the job, knowing the importance of getting it finished before the winter set in. Elsa had treated many of the men and saved many of their lives so they wanted to make certain that their healer had a good sound place to do her healing.

Elsa was another one he had saved from death, only she had been about to be burned for being a witch. A sickness had wiped out almost an entire village where she had been a healer, and the remaining few people had blamed her for their loss. A hefty purse had stopped the byre that was about to be torched. And there had not been a day that he or his men had regretted it, though his men had grumbled at first about a witch joining them. It had only taken one day of Elsa saving two men who they had all thought were at death's door for the men to change their minds. Now they all protected her with their lives.

"My lord," Elsa said with a bob of her head when Cree entered the cottage. Two other women, one skinny and the other wide in the hips bobbed their heads as well and kept their eyes downcast. "Is this a visit or are you in need of care?"

Some thought Elsa too blunt, but he liked that she always got right to the point as did he. "A private talk, Elsa."

"As you wish, my lord." She turned to the two women, snatching up a basket covered with a cloth on the table. "Ann, Lara, please take this to Lila and Paul and see if all goes well with the new babe."

Lara took the basket and with another respectful bob to Cree the two women hurried out of the cottage with what appeared to be relief.

"As always, Elsa, your cottage smells delicious," Cree said taking a seat at the table not far from the hearth.

Elsa beamed with pride. "Freshly baked bread for those in need of care. Would you like some?"

"I'm not in need of care."

"We can all use some care now and again," she said and joined him at the table. "Dawn, though, is one you would think needs much care when in truth she seems to give care to others."

Sometimes Cree wondered if Elsa was a witch. She possessed an uncanny sense of knowing. "You know that I came to speak with you about her."

"Tongues are busy this morning talking about what she did for Dorrie last night. Dawn is a brave woman."

"Bravery and foolishness are closely linked."

Elsa laughed. "Aye, it sometimes takes a fool to be brave?" Her laughter faded. "Then there are those who are born brave."

"Or those made brave by circumstance."

"Like Dawn," Elsa said shaking her head. "To be born without a voice, to never utter a single sound is beyond comprehension to me, and yet she has learned to communicate with others and to live with integrity. A remarkable feat."

"She will never have a voice?" Cree asked not hearing the hopefulness in his tone.

"It is unlikely since she was born without one."

"Why is someone born that way?"

"Most people would say that it is God's will. But who is to truly say why?"

Cree asked the question he hadn't thought would be relevant to him before last night. "Will she pass her affliction onto her own children?"

"I could not say for sure. Not having a voice, not being able to make a single sound is rare. Dawn is the only person I have met with this affliction that cannot at least grunt or groan. But having birthed many babes, I can say there is much that parents pass on to their off springs. So if you wonder if there is a chance that Dawn could give birth to a child who would have no voice, then I would have to say that there is a chance, rare as it is."

Cree cursed himself a million times over. He should have never allowed his passion to rule, never allowed himself to empty into her over and over. He could not take the chance again unless...

"Is there anything a woman can take to prevent getting with child?"

His question didn't surprise Elsa; he hadn't thought it would. She no doubt expected it, and he hoped that perhaps this was one of those times that her witch ways could help."

"There is, but if the woman is already with child and ingests the concoction, then she chances aborting the babe."

He hadn't expected his stomach to clench as if someone had hold of it and was twisting it unmercifully. And that disturbed him. He had spent only last night with her, he reasoned with himself, one night. But how many times had they coupled? Still it was only last night, and if she took something now... his stomach clenched again.

"Shall I speak with Dawn?" Elsa asked.

"That would be good," he said and stood, not wanting to discuss it any further and left without saying another word. His one and only thought... would she even want to bear his babe?

The horses were waiting at the front of the keep. William was there as well sitting atop his horse. Six of his men were also mounted and ready to go. He was glad for this time away from the village, time away to free his thoughts of Dawn, for she was on his mind much too often.

Cree mounted his stallion and from his impatient prance he could tell the steed was ready for a good ride.

Just like Dawn had been last night.

He silently cursed the thought and explicit visions it brought with it.

He gave a wave, anxious to leave, and they rode through the center of the village, the villagers' heads bowing in respect as they moved out of the way of the horses. He was surprised to catch sight of Dawn, no doubt headed for Lila's cottage. How had she gotten passed the guard? The window again? She had stopped like the others and bowed her head waiting for him to pass. He was annoyed that she had slipped past the guard, though he was more annoyed that the sight of her had grown him hard much too quickly.

Without thought to his actions, he spurred his horse and rode directly at her. He didn't stop as he came within reach of her. He leaned over the side of his horse, swung his arm out, and scooped her up around the waist, planting her in front of him on the horse.

Chapter Twenty-five

Dawn was too shocked to do anything but throw her arms around Cree's neck as he planted her sideways in front of him on the stallion. Her breath was locked somewhere in her chest, and it took her a moment or two to find it and expel it. In the meantime her grip got tighter around his neck.

With a slight shift, he tucked her solidly against him, his arm around her waist keeping her firmly in place. His chest was a wall of muscle and while rock-hard, it was comfortable to rest against. And she could certainly attest to that since she had rested against it most of last night.

She was relieved that with her face tucked against him that he could not see her cheeks heat from the intimate memories. Never had she thought she would enjoy coupling so very much. Never had she thought that she'd respond so readily to Cree's touch. And it seemed that the more he touched her the more she responded, and the more she wanted him. Whether it was his arm around her waist as it was now or a gentle touch to her arm, or a light kiss or the brush of his arm against hers, passion flamed. And she wondered if she would ever get enough of him.

"Are you all right?" he asked.

Dawn was beginning to realize that he always sounded as if he demanded. It seemed to be his way, and she knew she must learn not to let it bother her.

She answered yes by pressing once against his arm.

"How did you get passed the guard? Let me rephrase that... did you climb out the window?"

She smiled, once again relieved that he could not see her face and pressed once on his arm.

"I suppose I'm going to have to have that window boarded up."

She shook her head vehemently as she raised it off his chest. The shaking slowed, then stopped when her eyes met his. How could they be so dark and cold, yet so heated and lustful? His eyes warned and yet promised, and her body quivered at the thought.

"You are not a prisoner. You may go where you like and the guard will accompany you."

She tapped her chest and shook her hand.

"You may think you don't need a guard, but I think you do, so you shall have a guard at all times until I say otherwise."

There was no point in arguing with him. He would have his way no matter what, and she much preferred not to have the window boarded shut. She already felt a prisoner; a boarded window would only make it worse.

She acquiesced with a slow nod.

Cree felt her relax in his arms. He did not know what had made him scoop her up and bring her along. He only knew that he had not been able to resist the urge, and he was glad he hadn't and that she was now here with him.

Of course growing hard against her as he was doing did not help, but then he was already thinking of getting her alone and making love to her. He had thought he had had his fill last night, but his urge for her was like that of a starving man. And the more he had her, the more he wanted her.

He slipped his hand beneath her breast and cupped it, giving it a firm squeeze and whispered, "I want to feel you grind beneath me again."

Her body grew taut and she cast her eyes down.

"Look at me," he ordered and her eyes shot up. He inhaled sharply. "Passion burns in you as it does me."

He was right, and it made her feel all the more a wicked woman. What was the matter with her, craving Cree the way she did? Did she forget that the devil was tempting her soul? Nothing good would come of their lust. He would never wed her, and one day he would leave her, and then what? But at the moment what choice did she have? He was the new Earl of Carrick, and she could not deny him, and Lord forgive her, she did not want to.

She pressed her finger once against his arm, holding it there longer than necessary, letting him know that he was right.

"You belong to me, Dawn. I and I alone will touch you. And I alone will decide your fate."

Her stomach churned at the thought that her fate lied in Cree's hands, and she shifted slightly as if putting a bit of a distance between them would make a difference. She winced, though silently, when she accidentally settled against his bulge.

"You're sore."

She ignored his curt tone and nodded.

"You will go see Elsa when we return."

Another terse remark she ignored and nodded to appease him. She would go see Elsa when she felt it was necessary or at least put it off until he forced it upon her. Where did this feeling of defiance come from? She had always obeyed without question. She had had little choice. It had been either that or suffer harsh consequences. Did she think that Cree wouldn't punish her? Or was she finally feeling her own strength and relying on it?

She looked around her, wondering where they were headed and her heart gave a catch at the beauty of the land that stretched out around them. The rolling hills gave way to meadows falling dormant in preparation of winter. The last of the heather was fading fast and some of the trees were already barren while the pine remained ever green.

Her mum had traveled over this land with her when she had been only a babe. She had made the journey alone, her da having died before she was born. Her mum had told her that she had gone in search of a better life for them both. And life had been fairly good until Colum had arrived. Now there was Cree.

She tilted her head to peek up at him and found him staring down at her.

"You have something to say?"

It pleased her that he spoke with her as if she had a voice. And yes, she had much to say to him, but not here, not now... in time. She nodded and pointed ahead, then shrugged.

"You wonder where we go."

She nodded and smiled, pleased that he understood her.

"You saw the drawings for the keep that I intend to start building in the spring. We go to where that keep will be located. William has come along as well so that he and I can go over some details."

Her hands immediately began moving.

"Slow down," he said with a smile, "so that I may understand you."

Her gestures slowed, though more so because of his smile. He was smiling more often when he was with her and that pleased her as did the fact that he seemed all the more handsome when he smiled, if that was possible. Or perhaps it was more than that, perhaps on these rare occasions his heart got a chance to shine through, which might suggest that his soul wasn't as evil as everyone believed.

He followed her gestures more easily than he had expected. "You would like to see the drawings again and hear what William has to say?" Her nod had him continuing. "Since I intend to keep you by my side while we are away from the keep, I would say that is a distinct possibility."

They arrived at the location a short time later and Cree dismounted. Then he reached up, took hold of her waist and slipped her off the horse. He did not release her right away and Dawn could have sworn he was going to kiss her. And she was disappointed when he didn't, but then here and now in front of his men was not the time or place for such intimacy. The sensible thought did nothing to quell her desire. Her lips ached, her stomach fluttered and that damn tingle rushed to tease between her legs.

If she was not already speechless, she would have been struck so when he took her hand in his and tugged for her to follow beside him. His hand was warm, his grip strong and a tad possessive, as if he intended to never let her go. And foolish as the thought was, it brought a smile to her face and lightened her heart.

Dawn noticed that his men fanned out, without any instructions from Cree, and formed a perimeter around the area. William rushed up to meet Cree, rolled parchments flapping under his arm.

"My lord," he said with a brief bow. "Once we discuss further options today, I will be able to complete my list and if I have your permission, I would like to take my leave before winter sets in so that I may locate the necessary craftsmen and purchase the necessary material for work to begin in the spring."

"If all proves acceptable you may leave before the first snow falls," Cree agreed.

With her hand still firmly in Cree's she walked along with the two men as they talked, but her interest soon drifted to the view as they followed up the rise. And once they reached the top of the bluff her eyes turned wide. The view was breath-catching. You could see Ben Loyal in the distance and beneath the bluff flowed the Kyle of Tongue. With water so close, any village built here would prosper.

"The river will make it easy to bring the materials and furnishings by boat and is perfect for the trade you have in mind. I have drawings for the port you spoke about," William said rifling through his drawings.

Trade? Port? Cree certainly had plans. What other plans did he have? A wife? Children to pass all of this onto?

Dawn needed distance from what she was hearing, and what it would mean to her, and tried to slip free of Cree's grasp. He looked with questioning eyes at her, and she pointed to an area of large stones. He nodded his consent, though he released her hand with some reluctance.

There was a slight breeze on the bluff and, though the sun was strong today, there was a chill in the air. She wrapped her dark green wool cloak around her and was glad for the dark blue wool skirt and white linen blouse she had donned this morning. She had forgone the wool leggings not liking the feel of them, preferring her legs bare beneath her garments. It afforded her the opportunity to remove her boots and let her feet enjoy the feel of the grass or the rich soil when ripe for planting.

But she had no thought to remove her boots when she sat on the flat stones. Her thoughts had lingered as to who would be by Cree's side when the castle was finished, the village built, the port flourishing. And why did she let the thought disturb her? He would never wed her. She could bring nothing to a marriage. And why would she even think such a foolish thought.

She, like the other villagers, served Cree. Each and every one of them did as he dictated and that would always be the way of it. Feeling maudlin, she found a rock with a pointed edge and began to draw in the dirt.

Cree watched her as he listened and spoke with William. Something had changed within Dawn when they had reached the top of the bluff. Her enthusiasm for the castle drawings had waned, and she seemed upset, though he could not fathom why.

William had more sketching he wished to do while here, and Cree had hoped to walk with Dawn to a small secluded area where they could enjoy a moment of intimate privacy. Very intimate privacy. Deep, penetrating intimate privacy. He grew hard thinking about it.

Cree asked William more questions and made some suggestions to the port drawing. It was essential that the port be built. He had plans, big plans and the

King had agreed with him. And the King knew that he would see the plans done. Another reason he had awarded him this land and arranged a marriage. One he had no choice but to enter into.

He rarely heard the thud of his heart so when he did, he found it odd. It was almost as if something was awakening in him, and he wasn't happy about it. He did what he had to do, and he did it well and did so because he did not allow himself to care.

He had stopped caring the day he had buried his mother and had placed his sister in the convent. And with each visit to his sister, he had grown more distant, and she to him until... it had been four years since he'd last seen her. And the thought suddenly disturbed him.

William rolled up the maps and cast a nod at Dawn. "She has a remarkable talent. May I see what she is drawing, my lord?"

He was just as curious, so they both walked over and peered down.

"Good Lord, that is fantastic," William said startling Dawn, though she smiled at his compliment. "My lord, if she does such an amazing drawing of you in the dirt I cannot phantom what talent she would have with a brush. You should have her paint a portrait of you to hang in the Great Hall of the keep. I would be only too pleased, while on my journey, to gather the necessary items she would need to paint and draw."

Dawn cast hopeful eyes on Cree. She would love to have the materials to draw with and to paint. They had been luxuries out of her reach, but now and again she would dream.

"We will see," Cree said and his heart thudded again when her hopeful expression faded. And he scowled. "Finish, William, we leave shortly."

William bowed his head and hurried off.

"Come," Cree said holding his hand out to Dawn while casting one last look at his image. Stern? Authoritative? Stalwart? This is how he appeared to her?

She took his hand with reluctance and was surprised when he issued orders to his men in French. At that very moment she was grateful to her mum for having taught her to understand French and Latin as well.

Cree ordered his men not to disturb him unless necessary, which had Dawn wondering his intentions, though the grins on the warriors' faces had them assuming the obvious, and she blushed with embarrassment. But didn't everyone know by now that she was Cree's woman?

They entered the woods that bordered the north side of the bluff, and Cree walked with such confidence that it was obvious he was familiar with the land. If that was so, then he had to have come here often or could he have lived his younger years in this area?

There was so much she didn't know about Cree. And what she did know, she had learned through gossiping tongues. Some of the tales were proving true while others had proved false. Who truly was this man that she had willingly surrendered to and who was stealing her heart a little bit at a time?

He stopped abruptly a few feet into the woods and turned to her. "What's wrong?"

She scrunched her brow, not quite understanding.

"You had been thrilled about talking with William and looking over the plans for the castle and suddenly you sulk off to sit on a rock and draw a portrait of me. So what is wrong?"

Her eyes widened startled that he had noticed and that it had disturbed him enough to ask her about it.

"You are surprised that I noticed." He reached up and stroked her cheek with his finger, then ran it faintly across her lips. "I notice everything about you."

The tingles emerged in a gentle throb between her legs.

"Your dark eyes glow with lust every time I touch you, and it makes me want to touch you even more, but first... what upset you?"

That he cared enough to pursue an answer warmed her heart, but she could never tell him that it hurt her to know that another would share his new home with him and that she would be left on her own, alone.

He slipped his finger under her chin and forced her head up. She hadn't even realized that her head had drooped or that her shoulders had sagged with the weight of her problem.

"Tell me," he whispered and leaned down and brushed a soft kiss across her lips.

She couldn't tell him. He would think her a fool. She was his mistress, nothing more and only for however long he desired her. And right now he desired her, his lust potent in his eyes. Instead of answering his question, she responded to his passion.

She changed the gentle kiss from soft to eager as she moved closer, her arms going around his neck and her body pressing intimately against his.

He tore his mouth off hers. "You will not distract me; I'll have an answer."

He left her lips pulsing for his and instinctively

her tongue slipped out of her mouth to slowly stroke her aching lips.

His groin tightened like never before, and he thought he'd come right there and then as he watched her slim tongue play across her already moist lips. His hands shot out, grabbing her face. "Damn it, Dawn," he said though it sounded more like a feral growl, and then his mouth clamped down on hers.

They were both eager and hungry for each other, and his hands were soon at her backside, urging her against him.

"I want you. Here, now, hard and fast," he said having released her mouth with more reluctance than he had ever known. And he wished, oh how he wished she could tell him that she wanted him.

She smiled, and her hand slipped down and under his tunic to squeeze the hard length of him.

He gave a brief, rough laugh and rested his brow to hers. "I love when you speak to me so clearly." And he titled his head to kiss her again when an arrow sped past just missing the top of Dawn's head.

Chapter Twenty-six

It took all but a second for Cree's arm to go around her waist, shove her to the ground, and shield her body with his. A second arrow grazed his leather tunic at the shoulder and he let out a blood-curdling roar.

His men arrived in a flash and before they could surround him he yelled, "Two stay and the others go find the bastard!"

Cree was furious. His heart pounded in his chest and every muscle in his body turned rigid with anger. He silently berated himself for not having a larger contingent of warriors with him, and he was even more of a fool for walking off with Dawn alone when danger still existed. Until the culprit could be found, he intended to see her well-guarded and that damn window boarded.

He moved off her and asked, "Are you all right?" He didn't need an answer. She had lost all color in her face and she shivered slightly. He was about to take her in his arms when an all clear signal sounded from one of his men.

He reached out and, with his hands around her waist, eased her to stand along with him. He kept his arm firmly around her, not trusting her to stand on her own. All but two men returned and the news did not please him.

One of the warriors informed him that they had picked up a trail and that two of the men were following it, though it did appear as if the archer was headed back toward Dowell.

"We return now," Cree ordered and with his arm remaining firm around Dawn, he hurried her to his horse.

In minutes they were on their way, Dawn once again sitting across the front of his lap as he sped through the countryside. He wanted back to the village where he could keep her safe and then...

The person responsible for this would live only long enough to tell him what he needed to know, and then he'd beg to die. And Cree would be the one to deliver the final blow.

Dawn kept her head tucked in the crook of his arm and her face pressed firmly against his chest. She couldn't stop shivering. It wasn't that she was cold, it was more from fear. Had someone truly targeted her for death? And if so why?

She didn't have time to ponder. They were entering the village at a good speed and villagers were rushing out of their way, their eyes wide with curiosity and fear. She had expected Cree to deposit her at her cottage, but instead he scooped her off the stallion after dismounting and, with a firm grip on her arm, hurried her into the keep and to the Great Hall.

He shouted for Sloan and a couple of servants rushed off, no doubt, to find him. He all but shoved her to take a seat on a bench at a table closest to the large hearth. He then yelled for hot cider and a flush of servants appeared not only with pitchers of hot cider, but platters of food.

William wandered in appearing as pale as Dawn along with several warriors while more warriors followed behind. William took a seat across from

Dawn and, with shaking hands, accepted a tankard from one of the servants.

Dawn cupped a tankard in her hands, but she had yet to drink.

Cree leaned down in her face and ordered, "You're chilled, drink."

His dark eyes flamed with such fury that she immediately obeyed as did William, though Cree's edict had not been directed at him.

When she finished taking a swallow, Cree leaned down in her face again. "You will stay here. You will not move until I come for you. *Understand*?"

Dawn nodded, his eyes so feral with fury that he actually frightened her. And at that moment she wondered if perhaps he didn't have a heart after all. She was relieved when he walked away to talk with his men. It was as if she could finally breathe again.

"That was a frightening ordeal," William said in a near whisper.

She nodded, the hot cider finally chasing away her chill or perhaps it was her fear dissipating. Whatever the reason, she was feeling comfortably warm and let her cloak fall off her shoulders, though she kept it tucked around her waist and over her legs that still trembled a bit.

"Have you always liked to draw?" William asked.

Dawn's face lit with a smile and she nodded.

William smiled as well. "It is a God-given talent you have."

She placed her hand on her chest and bowed her head briefly, thanking him.

"You are most welcome," he said understanding her, and then lowered his voice. "I will make certain that I bring you some drawing tools. Your talent is too amazing to waste."

It was thoughtful of him, and so few people were thoughtful of her that she wished to show her appreciation. So she reached out and gave his arm a squeeze.

Cree appeared out of nowhere. "Does William not understand you that you need to touch him?"

Dawn froze, his face only inches from hers and that feral look in his eyes worse than she remembered. She blessed William a hundred times over when he offered a reasonable explanation.

"Forgive me, my lord, Dawn was gracious enough to offer me comfort after this most upsetting ordeal."

"Busy yourself with your designs and you will have no time to dwell on it," Cree ordered. He planted his hands on the table, blocking Dawn from William's view and whispered harshly in her ear, "You will touch no one but me."

He walked away, leaving Dawn to stare after him.

"Would you like to look at the drawings?" William offered. "Perhaps my lord is right and we would be better off with our minds occupied on other things."

Dawn nodded. Her eyes remained locked on Cree's back until her shivers returned and distracted her. She reached for her tankard and drank in hopes of chasing them away once again.

She was grateful for William's endless chatter, and she soon became engrossed with the drawings and the plans he so graciously detailed.

Cree kept a watch on Dawn out of the corner of his eye. He had had to restrain himself when he had seen her touch William. It had been a simple gesture more than a definitive touch and yet it had infuriated him. And he was even more infuriated that the archer had yet to be found.

"He eludes us at every turn," Sloan said.

"Have you and the men become so complacent that you allow one solitary man to evade you?" Cree accused, his temper still much too close to erupting.

Sloan wisely refrained from debating the issue and said, "No, my lord."

"And you have yet to find him," Cree said, though didn't allow for a reply. "I'm going to take twenty men and see to this myself. You will make certain that Dawn is kept safe while I am gone."

Sloan gave a nod, and Cree could see that he was not pleased with his decision, but he would not dare challenge him. He would obey.

Cree looked over at Dawn. She was engrossed with the drawings. He thought of going over to her, warning her to obey Sloan, but decided against it. His obsession with her had to stop. He turned and without another word to Sloan, stormed out of the Great Hall, his anger growing ever darker.

Sloan walked over to Dawn, intending to make certain she understood that she was not to go anywhere without a guard. But when he approached the table and caught sight of a change she was making to William's drawing, he stared in awe at her remarkable talent.

"A double battlement, I would have never imagined and yet it makes sense," William said staring in just as much awe as Sloan.

The three were soon discussing other changes that Dawn had made, and it was an hour later that William nodded and said, "These changes are good. I will present them to Cree."

"He'll approve," Sloan said with a nod.

William rolled the parchments and stood. "I have

more work to do." He gave a nod to Dawn. "It has been a pleasure working with you and I hope to do so again."

Dawn smiled, patted her chest and pointed to him to let him know that she had enjoyed working with him as well.

William smiled and gave another brief nod and left the Great Hall.

Sloan turned to Dawn and delivered Cree's edict. "You are to go nowhere without a guard and until Cree returns it would be best for you to stay to the keep or your cottage."

Dawn knew without being told that Cree had gone with his men to find the culprit who had attacked them. And she did not want to think about what he would do to him once he found him. She also did not want her movement limited to two places. She wanted to visit with Lila, see how baby Thomas was doing, get to hold him, and get to talk with her friend. She also wanted to see how Flanna was doing, but she felt odd going to the kitchen and taking what food she wanted, though it would give her a reason for being there.

She gave Sloan a nod and let him know that she understood. He hadn't ordered, only suggested it would be best that she limit herself to the keep and her cottage. Therefore, she was free to go other places if she wished as long as a guard accompanied her. She suddenly looked forward to the rest of the day.

Sloan rubbed his jaw and stared intently at Dawn. She could see that he debated about asking her a question. She wondered if he didn't because he worried about understanding her gestures. She had found it to be a common reaction in people and the reason many ignored or made fun of her, flailing their hands and arms in mock facsimile of her gestures.

Whatever the reason for his hesitation did not matter to Dawn, she was more curious to know his question. And so she pointed to him and shrugged.

Her gesture had him smiling and responding. "You make yourself understood remarkably well for one without a voice."

She smiled and gave a nod of thanks, then pointed to him again and shrugged.

"And you're persistent to boot, but then most women are."

She was pleased that he included her with other women. It made her feel less different from them.

"I have a problem and I was wondering if you might be able to help me, since you probably see more than most as to what goes on around here."

That was true. People constantly assumed her deaf since she was voiceless and often spoke freely around her even about her, as if she wasn't present. She was delighted that Sloan should ask her for help, and she nodded eagerly.

"I need to find a woman who can handle the daily running of the keep. It would require someone who could be firm with the servants and see that all chores got done to specifications, someone who could give orders as well as take them. Would you know anyone capable of handling such an important chore?"

Dawn nodded, having known instantly who would be perfect for the important task.

"Can you bring her here to me?" Sloan asked his face lighting with a smile. "Let me get a guard to accompany you."

Dawn shook her head as she swung her legs over the bench and stood. Then she pointed around the room.

"She is here in the keep?"

Dawn nodded.

"I'll go with you. Where in the keep is she?"

Dawn hooked her arm out and made a motion as if stirring in a bowl.

"The kitchen?" Sloan's smile faded. "I'll wait here while you go get her. Go straight to the kitchen and return here right away. If Turbett should give you any trouble, tell him that Cree has ordered the woman's presence."

Dawn nodded, though doubted Turbett would understand her gestures. Flanna, on the other hand, would. She entered the kitchen a bit apprehensively and was surprised to see Dorrie, her eyes teary, chopping wild onions. As soon as Dorrie saw her, she smiled and bobbed her head. Dorrie had never acknowledged Dawn so pleasantly. Usually it had been a disparaging remark that Dorrie had greeted her with, but it would appear that she had had a change of heart.

"Can I get you something, Dawn?" Turbett asked as he approached her.

Turbett's girth could intimidate, especially when one realized that his thickness was mostly muscle. His direct manner could also be disconcerting, but she had to remember that she was allowed to be here and allowed to have what she wanted from the kitchen.

Dawn pointed to Flanna.

"Cree ordered that you can have whatever food you want from the kitchen, but I will not allow you to disrupt my staff at your leisure."

His words were clipped and stern and for a moment she thought of turning away and getting

Sloan. But she dismissed the idea and stood her ground, though on trembling legs.

She waved Flanna over.

"I have not given her permission—"

Dawn's hands started moving before he could finish, and Flanna was by her side then and interpreted. "Dawn asks that I explain what she says."

Turbett gave a reluctant nod.

Dawn kept her expression concise, Flanna not understanding her as well as Lila, but then few understood her so well. *Cree was beginning to.* The thought startled her, though she didn't allow it to show.

"My presence is requested in the Great Hall," Flanna said, her eyes turning wide with fright.

"Go and return here as soon as you are done," Turbett ordered and shooed them away as if they were annoying flies.

The two women didn't hesitate, they hurried off, though Flanna grabbed Dawn's arm once they were a few feet through the stone passageway and stopped.

"Am I in trouble?"

Dawn realized that every single villager had feared being summoned to the Great Hall when Colum had ruled and for good reason. The person always suffered harsh punishment, leaving everyone fearful of receiving such a summons.

Dawn shook her head and smiled wide.

"Something good?" Flanna asked hopefully.

Dawn nodded.

Flanna ran her fingers through her hair and took her apron off turning it to the other side that was less stained and retied it around her waist. Then she grabbed Dawn's hand. "I'm ready."

Dawn patted her hand and nodded vigorously.

Flanna smiled and hurried to the Great Hall.

Flanna answered every question Sloan asked her, and then stood speechless when he told her that she would be in charge of the keep's servants. And that she would be answerable to him and of course Cree.

Sloan cleared his throat and added, "You would need to deal with Turbett as well, making certain all flows well between the servants and the kitchen."

Flanna grinned. "I can do that."

"You can?" Sloan asked shocked, and then caught himself. "Good, that's good."

Dawn bit back a smile. It was obvious that Sloan feared Turbett and was relieved that Flanna would be dealing with the daunting man. And she had no doubt that Flanna was looking forward to every minute of it.

"You will begin your duties right away," Sloan instructed. "Inform Turbett, and then gather the servants so that I may instruct them that they will now be answerable to you. And as I mentioned before Cree will not tolerate dirt or foul odors"

"No worry, sir," Flanna said with a sharp nod. "The keep will sparkle and smell heavenly."

"A good choice, Dawn," Sloan said turning her way. "Flanna seems more than up to the task. Thank you for suggesting her."

Flanna beamed a wide appreciative smile at Dawn, and then bobbed to Sloan. "I will go collect the servants."

Dawn returned to the bench where she had been sitting and watched Sloan talk with a few warriors. Servants began entering the hall, mulling around whispering, wondering and worried over the summons. When they had finally all gathered Sloan stood in front of them to speak. Relief flooded their faces as he introduced Flanna.

With everyone occupied, Dawn decided it was time for her to be off on her own for a while, so she left the keep. She didn't bother to see if a guard followed her, she assumed one would and though she had planned on going to visit Lila, she changed her mind.

She meandered through the village taking note of how busy everyone was, though they smiled as they went about their chores. It had been almost a week since Cree had attacked the village, and yet it looked as if it had been prospering for weeks. Apprehension still filled some faces, but fear was not as prevalent.

Children's laughter filled the air and Dawn stopped to watch a group of young ones at play. It had been many years since anyone had seen the village children play with such careless abandonment, and it was good to see.

Two women, baskets on their arms, nodded pleasantly at Dawn as they passed her, and she quickly returned the greeting, though she almost stumbled over her own feet, she was so surprised by their acknowledgement.

What had caused their change of heart toward her? Was it what she had done for Dorrie or did they fear repercussion from Cree if they treated his mistress badly? The thought troubled her, but she refused to linger on it. It was a beautiful day and she intended to enjoy it.

Free time was not something Dawn was used to. She had worked hard as long as she could remember. So to be carefree with no worry of getting chores done was a bit disconcerting to her. Her mum had warned her often that idle hands brought trouble. With that reminder, she decided to collect some heather and dry it for the coming winter. It would keep her cottage smelling fresh.

She retrieved a basket from her cottage and headed to the small hill on the outskirts of the village, not far from the fields the men tended. She was not concerned for her safety, having spotted a warrior trailing her. Besides, she didn't intended to linger. She would collect extra and stop to give some to Lila on her way back. It would give her a chance to visit with baby Thomas.

Dawn took longer than she intended, the sunny day, the lovely scent of heather, the light autumn breeze all served to delay her return. When her basket was full to overflowing, she smiled and realized she had lingered long enough.

The warrior must have thought the same for he approached her.

"Time to go," he said.

She nodded and smiled, feeling a bit guilty. He surely must have been bored waiting for her.

He reached out and took the basket from her, and she was about to thank him when he tossed it aside and grabbed her arm.

He grinned. "Why don't you scream?"

She turned to see if anyone was in sight. Men were working in the field, three women lingered to talk beneath a large tree, but they were all at a distance, though not that far away to help her if she could scream.

His grip was so tight, she could not break free, and he forced her to walk alongside him. Her eyes widened when she saw that they were headed to the woods. She glanced around, hoping someone would look their way, see her frightened face, and help her.

The warrior leaned his head down. "You're the devil's whore. Why would anyone help you?"

Chapter Twenty-seven

Cree's warriors circled the trembling young man. The only escape for him was death and when two warriors parted to let Cree enter, he knew death would be a welcome relief.

"Tell me what I want to know and I will I kill you swiftly," Cree said walking slowly around him. "Tell me nothing and I will make you suffer the torments of hell."

The young man's mouth went dry and fearing he would not be able to speak, he nodded.

Cree stopped in front of him, close enough to smell his fear. "Who wants the voiceless one dead?"

The young man licked his lips, though they remained dry, his mouth parched. "I—I don't—"

"Lie to me again and I will slice your arm open from shoulder to wrist." His hand went to the handle of his dirk in a sheath at his waist.

"Please, I beg, mercy, please."

"You beg for your life when you had no qualms about taking one," he shouted in the man's face and he paled.

"I—I—I did not try to harm the woman. My task was to lead you astray."

Cree's hand snapped out and grabbed the startled man by the neck. "What do you mean?"

He choked out the words. "Two of us were instructed to keep you on our trail, away from the village, while the others went for the woman."

Cree released him so suddenly that the man stumbled and collapsed to the ground, choking to regain his breath.

"You know what to do with him when you get him back to the keep," Cree said to two warriors." The rest of you follow me. We ride hard and fast."

12. ~~~

Sloan had several warriors comb the village for Dawn. She had left the keep before he could assign a warrior to her. Cree would kill him if anything happened to her, and he would deserve it. He had been ordered to keep her safe and what had he done? After dealing with Flanna and the servants, he had been summoned to handle a problem at the mill. It wasn't until he had returned to the keep that he had thought about Dawn.

A warrior rushed toward him, and Sloan flew off the steps to meet him.

A few words were exchanged and the two men took off, Sloan shouting to other warriors who fell in behind them. When he reached the spot where the basket lay on the ground, heather strewn about, he shook his head.

He looked around at the group of warriors waiting for orders. "We don't return until we find her. And remember she has no voice." They all nodded, knowing full well they would rather search the woods all night than face Cree's wrath if they returned without her.

Twenty or more warriors gathered at the edge of the woods, spread out, and headed into the forest at a fast pace.

13.

After they were only a few feet into the woods Dawn stumbled on purpose, and the warrior released her, letting her fall.

"Here is as good a place as any," the man said and reached for his sword.

She dug her hand into the dirt, grabbed a handful, and threw it in his face as she jumped to her feet, and then she ran. She hiked up her skirt and cloak as she went, so they wouldn't impede her speed and kept running, knowing that she ran for her life. The woods were familiar to her and she had managed to skirt past the warrior, as he choked and wiped away the dirt in his eyes, and headed back toward the village. She didn't have much time before he followed, and she prayed that once she broke past the woods someone would see her and help.

Dawn's stomach roiled when she heard heavy footfalls until she realized that they weren't coming from behind her. Were there more warriors after her? She was about to change direction when she stopped and first caught sight of Sloan, and then other warriors came into view behind him.

She wanted to drop to the ground in relief, but she didn't dare. She ran straight for Sloan, stopping in front of him, breathing heavily and pointing behind her.

"How many?"

She held up one finger.

"Get him," Sloan ordered. He wasn't about to leave her safety to anyone else. He intended to keep her by his side until Cree returned.

He watched as she paced back and forth, fighting to slow her breathing. She pressed her hand to her side, and he wondered if she had suffered a blow there.

"Are you all right?" he asked anxiously.

She nodded.

"Did he hurt you?"

She shook her head.

"How did you get away?"

Dawn pretended to scoop up some dirt and throw it at Sloan.

He smiled and nodded. "Wise move."

Dawn took a heavy breath and returned his smile. She pointed to herself, and then toward the village.

"You want to go home?

She nodded vigorously, though home wasn't exactly what she would call her new cottage. She turned as did Sloan when they heard the warriors returning and in the middle of the group was the man who had abducted her. His nose and mouth were bleeding and his hands were tied behind his back. He tried to walk, but the warriors took turns shoving him, and he stumbled more than walked.

Sloan wanted to roar with relief. Dawn was safe and the culprit was caught, though that wouldn't completely appease Cree, it would help. He would still be furious that she had been taken from under their very noses.

Sloan went to help Dawn, but she was already several feet ahead of him, and he ran to catch up with her. The woman certainly had courage. He had expected her to collapse at his feet crying when he had seen her running toward him. That she had immediately let him know what had happened had surprised him, and he admired her tenacity.

Once out of the woods, they headed for the village. Clouds had blotted out the sun and looked as if they were there to stay. The once beautiful day was no more, and Dawn suddenly felt the weight of the day upon her. Her pace slowed and her shoulders slumped and she wished she didn't have to take another step. And she didn't.

Everyone had stopped suddenly, and she followed suit looking to see what had halted them in their tracks.

Cree.

He had come over the rise, his men following behind him, though not able to keep pace with him. His beast of a stallion was fast and he rode hard. And Dawn wondered over his anxious return.

No one moved. They waited as their fearless leader approached with lightning speed. Sloan stepped forward as Cree brought the large animal to a halt in front of them. The black beast pawed the ground and snorted, as if annoyed that he'd been stopped.

"We caught the culprit," Sloan said and two warriors pushed the man forward and down on his knees, then grabbed a handful of his hair and yanked his head back to look up at Cree.

"Take him to the stable area, secure him and post extra guards. The rest of you return to your duties," Cree ordered and turned to Sloan. "Why is Dawn here and why does she have twigs and leaves all over her?"

Dawn had grown accustomed to people talking about her, in front of her, as if she wasn't there, as if she could not hear them, as if she was incapable of participating in the conversation. This time, however, it annoyed her. Why had he not acknowledged her? Was this what she was to expect from him being his mistress? Would he only be courteous to her when they were alone and ignore her other times? And would he forever scowl at her?

She did not know what gave her the temerity to step forward, perhaps it had been all she had been through lately or perhaps she did not fear Cree the way she once did. Whatever the reason, the one small step was liberating.

She began gesturing with her hands, no doubt too fast for him to understand, but her intention was to show him that he was not the only one annoyed.

"Enough," he warned frustrated. "I asked Sloan to explain, not you."

Dawn slapped her chest several times and tapped her mouth repeatedly, then stamped her foot."

"That I understood, and I do not care if you want to speak for yourself. I asked Sloan to explain—"

Dawn shook her head and pointed to Sloan. How could he explain? It hadn't happened to him. It had happened to her.

"Be quiet," he snapped.

She caught her smile before it could surface. Never had she been told to be quiet, and it thrilled her.

Sloan wisely spoke before Dawn could object. "Dawn had gone to collect heather and was abducted."

"Tell me that her guard was killed trying to protect her because if he wasn't, I'll kill him myself."

He wouldn't, Dawn thought, but the murderous look in his eyes told her otherwise.

Sloan shook his head. "She had no guard."

That brought Cree off his horse to stand directly in front of Sloan. "You failed to carry out my orders?"

Dawn tapped Cree on the arm.

"Not now," he snarled, his eyes fixed on Sloan.

This time she gave him a shove, and it did the trick. He turned slowly to glare at her.

"Did you just shove me?"

She nodded, pointed at him, pointed at her ear, and then to herself.

"I should listen to you."

She nodded.

"Is that an order?" he asked caustically.

She gave a sharp nod of command and Sloan laughed, unfortunately not soundlessly.

Cree turned on him. "I'm not finished with you."

Sloan respectfully and wisely bowed his head.

Cree signaled to a warrior who stood nearby, and Dawn realized that there were always warriors near Cree to do his bidding. He directed the man to take care of his horse, and then he grabbed Dawn's hand and dragged her alongside him. Sloan followed.

Dawn didn't have to be told where they were going. She knew he was taking her to Lila so that she could interpret. It annoyed her that he felt the need to do so. He had understood her gestures well enough and with time... perhaps he didn't plan on spending that much time with her. And the thought saddened her, which troubled her all the more.

People were clustered in small groups as they passed through the village and one look from Cree had them scurrying off. Lila stood just outside her open door with baby Thomas cradled in her arms sound asleep. She stepped inside at their approach. Once they entered, Dawn yanked her arm free and started gesturing before Sloan even had a chance to close the door.

Dawn let all her frustration loose, letting her friend know what a stubborn fool Cree was and how he refused to listen to her, or take the time to become familiar with her gestures. That all he truly was interested in was satisfying himself between her legs. Her last complaint broke her tirade and she shook her head, she wasn't being fair to Lila. These weren't things she should be saying to Lila, at least here and now, in front of Cree.

Pushing her frustration aside, she began to explain what happened, and Lila, with a look of relief, interpreted.

"A warrior followed behind her, and she assumed that he had been assigned to protect her. He waited for her to finish collecting heather and told her it was time to go. That was when he slapped the basket out of her hand and dragged her into the woods."

"Did he say anything else to you?" Cree asked and her body responded by turning rigid. "Tell me," he urged his tone less angry. He watched her gestures as Lila spoke.

"When he forced her into the woods, she looked around hoping someone would see them and he told her—" Lila stopped her eyes filled with sadness and shook her head.

"Lila," he said curtly, anxious to know what had stopped Lila and filled her with such sorrow.

"He told her that she was the devil's whore and no one would help her."

Rage roared like a fiery blast through Cree. He kept his lips firmly locked so that it would not erupt and clenched his fists eager to turn his wrath on the man. He tempered his anger before he said, "He was wrong."

Dawn thought she saw pain in his dark eyes, but it

was so brief that she couldn't be sure.

"How did you escape?"

"She threw a handful of dirt in his face and took off running and ran right into me," Sloan answered to Cree's surprise. Sloan pointed to Dawn. "She told me about it while the men went after the culprit."

That seemed to agitate Cree and his scowl grew darker. "Had you assigned someone to Dawn?"

"No," Sloan admitted reluctantly. "There was a problem at the mill and the last time I say her she was in the Great Hall, and I had advised her to remain in the keep or close to it."

"And you saw fit to ignore him?" Cree asked turning his scowl on Dawn. Before she could start gesturing, he held up his hand. "I've heard enough from the both of you. Sloan, go and prepare the prisoner for questioning and also the men should have returned by now with the man we found, so prepare him for questioning as well. Assign Neil to guard Dawn. Have him wait outside her cottage. And be ready to discuss your poor handling of the matter later."

Sloan gave a quick bob and was out the door, closing it quietly behind him.

Cree's eyes fell on Lila. "Now you will tell me what Dawn said when we first entered your cottage."

Chapter Twenty-eight

Lila paled and so did Dawn. The thought that Lila would repeat any of what she had said turned her legs weak. The thought of what Cree might do to Lila if she didn't made her stomach churn. She had allowed her frustration to get the better of her and now look at what her lack of restraint had done. She was stuck with the mighty warrior and had been since he had entered the village a week or so ago. Had it only been such a short time? It felt as if she had known Cree much longer, even more so since they had become intimate. Her cheeks flushed at the thought.

"I never ask twice," Cree warned when the silence lingered.

Lila answered, though hesitantly. "Dawn ," —she sent an apologetic glance to her friend— "feels you are a stubborn fool for not listening to her and for not taking the time to become familiar with her gestures."

"What else? And don't lie and tell me that there is no more. You have worried at your lower lip until it is quite red," Cree said his eyes fixed on Lila.

Lila sighed, rolling her eyes heavenward.

Dawn was angry with herself for placing her friend in such an awkward situation, and she sought to correct it. She began gesturing.

"Dawn says she will repeat her words for you so you know they come from her."

"Why? Would you lie for her?" Cree asked.

"No, my lord," Lila answered shaking her head

and repeating again. "No, my lord."

Dawn walked over to Cree, poked him in the chest, pointed to her ear and slapped her chest, then threw her hands up.

"She says—"

"She's made herself very clear," Cree said. "She says that if I had listened to her none of this would have been necessary."

Dawn nodded.

"I'm listening now," he said stepping closer, his scowl gone and his dark eyes devouring her.

For a moment Dawn's breath caught and a tingle ran through her to settle between her legs. He had to be the devil's own to make her desire him with the slightest look. She had to be done with this and leave Lila in peace. This was not her problem, and Dawn should have never brought this into her home.

Dawn began moving her hands and Lila quickly interpreted. "Dawn says that all you're truly interested in is," —Lila paused a moment and hurried to finish— "satisfying yourself between her legs."

Cree brought his face so close to Dawn's that their noses touched. "Are you telling me that I failed to satisfy you last night, because from what I recall you seemed more than satisfied, especially since one coupling was not enough for you?"

Her mouth dropped open and she stared at him shocked.

"Speechless are you?"

Dawn nodded, her cheeks flaming red.

"Is there anything else you wish to tell me about when it comes to me bedding you?"

Dawn immediately and most vigorously shook her head.

Cree took hold of Dawn's arm. "You have proven your fealty, Lila, and I will see you rewarded for it." And with that he escorted Dawn out the door.

His pace was quick, and Dawn had to hurry to keep up with him. He did not say a word to her and when they reached her cottage, he stopped to speak to the warrior guarding the front door.

"She is not to leave this cottage without my permission, Neil."

"She'll not get passed me, my lord."

"I'm confident of that, which is why I have assigned you to the task."

A prisoner. she was a prisoner. He had known what it was like to be kept locked away. Why was he forcing the same punishment on her?

She glanced at Neil, wondering if he would be at all malleable. He was not tall, perhaps a mere inch or more in height than herself, but he was thick with muscles and a narrow, well-healed scar ran down his right cheek. He appeared stoic, not at all approachable.

Cree hustled her into the cottage, closing the door behind them. She turned ready for a scolding and warning to behave. So she was surprised when he reached out, his hand wrapping around her neck, and pulled her to meet his hungry mouth.

He kissed her with urgency, as if he had been away from her far too long and had missed her and needed to familiarize himself with her again. His demanding tongue stirred her hesitant one to life, and they mated in an intimidate dance that stimulated all her senses. Her skin prickled with pleasure and her nipples hardened so tight that they poked at her linen blouse, and she grew wetter as the kiss lingered on.

Cree tore his mouth away from hers, biting at his

bottom lip as if to stop himself from kissing her again. His large hands quickly cupped her face, squeezing it. "Are you all right?"

His question surprised her as did her answer. She nodded as she touched his arm and pointed to the room.

"Now that I am here with you?"

A small smile surfaced as she nodded slowly.

"I have matters that I must see to, then I will return and I will be staying the night with you." He kissed her again, fast and brief, and Dawn felt his absence down to her bones when he stepped away.

He stopped, his hand on the latch. "I do not use you only to satisfy my lust and tonight I will prove it to you."

Her body shuddered as she throbbed unmercifully between her legs, and she couldn't stop herself from rushing her hand to press at the taunting sensation.

Cree groaned as he watched her touch herself and in two quick strides he had her up and on the table in a blink of an eye, hoisted her skirt, pulled his leggings down, yanked her legs up and apart, and then with one thrust buried himself in her sweet wetness. Lord, but he had wanted to do that since he had first caught sight of her when he had come over the rise. The vision of her alive and well had turned him hard, and he had wanted her with an urgency he had never felt before.

He took hold of her hips and held them firm as he continually rammed into her over and over, watching her passion grow out of control along with his own.

"God damn, Dawn, what the hell are you doing to me?" He gritted his teeth and squeezed his eyes shut as he felt her tighten around him.

She gripped the edge of the table and rolled her head from side to side, wishing she could scream out her pleasure. Her passion spiked with each forceful thrust and she had no doubt that she would come more than once before he was through.

"I can't hold back. God help me, I want to pour myself into you."

His words sent her tumbling over the edge, exploding in a wild frenzy that had her body bucking against his from the force of her climax and sending him toppling over the edge along with her. And when Dawn thought herself done, another climax erupted, exploding in a rush of tingles that shivered her body.

Cree had collapsed over her, his head buried in the crook of her neck. She wrapped her arms around his broad back, not that they fit completely around him. He was warm and breathing heavily and still buried inside her, and she wanted to keep him there just as he was, for a few moments at least.

He nuzzled her neck with gentle kisses, and she smiled.

He, however, wore a scowl when he raised his head. "I lose myself when I'm with you."

He sounded as if he was trying to decide if that was good or bad. She liked to think it was good, for she had certainly lost herself in him and had never felt anything so satisfying.

With a quick kiss to her lips, he was off her, pulling up his leggings and pulling down her skirt. He gave her his hand to help her off the table and when she stood he kissed her again only this time it was a gentle, lingering kiss.

"I will see you later. Stay put. I will have supper sent to you."

She stared at the closed door for several minutes

after he left, and then she dropped down on one of the chairs. She pressed her hand to her chest. She hadn't wanted him to leave. She had wanted him to stay with her and make love to her again and again. How was it that she could not get enough of this man who she only recently had feared? How could the infamous Cree have become so necessary to her?

She wasn't sure if she liked were her thoughts were going. It would, after all, do her no good to...

No, it was not possible. She couldn't be falling in love with the devil. Cree was no devil. He provided well for his people whether it was shelter, sustenance or a healer to tend their ills. He had a celebration feast after claiming the village and provided the people with food, drink and— hope. That is what he had been giving them—hope.

She stood and removed her cloak and after hanging it on the peg, she picked the twigs and leaves off it. Hope filled everyone's heart in the village, everyone except hers. She had to keep reminding herself that this was her lot and she would need to accept it.

How did she do that if she was falling in love with Cree? How did she remain his mistress always wondering when he would discard her in favor of another? How would it be when he took a wife and had children... and what if she bore him children?

Dawn shook her head, the thoughts too heavy to linger on. Her day had been troubling enough. She didn't need to add more angst to it. She would keep herself busy.

Idle hands, she heard her mother's warning strong in her head and held her hands out in front of her. They were dirty, one worse than the other and it reminded her of how she must look from her scuffle in the woods.

She frowned. Why did someone want her dead? It made no sense. She grabbed the rope handle of the bucket near the hearth and went to the door. She startled when she opened the door. Neil stood in front of it, his arms braced across his chest.

"You'll not be going anywhere," he said bluntly.

She held up the bucket to him, and he snatched it out of her hand.

"Close the door," he barked and stood there waiting until she did.

If she thought that had been even a small possibility of getting passed him, she quickly discarded it. She wished Elwin was still her guard. He was pleasant, perhaps if she requested him.

A rough knock at the door had her jumping. She opened the door and Neil shoved the full bucket at her.

She nodded her thanks and shut the door, her thoughts drifting back to why Neil was stationed there in the first place. She was unimportant, one among many peasants. It was truly a puzzle why anyone would want her dead. She was so insignificant.

Her troubled thoughts soon vanished as she began to wash herself replaced by thoughts of Cree's return, and her body began to tingle all over again.

14. ~~~

Cree stood in front of the two men tied to posts in a pen. He tapped his fisted hand against his mouth, staring at the two. The younger one was scared to death, already having wet himself. The older, and obviously more seasoned warrior, stood defiant. Cree didn't trust either one of them.

He unfurled his fist and rested his arms across his chest. "I do not repeat myself. So when I ask you a question, I will ask it only once. Answer it and you'll spare yourself suffering. Don't and I promise you that you'll pray for death?"

The younger one started babbling immediately. "I don't know anything. I was instructed to lead you on a chase until you chased no more. I don't even carry a weapon. And I never met this man." He gave a nod to the prisoner next to him.

"Then how was it that you knew exactly where and when we would give pursuit?"

The young man paled.

"The truth or suffer the consequences," Cree threatened.

It was the seasoned warrior who spoke up. "Either way we're dead men."

"True, but it is how you wish to die that is your choice; agonizing pain or quickly."

The young man babbled once again. "We were each hired by different people and sent to meet at a designated spot."

"How many?" Cree asked.

"Four of us. One issued the instructions, though never gave us any reason why the woman was to die."

Cree's hand fisted and his stomach clenched.

"We would have been done with our mission and on our way if you hadn't shown up," the older warrior said with a bitter sneer. "Between Colum watching over her and you rutting with her so—"

The warrior's head snapped back from the fierce blow Cree landed on his jaw. The second one came just as fast and sent his head lolling to one side where it stayed.

Cree turned away from the man, his eyes going to Sloan. "Revive him."

Sloan took a bucket of water and threw it in the man's face, then grabbed him by the hair and slapped his face until he opened his eyes.

"Who sent you?" Cree demanded coming to stand in front of the man again.

"Go to hell," the warrior spat.

"Wrong answer." Cree hit him again, only this time much harder. He split his bottom lip wide open and blood poured out. He stepped away from him for a moment and when he turned around he held a dirk in his hand.

The warrior started talking. "You'll need to find the one we met up with and told us what to do." He spit blood that was filling his mouth. "He has the information you seek."

The younger man kept bobbing his head agreeing.

"He's one of the two out there?" Cree asked.

The older warrior nodded. "A sly one he is. He's walked among you and you didn't even know it." He grinned, blood covering his teeth. "Kill me now and be done with it. I'm tired of living this miserable life."

"I'm not, I'm not," the younger one begged. "I don't want to die. Please, I beg you don't kill me. I'll join you. I'll pledge my fealty to you, but please, please don't kill me."

Cree stepped away from them and nodded for Sloan to follow him. "Get Dorrie and bring her here," Cree said for their ears only.

It didn't take long for Sloan to return with Dorrie and when she stopped in front of Cree, she bobbed her head. "My lord."

"Tell me if you recognize that man, Dorrie." Cree pointed to the younger one.

Her eyes turned wide. "That's Seth, the one who gave me the message for Dawn that night."

Dorrie was whisked away by one of Cree's warriors as he watched Seth's demeanor change. Gone was the groveling, frightened young man and in his place was a warrior who held his chin high, his shoulders back, and showed not an ounce of fear.

"How did you know?" Seth asked.

"You pleaded far too much for your life and this one," —Cree nodded at the older warrior— "confirmed it for me when he told me to kill him. He knew that once this mission was done you would kill him."

"How would you know that?" Seth asked.

"Because he was told the same thing and whoever arranged this no doubt hoped you would both finish each other off, leaving no one to tell the tale."

Seth snapped his head to the side to look at the older warrior. "Were you told that, Rem?"

"Didn't it for once cross your mind that if you were told to kill me that I had been told to do the same to you? Or did you think yourself better than me? Go on, keep protecting whoever hired you and suffer a miserable death. Me? I'll go quickly and meet my maker."

Seth strained with anger against his ties.

"Does Colum or Goddard have anything to do with this," Cree asked.

"They are both fools," Seth said, "and had not an inkling of why I had joined their worthless warriors. This all would have been over and done if Goddard hadn't interfered and attacked Dawn that night, though I saw that he suffered for it. The wound will either kill him or he will suffer a limp for the rest of his miserable life."

Cree was pleased to hear that, though he much preferred the previous fate to the latter.

"So Colum has no knowledge that someone wanted Dawn dead?" Cree asked.

"He was too caught up in filling his own coffers than caring about anything else. And since he and Goddard lingered in the area after your attack, I assumed that he hadn't had enough time to collect his wealth before he left."

Cree had yet to find time to collect and discover what the chest contained that Old Mary had informed him about, though now he had a fairly good idea. He had however seen to making sure that the secret passageway had been secured.

Cree had heard enough for now and with the overhead clouds turning darker rain was imminent. He'd let them both suffer through the night outdoors, tied to posts, and see if tomorrow they would be more forthcoming with information.

"We will talk more tomorrow," Cree said.

Rem laughed, then broke into a cough, blood gushing from his spilt lip. "You talk, Seth, and try uselessly to save yourself. I've said my piece and I'm ready to die."

Cree turned to Rem. "You're in an awful hurry to die."

"I'll take death over agonizing suffering any day."

Cree rubbed his chin. "What aren't you telling me?"

"I confessed everything I know about this mission, except one thing," —Rem coughed and spit out more blood— "whoever is behind this won't stop until that woman's dead."

Chapter Twenty-nine

Cree entered the Great Hall with Sloan and went directly to the dais and poured himself a tankard of ale.

Sloan followed suit, though before he took a swig he said, "This isn't about you. It's about Dawn, but why would someone want a voiceless peasant woman dead?" He shook his head. "Perhaps she knows something she doesn't realize."

"It is a possibility. Many assume her deaf as well as mute, so speak freely around her." Cree refilled his tankard. "None of it makes any sense at all. And what troubles me the most is that someone is determined to see Dawn dead and will not stop until she is. Her death is a priority to someone, but why?"

Sloan shrugged. "There are only truly two reasons why someone would want someone else dead. The person knows something that threatens another or the person wants to do harm to the other one. And neither appears to explain this situation."

"Unless there is something in Dawn's past that now threatens her."

"Do you know much about her past?"

"I know that her father is dead and that her mother brought her here, though I don't know how long ago that was."

"Lila or Paul would know," Sloan said. "I could talk with them."

Cree nodded. "And I will talk with Dawn about

it."

"She does communicate well for one who has no voice," Sloan said. "She helped me find someone to fill the position of head servant for the keep. And I must say, the woman Flanna has been at it only a few hours and she has everyone hopping." He grinned. "She's also dealing with Turbett."

"A relief for you, I'm sure," Cree said and sat his tankard on the table, then turned a scowl on Sloan. "Now about failing to protect Dawn."

15.

Cree returned to Dawn's cottage later than he had planned. He had spent a good hour berating Sloan for his mistake, though he couldn't entirely fault him since Dawn had seen fit to go off on her own without making certain a guard went with her. Still, Sloan had had a duty that he had failed to carry out and that was unacceptable to Cree, and it was to Sloan as well. They both knew the value and necessity of being able to depend on each other, but then they had never faced a situation with a woman like Dawn before.

In the end Cree had been lenient, though Sloan had offered numerous apologies and swore on all that was holy that he would never allow it to happen again. And if necessary, he would give his life to protect Dawn.

Cree didn't have to hear anymore. With that promise, he knew he need not worry that it would happen again. He had been about to leave after that when Flanna had entered the Great Hall and Sloan introduced her. Within minutes the woman was praising Dawn and blessing the day that she and her mum had arrived at the village, which he had learned was ten years ago when Dawn was nine.

Cree wondered where Dawn had spent the first nine years of her life and how old she had been when her father had died. He planned on asking her after they made love. He couldn't wait to bury himself inside her. It had been a long, tiring day with too much left on his mind to think about. Once inside her, his thoughts would vanish and there would be only the two of them and the exquisite pleasure they would share.

Neil nodded to him as he approached the cottage.

"You're relief will be here shortly," Cree said.

"I can stay the night, my lord, if you wish," Neil said with a bob of his head.

"I prefer that you get a good night sleep and be here bright and early so that you can keep a watch on her all day tomorrow. She can be quite a challenge."

"No worry, my lord, she's safe with me."

"Good to hear," Cree said and entered the cottage. The room was quiet and Dawn was nowhere to be seen. He panicked for a moment, and then took stock of the room. A bucket sat near the door with a cloth in it and her clothes were draped over two chairs. The food on the table had been picked at and Cree smiled.

He walked to the other room, knowing he'd find her in bed, tired after her ordeal, though taking the time to refresh herself with a wash and some food first. He stopped just inside the room. She lay in bed asleep, tucked under the warm wool blankets, and he wondered if she was naked.

He shed his garments fast and eased beneath the covers, a smile spreading across his face when he wrapped himself around her warm naked body. He grew hard instantly and was about to tease her awake when she turned in his arms and snuggled against him, resting her face on his chest.

Her body relaxed against his, and he felt a jab to his gut, his heart lurch, and his arousal thickened. Her actions showed just how much she trusted him, felt safe with him, and as much as he wanted to wake her so that he could make love to her, he couldn't bring himself to do it.

She was exhausted from the day's events and needed to rest. He wrapped his arms around her, tucked his leg over hers and though he thought he'd lay awake for hours unable to sleep, he didn't. He closed his eyes and was asleep in no time.

Dawn didn't know what woke her. It was as if someone was nudging her and she refused to open her eyes. She didn't want to wake yet, she was warm and snug and so very comfortable all wrapped up in...

She smiled, realizing that she was in Cree's arms. He had come to her, slipped in bed beside her and joined her in sleep. He hadn't turned away when he found her sleeping or had he woken her to couple. He lay beside her content, and it filled her heart with joy, for it meant he wanted to be there lying beside her whether they made love or not.

The thought stirred her passion and that was when she realized what had nudged her awake. He was hard and his arousal poked at her. She eased her head off his chest to gaze up at him, expecting to find him awake, but he was sound asleep.

He was handsome beyond words, but at the moment that seemed unimportant to her. What mattered was that caring side of him. He had demonstrated it time and again, and it had her curious. Who was he? She knew so little about him and she suddenly realized that she wanted to know...

as much as possible.

After all, she should know about the man she was losing her heart to little by little. The thought should have warmed her, but it chilled her instead, and once again she rested her head on his chest. She would not dwell on what it meant to give her heart to Cree, for what good would it do? It would not stop her from falling in love with him. Her heart had already taken the plunge and she could not snatch it back nor did she want to.

Love will find you. Those were her mum's words and though she had doubted them, her mum had been right. Love had found her and there was nothing left for her to do but welcome it.

She snuggled contentedly against him and felt his arousal poke her again. She smiled suddenly feeling wicked or perhaps it was her own rising passion that had her hand drifting down to stroke him.

She was surprised at how good he felt and how caressing him simulated her own senses. She soon found herself exploring him more intimately. She slipped her hand lower and cupped his genitals weighing them gently in her palm and enjoying the feel of them. She then eagerly returned to run her hand over the length of his rigid arousal. He was big and thick and she gave it a squeeze, thinking how she'd love to have him inside her. And the thought brought with it a rhythm and setting her grip tight around the length of him, she followed pace, her own body joining in.

His moans turned her daring or perhaps it was her own passion that made her react so wantonly, though whatever it was at the moment she didn't care. She pushed him on his back and climbed on top of him, his eyes opening wide. She guided him inside her, her mouth dropping open as if she cried out in pleasure when his thick hardness pierced her.

"I want that mouth on mine," he groaned and grabbed the back of her neck, forcing her head down and claiming her lips in a brutally erotic kiss.

Dawn pushed him away after a few moments, her need to ride him too great to ignore. She threw her head back and braced her hands on either side of him and lost herself in a rhythm that was as natural to her as breathing.

"Good God," Cree moaned and reached out to squeeze her breasts and tease her nipples with his fingers.

She planted her hands on his chest, and he clamped his hands on her hips and together they set a rapid pace.

"Damn, woman, I'm going to come, tell me you're ready."

She threw her head back in pure ecstasy, and Cree's powerful hands brought her down on him even harder. His groan grew and when he shouted out her name, she burst again and shuddered against him in another climax.

She collapsed on top of him and he hugged her tight, but only for a moment. He needed to regain his breath and so did she, so he rolled her off him to rest at his side, his arm wrapping protectively around her.

When his breathing finally calmed, he turned to look at her and she smiled. He did the same, though he had a feeling that his grin was much wider than hers.

"You can wake me anytime you want like that."

He couldn't hear her laugh, but he saw it on her face.

She poked his chest and nodded.

"Did I enjoy it?"

She nodded again.

"Words cannot describe how much I enjoyed every minute of it."

He could see again the laughter in her eyes. "And you?"

Her grin turned wide and she nodded vigorously. Then she tapped her chest and placed her hand on his now limp shaft.

"You like touching me?"

Again she nodded vigorously.

He kissed her gently. "I love the way you touch me, and I give you permission to touch me whenever you like."

Her smile was interrupted by a yawn.

"You need sleep after such strenuous activity," he teased and she cuddled against him. He kissed the top of her head as his arms tightened around her. "You belong to me, Dawn, always remember that."

She could not argue with that. She did belong to him... but did he belong to her?

Chapter Thirty

Cree woke with the first light of day, Dawn curled around him. Damn, but he loved her there in his arms, in bed with her, and damn if he didn't want to make love to her again. His lust was insatiable when it came to her. He couldn't remember wanting any woman with the voraciousness that he wanted her.

Your seed will grow in her soon enough. The thought startled him and concerned him. It would not be good to get her with child. He would not only worry over her, but for the child as well. He would not want a son or daughter to suffer as she had. And being his mistress and not his wife would make it all the more difficult for any child born of their union. He shook his head. He needed her to talk with Elsa so that he did not have to worry that his seed would take root.

If only things were different... but they weren't. He expected to hear from Roland Gerwan any day now. The King no doubt had cautioned him to react wisely to his new circumstances and obey his command or suffer the consequences.

Cree had been more concerned with Colum than Roland Gerwan. Colum had seen an opportunity and had taken advantage of it. Gerwan was old, too old to tend his lands as well as he should. Colum had ingratiated himself with Gerwan and had convinced him to appoint him liege lord, with intentions of gaining more and more control.

However, Colum had not known that the King had other plans for Gerwan's land, and he wasn't part of those plans. As long as Colum didn't convince Gerwan to lodge an attack against Cree, a foolish move, then all would go smoothly. It was the reason the King sent an immediate message to Gerwan telling him that Cree was now the new Earl of Carrick and that his daughter was to be his bride sealing the title.

The plan had been flawless—that was until Dawn.

He glanced down at the sleeping woman in his arms and wondered what magic she had worked on him, for he could not comprehend his maddening desire for her.

Love. He grew annoyed at the foolish thought. He promised himself many years ago that he would never fall in love. He had no time for such folly. He had committed himself to forging a future, a good future for himself, his sister, and his men. He could let nothing stand in the way— not even love.

That he should even think that he could love Dawn was surprising. He had turned his heart so silent that he hadn't thought himself capable of loving. Had she proved him wrong?

She certainly had made him view things differently of late. That she had forgiven Dorrie and helped her, that she had seen that Flanna had gotten a new position, had protected Old Mary, and had made certain that her friend Lila did not suffer because of her, all had made him aware of her forgiving and generous heart.

Had her heart stirred his? Had she awakened it to feelings he had long kept buried? Those were questions he was not sure he was ready to answer.

She stretched herself awake beside him, her arms reaching above her head and her toes bent as she stretched her legs. She rolled on her back, and Cree threw the covers off them so that he could watch her body unfurl like a flower greeting the morning sun.

She was beautiful, long limbs, soft flesh, and pert breasts that tempted him to taste, and of course he did.

Her fingers wound their way in his hair, pulling him closer, and her legs wrapped around him, drawing him against her.

Cree didn't hesitate. He slipped over and into her, knowing she'd be wet and ready for him, and she was.

16.

Dawn remained abed when Cree left. She hadn't wanted him to leave and she thought that he felt the same, though perhaps that was wishful thinking. He was the new Earl of Carrick and had responsibilities to attend to. He could not linger in his mistress's bed all day, though a wife's bed would be different, for many would expect him to produce an heir as soon as possible.

Her hand went to her stomach. What if he had already gotten her with child? What would she do? What would he do? She pushed the disturbing thought from her mind. She did not want to think about it.

Before he left he had mentioned again that she should talk with Elsa the healer. He had not stated why, though he seemed adamant about it to a point where he had made it sound more an order than a suggestion.

Curiosity had her wondering over it, so when she

finished a quick morning meal of porridge that had been delivered to her door and had been far tastier than she had thought possible, she slipped on her cloak and opened the door.

Neil blocked the open doorway. She smiled pleasantly and gestured with her fingers, as if taking a walk, and then scrunched her face and held her stomach.

"You need the healer?"

She didn't bother to correct him about needing the healing versus visiting the healer since he nodded and stepped aside to let her out.

"I'll be walking right behind you. I'll let no one hurt you."

His adamant words not only startled, but endeared her to him and made her feel safe. She nodded, smiled, and pressed her hand to her chest in a show of gratitude.

He bobbed his head and his cheeks flushed red, letting her know that he understood her.

The day was overcast, blustery and more than a chill stung the air. Still, villagers were busy going about their chores and most wore smiles. Children scampered around laughing and found fun in almost anything. The village Dowell appeared brighter and happier than it had in a long time and oddly enough they owed it all to the devil.

Dawn took her time admiring the changes that were taking place. Roofs were being repaired, fences mended, peat and wood stacked for the coming winter, and new furnishings being made by skilled hands that had been kept idle too long. The village actually looked alive.

When she reached Elsa's place, she wasn't surprised to see that the room being added to her cottage had been finished and that her two helpers Ann and Lara were busy sweeping it out, making it ready for use.

When Elsa saw her approach, she signaled the two women and before Dawn reached the cottage the two women were on their way each with baskets on their arms. It appeared that Elsa planned on having privacy when they spoke, and Dawn wondered why.

Neil waited outside the cottage a few feet away, he also granting them privacy.

"Sit," Elsa offered, pointing to a chair at the table once she closed the door.

Dawn slipped her cloak off, draping it over the back of the chair and sat while Elsa prepared two hot ciders for them.

"I am so glad you stopped to visit. I was hoping to speak with you," Elsa said, joining her at the table.

Dawn threw her shoulder back, puffed out her chest and scowled, then tapped her chest and pointed to Elsa.

The woman laughed. "You're telling me that Cree sent you."

Dawn nodded and shrugged, asking why.

Elsa retained her pleasant smile as she said, "You are aware that everyone knows of your new status in the village."

The woman was kind not calling her what she was certain many did, a kept woman or as her attacker had said the devil's whore. Cree's mistress, of course, sounded much nicer, though she was what she was and, no matter what way you put it, she belonged to Cree.

"Naturally, with coupling comes the chance of a babe. Have you given that thought?"

Dawn stared at her with a blank expression not believing that the woman asked her such a personal question. And why? Then the thought hit her. Had Cree talked with Elsa of the possibility of her carrying his child, and if so why? She shrugged and scrunched her brow.

"Why, you ask?"

Dawn nodded.

"I wondered if perhaps you wished to prevent pregnancy. If so there is a plant, wild carrot that works well, though there is one thing that you must consider before using it. If you are already with child, then it will abort the babe. Of course the choice is yours as to whether you wish to make use of it or not."

Did Cree worry she could be with child? The question tolled like a loud bell in her head. Cree had not spilled his seed in her at first and now that he had, did he worry that it had taken root? Did he want her to abort his babe that might already be growing within her? Did he fear having a son or daughter like her—voiceless?

The joy she had woken with this morning quickly vanished and once again she felt trapped—a prisoner—for though Elsa made it seem it was up to her, it wasn't. If Cree so chose, he could dictate otherwise.

"The bruises on your face heal nicely. They will soon be gone," Elsa said and though she easily changed the subject, it was not so easily dismissed.

Dawn knew it would linger there to haunt her, especially if she was with child, for there would be no way that she would abort her babe.

"You are feeling well?" Elsa asked.

Dawn forced a smile, nodded vigorously then

jumped up, gesturing before she slipped on her cloak.

"You're going to visit Lila."

Dawn nodded, relieved that Elsa understood her. All she wanted to do was leave and rush to talk with Lila. She kept her smile tight and nodded her thanks to Elsa as she walked to the door.

"Dawn," Elsa said before her hand touched the latch.

Dawn kept her chin high and her smile bright as she acknowledged the woman with a nod.

"I am a healer and I am here to help. I hope you will remember that and come to me whenever you feel the need."

Dawn saw sincerity in the woman's soft blue eyes, but there was also sadness there and that disturbed Dawn. Elsa knew as well as she did that no matter what either of them decided, in the end Cree would have the final word.

Dawn rested her hand to chest and nodded.

"You are most welcome, and please do visit again."

Dawn gave another nod and out the door she went. Neil was immediately at her side and followed along as she made her way to Lila's cottage. She had intentions of discussing the matter with her friend, but when she recalled the predicament she had placed Lila in the last time she had foolishly complained to her, she thought twice.

Besides did she truly want anyone, even her dearest friend to know how Cree felt about her carrying his child? It was best she kept this to herself, so she wore a smile when Lila opened the door and greeted her with a hug.

Neil waited outside, though Dawn brought him a

hot cider to keep him warm while he stood guard.

Dawn was disappointed that Thomas was asleep in his cradle or perhaps it was better that he was. If she held him, she might break into tears thinking that she would never have the pleasure of holding her own babe.

Lila started talking as soon as Dawn had entered, chattering on about what a wonderful babe Thomas was and she hoped to have many more like him. Dawn listened, smiling, nodding, and gesturing now and again.

"Enough," Lila said, "what's wrong?"

Dawn's smile faded and her shoulders sagged. She should have known better than to think she could hide anything from Lila, though his time...

Dawn shook her head.

"Don't think you can keep anything from me. Tell me. We will talk and you will feel better."

It was tempting to spew all her frustration and worries to Lila as she had done many times through the years, but it was different now. She could not take the chance. And so she shook her head again.

Lila reached out and placed her hand over Dawn's. "We have shared everything. We have laughed and cried together. There isn't anything you don't know about me or I don't know about you. The only reason I can think of you not telling me is to keep from placing me in a difficult position."

Dawn's smile was brief and her eyes teary when she nodded and squeezed her friend's hand.

"It's not fair. Life has improved for all except you."

Dawn shook her head and scrunched her brow. With gestures Lila easily understood, she told her that life was not bad for her. That she had much to be grateful for and she was happy that the village and villagers were prospering.

"Cree ordered plaids to be weaved for all. He is having more spindles and distaffs made and he has appointed me to gather other weavers and oversee the project that will take the winter to complete. He wants to unify us as a clan." Lila sighed. "I feel a traitor to you, Dawn. I am grateful that Cree is here and life has improved, but I hate that you have been forced into a situation that has no—" She shook her head.

Happy ending, Dawn finished what her friend couldn't. She suddenly felt confined, trapped, a prisoner more now than she ever had, and the need to escape overpowered her. She stood abruptly and grabbed her cloak.

"Stay, Thomas will be awake soon and he so loves when you hold him."

The last thing she wanted to do was hold a babe. She shook her head, slipped her cloak on, and hurried out of the cottage to bump into Old Mary.

"I've been looking for you," the old woman said and slipped her arm around Dawn's, forcing her to follow along. "I owe you much."

Dawn shook her head. She didn't want to hear from anyone else how good life had become for them. She wanted to go back to her cottage, not her home, but a cottage Cree had forced on her and let her misery consume her.

The next thing Dawn knew, they were turning up the path to her old cottage and she felt her heart catch. This was home to her; this was where she belonged. And she entered willingly as Old Mary urged her through the door.

Dawn stood, her heart thumping madly in her

chest as she looked around to see a table and two chairs and a narrow bed with a fine stuffed mattress occupying the spot that her sleeping pallet once had been.

"I have a fine cottage, right here in the village because of you," Old Mary boasted and shoved her gently to the bed. "You should rest. You look tired and you will have a good rest here in your old home."

The old woman was right. She felt drained, as if she hadn't slept all night, but then she had only slept part of the night. And being here—being home—she felt a certain comfort.

Dawn stretched out on the bed and Old Mary reached out to stroke her forehead. "You were born very special, Dawn, you must always remember that."

For a moment with her eyes drifting closed, she thought it was her mum talking and telling her, as usual, how special she was, and she slipped into a peaceful slumber.

17. ~~~

It hadn't taken much to get Seth to talk. Cree supposed it was because as he did, Seth realized himself that whoever had hired him had never expected him to return. Had never expected to pay him the large sum that had been promised after the mission had been successfully completed and that the fools stupid enough to take on the task would, in the end, not survive. Seth had grown angrier the more he realized he had been duped, therefore, he became more talkative, more forthcoming. And it made him wiser to the fact that once Cree had what he needed from him, his life would be worthless.

Cree was not at all surprised by what Seth

proposed when that time came.

"I can find the others for you and any more men that are sent."

Cree stood, his arms folded across his chest, a scowl on his face, staring at the bloodied young man still tied to the post. He appeared to mean every word, though Cree still did not trust him. He did, however, intend to use him to find the others who had been sent to harm Dawn.

"I will pledge my fealty to you and serve you well if you let me."

"It is easy to pledge fealty when you are about to die," Cree said.

Seth paled. "A chance, just give me a chance to prove that I am true to my word.

Cree appeared to consider it, though his decision had already been made. Then he looked to Sloan. "Get him cleaned up, fed, and take him to the shack. Tomorrow he's to go with the troop of warriors to find the other two." Cree eyes fell on Seth whose relief was obvious. "You go back on your word and I will cut your tongue out and force it down your throat before I slowly kill you."

Seth shuddered. "I will serve you well, my lord. I swear it"

"We will see, for you have not escaped death yet." Cree walked away, Sloan following him. "Keep him locked in the shack with two guards on it at all times and send two extra men with the troop tomorrow, their sole mission to stay atop Seth."

Sloan nodded. "You think he means to run or finish what he started."

"I don't think he's a fool, especially after what he learned himself. And we have picked many a man up along the way that could not at first be trusted, but proved their worth."

"More like they saw that you were a man of your word and that they were well compensated for fighting alongside you." Sloan grinned. "Of course it didn't hurt to see what you did to those who betrayed you and was the reason many believe you the devil."

"Fear is a good comrade to send into battle before you. Now what of Rem?"

"He's enjoying a good meal, I assume his last, while he waits for you in the Great Hall, though I have never known you to give a condemned man a last meal. Is there something I missed about Rem?"

"He gives no thought to suffering or death. He is a desperate man and I want to know why."

A few minutes later Cree and Sloan entered the Great Hall. Sloan joined Rem at the table while Cree stood.

Rem raised his tankard to Cree. "The devil is generous, providing me with a fine meal before I die."

"I've decided to delay your execution."

"Why?" Rem demanded, pounding his tankard down on the table. "I've told you all I know and all I've surmised from meeting the others. This is no fool who hired these men. He knows what he does and he is determined in what he wants, and he wants the voiceless one dead."

"You have no idea why?" Cree asked.

Rem shrugged. "Who knows why madmen kill innocents?"

"You tell me since you were about to kill an innocent."

"A goodly sum tempts even the most honorable man," Rem said.

"True honor is never tempted."

"Honor does not fill an empty belly."

"So you do this to feed yourself or your family?" Cree asked.

"I am alone and care for no one."

"I have more questions for you, but they can wait for another day." Cree turned to leave.

"Going to rut with your whore?" Rem shouted and every servant in the room froze.

Cree swung around and Sloan jumped up.

"I wish I had had more time with her. I would have given her a good poke before I sliced her throat and watched her slowly bleed to death.

Cree lunged at the man, his fist slamming into his face and knocking him to the ground.

"Take him outside. I want all to see what happens to someone who dares to speak to me that way," Cree ordered.

Rem was dragged outside, his arms tied tightly behind his back. People were already gathering, the servants having spread the news fast that one of the prisoners were being punished.

A block of wood was set up and Rem's head smashed down on it. And all wondered if the man would have his head chopped off. Then two warriors forced a metal cage type device in his mouth and one took a pair of long metal tongs and grabbed hold of the man's tongue. They all knew then what would happen. He would have his tongue cut out.

18. ~~~

"Wake up, hurry, Dawn, wake up."

Dawn opened her eyes, not sure where she was at first, and then smiled, realizing she was home. But what was Old Mary doing in her place? Then she remembered that this was no longer her home.

"Get up. Get up," the old woman urged. "The devil is about to punish one of the prisoners and everyone is gathering to watch."

Dawn had been forced to watch too many punishments. She did not want to see this one, whether he deserved it or not.

But Old Mary forced her out of bed and shoved her cloak at her. "The devil is going to cut out the prisoner's tongue."

Dawn paled, dropped her cloak to the ground and, without thought to her actions, rushed out the door. Neil could barely keep up with her, she ran so fast. She saw the crowd gathered and heard Cree's voice announce that no one will threaten anyone who belongs to him.

She froze when she heard whispers that he meant Dawn. That this man's tongue was being cut out because of something he had said about her. She knew then it was the prisoner who had taken her into the woods to kill her, but it didn't matter. If Cree wanted to punish him let him do it a different way, but cut out his tongue?

Dawn pushed her way through the crowd and as she burst through to the front she almost got sick at what she saw and without hesitation she ran forward and threw herself over the man as Cree brought his blade down.

Chapter Thirty-one

Cree swung the blade away, but he didn't have enough time to avoid missing her completely and caught the edge of her shoulder. Blood immediately poured from the rip in her blouse and began to seep into the linen. He hurried to yank her off Rem and when he saw her pained expression, he let out a roar that had the people running in fright.

"Finish this," he ordered Sloan and went to scoop up Dawn and rush her to Elsa, but she slapped him away and began to gesture.

Cree was relieved when Lila appeared since he was having difficulty understanding Dawn. And he was concerned with the way her sleeve was getting soaked with blood.

"My lord," Lila said respectfully.

"Tell me what she says," he ordered anxiously.

Lila turned to Dawn. "My God, Dawn, your bleeding badly, you must go to the healer."

Dawn shook her head.

Lila spoke as Dawn gestured. "She refuses to go anyway until you give her your word that you will not cut this man's tongue out. If he needs to be punished—punish him—but she begs you not to cut his tongue out."

Cree glared at Dawn furious that she stood here arguing with him when her wound needed tending. He was also furious that she had dared to interfere with his command. He understood why she had objected to the punishment, but her actions had left him in a difficult situation. It would be a sign of weakness if he showed mercy, showed that he allowed a woman to sway his decision. He could not let that happen.

He stepped toward her, and her hands began gesturing again.

Lila was about to interpret when Cree said, "It matters not what she says. My word is law." He then scooped her up into his arms and when she tried to struggle, he whispered in her ear, "Fight me and he'll suffer for it."

She stilled instantly and turned to look at the man. His head remained twisted to the side, his face plastered to the block by a booted-foot.

"Tongue, eyes, limb, take what you want and be done with it," Rem said with a laugh that turned to a cough until he choked and could not stop.

Elsa suddenly appeared and looked from Dawn's blood-soaked blouse to the choking man on the block. She turned to Cree. "Dawn needs immediate attention, my lord, and that man is about to choke to death. Do you wish his death to be that swift?"

With a signal from Cree, Rem was yanked to his feet and dragged away as Cree hurried Dawn to her cottage since it was the closest place.

"Sit her in a chair," Elsa ordered following them inside.

"Shouldn't she be in bed?" Cree asked.

"Not yet, now leave me to do my work."

"No!"

Elsa's eyes rounded at his sharp retort and she wisely nodded, "As you wish, my lord."

He helped her remove Dawn's blouse, his eyes

narrowing when he saw that blood not only covered her shoulder and arm, but her lovely breast as well.

"It is worse than it appears," Elsa assured him after a quick perusal.

"It must pain her," Cree said and then shook his head. He was doing what everyone did to her, talking as if she wasn't there or could not hear. He hunched down in front of her and was about to ask if she was in pain, though didn't bother, her eyes answered for her. He stood. "She's in pain do something."

He hunched down again when he felt her hand slip around his and he squeezed it lightly. "Elsa will take care of you, she will stop the pain, and you will be fine."

She blinked and scrunched her face when Elsa touched her shoulder, and she quickly laid her head on Cree's shoulder, gripping his hand more firmly.

"Do something for her," Cree demanded.

"I am doing all I can and the wound is minor. Her pain comes from the blow to her bone where the blade struck it. I have tended many such wounds and the abrasion will heal long before the soreness leaves her shoulder."

"What about the bleeding?" Cree asked seeing that blood still dripped down her arm. "Does the wound need to be seared with a hot iron?"

"Am I the healer or are you?"

Cree sent Elsa a scathing look.

"I am sorry, my lord, but I need to focus on Dawn, not your endless questions."

"That you do, but watch your tongue with me, Elsa."

"Again my apologies, my lord."

Dawn had enough of their bickering. She threw

her head back, slipped her hand out of Cree's and waved it from one to the other, and then brought her hand to an abrupt halt in the middle.

"I believe she's heard enough from the both of us," Cree said.

Dawn nodded, and then dropped her head against Cree's chest.

Elsa worked in silence after that, Cree remaining hunched in front of Dawn, his hand firmly wrapped around hers.

"It is as I first thought," Elsa said after a while. "It is not as bad as it seems and the bleeding has stopped. I will apply a poultice of herbs to help the wound heal, and I have something that will help ease the pain a bit. First, let me clean the blood away."

"I'll take care of it from here," Cree said.

Elsa looked ready to protest, but when she met his intense eyes, she simply nodded. "As you wish, my lord. I will leave the wrapping for you and will set water to heat along with the brew."

She hurried to complete the few tasks before gathering the bloodied cloths and with a quick bob of her head, she said, "I will return on the morn, though if you should need me..."

"I will summon you," Cree assured her. "And, Elsa, go tend the prisoner."

As soon as the door closed behind Elsa, Cree went to work. He had seen his share of blood on the battlefield, had tended many of his own warriors when necessary, so tending Dawn was no chore. He was relieved that the wound had been minor, though he was still angry that she had interfered with his decree.

The blood had dried in a few spots, so it took a bit of scrubbing to remove it. When it came to her breast, he held it gently as he wiped it clean going over it twice to make certain not a spot remained. He wanted no taste of blood to linger there, for when his mouth settled on her nipple he did not wish to be reminded that he had been the cause of her pain.

He applied the poultice to the wound, and then wrapped clean cloth around her shoulder tying a strip around it to keep it in place. Then he poured the brew that Elsa had left in a tankard and handed it to Dawn.

She shook her head.

He scowled and took hold of her chin. "You will drink this. It will ease the pain."

She clamped her mouth closed, again shook her head, and gently pushed the tankard away.

He did not understand her reluctance to take it, but he would not force her. She'd been through enough. He sat it on the table. "It is there if you want it."

She nodded.

He left her a moment to fetch her night dress from the other room. He helped her to stand and when his hands went to her waist band, her hand stilled his. She tapped her naked chest.

"No, you will not do it yourself. I will do it." He brushed her hand away and slipped her skirt down over her hips. She shivered, and he quickly got her night dress over her head and gently helped her get her arms in the soft wool sleeves.

Her brow scrunched, and he winced aloud for her when he eased her wounded arm in the sleeve. He had her sit again as he gathered her skirt from around her feet and placed it on the back of a chair. Then he gently removed her boots.

"You should wear your wool stockings. It grows

colder." He looked up at her. "You are to stay abed until Elsa says otherwise."

Dawn stared at him, a pressing question on her mind. She had not given thought to her actions and had blatantly interfered with his ruling. It was cause for severe punishment, and she wondered how he would punish her. She was afraid to ask, though she was afraid not to ask. If she didn't, she would not know a moment's peace until she found out.

"Something troubles you?"

She nodded.

He lifted her gently in his arms and carried her to the bed in the other room and rested her back against the pillows to sit. He tucked the blanket up and around her waist before he asked, "Tell me what troubles you."

He sat beside her waiting, his hand resting on her thigh, his dark eyes intense.

She pressed her hand to her chest and bowed her head.

"You're sorry."

She nodded, and then pressed her fingers to her mouth and pretended to shudder.

"I understand that you were upset with the punishment I meted out, but it is not your place to interfere."

Fear trickled through her as she placed her hand to her chest, scrunched her brow, and shrugged.

He seemed perplexed at first and then his brow shot up. "Are you wondering if I will punish you?"

She nodded slowly.

"You deserve a lashing for interfering in my decree, especially since it is the second time you have done so."

She paled. She had seen those that Goddard had

lashed under Colum's order. The man had appeared to enjoy meting out the punishment. Out of the few who had suffered the sting of the lash, one had died.

"My word is law," he reminded.

She bobbed her head.

"He intended to kill you," Cree said. "He deserves a fitting punishment."

She nodded, and then shook her head and pointed to her mouth.

"You made yourself very clear when you threw yourself over the prisoner. Punish him, but don't take his tongue."

She nodded and began to gesture and Cree was pleased that he understood her.

"You think he may have more to tell me?"

She nodded and continued gesturing.

Cree scowled after she finished. "Yes, I thought the same myself—he seems in a hurry to die."

A scrunch of her brow and a shrug had Cree voicing Dawn's query. "Why is a good question, perhaps he does have more to tell us."

Relieved that Cree would not carry out his edict and her shoulder throbbing, she closed her eyes a moment.

When she opened them Cree's face sat only an inch or so from hers. She could not tell if it was anger, passion, or sorrow she saw in his dark eyes, but whatever it was, it burned deeply within him.

He took hold of her chin. "I will lash you myself if you ever do something so foolish again." He dropped his brow to hers. "I could have killed you." His whispered words brushed across her lips before he kissed her, then said, "I would have never forgiven myself."

He kissed her again, gently and lovingly, but it had been his heartfelt words that touched her the most. That he would have regretted her death made her wonder if he possibly cared for her.

"Rest," he ordered as he stood. "I will return later."

How could she rest when there was so much on her mind? She nodded nonetheless and when she heard the door shut in the other room, she slipped out of bed and went to sit in front of the hearth. She drew her knees up to her chin and wrapped her arms around them. It was a habit of hers to sit that way before the fireplace whenever she was troubled. Her mother had often joined her and comforted her.

Her problems had been nothing compared to what they were now. As for solutions? There were none. She belonged to Cree and he could do with her as he saw fit. And yet when she thought about it, he had done nothing more than treat her well and protect her. But then as he often reminded her... she belonged to him. And while the thought sent a shiver through her, it was for a far different reason than she would have imagined. As much as it alarmed her to think about it, she truly felt that she wasn't falling—but had fallen—in love with the devil.

19. ~~~

Cree had almost made it to the keep steps when he turned around and returned to the cottage. An overwhelming need had forced him to go back. He had no idea the reason for it, but he had learned a long time ago to follow such potent instincts. Of course, there was also the fact that he had not wanted to leave Dawn in the first place.

The guilt for having caused her harm had overpowered his anger at her foolish actions. He would have loved to have throttled her for what she had done, and how she had scared the life out of him, but he would never lay a hand on her that way. He was relieved that her wound was not severe and only painful. Perhaps the pain would remind her to think before she acted so foolishly.

He entered quietly, so as not to disturb her, and when he stepped into the other room and saw her sitting in front of the fireplace as he had found her on another occasion, he stopped. He watched her a moment and ascertained that she was not crying. Why then was she sitting there with her knees drawn up so tightly to her?

Dawn," he said softly as he approached not wanting to frighten her.

She startled nonetheless and turned.

He scooped her up in his arms and held her close as he sat on the edge of the bed. "No tears this time, but obviously something troubles you."

She was surprised by his return, pleased actually, and also pleased that he cared enough to ask what troubled her, but did she tell him? Did she let him know of her need for him? Did she let him know that she favored him by her side, in her bed? Did she let him know that she had fallen in love with him?

"If it is punishment you fear, worry not. The pain and discomfort your wound brings serves punishment enough and will be a lingering reminder."

Did she allow him to think that was what concerned her?

He pressed his cheek to hers, and then brushed his lips over hers. "I can see that wasn't it. And since you know full well that I never ask twice, I wait on the truth. A reminder—there isn't anything that you cannot confide in me. Tell me your worry, all your worries. Tell me even if you think it unimportant or foolish. Tell me whether it be sorrow, happiness, regret or..." He kissed her softly. "Tell me, Dawn."

His words and his kiss gave her the courage to admit what she had tried to hide from herself. There was one gesture she used to let people know that she loved them, but her love for Cree was different than for anyone else. She wanted a gesture that was meant to show her love—for him and him alone.

She pressed her hand to her heart, and then with the same hand pressed it over his heart.

He stood abruptly and dropped her on the bed. "Do not be so foolish to tell the devil that you love him."

He walked out of the room and when Dawn heard the door slam shut, she began to cry.

Chapter Thirty-two

"*Damn her*," Cree mumbled beneath his breath as he vaulted up the keep steps and straight through the Great Hall to his solar without acknowledging anyone. He slammed the door shut and went to the pitcher on the table and filled a tankard to the brim with ale. He downed half without stopping.

He then dumped himself in a chair before the hearth and let out a heavy sigh. How could she love a heartless bastard like him? He had almost killed her and what does she do? She tells him that she loves him.

He had encouraged her to tell him anything—anything other than she loved him that was. He squirmed in the chair. He understood immediately, or perhaps it was instinctively, her silent words when she had placed her hand to her chest and then to his.

Love.

He wasn't capable of loving. He had turned his heart silent a long time ago and yet...

He downed the rest of his ale and stared at the flames. He had been drawn to Dawn from when he had first seen her. He had allowed Colum to capture him, allowed him to put him on display in front of the village, allowed the fool to think that he had actually captured the infamous Cree.

He had seen Dawn as soon as they had entered the village. She had stood tall and proud, even if she hadn't realized it. She had a regal poise to her and though she wasn't beautiful, there was something about her that drew the eye and made it linger. He had had plans to seek her out after the attack on the village. but was spared the delay when Colum had chosen her to tend him.

When he had discovered that she had no voice, he had admired her all the more. Dawn was special in so many ways and he wanted her in his life now and forever.

The thought jolted him, and he bolted out of the chair and refilled his tankard.

Forever was a long time and he had never thought that way about a woman—until Dawn. He did not want to think about life without her. The closer they became the closer he wanted to become. There was something about her that... soothed his soul.

He felt a comfort with her that he had not known in a long time. A comfort he thought never to know again.

Love.

Damn that word refused to leave him alone and he refused to give it credence. He couldn't. He didn't want to hurt Dawn and in the end if he allowed himself to love her, he'd only hurt her and that he could not bear to do.

A knock sounded at the door and he reluctantly bid the person to enter.

Sloan closed the door behind him and stopped halfway across the room and stared at Cree. He looked about to say something, but Cree's scowl darkened and he wisely made no comment. Instead he walked over to the table and poured himself a tankard of ale and joined Cree in a drink.

Another knock sounded and Cree sent Sloan a

murderous look. He would have preferred to have been left alone for a while, though the only place he had undisturbed time was at Dawn's cottage.

Sloan ignored Cree and walked over to open the door.

Cree was surprised to see Elsa.

"My lord," she said with a bob of her head. "I thought you would want to know about the prisoner."

"Is he well enough for me to kill him?" Cree asked without a shred of remorse.

"It would be merciful of you."

"What do you mean?"

"Rem is ill and dying. His death will not be pleasant. He will suffer."

Cree turned to Sloan. "That was why he took this job. He knew it would end in his death. And once captured, he baited me so that I would see that he would die fast and end his suffering. Now the bastard can suffer until he dies, a much more fitting punishment."

"As a healer I cannot see him suffer—"

"Then don't watch."

"May I at least tend him on occasion?"

"No," Cree snapped. "He will pay for what he has done or planned on doing to Dawn."

"I have not known Dawn long, but from what I do know of her, she would not want to see this man suffer."

"It isn't her choice and has Dawn suddenly become some angel of mercy who will save everyone from the devil?"

Elsa quickly bowed her head and kept silent.

"I'm glad I didn't kill him yet. Now he will get what he deserves," Cree said and with a wave of his hand was about to dismiss Elsa when he stopped. "Is there any reason you know why Dawn would refuse to drink the brew that would ease her pain?"

Elsa cast a quick glance to Sloan and then down at the floor.

"Sloan, leave us," Cree ordered.

Sloan hurried out the door.

"What is it?" Cree asked.

"Dawn came to me and we talked about preventing conception."

Cree didn't know why, but her words disturbed him, though he said nothing.

"I explained that there was a plant that would help prevent a babe from taking root, though I warned her that if she was already with child, it could very well abort the babe. I told her that the choice was hers."

"Her response?"

She never answered me, though by not answering her response was clear. She would not dare threaten the life of a babe that might already be growing inside her."

"So she worries that the brew you fixed for her could be the one you had spoken of and would harm a babe that might already being growing inside her. And she would suffer the pain rather than take the chance of causing harm to the babe."

"I assume so," Elsa said.

Cree's scowl deepened.

Elsa shook her head. "I gave her no such brew, my lord. I told her that the choice was hers."

Cree dismissed her with a brief wave of his hand and returned to the chair in front of the hearth. So she would protect a babe of theirs that she may carry even to the point of pain, unsure if the brew would harm the unborn babe. Dawn certainly was a brave one, and the thought that she would suffer for their child made him more aware of what a loving and faithful person she was.

A knock at the door and a shout from Sloan had Cree bidding him entrance. In minutes the two men were making plans for the morrow when Seth would accompany Cree's warriors and track the other two men lurking in the woods.

20.

Dawn rested the reminder of the day and when supper was brought to her she waited, thinking Cree intended to join her. When he didn't, she nibbled on some of the food, finding she had little appetite.

She feared she had made a terrible mistake by telling him that she loved him. She now wondered why she had done such a foolish thing. He certainly had encouraged her to confide *anything* in him, and she had taken it to heart. She had believed he had truly meant it. And she had foolishly thought that perhaps—just perhaps—he could possibly feel the same.

The hours wore on and as it grew later and later, Dawn realized that Cree had no intention of returning to spend the night with her. Had her declaration of love driven him away? It was too late now. She could not take it back and she didn't want to. She had spoken the truth. She loved him. And that wasn't going to change.

A couple of hours later, Dawn slipped into a fitful slumber.

Cree stood watching her from the doorway. He didn't know if her wound was causing such a restless sleep or if perhaps dreams disturbed her. Whatever the reason, her sleep was far from peaceful.

He hadn't planned on returning to her bed tonight. He had given thought to not returning to her at all, but he had discovered after only a short time in his bed alone that that wasn't possible. He had actually missed her. He had turned on his side, his arms reaching out for her when he had realized that he was in his own bed alone. The idea that he didn't have her beside him to wrap himself around had angered him, so he had come here to her cottage.

He hadn't debated the matter, argued, cautioned, or stopped himself. His one and only thought was to crawl into bed with her, wrap himself around her, and go to sleep.

Mostly, his thought would have been solely on making love to her, but not this time. She had been wounded and needed rest, and he felt worn out himself. He simply wanted the comfort of her body against his. And to make certain she was protected even though he had guards on her. No one could protect her like he could.

He shed his garments and eased himself in bed beside her. She lay on her side and he moved up against her, his arm draping around her to tuck her close against him. She tried to turn in his arms, but winced as she did, her wound too fresh to lie on.

"Shhh," he whispered, "you're safe in my arms." He pressed her back flat against his front, and draped his legs across hers, stilling her restlessness.

She settled into a peaceful sleep, her hand moving to rest on his arm and her one finger giving it a tap.

He smiled. He liked that in her sleep she acknowledged that she agreed. Yes, she was safe in his arms. His smile slowly faded. How had this voiceless woman become so important to him? He had no answer and he presently didn't care. The only thing that mattered was that he was here wrapped around her, and he planned on never letting her go.

Chapter Thirty-three

Dawn walked through the village, a basket on her arm and Neil tagging close behind her. She had gotten permission from Cree to go into the woods and gather the makings for a wreath. The air had the scent of snow to it and with the grayness of the sky, snow definitely seemed likely.

It had been two weeks since her injury, and her wound had healed well, though her shoulder ached slightly. Daily life had settled into a pleasant routine for all and smiles were seen far more often than frowns. Everyone worked to make certain food supply would be plentiful for the winter. And Cree saw that hard work was rewarded. Fear for their new lord had been replaced with respect and admiration. The first session Cree had held to hear grievances had gossiping tongues wagging about what a fair lord he was.

The villagers were also pleased that Cree had ordered plaids made for everyone in the village, so that they would unite as a clan. Even the smallest child would have one. Lila had been made overseer of the project and four women were appointed to work with her.

Dawn hurried her pace. Cree had warned her not to dally. Even though the other two men sent to eliminate Dawn had been caught with the help of Seth, Cree still kept a guard on her. Seth remained a prisoner as did Rem.

Dawn was still perplexed as to why someone would want her dead. And though she had tried to engage Cree in discussion about it, he refused. He told her not to worry about it. He would let no one harm her. The question, however, continued to nag her. Why would someone want a peasant lass dead?

She entered the woods and got busy gathering what she needed, though when she spied the tree where Cree had braced her against that one day and had brought her body to life, she stopped to stare.

So much had changed since that day. No longer did he spill his seed outside her. Each and every time—and there were numerous times—they made love, he remained buried deep inside her. And she—fool that she was—grew to love him more and more.

Though Cree was mostly a stoic man, rarely letting his guard down, there were times his shield would fall and she would see a different man. Tender, kind, and so very loving. And it fed Dawn's hope—her dream— that someday he could possibly love her at least half as much as she loved him.

She kept her foolish hope to herself. She did not even trust Lila with it, for though her friend would never laugh at her, she would certainly pity her for wishing the impossible.

Dawn shook the troubling thoughts from her mind and returned to finishing her task. Satisfied that she had gathered enough she headed back to the village, Neil in tow. Her thoughts returned to Cree, though when didn't she think about him? He was forever on her mind and much too deep in her heart. It still amazed her to think that she loved him. She smiled and pressed her hand to her chest, as if guarding her secret and keeping it safe.

They had barely entered the village when the bell tolled an attack.

Neil grabbed her arm. "Get to the keep and stay there." He gave her a shove, and then took off joining a group of warriors headed to the entrance of the village.

Women dropped what they were doing, grabbed their children and ran for the keep, following the protocol that Cree had set down when he had spoken to the village one day. The village men gathered weapons and took their defined positions ready to defend their families and homes.

Dawn spotted Lila, Thomas cradled protectively against her chest, in the middle of a group of women heading for the keep. Lila waved for her to join them, and she was about to when she saw Cree astride his horse, his eyes searching the crowd. She didn't know if he searched for her, but in case he did, she waved his way to get his attention.

He nodded at her with what she thought was relief in his eyes and pointed to the keep. She nodded in return, and then he took off, a large group of his warriors following behind him. She turned, anxious to join Lila when she spotted Elsa arguing with one of the warriors. She shook her finger at him and turned to enter her cottage. The large warrior grabbed her by the arm and forcibly dragged her away, ignoring her adamant protests.

Dawn recalled that the prisoner she had saved from having his tongue cut out had been moved to the room that had been added to Elsa's cottage, his illness having worsened. She didn't know why she felt compelled to see the man, but she couldn't seem to stop herself. Did she hope that he would have something more to tell her that could help her solve this riddle? A moment that is all she would dare take, and then she would join the other women in the keep.

She pulled the hood of her cloak up over her head, concealing her face so that none of the warriors would spot her and force her to the keep. She made her way around the crowd and hurried up the short path to Elsa's cottage. She entered the room to find the man sitting on the edge of the bed. He was pale and took several heavy breaths. She threw back her hood and hurried over to the bucket of water near the bed to fill the ladle and hold it out to him. He reached for it, but his hand shook too badly for him to hold it so Dawn held it to his mouth for him to drink.

When he finished, he struggled for more breathes and said, "What's happening?"

Dawn did her best to gesture an attack and was relieved that he understood.

"You must go and keep safe, but first—I'm sorry."

She shrugged and knitted her brow, hoping he would understand that she asked why.

"I did bad things most all my life," —he shook his head — "then I fell in love with a good woman and she bore me a beautiful daughter." He stopped again, though this time tears filled his eyes. "Someone I wronged badly sought revenge and took from me what I had taken from him." Tears spilled down his face. "God heard me when I told him that I didn't want to live any longer. Though he did not believe that I had suffered enough, and so he gave me an illness that would slowly torture me to death," —he drew a few more breathes— "I thought to fool him and shorten my suffering, but instead he sends an angel to protect me from losing my tongue, and now she sees to my care when she should see to her own."

"You are pathetic, old man."

Dawn turned to see Seth standing in the open doorway.

"And you are more the fool if you think Cree trusts you," Rem said.

Seth shook his head. "Of course he doesn't trust me, but that doesn't matter since my plan worked. Goddard freed me while that ignoramus Colum charges head first to his death, thinking to regain Dowell and save face with Roland Gerwan. In the meantime, I will succeed in carrying out my mission and be paid handsomely for it."

"You are an idiot," Rem said and started coughing.

Dawn sat on the bed beside Rem, patting him on the back. Her helpful gesture wasn't for Rem alone. She wanted to be sitting. It gave her closer access to the dirk in her boot she had taken to carrying, never wanting to be caught without protection again.

"I will finish what Cree failed to do—cut out your tongue—though I will not give you the satisfaction of killing you."

"Do what you will. You're still a dead man."

"Cree will never find me. I will be long gone before he realizes I'm missing."

"You idiot, it isn't Cree who will kill you. It is the person who hired us. He wants no one left alive who can speak of this. We were dead men as soon as we agreed to kill this woman."

"Not me," Seth sneered. "I will let no one take my life. I will get what I deserve."

"That you will," Rem said and began coughing so badly that he doubled over.

"I have no time for this," Seth raised his sword

and charged toward Dawn.

Dawn was suddenly slammed back on the bed, and she watched wide-eyed as Rem jumped up, her dirk in his hand, and as Seth's sword pierced his chest, Rem drove the dirk into his neck.

Seth stumbled backward, his eyes wide with shock and collapsed to the ground. It took only seconds for him to take his last breath.

Dawn jumped off the bed, grabbing Rem and going down with him as he crumpled to the floor.

He grabbed her hand. "I have no right... but... please... I'm afraid to die alone."

She patted his shoulder and gently lifted his head to rest in her lap, then took hold of his hand.

He squeezed it tightly. "I hope God forgives me and lets me see my wife and daughter again."

Dawn nodded vigorously, patting her chest and pointing to Seth.

"You believe... I redeemed... myself... by saving... your life."

She nodded again.

"You are... an angel... and I am grateful to you... for forgiving me. Be careful... someone... wants you dead." He squeezed her hand even harder. "And be... even more careful... the devil... loves you... and will never... let you go."

Rem coughed, smiled at Dawn as if he had found peace, and died clutching her hand.

She sat there frozen, too numb to move, too numb to barely think, though Rem's last words echoed loudly in her head... *the devil loves you and will never let you go.*

What would make him think such a thing?

Elsa appeared in the doorway, though Dawn had

no way of telling if it had been minutes or hours that had passed. The woman took in the scene in one glance, then stepped back out, shouting. The next thing Dawn knew, Cree was there filling the doorway.

She hadn't known she was crying until Cree knelt beside her and gently wiped away her tears with his finger.

"Are you hurt?" he asked.

She shook her head, patted Rem's head, pointed to Seth, and then tapped her chest.

"Rem took the sword meant for you?"

She nodded and the next thing she knew, she was lifted into Cree's strong arms. She pointed to Rem.

"He will be given a decent burial."

Dawn nodded, pleased, and rested her head on Cree's chest as he carried her out of the cottage. Her head popped up once outside. She was surprised to see that no damage had been done to the village. And there looked to be no wounded. Men walked laughing toward the keep to collect their wives and children. Another rule Cree had lain down. No women or children were allowed to leave the keep after an attack until their husbands or fathers came for them.

She looked to Cree and shrugged.

"Curious as usual."

She nodded.

"It was no fight at all. Why the fool Colum thought he could retake the village with such few men bewilders me."

Dawn shrugged again, wondering over Colum's fate.

"Colum got what he so richly deserved and what I had wanted to do to him ever since he laid a hand on you. He will never hurt anyone again."

Dawn now understood why the men laughed and

appeared so joyous. Colum was dead. There was no fear that he would one day return. He was gone forever.

Once in her cottage, Cree lowered her to stand, though his hands went to clasp at her waist. "Are you sure you're all right?"

She smiled and patted her chest.

He grinned and gave her a quick kiss. "You are a courageous woman."

He sounded as if he admired her and the thought caused her breath to catch.

"The warrior guarding Seth was knocked on the head from behind and never saw his assailant. Did Seth say who freed him?"

Dawn gestured as she did once before when she wanted to identify Goddard to Cree, and he remembered.

"Goddard. I thought as much. He was nowhere to be found."

Dawn tensed.

His hands tightened at her waist. "Do not worry. I will find him and put an end to him. Then he will trouble us no more."

Us. It thrilled Dawn to hear him refer to them as us. Could Rem have been right? Did the devil love her?

"I'll return later," he said and lowered his lips to hers to savor for a moment.

It was far too many minutes before they broke apart and reluctantly, then quickly joined again. She knew he had to go, though she wished he wouldn't. She wished he would stay and...

The thought that perhaps she could make him stay if only for a short...

Dawn didn't think on it, she daringly acted, slipping her hand over the bugle between his legs, teasing it. He groaned and his kiss deepened as his mouth grew hungrier against hers. She felt empowered by his eager response and she continued tormenting him into submission.

"Damn it, Dawn." He all but moaned as he tore his mouth away from hers. "I have no time—"

She hurried to the table, hopped up on it to lie on her back and spread her legs and stretch her arms out to him.

Cree grinned and didn't hesitate to accept her invitation. He planted himself inside her quickly, an easy plunge since she was so wet and ready for him, which excited him even more. It wouldn't take long for either one of them, another thought that had him thrusting in her even harder.

Damn if he didn't enjoy her more and more each time they coupled. And damn if he wasn't building to an explosive climax as always. And one final damn if he didn't lov—

He burst in a blinding climax as she wrapped her legs more tightly around him, forcing him to plunge even deeper as she tightened around him. He shuddered as his climax ended, and he pulled out of her so quickly that her body startled and her eyes grew wide.

He didn't say a word to her. He adjusted his leggings and stormed out of the cottage, leaving her staring after him.

Chapter Thirty-four

Dawn was bewildered. What had she done wrong? Cree had been as eager as she had been to make love. So why had he stormed out of the cottage so quickly when they had barely finished. If he had remained inside her just a moment longer, she would have reached a second climax.

She grew annoyed at what she didn't know. What she did know was that she didn't intend to remain in the cottage and sulk or linger on having watched two men die today. She quickly adjusted her garments and was out the door expecting to see Neil or another guard stationed there. When she saw none; she smiled. She was on her own, for how long she didn't know, but she intended to relish her freedom.

It didn't take long for her to decide where she was going. First, she would retrieve the basket she had left by Elsa's cottage, and then she would go and see how Lila and Thomas had faired through this all.

A few injured warriors lingered around Elsa's cottage waiting their turn to be tended. There seemed to be only minor wounds that needed attention. Dawn did not want to be in the way, so she grabbed her basket and walked around to the back of the cottage and headed to Lila's.

She had taken only a few steps when she was grabbed by her hair and around the waist. She fought her assailant, twisting and throwing punches that caused him to lose his grip and stumble. When she saw that it was Goddard, she fought even harder. He had caused her immeasurable suffering, and there was no way she'd let him hurt her again.

She couldn't scream, but she might be able to...

She twisted quickly in his arms and when he went to hit her, she grabbed his arm and sunk her teeth into it hard. He did exactly what she hoped he'd do, and what she couldn't do... scream.

Cree had joined Sloan at the top step of the keep when he heard the scream. Both men turned to see where it had come from and saw the warriors at Elsa's cottage run around back. Cree and Sloan flew off the steps.

Cree couldn't help it; his first thought was of Dawn. He had left angry, not at her but himself. He could not let love interfere with commitments he had made. He wasn't even capable of loving. He had turned his heart cold long ago and had no intentions of ever warming it to anyone.

The sheer idea that Dawn could have possibly cracked the ice and slipped in filled him with dread. She would be the one to suffer if he allowed himself to love her, and he would not allow that.

Cree ran ahead of Sloan, following around to the back of Elsa's cottage where all the commotion could be heard.

"I'll kill you, you bitch!"

Rage hot and furious raced through Cree when he saw that Goddard had pinned Dawn to the ground, his hands tight around her neck and his men fighting to get him off her. Cree let out a vicious roar and raced at Goddard, slamming into him with such force that the blow knocked Goddard off Dawn and sent the two men tumbling. Cree scrambled to his feet and was on

Goddard before he could stand. In one swift twist he broke Goddard's neck and let his body crumple to the ground.

"Put him where the animals can feast on him," Cree ordered and two warriors did as he bid, carrying the body off into the woods. He walked over to drop down next to Dawn. "What the hell are you doing going anywhere without a guard?"

Dawn barely had regained her breath, barely had time to register what had just happened when Cree had turned his temper on her. She had had enough. She had witnessed death too many times today to dismiss it so easily. And then there was the issue of Cree having made a hasty exit after what had been to her a mutually enjoyable joining. Now he was insinuating that it was her fault that she'd been choked because she had gone without a guard.

She was furious and she tapped his chest hard, shook her head, and then tapped her chest.

He scowled. "Are you telling me that I can't tell you what to do?"

Dawn struggled to her feet, pushing his hands away as he tried to help her up. He would have none of her protests. He grabbed her around the waist and lifted her to her feet.

"Answer me," he demanded.

Dawn caught the way his men looked at him as if he was crazy for thinking that a voiceless woman could answer him. But Cree hadn't thought that. He had spoken to her as if she was no different than anyone else, and damn if that didn't warm her heart... a little.

She gave a curt nod.

"Leave us!" Cree shouted and his men scurried

off. "Haven't you gotten yourself into enough trouble today?"

Dawn turned her eyes wide and slapped her chest. "Yes, you."

She gritted her teeth, scowled at him, and turned and walked over to pick up the spilled contents of her basket.

"I am speaking to you," Cree said sternly.

Dawn turned patted her chest, tapped her lips, shook her head, and pointed at him.

"You're not speaking to me?"

She smiled, nodded, and resumed her task.

His strong grip on her arm stopped her. "I would not advise that."

She questioned why with her usual shrug.

He let go of her arm to stroke her neck, angry with the light bruising he saw there. "Because I want no silence between us."

His words stunned her. Did he truly feel as if she actually spoke to him? Did he hear her voice as silent as it was? Her anger melted and she pressed her finger to his lips, and then to hers and shook her head.

"I'm glad you feel the same. I would miss speaking with you."

He stunned her again and her reaction was instinctive, she wrapped her arms around his neck and kissed him. And all she could think about as she did was how very much she loved this man... not the devil... not the infamous Cree... but this man who would miss talking with her.

When the kiss ended Cree was quick to say, "You'll come to the keep with me and enjoy the warmth of the fire while I tend to some matters."

Dawn did not relish the idea of sitting in the Great Hall while Cree was busy. She wanted nothing more than the solitude of her cottage. She shook her head and pointed to her basket and the contents lying scattered about.

"The wreath," he said with a nod. "You wish to return to the cottage and work on the wreath?"

She smiled and nodded.

"You promise me that you will stay there?"

She crossed her heart with her finger.

"I will join you for supper."

Her smile grew and she nodded vigorously.

Cree smiled as well and teased, "That hungry are you?"

Dawn felt playful and a bit wicked, and so she licked her lips ever so slowly as she nodded.

Cree watched the play of her tongue along her lips, leaving them moist in its path, and he couldn't help but wonder how her tongue would feel licking his—

"Enough," he said with a low growl, the image it evoked growing him hard. He shouted and a warrior appeared. Cree instructed him to help Dawn gather her twigs and pine cones and see her to her cottage. He then turned to her. "I will see you later and make sure to stay put this time."

With that he was gone, Dawn disappointed that he would not walk her back to the cottage. She had hoped to coax him inside and...

She turned away, dropping down to refill her basket and hide the blush that surfaced. She had turned into a sinful woman and if she was not mindful of her thoughts, she would surely suffer for it.

It didn't take long for her to collect the spilled contents and return to her cottage. She was grateful for the solitude and for the chore that not only kept her hands busy, but her mind as well.

The knock interrupted her peace, though when Old Mary entered, she smiled greeting the old woman.

Old Mary shut the door behind her and rubbed her gnarled fingers. "Snow's coming for sure."

Dawn pointed to a chair and poured her a tankard of cider from the pitcher being kept hot by the hearth.

Old Mary accepted it with a grateful nod. "I used to make wreaths, and oh how I loved to weave baskets, but these old hands won't let me do that anymore."

Dawn patted her chest and pointed to the woman.

"That is sweet of you to offer to make me one." Old Mary took a sip and remained silent for several minutes.

Dawn patted the old woman's arm and shrugged wanting to know what was troubling her.

"You are perceptive. You know people, understand them better than most, but then you have no choice but to listen." Old Mary reached for Dawn's hand. "Listen well to me, Dawn. Things are not what they seem to be—they never were. You must be careful. You must not trust anyone."

Another knock at the door had Flanna entering with two servants and baskets of food. Her entrance not only turned Old Mary silent, but had her bidding Dawn good night. Dawn tried to get the old woman to stay and partake with her, but Old Mary was adamant about leaving. Dawn was disappointed, she wanted to know what the old woman meant by *things are not what they seem to be and never were.*

Old Mary's warning made her nervous. Of course, they could just be ramblings that meant nothing, but Dawn had known Old Mary too well to believe she rambled. Her mind was sharper than anyone realized or that she led anyone to believe.

Flanna fussed over her after ordering the two servants to return to the keep. "I want to thank you again for helping me get this position. I am very happy with it and happy that Turbett cannot order me around anymore."

Dawn smiled and patted her chest to let Flanna know how pleased she was for her.

"It is an important position and it has earned me respect with the villagers. Turbett even treats me differently." Flanna smiled. "He had a separate table set for us where we could eat while we discussed the keep's menu for the coming days. He served me a special mixed cider that he wanted my opinion on. It was delicious."

Dawn's eyes lit with joy. Could the unlikely pair be finding common ground? She hoped so. Flanna deserved to find someone to love her. She could be stubborn at times. but she had a caring soul.

"Cree is deep in conversation with Sloan and food has been served to them, so I'm not sure if he will be joining you tonight."

She was disappointed to learn that he might not share supper with her, though she would not let Flanna know that. She pointed to the array of food spread across the table and shrugged.

"I make sure the meal is plentiful in case Cree does join you."

Dawn pressed her hand to her chest and nodded in thanks.

Flanna grabbed hold of her hand. "You owe me no thanks. It is I who am indebted to you. Now I must go and tend to my duties and later Turbett asked me to share a meal with him. He has cooked something new and wishes my opinion."

Dawn hugged Flanna and the woman almost squeezed the breath out of her when she hugged her back.

"You are a good woman, Dawn," Flanna said sniffling back her tears and hurried out the door.

Dawn sat looking at the abundance of food and shook her head. She had lost her appetite as soon as she heard that Cree might not be joining her. Wind whistled around the cottage and she wondered if it had started snowing yet. Then she recalled that a warrior stood guard outside her door and she quickly filled a tankard with hot cider. She also grabbed a hunk of bread and meat.

She opened the door and Neil was quick to step in front of her. A light dusting of snow covered his hood and cloak. She held out the tankard and food to him.

He bobbed his head and took them from her. "Thank you. Now back inside. It's going to be a cold one tonight."

Dawn reluctantly closed the door. It wasn't fair that Neil had to stand out in the cold all night. And the longer she sat in front of the hot fire, the more worried she became for the man. Not able to take it any longer, she grabbed a blanket from her bed and went to the door.

Once again Neil stepped in front of the door. She held the blanket out to him.

Neil shook his head. "I'm fine. Don't worry yourself about me."

Dawn shook her head and proceeded to wrap the blanket around him.

"A little snow is too much for one of my warriors?"

Neil quickly pulled the blanket off him and shoved it at Dawn before turning to acknowledge Cree with a nod. "The snow does not bother me, my lord."

Dawn looked to Cree, ready to protest, but his dark scowl made her realize it was not her place to interfere when he spoke with his warriors.

"I thought as much," Cree said, "though you know the protocol for guard watch when it snows."

"Aye, my lord," Neil said with a bob of his head. "Guards are to be changed every thirty minutes."

"That starts now," Cree ordered with a wave to a warrior that stood a few feet away. "You have been here long enough. Kirk will relieve you, and you go see Sloan for the night's schedule."

Neil nodded and turned to Dawn. "Thank you for your generosity." He took off then disappearing into the swirling snow.

Dawn retreated several steps as Cree entered the cottage.

He closed the door and scowled at her. "Do not coddle my warriors."

Dawn hugged herself and shivered.

"I know it's cold outside, but they are seasoned warriors and do as they must under any conditions. They have been through much worse than this minor snowfall." He walked over to her, his arm going around her waist and drawing her close to him. "Are you as ravenous as I am?"

She smiled, ran her hand along his chest and nodded.

"It will take much to appease my appetite tonight," he cautioned with a whisper.

Dawn tapped her chest lightly, and then tapped

his.

"You will appease me?"

She crossed her heart.

"That's a promise?"

She nodded.

He brushed his lips over hers. "I will hold you to that promise."

He kissed her and she returned it with an eagerness that had their passions mounting in leaps and bounds.

A pounding at the door had Cree swearing as he reluctantly tore his lips away from hers. "Who disturbs me?"

Sloan's voice rang out. "The messenger you have been waiting for has arrived."

"Damn," Cree mumbled, his hands falling away from Dawn. "Fortify yourself with food or rest whatever it takes, for you will get no rest when I return."

Dawn smiled, crossed her heart, and shrugged.

Cree's arm shot out going around her waist and yanking her hard against him. "You want a promise from me?"

Her breath caught deep in her throat as she nodded. He was hard against her, and she was already wet with the want of him.

"I promise that you will never forget tonight."

Chapter Thirty-five

Dawn waited until she could no longer keep her eyes open. She sought her bed disappointed that Cree had yet to return to her. The message must have been of great importance. She only hoped it wasn't bad news and that all would be right with the village. She, like many others, worried that perhaps Robert Gerwan would be given his land back and life would once again turn harsh.

She added two more logs to the already roaring fire not wanting it to burnout in the middle of the night, especially with the snow still falling. The wind had grown stronger as had the snowfall. She had taken a peek hoping to see Cree headed to the cottage, but all she had caught sight of was swirling snow and the guard bundled in a fur-lined cloak and huddled close beside the front door.

The bed welcomed her with its warmth, though she wished it was Cree's arms and his naked body that held her snug. He would come, she had no doubt. After all he had promised her and she knew that Cree would not break his promise to her. He was a man of his word.

Trying to remain awake proved difficult, and she succumbed to sleep sooner than she planned with hope that Cree would wake her soon.

Cree dismissed all guards for the rest of the evening. The snow was falling heavily and it would be impossible for anyone to find their way through it in the dark. The guards would resume their duties at first light.

He entered the cottage quietly and secured the latch that was usually left unlatched. He wasn't surprised to find Dawn abed, and he disrobed with haste, though when he approached the bed he stood there staring down at her.

It had taken longer than he had expected to return to her and if he hadn't promised her that he would return he didn't know if he would have tonight. It wasn't that he didn't want to return. He was hungry for her and had been sense he had left her, but then when didn't he want her. He wondered over his perpetual state of arousal whenever he was around her, and he also wondered if she felt the same since she was always eager to couple with him.

It had been the message that had stalled his return. He thought of telling her the news tonight, but worried that once she learned of it she would not be so eager to make love with him. He had decided to wait and tell her the news tomorrow.

He eased into bed wrapping himself around her, his hand cupping her breast to gently squeeze it. He ran his thumb over her nipple and licked his lips eager to take the hardening bud into his mouth.

She turned as he knew she would. She always responded to his touch, no matter in bed, before the hearth, on the table. He grinned at how adventurous she was and planned on enjoying many more adventurous couplings with her.

He took her hard nipple in his mouth and teased it with the tip of his tongue while his hand roamed down along her body, relishing the feel of her velvet soft skin. He loved touching her, every inch of her.

The exquisite feel of her not only aroused him, but brought him a strange comfort. He wasn't sure what it was or perhaps he did not want to admit it, but it was as if he was home when he was with her... a safe haven.

His fingers inched their way between her legs, itching to dip inside her and bring her body to life. He sighed when he felt her moistness. It was as if she remained forever ready for him, only him. While his fingers played inside her, his thumb searched out the small nub that he would tease awake.

She might not be able to make a sound, but the way her body responded to him spoke louder than words ever could. Her body possessed a magical rhythm that enticed and enthralled and that responded only to his touch. But then it seemed the same for him. His body responded to her exploring hands and tongue like no other, and he wanted no other but her.

A dark thought intruded and he pushed it away. Tomorrow was time enough to tell her.

Her eyes fluttered open and her body stretched awake, moving to the gentle rhythm he had set.

She smiled, tapped his chest, waved her hand around the room, nodded, and crossed her heart.

"I am pleased to know that you had no doubt that I would keep my promise and return to you tonight."

Her smile grew as she slipped her hand down between them to grasp hold of him and rub the tip of him against her.

"You're a hungry one," he teased.

She patted his chest.

The loving passion in her eyes spoke more than her gesture.

"Only for me." His hand slipped out of her and

pushed her hand off him, replacing it with his own and rubbing himself against her moist entrance. "I can't wait. I want you now." He kissed her hungrily. "Then again." He kissed her as if starving. "Again and again and again."

He turned her on her back and as soon as he climbed over her, he thrust into her and she bucked beneath him taking him even deeper into her.

He gasped. "Damn it, woman, you'll make me come fast if you keep that up."

Wickedness rose in Dawn and this time she paid it no heed. She loved being able to bring him to climax. It made her climax that much stronger. And so she set a rapid rhythm, squeezing him tight and forcing a groan to erupt from his lips.

"You witch," he whispered before he claimed her mouth in a demanding kiss that she responded to with even a greater demand.

Cree finally pulled back and braced his hands on either side of her head. "Hold on, I'm going to ride you hard and fast."

She grabbed hold of his arms and wished she could scream out the immense pleasure each and every one of his deep thrusts brought her. She let him know the only way she could by tapping at his arm over and over and over... until.

She exploded in such a blinding climax that she locked her hands on his, threw her head back, and bucked against him, squeezing tight to relish every last tingle that rushed through her.

Cree felt as if he exploded over and over and over, he came so hard. It was so amazing that he didn't want to pull out of her. He wanted to remain in her for the entire night.

And he almost did. It seemed as if neither could

get enough of each other.

He loved when he bent her over the bed, grabbed her backside, and drove into her until she tore at the blankets in a never-ending climax.

In between the bouts of love making, they ate to fortify themselves and when Dawn pushed him back on the chair and straddled him, he welcomed her with a grin and nibbled at her nipples while she bounced up and down on him.

The last time they made love was with gentle, exploring touches and soft, lingering kisses. Until finally Cree slipped tenderly into her, his movement slow and measured, allowing their passion to climb slowly when finally they burst together in a lasting climax that had them shuddering in wave after wave of pleasure.

Wrapped in each other's arms, they drifted off to sleep more content than either of them had ever known.

Dawn woke with a stretch and winced, then smiled at the soreness between her legs. She turned, wondering why Cree wasn't wrapped around her as usual and found the bed empty. A shiver ran through her as if something dreadful had just happened, and her stomach roiled.

Her stomach grew queasier and she hurried out of bed to dress in a warm wool skirt and blouse. She didn't bother with leggings. She simply slipped on her boots. Her stomach hadn't settled by the time she finished braiding her hair. And when she entered the other room, she ran for the bucket and heaved, though there was nothing in her stomach to come up.

The thought hit her like a splash of cold water. She had not bled when she should have and now this.

There was no denying the obvious—she carried Cree's child. Now what? She feared telling him, for she was unsure of his reaction.

A knock sounded and a servant entered with food enough for one. Dawn was glad when she left, for she heaved once again, the food causing her stomach to protest. Also the young lass had looked at her oddly and Dawn feared that she might suspect something since she probably looked paler than usual. She was also relieved that Cree wasn't here to see her like this. He would know right away the cause, and she wasn't certain if she wanted him to know just yet.

She supposed she was hoping for a miracle. That somehow he would proclaim his love for her and wed her. It was a foolish dream, she knew that, but she could not help but hope.

Another knock sounded before the door swung open to admit Lila.

Dawn smiled and cradled her arms, asking where Thomas was when she realized that Lila appeared upset.

Dawn went to her and Lila reached out and hugged her tightly. Something was wrong terribly wrong. She eased Lila away and shrugged.

Lila's eyes turned wide. "You don't know?"

Dawn felt her stomach clutch and she prayed that she would not heave in front of Lila. She shook her head.

Lila took hold of her hand and tried to get her to the table to sit, but Dawn shook her head and gestured insistently for Lila to tell her now.

Lila nodded and kept hold of her hand. "Cree's future bride arrives in a week."

Dawn's legs turned so weak that she would have collapsed if Lila hadn't slipped her arm around her.

Lila got Dawn to a chair and sat her down, then pulled a chair beside her and sat.

"The whole village is talking about it. He's to wed Robert Gerwan's daughter by the King's decree and all Gerwan's holdings will revert to Cree along with the title."

With her dream shattered before her eyes, Dawn suddenly feared for her unborn child. No new bride would want her husband's bastard child in the village for all to see.

The door opened and Cree stood in the doorway, a light snow covering his cloak.

"Leave us," he ordered sternly and Lila scurried out after giving her friend's hand a squeeze.

Dawn grew even more upset when she realized Cree knew this last night, knew it all along and had never said a word to her about it. Not that he had to, but she had thought that they were—what a fool she had been.

Cree stepped further in the room after closing the door. "You've heard."

She nodded.

"This changes nothing between us. You are my mistress and will remain so. Elsa will be here shortly. She will provide you with the plant that prevents conception. Make certain to take it."

Was he telling her to get rid of any child that might be growing inside her? But of course he was. He would not want a son or daughter born voiceless like her.

He walked over to her, though he did not reach out to touch her. "I will treat you well and keep you safe."

Dawn wouldn't look at him; she couldn't. Her

heart was breaking. She simply nodded.

His hand moved to touch her face, and she braced herself not to cringe and blessed the heavens for the knock at the door that stopped him.

"That will be Elsa. Take what she gives you and we will talk more on this later." He opened the door and let Elsa in. "We have discussed this. She knows what is expected of her."

Elsa nodded and when the door closed she walked over to Dawn, setting her basket on the table.

Dawn would accept the plant, but had no intention of taking it.

Elsa explained to Dawn how to brew the leaves and how often to take it. "But remember if you are already with child it will abort the babe." Elsa took a pouch from her basket and placed it on the table. "I will bring you more next month."

Dawn nodded.

"Think on this Dawn, for any decision you make will have repercussions."

Dawn realized then that the woman knew that she was already with child and leaving the decision to her.

"I am a healer and I heal. I cause harm to none for I am all too aware of the consequences. Think on it, Dawn, and do in your heart what you feel is right for you."

Dawn wanted to hug the woman for giving her a choice, but she didn't. She simply nodded and pressed her hand to her chest to show her gratitude while she fought back the tears ready to spill.

Elsa squeezed her hand before she stood. "I am here if you need me."

Dawn nodded and tried to smile, but it barely reached her lips. As soon as the door closed she burst into tears. She spent the rest of the morning sitting in front of the hearth too numb to move.

When Sloan arrived telling her that Cree wanted to see her in his solar, she gestured that she was sick and could not go.

"It isn't a request," Sloan said.

Dawn was pleased that the babe decided to protest just then and she ran to the bucket and heaved.

To her relief, Sloan left after telling her he would inform Cree that she wasn't well.

Several hours later she heard Cree talking to the guard outside the door. She hurried into the other room, pulled her boots off, climbed under the covers, and curled into a ball. She didn't want to see him, didn't want to talk with him... she wanted him to leave her alone.

She heard him enter the room and walk over to the bed and lean over her.

His hand touched her brow. It was cool, his touch gentle and as always her body sparked to life, but she refused to acknowledge it.

"Dawn," he whispered.

She knew if she didn't open her eyes that he would persist, so she fluttered them open as if she was waking.

"Are you all right?" he asked with such concern that it touched her heart, but again she refused to acknowledge it.

She shook her head.

"I will send for Elsa."

She shook her head. Placed her hands together as if in prayer and rested them to her cheek.

"You just need to rest?"

She nodded.

"If you are not better by late evening then Elsa will see to you," he ordered and she nodded. He kissed her brow. "I will see you later."

Dawn nodded and closed her eyes to keep her tears from falling and sighed silently when she heard the door close.

The hours wore on until she finally felt the need to get away from the cottage and not with a guard. She slipped on the wool, fur-lined cloak, and then moved the trunk to the window, relieved that Cree had not had it boarded up, but then she had not given him cause to after the last time. Now however was different, and she didn't care about the consequences.

She eased herself out the window feet first so that she could grab hold and lower herself to the ground. She did not want to take a chance of hurting the babe by simply dropping to the ground as she had done the last time.

Once out, she snuck around the back of the castle. She knew where she would go—her safe place. It was where she went as a child when she wanted to escape and feel free. And she needed that now, a place to escape to and feel free if only for a short time.

Then she would return and face her fate.

Chapter Thirty-six

"What do you mean she's not there?" Cree demanded, his head coming up to scowl at the young servant lass.

The servant trembled as she spoke. "I could find her nowhere in the cottage, my lord."

Cree stood towering over the woman. "You looked in the other room?"

She bobbed her head. "After I called out to her and got no answer, I went in the other room to make certain she was all right, but it was empty, though the window was open."

Cree waved the lass away and turned to Sloan. "Come with me."

They arrived at Dawn's cottage in no time and followed the footprints beneath the window until they dissolved into an utter mess.

"She covered her tracks well," Sloan said.

"You sound as if you admire her," Cree snapped.

"She does have a sharp wit."

"Let's see if your wit is sharper—*find her*!" He turned to storm away and stopped abruptly, pointing to the window. "Board it."

Two hours later and no success in finding Dawn, Cree stormed into Lila's cottage causing Thomas to cry out. Elsa stepped in behind him. "Take the child."

"No, my lord, please," Lila begged, hugging her son tightly against her.

Elsa reached out for the babe and whispered, "Do as he says and your child will be returned to you."

Lila gave Thomas to Elsa and she left the cottage, Cree closing the door behind her.

Lila couldn't stop her tears from falling. She feared she would never see Thomas again.

"You were the one who told Dawn that my future bride was on her way?" Cree accused.

Lila bowed her head. "I thought she already knew—that you had told her—and only sought to comfort her."

"She was upset?"

"Aye, my lord, her legs grew too weak for her to stand."

Cree let loose a low growl. "Where would she run to?"

Lila shook her head. "She would not run. There is no place for her to go, though..."

"What? Tell me."

"There is a place she would go as a child when she wanted to feel safe, feel free."

"Where is it?"

"I do not know. She never told me. She never shared its whereabouts with anyone."

"Don't lie to me," Cree warned.

Lila stiffened with fear. "I do not lie, my lord. If I knew where it was, I would tell you. Dawn was very protective of it. She told me once that the only person she would share her safe place with would be the man she loved and wed."

Her words stabbed him like a sharp knife to the gut. She would never wed, for he would not let her. But she would share her safe place with him—he would make certain of it.

"If she didn't want to return to the cottage, where

do you think she would go?"

"The only other place she felt safe," Lila said sadly. "Home."

21. ~~~

Dawn sat holding her cold hands out in front of Old Mary's hearth—her old hearth. She had taken her boots off, her feet cold as ice. She had stayed too long at the glen, but it had been so peaceful that she hadn't noticed that dusk had been fast encroaching. Night had settled on the land by the time she had reached the village. Not wanting to return to her new cottage, she decided to go home and Old Mary had greeted her with a smile.

She rubbed her hands together and looked at the old woman sitting in front of the hearth on the floor beside her. She was wizened with age and knowledge, and Dawn took this opportunity to question her about what she had said when last she had visited Dawn.

Before she could gesture, Old Mary laid her hand on Dawn's knee. "He's coming for you and he's angry."

Dawn scrambled to her feet, slipped her boots on, and headed out the door, stopping abruptly when she caught sight of him.

He came out of the shadows of the night his cloak flying out behind him as he hurried toward her. Instincts took over, and she ran.

She didn't get far. He scooped her up in his arms and headed straight for her cottage. Dawn was glad night had fallen. There were fewer villagers about to see his fury and gossip about her dilemma, though no doubt she was already talk of the village. Everyone was probably wondering about her fate with the imminent arrival of Cree's intended.

He kicked the door shut to the cottage and after setting her down on her feet, though keeping hold of her wrist, he latched the door. He then shoved her into the other room.

"Disrobe, and I will not tell you twice," he ordered.

The fury in his dark eyes warned her not to argue or protest, so she did as she was told. She shed all her garments to stand naked in front of him.

He walked over to her and grabbed her wrist, yanking her against him. "If I must keep you naked so that you don't run off I will." He shoved her onto the bed and hastily shed his clothes. He then dropped down over her, pinning her arms above her head.

He kissed her then, but so much more gently than she had expected and angry as she was, as much as she wanted to resist him, she simply couldn't resist his loving tenderness. And either could her body. She heated with passion as his kiss deepened and when his hand began to touch her, gently, loving... she surrendered.

It was as if he paid homage to her body; kissing, tasting, touching and entering her with a tender control that had her writhing beneath him. When all was done and he had brought her to climax several times, he moved off her and rested on his side. He eased her over on her side, drawing her back against his chest. He wrapped his arm tightly around her and draped his leg snugly over hers.

Then he whispered in her ear. "You're *mine*; you *belong* to me. I will *never* let you go."

Cree and Dawn's story continues in ***Forbidden Highlander***, book two of the Highlander Trilogy. Available now.

Titles by Donna Fletcher

Single Titles

San Francisco Surrender
Untamed Fire
Rebellious Bride
The Buccaneer
Tame My Wild Touch
Playing Cupid
Whispers on the Wind

Series Books

The Wedding Spell (Wyrrd witch series)
Magical Moments
Magical Memories
Remember the Magic

The Irish Devil
Irish Hope

Isle of Lies
Love Me Forever

Dark Warrior
Legendary Warrior

The Daring Twin
The Bewitching Twin

Taken By Storm
The Highlander's Bride

Return of the Rogue (Sinclare brothers' series)
Under the Highlander's Spell
The Angel & The Highlander
Highlander's Forbidden Bride

Bound To A Warrior (Warrior King series)
Loved By A Warrior
A Warrior's Promise
Wed To A Highland Warrior

Highlander Unchained
Forbidden Highlander

About the Author

Donna Fletcher is a *USA Today* bestselling romance author. Her books are sold worldwide. She started her career selling short stories and winning reader contests. She soon expanded her writing to her love of romance novels and sold her first book SAN FRANCISCO SURRENDER the year she became president of New Jersey Romance Writers. Donna is also a past President of Novelists, Inc.

Drop by Donna's website www.donnafletcher.com where you can learn more about her, find out Book News, get a printable Book List, and read her blog.

Want to be alerted to Donna's book releases? Sign up for Book Alert. Send Donna an e-mail at donna@donnafletcher.com with Book Alert in the message box and you're all set.

Made in the USA
Lexington, KY
24 November 2015